FYRIAN'S FIRE

EMILY H. JEFFRIES

FYRIAN'S FIRE

Published by Sheepgate Press, Atlanta, Georgia
http://www.emilyhjeffries.com

Edited and Designed by Girl Friday Productions
www.girlfridayproductions.com

Editorial: Tegan Tigani, Kelley Frodel, Amy Snyder
Interior Design: Rachel Marek
Cover Design: Paul Barrett
Image Credits: cover and interior illustrations © Rachel Grantham

ISBN (Paperback): 978-1-7333733-0-2
e-ISBN: 978-1-7333733-1-9
Library of Congress Control Number: 2019911299

First Edition

Printed in the United States of America

To Husband Hill—fairytale princes have nothing on you.
And to Editor Adair, who loved Tess first.

Continent of Diatonica

ATHOES
←

Militia
Headquarters

Council of
the Nest

Ruby Creek

HINGE FOREST

Den V
"Back Door"

The Ruins

**SOUTHERN
WOODS**

Birch
Grove

Crescent
Lake

THE HILLS

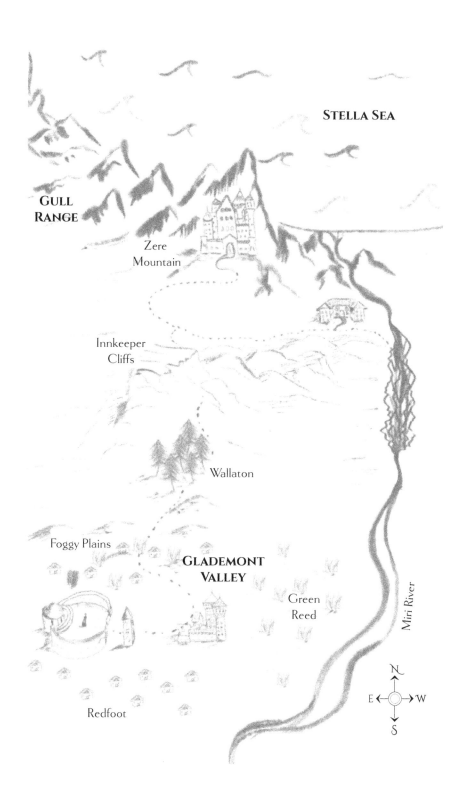

STELLA SEA

GULL
RANGE

Zere
Mountain

Innkeeper
Cliffs

Wallaton

Foggy Plains

GLADEMONT
VALLEY

Green
Reed

Miri River

Redfoot

N
E ← → W
S

PROLOGUE

On the first night of the wedding festival, a foreigner ambled from the untamed lands west of Glademont Castle. His stubble grew thick for a man no older than twenty. Cool wind blew leaves against his long legs, which parted the swaying grasses of a yellowing meadow. Thirty paces away lay Glademont's main highway, where villagers sang patriotic songs on their way to the royal wedding.

A crow with clouded eyes hunched on his shoulder. It unfolded a wing and shifted on its talons. "When you find her, don't touch it." The bird's throat caught on a perpetual scratch. "Cut off her hair and put it in your pouch. Escape unseen and bring it to me."

The young foreigner hoisted his faded checkered trousers and scowled at the Glademontians with their colorful trappings and prim feathered hats. "I confess, I never thought I'd be wearing my seaman's rags again," he said.

The crow's rasp intensified. "There will be citizens from all four corners of the dione, not only the wealthy. You're to blend with the peasants, boy. Look no one in the eye, and keep moving."

The man clicked his tongue and lengthened his stride.

Merchants and commoners from the valley called to one another from the backs of braided ponies. Powdered aristocrats emerged from their carriages, opting to parade through the boxwoods on foot. Had any of the guests glanced beyond the hedges toward the forest, they might have caught the foreigner's sunned stubble creasing into a smirk. An old saying from his home continent sprang to mind:

How brightly burn the blind.

Just another ignorant people, adoring a predictably corrupted royal class.

The setting sun warmed the foreigner's shoulders. He dug a pipe and a pouch from his trouser pocket and stuffed savory leaves into the bowl—a habit he'd picked up at sea from men twice his age. Nearing the castle gardens where guests poured in by the dozens, he spotted elaborate bronze torches lining the drive. He smirked again, flashing a dimple on his left lower cheek. Would Glademontian sensibilities allow for lighting one's pipe on a royal torch? But a rustling on his shoulder forced him to consider his delicate mission this evening.

"What if she uses the thing against me?" He strained his neck to avoid the musty bird smell so near his nostrils.

He cawed. "She'll be too weak, if she isn't dead already."

The foreigner held his pipe to his nose and shook his head. Even nature's handsomest fragrance couldn't mask the old crow's sour feathers. "And the castle plans?"

"Yes, yes. If you come back with nothing to show the king, he will be suspicious. Map as much of the castle as you can."

The foreigner's tanned face hardened. "I hope I need not remind you that I have your word that when Nabal claims Glademont, he shan't interfere with me. I'm through roaming between continents like a hunted seal."

The crow clacked his beak the way he always did when a plan neared execution. "I have promised. He will not send you back to the sea. Do as I say, and this will be your home."

They joined the Glademontians among clipped shrubs in various sweeping shapes. Early evening wind seeped between the thin fibers of the foreigner's tunic. A fine carriage passed on creaking wheels. To the right, a balding horse breeder with a jug in his hand howled at his own anecdote. Ahead, an elderly woman wearing a burgundy gown glared at the crow. The foreigner flashed a smile in return, and the woman started at his rustic dress. But his smile persisted, and the next instant she melted, fluttering a pair of gray eyelashes at him. He moved toward a torch, lit his pipe, and winked.

The crow took to the air without another word, leaving his companion to thank the skies and shake the tension from his arms. Then, scratching at his chest, the foreigner indulged in a draft of autumn air.

Locate the queen and secure the object—he had navigated greater challenges than this.

He scanned the top of the castle's outer wall. Six sentries with spyglasses, each more ridiculous than the last. The old crow was right: Glademont wouldn't stand a chance in battle. They'd be ash in Nabal's fist before first snow.

The young foreigner saluted to a swarm of royal servants and passed through the outer wall, taking a long drag on his pipe.

PART I

CHAPTER 1

Sundown meant only an hour remained until the start of Lady Tessamine Canyon's wedding festival. She waited on the bridge leading to her home, her fingers clenching the warped oak railing in front of her.

Of course something like this would happen.

"Lady Tessamine," barked Colonel Regency Thorn—Reggie, as Tess and her siblings liked to call him. The stout salt-and-pepper terrier was the Canyons' governor, and as canine monitor of the family, the Colonel stood on ceremony at all times. "You have caused a scandal, standing outside in the damp. What will your mother say?" A moth fluttered in front of the Colonel's nose, and he repelled it with a snort.

"I'm staying out here. The man should know how much distress he has caused us." She twisted her engagement pearls around her finger.

Autumn wind bit at Tess's ears while scathing thoughts churned in her head. Her younger brother, Ryon, pulled himself up to sit on the bridge railing beside her, letting his polished boots dangle over the brook. At twelve, he was still small enough for the railing to support his weight.

"At least you'll get to dance tonight," he said. "Show off all your fancy training."

"There will be no 'showing off,' Master Ryon," the Colonel said, his beard quivering importantly. "If her ladyship must dance, it will be with the prince, and it will be in the old way. Without the theatrics of a city ballet. Now, I will wait for His Highness inside so at least *some* of the family will be seen as respectable." His cropped tail swayed as he trotted toward the mansion.

Tess's freckled face darkened. Her plans to become Redfoot's most acclaimed dancer had been stalled by the marriage proposal. This new future hovered before her like a mist, obscuring her once clear view. Yet, how could she have refused such a gift from the skies? Surely the prince would never have asked her if he were indifferent toward her.

Ryon tossed a pebble in the brook, sending droplets onto Tess's marigold slippers. The stains pulled Tess from her musings. "Stop swinging your legs like that," Tess snapped. "You'll get mud on my gown." She glowered at the road through the bare trees. Still no prince.

"Let's go inside," Ryon said. "Reggie will come huffing back out here any minute."

Behind them, three stories of fat black stones and tall rounded windows stretched southward into a stately horseshoe-shaped home called Canyon Manor. For sixteen years, Tess dreamed of leaving to begin her own life. Yet, here she was on their old wooden bridge, the same brook babbling under her feet, and away to the right, the same two rows of apple trees marking the entrance to the grounds. Tess pursed her lips at those unfeeling trees.

Would she really ever leave?

Seeming to sense her restlessness, Ryon gently elbowed her ribs. "Hey, look. I've got something that might cheer you up." After reaching into his trouser pocket, he held out two braided grass strings coiled around a thin leather pouch. The leather bore the branded seal of the Dione of Glademont.

"Vermin and vinegar," Tess exclaimed. "A weapon."

"It's a sling," Ryon corrected. "Isn't it something?"

"Papa will never let you keep it. Get rid of it."

Ryon's face fell. "The prince gave it to me. I'm already learning how to use it." He hid his eyes under his mop of heavy cinnamon waves. "I'm pretty good."

Tess twisted her ring again—seven Miri River pearls for the seven days of the marriage festival. "Why on the continent would he give you a weapon?"

Ryon shrugged. "At that court supper, he was talking to Father and said he thought it was wrong to assume all sport made men violent. When I agreed, he seemed pleased. Then this parcel arrived. . . ."

"You know how dangerous it is to fool with weapons. Why do you think no one in the dione makes them?"

"The prince doesn't think they're dangerous."

"The prince doesn't think at all."

The quiet jingling of horse tack interrupted their debate, and a large covered carriage inched into view between the trees. The low, keen sun flashed on its wheels. The carriage, drawn by four black horses and painted in blue and silver florals, slowed to turn into the Canyons' apple orchard.

Tess retreated to the steps of her home, so as not to appear overly anxious. She did her best to flatten her thick black curls and pulled a plush hood over her moderately tamed hair, silently begging the crisp sky the prince would say something complimentary about her gown, for once.

The carriage rattled through the trees and over the brook. The horses snorted gusts of misty breath, easing to a halt in the gravel. A footman dismounted.

"Good evening, my lady," he said. "May Xandra's horn blow celestial blessings on you this first night of—"

"Thank you," Tess interrupted. By her count, there were three footmen, four horses, one driver, and no prince. "Where is Prince Linden?"

"His Highness has been detained with royal matters at the castle. He invites his betrothed and her esteemed family to attend tonight's festival in his carriage."

"Indeed?" Tess seethed. "There must be some mistake. I expected to arrive at Glademont Castle with the prince. He wrote me—"

Ryon stepped forward and bowed shyly. "His Royal Highness is very kind, isn't he, Tess? We, uh, shall be ready shortly." He tugged on Tess's cloak. Her throat tightened, but she didn't move. She glared at the footman.

"Is this not the first evening of our wedding festival?"

He bowed. "Indeed, my lady."

"I fail to understand how there could be a royal matter so urgent that it should prevent my groom from accompanying me to a celebration in my—in *our* honor." Her fur-lined hood fell from her face. With shaking fingers, she found her cloak hem and wrapped it across her torso. For how long would she be last among Prince Linden's priorities? Why on the continent did he even propose to her in the first place?

The door behind Tess opened, and the Colonel appeared at the top of the stairs. He approached the footman, too close to the ground to see inside the royal carriage.

"Ah, welcome to Canyon Manor. Does His Royal Highness wish to—?"

"He isn't here." Tess's eyes did not leave the footman.

"I see," the Colonel said slowly.

"Truly, my lady"—the servant remained unperturbed—"His Royal Highness seeks your pardon and sends his most joyous tidings on this magnificent occasion."

"You take liberties, sir." Her voice trembled. "Three months of barely answered letters and that empty carriage speak a different sentiment."

"Lady *Tessamine*," the Colonel said, trotting around her shins with a soft growl. "Inside at once."

The footman continued to stare politely at Tess. She dismissed him with a nod before following her governor into the manor. Arrive like a guest to her own festival? She could not bear it if Glademont's citizens discovered how little Prince Linden thought of her. There were already rumors of the dione's displeasure at his choice. They said she was too aristocratic to be a true "Commoner Queen." An advisor's daughter from Nobleman's Road wasn't truly of the people, they criticized. Her only consolation had been that, deep down, Prince Linden must love her. All her life, she had been taught that Glademont's princes and royal heirs chose their hearts' partners to wed. Surely, despite all evidence otherwise, Tess was no exception?

After pounding the solid door shut, Tess pressed her forehead against its iron hinges. The royal horses nickered outside, and Tess's chest shuddered with a mournful sigh. The first night of the rest of her life was nothing like she had dreamed.

She shook her head, dropping next to Ryon on a pillowed bench by the front doors.

The Colonel stood at her feet, his silky legs stiffening with purpose. "Well, your ladyship?" He snorted. "What are you waiting for? Put on your gloves, pull yourself together, and get in that carriage."

Ryon folded his jacket in his lap. "Prince Linden offered the carriage for all of us, Reggie. The whole family."

"All of us?" A moment passed as this information sank in. "*All* of us?" He raced up the stairs until the pattering of his nails disappeared above.

Tess leaned against the back of the bench and closed her eyes against the nightmare that was this evening. Ryon shifted next to her.

"I miss the academy." He pulled at his vest. "All these royal events make me itchy. First, all the banquets we have to attend with Papa. Now you . . ."

"You've been back a week, and already tired of home?"

Ryon blew a soft moan. "I could stay in the city for all four years without coming home."

"I used to feel that way," Tess said. "And when I graduated, I thought I'd be too busy dancing in all the best ballets to come back here very much." Tess leaned forward to put her forehead in her hand. Her ambitions had changed drastically in the past few months.

Ryon raised an eyebrow. "Are you thinking about when you went to school with Prince Linden?"

"No," she answered. "He was two years my senior and we hardly spoke." It was surprisingly similar to their current arrangement.

Ryon's tone softened. "I thought he knew you from school, and that was why he . . ."

The Colonel descended from the second story, whining and holding Sir Brock's dress gloves in his mouth.

"Thifs ifs disgraful." He growled through the gloves and paced on the landing. "Tardinesth becomesth not a creature of dithstinction."

"Let us hope all of Glademont begins its revelry early so as to mask our absence," came the cheerful reply of Sir Brock from the parlor door. He entered the foyer and took the gloves from the Colonel's mouth.

"All due respect, my lord," the Colonel said. "Even if every creature in the valley attends, their Highnesses will certainly notice if Lady Tessamine is not present." He resumed his pacing at Ryon's feet. "The royal carriage awaits us at this very moment."

"Are we all taking a royal carriage?" Sir Brock fastened an advisor's medallion to his solid chest. He winked at Tess. "I hope you won't mind our company, Tessy." Sir Brock was not tall, but he tended to walk about the house with official parchments under his arm, giving him an important air. He unrolled one such document and bent his head, revealing a rounded, exaggerated profile. He had a way of putting people at ease, even Tess.

Lady Matilde's petite figure descended the stairs next. She wore a brilliant royal-blue gown that draped at the shoulders. "No prince? He certainly seems preoccupied." As the mother of three and a native of a small fishing village in the valley, Lady Matilde was still unaccustomed to Tess's royal engagement. Sometimes, Tess suspected her mother secretly hoped the prince would forget about her.

"Who's preoccupied? That sounds unpleasant." Dahly, the eldest Canyon daughter, bounded down the stairs in a shimmering champagne gown. Her deep brown hair fell in large waves past her shapely biceps.

"We were speaking of the prince," Lady Matilde explained.

"That cad," Dahly said. "I wouldn't let my betrothed dismiss me the way he has you, Tessy." Dahly ignored the Colonel's growl, warning her against criticizing a royal. "The last time he was here was weeks ago, wasn't it? And he hardly stayed half an hour."

Dahly's frank sympathy made Tess feel more like a pitied child than the dione's successor to the throne. It was time to assert herself, or no one in the family would have an ounce of respect left for her.

"I'm going to have a talk with him," Tess said, holding her short, round nose high. "I cannot bear another minute of this neglect."

Sir Brock, Lady Matilde, and Dahly paused. Lady Matilde grasped the side of her neck. Ryon fiddled with his coat buttons.

"We'll discuss this in the carriage," Sir Brock said after a moment. "Matilde, are all the candles put out? Dahly, where is your cloak?" With furtive looks, Tess's family prepared to depart.

The sky behind the towering mountains had long since faded to navy by the time all five Canyons were ready. Before piling into the carriage, Tess lingered on the manor stairs. She sighed at the stables, wishing she could steal into Jesse's stall and ride to the castle on her own. Perhaps she could sneak past the crowds and find Prince Linden herself, without footmen or servants or parents to slow her down. Then she'd tell that man exactly what was on her mind. But there was no hope of slipping away tonight, not without embarrassing Papa. Tess sighed again and trudged toward the carriage.

They rolled onto Nobleman's Road. Through the window, Tess brooded at passing nobles in their curricles or on horseback, their gazes strained forward by good breeding. Ever since returning home from Redfoot Academy, Tess had sensed a new smallness about the cluster of distinguished homes atop Glademont's cliffs. Down in the city of Redfoot lived a more colorful array of people, from all kinds of families and walks of life. Perhaps the people were right to question Tess's authenticity as a Glademontian citizen, pampered as she had been up on the cliffs. But surely the prince had seen something in her that she would one day be able to reign with humility and understanding?

A full moon rose between thin clouds, and eventually the royal carriage turned north, revealing in the distance Glademont Castle at the base of Zere Mountain, the highest peak in the Gull Mountain Range. The castle, with its assortment of stout towers chiseled from the rock of the mountain, sparkled with lanterns and torches.

"Try to be calm," Lady Matilde said, smoothing her gown and pressing the strands of her twisted bun. "A lady keeps her emotions in check. Wait until you have a private moment, then kindly tell the prince how you feel. Do not accuse him, dear. He *is* the prince."

Sir Brock arranged his palms over his knee and leaned forward to catch Tess's eye. "A royal marriage is different than other unions, Tessy," he said with that serious tone he used when advising the queen. "As princess, you will not so much make demands as see to your duty. Prince Linden does just the same, as does Queen Aideen. Marriage, family, friends . . . your duty takes precedence over them all."

"Have they no duty toward me?" Tess said. "If not the queen, then at least the prince?"

"Of course," he said. "But in this case, as you are just beginning to know each other, I believe patience is your best ally."

Dahly cleared her throat and whispered in Tess's ear, "I could not disagree more."

The air in the carriage grew thick and hot, pressing on Tess's temples. "Thank you, everyone, for your concern. I am perfectly capable . . ."

The royal carriage turned and rolled between two towering holly trees. They had arrived at the royal lawn and gardens that stretched before the castle. Tess leaned her head against the glass to study her future home. Rough, weathered stones stacked thick and high on a rectangular wall loomed ahead. Only the broad coned roofs of the castle towers could be seen over the wall's silhouette. Was this the gleaming future she hoped for? In that moment, a thin dread tugged at her heart.

Then something atop the outer wall caught Tess's attention. Half a dozen sentries pointed spyglasses south toward the valley and west toward the Hinge Forest. Never had Tess seen so many sentries. Glademont was famously a peaceful dione. What were they looking for? Before she could speculate, the buzzing of a gathering crowd pulled Tess's attention to the castle's outer gate.

Dozens of cheering citizens greeted the royal carriage at the foot of Glademont Castle's imposing wall. The Canyons eventually lurched to a stop, and the driver shouted to settle the horses. Tess didn't expect to meet a crowd before entering the castle. Was there no one to escort her in?

The incessantly polite footman opened the door, and Tess waited for her family to step out before her. More and more citizens pressed in, peering around their neighbors and twittering with excitement. A happy ovation pealed from the crowd as her father stepped out—the queen's most trusted advisor. The people loved him, and he deserved their affection. Tess squeezed her eyes shut. She could do it, too. She could serve the dione well.

While the rest of her family exited the carriage, Tess's heart thumped so loudly the footman had to call for her attention. Fighting her apprehensions, she put on her best diplomatic smile and took his hand. Tess alighted on the cobblestones, and the citizens cheered and waved their hats. She nodded with regal gratitude, hoping her curls would not fly into view.

But when the carriage door closed behind her, the men replaced their hats and the women stowed their handkerchiefs. One of them murmured nearby, "Not so fine up close, is she? And no royal escort?" Her companion shrugged. "Stage performers are like that. So graceful from afar but terribly awkward in person." They pushed forward to pass through the gate, no longer interested in the royal carriage and its occupants.

The thumping in Tess's ears doubled. Why had Prince Linden not come for her? Was she really such a disappointment? She forced herself not to meet Dahly's eyes, in case she heard the gossips, too. Horrible busybodies.

Dropping her gaze to focus on her silk slippers, Tess saw they were half submerged in a puddle.

"This way, my lady." A royal servant with a striped feather in his hat offered his arm.

Struggling to regain her composure, Tess followed her family through the inner courtyard where stable boys and footmen hurried past one another to attend straggling guests. Dozens of torches and the protection of the wall made the courtyard mercifully warm. She stole a glance behind her at the sentries, high above. Were they laughing at her pitiful reception? Reaching the end of the cobblestones, Tess was ushered up the deep steps to the castle itself. Maple leaves, gourds, and golden beads garnished the great doors, and the servants who took Tess's cloak were similarly decorated.

General Frost Bud, the royal governor, pattered toward the Canyons inside the castle entrance. "Sir Brock, Lady Matilde, may Xandra bless you tonight and always." A stocky terrier with a fanned tail, General Bud displayed a colorful array of medals of honor on his breast. "Lady Tessamine." He lowered his solid, charcoal head. "May your marriage be starlit. The dione awaits the coronation with great joy." His tone implied that he was never joyful if he could help it.

Tess curtsied gracefully, covering her wet shoes with her crimson skirts. "Thank you, General. The stamina of the dione will certainly be tested, with six more nights such as this." She glanced at the floor and forced a playful smile. The voices of hundreds of guests trickled into the entrance hall from the left. Above Tess's head, shadowy, rough rock like a great cavern glinted dimly with mirrors and chandeliers.

"You are too kind." General Bud answered as though he were observing some disagreeable weather. "But I can assure you, Glademont is more than up to the task. A seven-day feast is nothing compared to the Jubilee Month. You may be too young to remember."

Lady Matilde poked at her bun while the servants carried away the Canyons' outer garments. "General, I hope we have not kept the prince waiting."

General Bud simply snorted—a short, businesslike noise—and led them to the left, out of the entrance hall and under the vaulted ceiling of the west hall. Four richly dressed servants shouted through the crowd. "Make way. Make way, there. To the side, citizens."

Soon the Canyons and their escorts arrived at the doors to the banquet hall and were asked to wait to be announced. Tess stood on her wet toes to see how the banquet hall looked on the first night of her wedding festival. At the far end, below the stained glass windows, a cramped orchestra played before a bony conductor with feathery hair. His already-small frame shrank under the soaring glass, where sacred constellations and moon phases hung in muted ripples. From a narrow endless table down the left-hand side of the room, smells of roast fish, vegetable pies, and sweet wines tempted Tess's nose. Guests had already begun grazing on the sumptuous spread, finding chairs or stools where they could.

"Lady Matilda Canyon and his lordship, Sir Brock Canyon, royal advisor to the queen," the doorman cried over the din. Tess's parents descended the staircase toward a circle of nobles. She smiled. Announcing an advisor after his wife broke with tradition, but Sir Brock insisted. Their unusual entrances had always made Mother bashful and Papa proud. Tess's usually upturned lips slumped to a frown. How could Tess's father respect her mother so much but insist Tess not seek the same respect from her betrothed?

Knowing there would be no announcement for them, Dahly and Ryon slipped into the banquet hall, leaving Tess to stand alone. She pulled her crimson sleeves at her wrists, dropped her shoulders, and assumed a demure yet elegant posture.

"Lady Tessamine Canyon, princess-to-be of Glademont," the doorman shouted. A few nearby scholars turned out of curiosity, but the majority of the attendees seemed not to hear. Tess stood a moment longer, twisting her pearls, then was escorted aside by an infuriatingly sympathetic servant. By the time the orchestra began the traditional royal anthem, another noble family stood at the banquet hall entrance. The doorman waved the orchestra off.

"Vermin and vinegar." Tess covered her face. "Of all the humiliating . . ."

Ryon appeared next to her, staring at his feet and tugging his hair. Large formal events always made him anxious. Tess clenched his upper arm, ignoring his wince.

"Come, we shall have a word with His Highness."

They started for the crowd.

CHAPTER 2

Tess and her reluctant brother edged along the banquet hall floor. She searched the throng, nodding to a few bowing citizens. The first evening of the wedding festival had drawn an enormous crowd. Nobles, scholars, advisors, and their spouses chatted and twirled across the floor. Clusters of children stood under the balcony while small yet imposing terriers patrolled, keeping behind the columns that ranged about the perimeter of the grand hall.

Villagers from the valley well outnumbered the nobles from the mountain. Mostly Redfooties from the capital had come, for they were used to parties and crowds. In addition to these, a few families from the fishing town of Green Reed had made the long journey from the rocky shores of the Miri River. Helping themselves to trays of wine, the friendlier pony breeders from Foggy Plains had shed their loose wools and rough shirts for finer clothes. But even damask fabric purchased from Redfoot could not conceal their ruddy complexions and windblown hair. Despite circulating complaints that Tess was too highborn to be a true Glademontian Commoner Queen, the plains folk were the most inclined to show Tess some appreciation when she passed. They were the most inclined to show appreciation anyway, pleased as they were to be drinking free spirits.

Across the room, Tess finally spotted Prince Linden making his way toward the orchestra. Even had he not been wearing his gold circlet, he would have stood out by his unusual height. She gathered her skirts and ushered Ryon forward.

"My lady." A breathless young villager blocked Tess's path and lowered herself into a clumsy curtsy. "Forgive my impertinence, but I have brought my daughter from the cliffs tonight just so she could meet you."

They were cliffdwellers—shepherdesses from the reclusive village of Wallaton—and the first from that poor area Tess had seen that evening. The woman who spoke held the hand of a tiny girl in a plaid jumper with a head engulfed in airy white curls. Her cheeks and neck were red as cherries.

"How nice." Tess nodded. Could Prince Linden have disappeared already?

"Her name is Belle. Her grandfather took her to Redfoot to see you dance *The Ashes of Dorian Minor* last spring. She's always asking to me to play the wise empress so she can twirl like a gem dryad. I can hardly get her to spin wool these days, she's so taken with the story." The woman flashed an enormous smile. A pleasant crease just under her lower lip reminded Tess of someone. . . .

"Did you enjoy it?" Tess asked Belle, forcing herself to be attentive. The curls bounced up and down. "I'm happy you did." Tess began to warm to her. "You know, I sewed the skirts for Fyrian's costume myself? My sister and I had a wonderful time dreaming up what a gem dryad might look like." Tess felt like laughing at the memory but found she couldn't.

"From what I have heard, it was a night for dreaming," Belle's mother said. She smiled and touched Tess's elbow, and suddenly Tess was overcome with the desire to stay in the company of these shepherdesses. How long it had been since someone paid her a genuine compliment. In fact, this was precisely how she had hoped the people of Glademont would receive her. A little girl wasn't exactly a parade in Tess's honor, but it was something.

"Would you care to dance?" Tess asked, grinning.

Belle shivered with delight, and the ringlets bounced again.

Tess turned to ask a terrified-looking Ryon to wait a moment. Stepping forward, she gently supported Belle's rough, small hand in her palm and placed another palm behind Belle's back. Leading with a simple three-step, Tess beamed reassuringly at her partner. The little shepherdess returned the smile with an awed gasp. The fluttering behind Tess's ribs felt good. She could sense the crowd's eyes on her. This was what it was like to be the princess. These were the whispers she had hoped to hear, the enraptured faces she hoped to see.

Then an image of Prince Linden bloomed in Tess's memory. She recalled the day of the betrothal ceremony, when Tess was officially presented before the queen. His expression was far from awed; it was annoyed. He looked at her like a fly in his soup. . . .

Someone let out a squeak at Tess's feet, and the gasps of the onlookers pulled her to the present. Her dance partner had tumbled to the floor. It seemed Tess had forgotten to shorten her strides for Belle. Horrified, Tess knelt to help. Then Belle's young mother appeared.

"No matter, my lady," she said sweetly. "May the stars bless you. Belle will remember this night for a thousand more." The woman gave her daughter a quick, comforting hug, and they disappeared back into the crowd. The fluttering in Tess's chest had turned to a panicked throbbing, and she found herself unable to meet the embarrassed gazes of the onlookers.

A gaggle of academy girls snickered and threw tipsy curtsies at Tess while they passed. The irony with which they offered their respects was not lost on Tess. The memory of Prince Linden's obvious disdain returned to Tess's mind. She covered her pearl ring with her palm.

The music ended, and Tess thanked the skies for a distraction. Across the room, beneath the stained glass windows, Tess heard the conductor arguing with his musicians. The brass players in the top rows gestured their disapproval, and Tess thought she heard one of them say, "Come now, sir. She is quite a talent."

One hand now gripping Ryon's shoulder, Tess crossed to the conductor's stand. When she could finally see the cause of the commotion, Tess shook her head with exasperation. In the percussion section of the orchestra stood Dahly with a sheepskin drum strapped across her shoulder. Tess thought it fortunate the Colonel was not present to bark a few choice words.

"This is an outrage," the conductor spewed. "The sister to the princess is not a hired musician." The crowd laughed, which only seemed to rile him further.

Amid the noise, a piccolo player seemed to come upon an idea. Putting his instrument to his lips, the portly fellow began a rendition of a folk favorite, "The Inn on Nobleman's Road." Dahly grinned and pulled her borrowed sheepskin drum to her hip. The rest of the orchestra rolled in with gusto. All around Tess, citizens raised their voices for the chorus:

> *Have you ever traveled far enough*
> *to reach the end of the road?*
> *The swinging bridge of tar and stuff*
> *will barely carry your load!*
> *But rest your head in the finest bed from the mead-*
> *   ows up to the sea.*
> *The moon and comets will tuck you in,*
> *and the winds will sing you to sleep.*
> *Oh! Have you ever traveled far enough*
> *to the Inn down on Nobleman's Road?*
> *Have you ever traveled far enough,*
> *in this land where the Heart is at Home?*

"My lady," Prince Linden said. Tess spun. The gold buttons on his ivory coat flashed as he bowed. When he straightened, he looked lanky as ever, still as angular in his movements. And he could still make Tess's heart gallop with his soft eyelashes and round, serious chin. He wasn't the handsomest man Tess had ever known, but something about Prince Linden's determined, earnest forehead made him irresistible. Curse him.

The nape of Tess's neck warmed under her bundled hair. She hoped the wisps had stayed flat since the last time she looked in a mirror. "Yes . . . hello," she said.

May I have this dance, she wanted him to ask. Instead, Prince Linden caught sight of her brother.

"Master Ryon, how did you like your gift?" he said, shaking Ryon's hand. Tess's brother beamed. It was just like Ryon to hate crowds but feel at ease with the crown prince.

"I've never liked anything better, Your Highness," Ryon replied. "Yesterday I shot a trout straight in the eye and ate it for lunch."

The prince grinned while Tess stifled her shock. "Impressive. You have better luck with it than I have with a longbow." The prince shook his head in mock despair.

"Your Highness," Tess said after a difficult swallow. "Forgive me, but you confuse my brother. Of course, Ryon, he does not mean he actually shoots a longbow."

A muscular fellow of about seventeen meandered into their circle. "His Highness shoots a longbow like my sister ties a *satin* bow." Nory Rootpine bowed, placed his goblet on a passing tray, and cracked his fingers against his jaw. "In other words, he needs more practice." He winked at the prince and then saluted to Tess. "Hullo, Lady Tessamine. Many blessings, and all that."

"Evening, Nory. Good of you to join us," Tess said with a cold glance.

"My pleasure." Nory clapped Prince Linden's back. "Rette and I have got all the papers ready, fearless leader."

"Oh, have you been arranging papers, Your Highness?" The words left Tess's mouth before she could restrain herself. "Was that what called you away this evening?"

The prince traced the circlet in his hair with nervous fingers. "My lady, I regret to have neglected you this evening, but there were serious matters to attend to. Masters Nory and Rette have been aiding me over the past months in an . . . endeavor."

"I doubt the lady is the slightest bit interested, Your Highness," Nory said. "Enjoy the remainder of the festivities, Lady Tessamine." Something about his tone made Tess nervous. He took another goblet from a servant's tray and wandered into the crowd.

Relieved to be rid of Prince Linden's friend, Tess checked her hairline. "Your Highness, would you care to join me for a dance?"

"I apologize for Master Rootpine's behavior," the prince said. He avoided her eyes. "We have been under some stress lately."

Tess looked pleadingly at the prince. She felt desperation creep into her voice. "Might I know what all this is about?"

The folk song was nearly finished, and Tess could hardly ignore the eyes of hundreds of citizens on her—no, on Prince Linden—waiting to see what he would do, waiting for his hand to touch hers. Would he show *any* affection for her? But the prince stood awkwardly beside her, apparently at a loss for words. Tess twisted her pearls around her finger. She glanced at Ryon, who seemed to be studying the prince's face.

"Citizens of Glademont," the conductor boomed from his stand. "Welcome to the first feast of the wedding festival." The citizens cheered, and the younger set glowed in Prince Linden's direction. Tess looked for Belle and her mother, but the crowd was too large.

"You have traveled far and wide to honor your prince, and to celebrate his happy union with an enchanting young noblewoman from right here on Zere Mountain," the conductor continued.

Polite applause.

"Let us hear from the bridegroom himself, who will offer a few words to open our celebration."

Prince Linden left Tess's side to replace the conductor. Enthusiastic applause, whistles, and squeals from the academy girls erupted. He looked as if he wanted to tug at his collar, but he resisted.

"Seeing such warmth and brotherhood grace this hall," the prince began, "is a blessing I do not take for granted. Glademont is a dione of kindness, beauty, hardworking creatures, and, of course, celebrations."

At this, the banquet hall erupted into the age-old cheers: "Glademont evermore!" and "Home of the heart!"

The prince nodded. "I do not relish speeches; they have fallen to the queen for so long." A note of sadness crept into the prince's voice, and Tess took Ryon's hand.

"But, the constellations have shifted in ways I could never have foreseen. And more changes are fast approaching." He wrapped his long fingers around each side of the conductor's music stand. The knuckles went white. "I regret to say the wedding festival must be postponed. Indefinitely."

A sudden humming rang in Tess's ears. She barely registered the hundreds of faces fixed on her, their jaws slack.

Until that moment, a small part of Tess had clung to the possibility that Prince Linden's indifference was imagined. But now there could be no doubt. He was spurning her in front of the entire dione. Tess envisioned herself floating away, dissipating into a freckled mist. The next moment, she felt she had gotten her wish but realized the blood had merely drained from her face.

Ryon's arm slipped around Tess and steadied her.

"The kingdom of Atheos conspires against us. Against the queen," the prince said. The hall filled with gasps, then nervous chatter. Sir Brock and Lady Matilde pushed through the crowd toward Tess.

"My sources report an assassin has crossed our borders." Prince Linden paused and wiped a damp caramel lock from his forehead.

One of the academy girls shrieked. Dahly shed her drum and rushed to her mother, who looked pale. The salty heat of anxiety masked the smell of foodstuffs and perfumes in the room.

Vermin and vinegar.

"I hope you now understand why I must postpone the festival," the prince continued. "Our dione may face its first crisis of this magnitude in centuries, and it is my duty as a son and a prince to ready our defenses. I will force no man to fight, but I ask for volunteers to enlist for training in an emergency militia." The prince pulled at his gold-embroidered lapel, then opened a palm to his left, where Nory and Rette stood behind a simple table. Papers, quills, and ink sat in tidy rows before them.

The crowd stood still. For a moment, nothing sounded but the scratching of silks and the clanging of bronze tableware. Then a man in velvet tails raised a wrinkled index finger.

"Your Highness, may I speak?"

Prince Linden pulled a satin handkerchief from his pocket and dabbed the back of his neck. "Judge Glasmilk, as you wish."

"I have served Her Majesty the queen for twenty-three years as judge of Redfoot, and your grandmother for twelve years before that," he said in a scratchy bass tone. "You know well how loyal I am to the Crown. But this decision is serious. Perhaps you've forgotten that our dione bears no weapons. It is the pure heart of our queen that protects us. And the Zere Mountain protects her, in turn. To take up arms would be to defy the constellations and betray the Crown."

Those who agreed shouted their affirmations. Tess thought of all the history classes at the academy, where her professors had lauded Glademont as the sole country on the continent that had successfully maintained its sovereignty without sword, shield, or arrow for two hundred years. She thought of Ryon's sling and wondered why the prince was so intent on destroying that peace. Was it even true that Atheos had sent an assassin? She leaned against Ryon's side, her arms shaking.

"Will there not be a council to weigh this decision?" the judge said.

"The decision has been made, Glasmilk." Prince Linden's voice cracked. "The queen's safety hangs between earth and sky, and I suspect this to be a plot to weaken our dione before an outright attack. It would not be the first time Atheos has assailed us."

"Your Highness, forgive me," Sir Brock called. "No soul in the whole of the dione does not mourn the loss of King Antony. But his death was not the result of any malicious scheme. As an advisor to the queen, I beg you to reconsider a council."

"Respectfully, Sir Brock, I decline."

A scholar called for the prince's attention. The black silk piping on her robes glinted in the candlelight. "Where is Her Majesty? We wish to see Queen Aideen."

Around her, a confident throng of scholars and noblemen chanted for the appearance of their monarch. Prince Linden's brow stiffened. He motioned for silence.

"If you wish to serve your queen and defend your families from whatever plot this assassin heralds, sign your name with Masters Rootpine and Cherrywater and remain in the banquet hall to begin your training immediately. We will need able bodies in combat as well as healers, builders—offer a skill and we will find a use for it. Any citizens wishing to exclude themselves from the militia, may the stars bless you. You are free to return to your homes and protect yourselves as you see fit."

A dazed, chaotic shuffle followed. While dozens of young men and women filed behind the sparse table to sign their names, the elders congregated in circles and spoke in low whispers. Mothers and governors shepherded children away from the commotion, clicking their tongues. Several fights broke out as baffled fathers attempted to restrain their sons from joining the prince's militia.

Tess felt Ryon's arm leave her waist as he started for the enlisting table. Sir Brock barred him with a firm hand. Ryon, too? What was happening to everyone? All this excitement and controversy, and yet no one had made the prince answerable for his promise to her?

As though her anger had summoned him, Prince Linden appeared at her side. He issued a dry kiss on her knuckles.

"My lady," he said, clearing his throat.

"How . . ." She pulled away from him. A dozen searing retorts came to mind, but she remembered her father's words in the carriage, and the intensity with which he said them. She must be patient and remember her duty. Perhaps she was further from a coronation than she thought, but she could still prove to this coldhearted boy she was made of the right stuff.

"Your Royal Highness." She inclined her head. "Certainly the queen should have been present for this . . . this interruption."

Prince Linden stared, then took a step forward. "Some dark magic has infected her."

Tess opened her mouth, but nothing came. Goose bumps materialized on her arms. The prince's eyes scanned the dozens of guests who were still watching him, then turned back to her.

"I understand you may have questions for me," he said, his mouth inches from her forehead. "Will you follow me to a more private setting?"

The humming in Tess's ears increased, and she was horribly aware of her own perspiration. She tried to curtsy, but her knees disobeyed.

"Certainly," she whispered, and the prince led her away.

CHAPTER 3

Tess hurried to match Prince Linden's long, stiff stride down the northward hallway of the west wing. He stopped at an elaborate set of blue- and silver-painted doors. One servant stood at either side, both holding tall iron candlesnuffers like lances.

The prince glanced at Tess. "I must ask you to wait a moment. Guards, I will summon her ladyship presently."

"Yes, Your Highness," said the servant on the right. But in his enthusiasm, he dropped his candlesnuffer. Prince Linden winced and disappeared behind the doors.

"Vermin and vinegar." Tess indulged in a soft growl.

Minutes passed while she paced outside. Occasionally, if she caught him staring, one of the "guards" would pretend to examine the ceiling. The sounds from the banquet hall were faint but distinguishable. Mostly young men and boys could be heard, buzzing with nervous laughter.

The doors opened.

"My lady."

Tess almost didn't recognize the prince. His circlet, sash, and formal coat were gone, revealing a high-collared shirt under a silver-threaded vest. His sleeves were rolled to the elbows. After inviting Tess in, he paced inside the elegant room, glaring at every vase and ornamental bowl as though ready to hurl it.

The carpet under Tess's damp slippers served as a welcome relief. Stern ancestral queens in oil paints and elaborate frames covered the walls of the sizable room. A glistening harp towered in one corner behind a green velvet chaise, where the queen of Glademont reclined under a blanket. Worrisome shadows marred her cheeks above her high lace collar. General Frost Bud snuffled regally at the legs of the chaise, making his presence known.

"Lady Tessamine"—Prince Linden forced the words through clenched teeth—"I believe you know my mother."

Tess tipped her head and extended her arms in a formal curtsy she knew only a few women could do well. Queen Aideen smiled under hooded eyelids.

"Forgive the prince, dear one." The queen extended her arm. "He and I have had a disagreement."

Tess approached to kiss the queen's icy knuckles. "Good evening, Your Majesty." She hoped she didn't look as thunderstruck as she felt.

"So, Linden has postponed the wedding," Queen Aideen said. Tess glanced at the harp and suppressed the urge to shove her own head through the strings.

"Yes, Your Majesty," she said.

"I was surprised to hear it. And I do not approve of his decision to organize a militia." Linden shifted to Tess's left and sat on a life-size sculpture of a sight hound, between the haunches and the neck. "But I am also dying. There is little time for debate," Aideen said.

Tess rose from her curtsy. "Your Majesty? Is it true? Prince Linden spoke of assassins and magic. . . ."

Aideen raised a palm. "As the future queen, you deserve to know the truth."

Linden and Tess exchanged tense looks. It was unclear whether he agreed as to the identity of Glademont's future queen.

"Three months ago, while journeying, I was ambushed by a counselor of the Atheonian court. He . . . he poisoned me with a dark spell. An ash spell, I think. And though I got away with my life, there are rumors this conspirer has crossed the Glademontian border to complete his mission." She calmly peered at Linden, who was still sitting on the sight hound and rubbing his face. "The prince feels he can protect me from this enemy. I do not share his confidence."

"My queen, I have stationed traders on the wall. They have all traveled to Atheos and can easily spot a foreigner. I assure you—"

"It was no mere man who wanted me dead, Linden." Wheezing, she held the blanket to her mouth as General Bud paced around the chaise, calling for a hot cloth from the servants. "Be still, General," she said, recovering her breath.

"Your Majesty, I do not understand." Linden stared hard at his mother.

"He is a master of red magic. A magician."

Tess wished someone would invite her to sit.

"Neither of you are familiar with magic." The corners of Aideen's mouth tilted, and a pleasant crease under her lower lip appeared. It reminded Tess of little Belle, the cliffdweller. Their dance together seemed ages ago. "That was how it was supposed to be, until Tess was princess. If you had just waited a few more days, Linden . . ."

"Mother, explain." Linden stood and waved the servants away, closing the inner door behind them. "This assassin—magician—could be at the castle doors right now, and I need to know how to defeat him."

General Bud barked a warning. "Your Highness will address the queen with respect, or not at all. Your Majesty, I must insist—" The queen rested a gentle wrist on the general's back.

"You cannot defeat him, Linden," she said. "Only Lady Tessamine can do that."

"What?" Tess and the prince said at the same time. Tess teetered on her feet a moment, and steadied herself against a standing glass globe. Aideen's hollow breath tore Tess's gaze from the carpet.

"Glademont does not maintain its peace without diligence. The queens of this realm have protected it, guarding it in secret. I have done so, as the mother of my husband did before me. We are a dione and not a kingdom, because kings cannot protect our people from enemies such as this. Our people believe there is something purer about a ruling queen—a queen who is not burdened with royal blood, which could make her arrogant. That is partly true. But the matter is more complicated than that. The truth is, a queen is needed to defend the dione from red magic."

"But how?" Linden demanded. General Bud growled. Linden rephrased. "Your Majesty, how have our queens protected us?"

"With this." Aideen reached behind her head and unwound something from an elaborate knot in her pewter hair. Her fingers trembled as she reached for Tess's wrist. "And now it's yours." A trinket dropped into Tess's hand.

Tess flattened her shaking palm and examined the object. It was not much: a long, thin leather strap, adorned on each end with a smooth copper ball the size of a large marble. The prince stooped for a closer look, and his soft hair brushed against Tess's arm. Despite her vexations, Tess found she could picture Linden as an attentive father, admiring some cherished object a child had found while playing.

The spheres ignited with a soft light, creating a warm buzz against Tess's skin.

"Thank the skies." Aideen leaned her head against the back of the chaise. "Fyrian's riddles have not evaded me. I've done the right thing."

"Your Majesty, what is it?" Tess felt a soft tingling spread from her fingertips to her collarbone.

"It is much older than Glademont," Aideen said. "We call it the *shenìl* after the ancient forest tongue, meaning *breath*."

"How shall I use it?" Tess whispered.

"You won't." Aideen grasped her neck and winced in pain.

"Your Majesty," General Bud pleaded.

"Another minute." The way the queen's brow bunched into determined wrinkles, she looked just like Linden the day he proposed. "I was going to begin your training after the wedding, but the constellations had other designs. No, dear one, for now your job is to hide the *shenìl*."

"Hide it?" The tingling faded.

"Yes. Until the danger passes and it is safe to travel to the Thane's Hold, where you can be trained properly."

"Mother"—General Bud snorted through a wiry beard at Linden— "Your Majesty, what if the danger doesn't pass? What if the magician reaches you before the militia is ready? If you're the only one who can use this, it seems foolish that you should give it away." Linden glanced at Tess out of the corner of his eye. He didn't trust her. She bent her left thumb to touch the engagement pearls. Why didn't he trust her?

"The *shenìl* has hardly responded to me for some months now," Aideen said, still massaging her neck. "And it must be kept from Pider at all costs. He could never wield it, of course, but if he were able to destroy it, Glademont would be lost. The entire continent of Diatonica would be lost."

"Pider?" Tess said weakly.

"The Atheonian. The magician. He knows about the *shenìl*. He knows its power, and he knows it resides in Glademont."

"This little object has been protecting our entire continent?" Tess said.

"Your Majesty"—Linden gave Tess another sidelong glance—"why can't the magician use the *shenìl*?" They all knew what Linden was really asking: Why couldn't the prince use the *shenìl*?

"It chooses its thane," she answered softly. "And the thanes have been Glademont's queens throughout the centuries. That is why Lady Tessamine must be your bride. That is why I insisted this wedding happen so quickly. No man can touch the *shenìl*. Its power stems from the dryads, and only a feminine spirit can move with its promptings. For our own protection, the *shenìl* will blind any man who wrongfully grasps it."

Tess hardly heard the queen's last words. She had gone numb. How stupid she had been these past months. Linden did not want her, had not chosen her over the other women of Glademont. His mother had forced his hand. Tess's thumb itched to touch her pearls again, but she was afraid of crying.

"Forgive me, my queen," she said. "But I could never marry the prince knowing he did not want me." Tess cleared her throat and stared at the ceiling so the tears wouldn't fall. She thought of the day Linden rode between her apple trees in all his regalia. She could smell the potted geraniums along the steps to her home, hear Dahly giggling behind her while Linden held out a velvet pillow . . .

"You misunderstand, my lady." Linden turned stiffly. "I simply have had greater concerns in recent months. The queen's health and the dione's security—"

"Linden, I have told you Lady Tessamine is vital to those concerns. She is the only person standing between Glademont and ruin." For a moment, a pinkish hue returned to Aideen's pale face. "We must hide her and hide the *shenìl*. Pider does not know this exchange is taking place. This is our best chance." Aideen lowered her eyelashes. A tear ran along her nose. "And you, Linden, must deliver my message to King Nabal."

The prince slammed a fist on the sight hound's head. "The man is a barbarian. The only reason he is in power is because . . ." He faltered, then cleared his throat. "The new Atheos suffers no negotiations, my queen, I promise you."

"As you say, Linden, I am still queen," Aideen replied, her eyes closed. "You will take the letter to Nabal, and you will tell him of Pider's plot. There is a chance he can be convinced to help us."

"I cannot face Nabal. Not after what he has done. Allow me to stay in Glademont. My work is here with the militia."

Tess gripped the copper orbs in her palm, her arm shaking.

"What does it do?"

Linden glared. "Whatever it does, it cannot possibly protect us from a ruthless magician and the might of the Atheonian army." He ran his fingers through his hair, pulling at what had developed into frizzy caramel tufts. "Old Glademont never left itself so exposed," he said.

"What do you know of Old Glademont?" Aideen's voice rose. "Old Glademont was laid to ruin because of red magic."

Tess let the tears quiver on her cheeks. She didn't care.

Aideen took a raspy breath and pushed against the arm of the chaise, sitting straighter. She addressed Tess. "Humans and animals are made of water, earth, and air, yes? But when you listen to that object in your hands, Tessamine, you become a blazing torch. You become fire."

Tess swallowed. Linden dabbed the back of his neck.

"What in the name of Luna is going on?" he said.

Aideen ignored him. "But that will come later. You are not the thane yet. When you are thane, you will know, dear one." Aideen pursed her lips and searched Tess's face. Was it a look of pity?

Tess looked down at the *shenil*. It repulsed her. Nothing made sense. The queen couldn't possibly mean the things she was saying. "My queen . . . please take it back." Tess extended her arm and hoped Linden couldn't see her trembling chin.

Aideen took the *shenil*, and for a moment Tess thought she might faint with relief. But the queen gestured at the floor beside General Bud.

"Kneel," she commanded.

Fighting the dread that rose in her throat, Tess obeyed. Aideen reached behind Tess's head and unfastened her thick black hair. The strands fell like bundles of rope. Slowly, Aideen wove the long leather strap of the *shenil* through a wide triple braid, with the orbs nestled together at the end of Tess's hair. Her cold fingertips worked haltingly, leaving glossy filaments to float at Tess's neck. Hovering just behind, the prince tapped the chaise arm in no particular rhythm. Tess could barely keep still, listening to his impatient taps and her queen's shallow, broken exhales. Finally, Aideen sank into her pillows, her head lolling to the side.

"Keep it safe."

"Mother." Linden knelt beside Tess, his shoulder brushing against hers. The queen was still breathing.

"That is quite enough," General Bud whispered ferociously. "Her Majesty is too weak to be pestered by you two any longer. You know your duties, now see to them." He pulled an envelope from a low console and placed it on Linden's knee. "Here is the message for Nabal. You must travel through the Hinge Forest, or it will never reach him in time. Don't stay in one place too long, and don't talk to the wild animals. If they try to detain you, you are *not* a prince and you are *not* from Glademont. You are a foreigner from the other side of the mountain, and you lost your way. Do you understand?"

Linden stood. "General, you know as well as I do the futility of this mission."

"I am bound to Her Majesty, and this is her wish. I shall look after her in your absence, and"—he glanced at the sleeping queen and lowered his voice—"I will oversee the training of the militia as best I can."

Linden raised an eyebrow. "Can you really help?"

General Bud shook his wiry beard. "Ah, you think our military ranks are empty titles, do you, Prince? Members of the Governor's Guild receive honors for our domestic service, yes, but our ties to combat are more real than you know. We terriers were warriors generations ago. In the days of Old Glademont. I think you'll find me more useful than not, Your Royal Highness."

In his astonishment, the prince could only nod his thanks. He touched his mother's elbow and started for the door. Tess didn't move, still kneeling and holding her new braid in disbelief.

"My lady," Linden said. "May I see you out?" He held out a stiff arm. The painted faces of queens and princesses looked down at Tess from the walls. Each one seemed to say, *You are not one of us.*

Tess thanked General Bud, though she did not know what for, and strode past Linden into the hall without touching his arm.

"I suppose you'll be wanting to get back to your family," Linden said as he closed the door behind them.

She spun, ignoring the hot flush rising to her cheeks. "What have I ever done to you?"

This was a nightmare—a vivid, catastrophic nightmare. How many times had Tess begged the red star for some sign that Linden loved her? And yet she was the furthest thing from his mind. Aideen was dying, a murderous magician hid stars-knew-where, the dione's greatest defense lay useless in her hair, and Tess had known none of it. Her coronation would have been in one week. If the queen had chosen her as princess of Glademont, thane of the whatever-it-was, why on the continent had no one thought to enlighten her until this late hour?

Linden straightened. Then, glancing at the servants by Aideen's door, he beckoned Tess down the hall to an alcove housing a potted tree. They stood on either side of the tree's peeling white bark, glaring at each other with suppressed rage. Linden stuffed Nabal's letter into his vest pocket.

"My lady, you speak too freely," he said in a low voice.

"Your Highness, you use my feelings too freely." Heat spread from her face to her neck. She knew this was not the tone her mother had in mind, but there was only so much Tess could take. "You could not have found a moment to speak with me about your plans to postpone the wedding? Or perhaps the fact that your mother had insisted upon our union?"

Linden ran a nervous hand through his hair. "As I've said, the situation here is one of unusual urgency. Certainly, had I the opportunity, I would have informed you of the state of affairs."

"What nonsense," Tess said. "You hardly thought of me at all. Your thoughtlessness has humiliated me countless times. And I saw your face when the queen gave me this." She lifted her braid. "You'd rather a goose have the *shenil* than I." Fresh tears formed at the edges of her eyes. "I repeat, what have I ever done to you?"

After a long moment, Linden's tall frame drooped. He looked away from Tess and gripped a branch with uncertainty. "My lady, you have never wronged me."

Tess wiped the wisps from her temples. The pearls around her finger grazed her forehead, and she suddenly had to know. "When the queen asked you to . . . to marry me . . ." The words, though barely audible, hung in the alcove like a thick mist.

He plucked a waxy leaf. Then another. "You must understand what pressures I have felt since the attack on Her Majesty. The fate of the entire dione is at stake."

"And she thinks I am our only hope, remember?"

"I do not agree." Linden ripped another leaf from the tree.

"Were you pleased? When she requested that we marry?"

"No, by the skies," Linden replied with sudden energy.

They stared. The prince's outline blurred in Tess's vision as she attempted in vain to process his words.

"You don't understand the world, Lady Tessamine. Your only thoughts are of royal fanfare and public admiration. You know nothing of diplomacy, of economy or trade, of the art of combat . . ." He swallowed.

The edges of Tess's vision sharpened again. She drew her shoulders back. "I don't want to be yours any more than you want to be mine, Your Highness. And you can have your diplomats and economy and pointless militia. You can run the dione to the ground, if that is your wish. When this is over, I will be glad to return the *shenil* to you. You will be free to give it to a girl with more worldly wisdom than me." She tried to steady her breath.

Linden's brow stiffened. With cold civility, he took her hand and bowed. Then, touching the letter in his vest, he strode away.

CHAPTER 4

Tess turned on her heels and ran, her heart thumping and her slippers clicking against worn sandstone. She needed a moment to herself before she had to face her family. They would want to know where she had been and what the prince had said to her. She couldn't bear that.

As Tess neared the door to the royal gardens, she began to breathe easier, knowing solitude would soon be hers. But from the corner of her eye, she caught a sudden motion. A strange man stepped into the corridor. He was perhaps three years older than Tess, with sandy hair combed smoothly from his forehead into a high, thick knot. In his mouth dangled a rough pipe. In his hands were a notebook and a piece of charcoal. He walked to a tapestry, looked behind it, and began sketching in the notebook. From the look of his faded linen trousers, Tess guessed he was a common villager—though she'd never seen anyone so young smoke a pipe.

Hearing her footsteps, the man clapped the notebook shut and stowed it in his trouser pocket. He took his pipe from his mouth and bowed low.

"My lady." The man's tone startled Tess. He spoke casually, as though the two had come upon each other in the market square. Though Tess could not place his velvety accent, she felt certain he was educated, if not a nobleman. But then why the humble costume?

"Sir, these halls are exclusive to the royal family," she said in her most authoritative tone. A tear fell onto her collarbone and she brushed it away.

"Forgive me, my lady," said the man. "I do so admire Glademontian architecture."

Tess desperately wanted to be alone, but something about the young man's face held her there. Light stubble grew under his sky-blue eyes. His expression was relaxed, playful. A dimple surfaced on his cheek as he grinned at her.

"I am Tynaiv, seafarer from across the Stella, my lady." He bowed again.

Tess inclined her head. "I am Lady Tess—Tessamine. Of Glademont. Ahem." Tess tugged at her sleeves. "You came by the Stella Sea? How did you cross the Gull Range from port? It must have been a harrowing journey." Why was she making light conversation with this man? There were so many more important things to worry about. And yet, his bright eyes looked on her with fascination, even awe. An unexpected thrill played in her chest.

"I was fortunate enough to find help through the mountains. And for that I am grateful, because tonight I am able to admire Glademont's finest works of art." He grinned again, staring unabashedly at her. She lowered her eyes.

"You flatter where you should not, sir. Remember I am betrothed to . . ." The words died on her lips. The thrill had gone.

"Of course. Do forgive me, your ladyship. I recall now that yours is the name of the prince's bride-to-be. I beg your pardon, on the grounds that I was too taken with your grace to remember my place."

"All is forgiven." Tess glanced over the man's shoulder at the door to the gardens. "In fact, as I'm sure you heard this evening, there may be no wedding at all. At least not between me and the prince. Will you excuse me, please?" She gathered her crimson skirts.

"Lady Tessamine," the man said, following behind. "Has the festival been interrupted?"

"The wedding is postponed and an emergency militia is being formed. Feel free to volunteer your service. Though you may not admire Glademont's architecture so much as to defend her in battle." Tess reached for the iron door handle.

"Lady Tessamine." The man's hand appeared on the door, barring her exit. "I trespass upon your time, but permit me to remain in your company. I dare say you are in some discomfort, and it may relieve your heart to speak of it. And if you must speak of it, speak to a poor seaman from a foreign continent, who wishes only to remain in your presence. What say you?"

The man held out his arm, and Tess smelled a wave of earthy tobacco. It comforted her, as did his firm forearm and soft dimple. She smiled meekly.

They walked together into the garden, down a pebbled path lined with rosebushes. The path led to the edge of a moonlit pond, where a simple stone bench overlooked the drooping trees beyond. The crisp autumn air filled Tess's lungs.

"Sit a moment, my lady." The man emptied his pipe and slid the stem into a breast pocket. "The breeze across the water will do you good."

"Thank you, sir," she said. Somehow, sitting made Tess feel guilty. But then her guilt turned to anger. It was *she* who had been wronged. Let the dione spin in a frenzy of foolishness for another five minutes.

"Thank you, Tynaiv," the man corrected. The dimple appeared.

"Tynaiv," Tess repeated. "That is an unusual name."

"Yes, my lady," he replied. "Even in Talon, where I was born, it is uncommon. It means, *forlorn*, or something like it, on my continent. My father and mother had mixed feelings about me, it would seem. Some are ill-fitted for parenthood." He pulled at the bowl of his pipe, but apparently thought better of it. Tess straightened.

"I am grateful for my own mother and father, then."

"Doting parents are a blessing from the skies, there is no mistake. What is their opinion of this postponement, my lady?"

Tess twisted her ring. "We've not yet discussed it. Tonight was the first I had heard of it. The prince has . . . pressing matters to attend to."

Tynaiv whistled. "That is rather unprincely of the prince. Had he no better explanation?"

Tess paused.

"Of course, my lady, feel no obligation to share the prince's doings with me. I only say what any honest man would, and that is that an intelligent woman such as yourself, with the world at your feet and the moon in your hands, does not deserve to be treated so carelessly."

A lump formed in Tess's throat, and she leaned ever so slightly toward Tynaiv's shoulder. "He may not be your prince, Master Tynaiv, but you must control your tongue. Although, a small part of me thanks the skies for this business with Atheos. I might otherwise have given myself too hastily."

"What is Atheos?" Tynaiv said as he picked a yellow three-pronged leaf from the ground. Tess stared at the curve of the muscles in his shoulders. How easily he moved, like a sandy-colored cat. Could he dance, she wondered? Tess felt the thrill again, and redirected her gaze to her lap.

"Atheos is the kingdom on the other side of the Hinge Forest. It is different there: uprisings and famine . . . And now it seems they have plans to overtake Glademont. Prince Linden is afraid an assassin has slipped through our borders."

"An assassin? By my prow. And who is this assassin's prey?"

"Queen Aideen. Have you seen her yet? She is beautiful, in her own simple way. And usually so wise." Tess touched her braid, which had fallen over her shoulder. She knew she should stop there, but Tynaiv was a stranger to their politics, wasn't he? He was right; a sympathetic, impartial ear would do her good.

"But she is not herself lately. She is sick from the assassin's first attempt."

Tynaiv shook his head. "How terrible." After a moment, he held up the yellow leaf. "In Talon, the women put leaves in their hair for wedding festivals. It is believed to make their spirits like trees, pushing roots deeper into their homelands and shading their loved ones with their branches. May I?"

Tess nodded as Tynaiv slipped the leaf behind her ear.

"The women in Talon look nothing like you, my lady," Tynaiv said. "Their hair is light, and the leaves are green. They are like fields, but you are like the night sky."

Tess laughed. "Such nonsense. But, I admit, it lifts my spirits."

Tynaiv came closer. His breath felt warm on Tess's skin. The wafting tobacco made her want to close her eyes. "The night sky, Lady

Tessamine, is black, deep, and shining. And it dazzles the most when a bright, yellow moon sits comfortably behind its ear."

He was inches from her, staring at her mouth and then settling on her eyes. Tess remembered something her mother once said: that Tess's eyes would land her in a mess of a tangle. They blazed under her thick eyebrows with all the vibrancy of a mosaic—a rich green in the outer rim of her irises, streaked by a starburst of amber. She wondered indulgently if Tynaiv was admiring them.

"Where in the sky is there an ear?" she whispered.

"I can't recall." Tynaiv pulled her to him and kissed her. Tess closed her eyes and relaxed her shoulders. This was the moment she'd imagined. But it was not Prince Linden stealing her breath. Nor was she wearing a cream gown covered in pearls, with a dione applauding before her. No, she was hiding in a garden with a stranger, trying desperately to forget all she had lost.

Abruptly, Tynaiv left her lips and put his hand to his chest. "Forgive me, my lady, but something has stung my ribs."

Tess flushed. "Oh, something in my hair. I am to hide it from . . ."

"Oh? May I see?"

"It's nothing. A token. I suppose Her Majesty felt sorry for me. . . ."

Tynaiv lifted her braid, started, and then dropped it.

"Master Tynaiv? Are you all right?"

Tynaiv's expression had changed entirely. His eyes were fixed on Tess's braid, his shoulders stiffened. "What is that?"

Tess clutched the *shenil* in her hair. "I—I don't know exactly." Her voice lowered. "I think I must take my leave."

Tynaiv slowly stood. "Certainly." His hand went to a pocket in his checkered trousers, but then he froze. He seemed to be deciding something.

The wind whistled through the rosebushes, and Tess felt the night press upon her shoulders. Tynaiv stared at Tess, his face stone-still. His easy posture had changed to paralyzed, even pained. He shook his head.

"If I may say so, my lady, it is not wise to trust the royals so blindly. Their interests are never what they seem."

It was time to go. After a hasty, silent nod of farewell, Tess gathered her skirts and started down the path.

"Take heed of my warning, Lady Tessamine. I do not give it lightly," Tynaiv called after her.

One stocking was falling down Tess's leg, but she didn't care. Her mind whirled as she charged into the castle. What had she just done?

Tess raced through the royal family's private wing to the banquet hall. There, young Glademontians still queued to volunteer for the emergency militia, while parents and scholars pleaded with them. Nory Rootpine called for more to step forward while Rette Cherrywater answered questions and told the men where to report. Tess pushed through the lines to the table.

"Nory," she shouted. "Have you seen the prince?"

"He left, my lady," Nory said, still beckoning men forward. "Said he'd be gone for days. Can you believe that? Left Rette and myself with the training. But we're up to it, eh, Rette?" Rette nodded a strawberry blond head and patted a thick leather vest that was clamped around his slim torso. Nory was wearing one to match.

"What are those? Where did you get them?"

"We made them," Nory said. "With His Highness, mind you. What do you think he's been doing all this time?" He winked. Tess felt sick. Everyone had lost their minds.

"Lady Tessamine." A black terrier appeared at her feet. "I advise you go home and stay indoors until further notice. I will send word to Colonel Thorn that you are to be under strict surveillance, by order of the queen."

"General Bud, I must speak with Her Majesty," Tess said.

"Out of the question," he said with a slight growl. "You have your orders. Now go to, young lady."

"Tessy." Dahly approached with a glum-looking Ryon in tow. "Where have you been? You changed your hair. . . ." The concern in Dahly's voice caused Tess's throat to catch.

"Xandra's horn." She gulped quietly. "Let's just go home." She looked over her shoulder for Tynaiv, but he had not followed her.

Tess and her siblings found their father debating in a circle of advisors, while their mother stood anxiously nearby.

"You have been so brave, dearest," Lady Matilde said. "It was prudent of you to take some time to yourself." Guilt gnawed at Tess's heart.

Ryon let out an exasperated groan. "Mother, let me volunteer. I can fight with the prince. I can—"

"That is enough." Sir Brock turned from his colleagues when he saw his family had been reunited. "This militia is illegal and borderline treasonous. I hate to speak against the prince, but I cannot understand what prompted him to take such a radical stance."

"The queen was attacked, Papa," Dahly said.

"First light tomorrow," Sir Brock addressed his fellow advisors. "This cannot stand." Then General Bud called out from the abandoned orchestra platform.

"Lords, ladies, citizens, and governors. I beg your attention once again. Her Majesty, Queen Aideen, requests a council in the court hall immediately. All advisors and judges are expected."

"Even better," Sir Brock said, kissing his wife's hair. "Good night. I shall be late, I think."

Mechanically, Tess followed the rest of her family to the castle doors and allowed the servants to cover her with her cloak and help her into the royal carriage. Crowds loitered outside the castle, some making hurried arrangements to depart for their homes, others begging the servants to allow them to stay in the castle, as they feared sleeping another night in the campgrounds. Through the carriage window, Tess saw Belle and her mother walking hand in hand. After the prince's speech, no one else would dare travel at night without a horse or caravan. But here they were, alone on the road, with nothing but a staff in the woman's hand.

Tess pressed her forehead against the windowpane. She did not deserve that little girl's admiration. She would never deserve Prince Linden's, either. The queen had chosen the wrong girl.

CHAPTER 5

Tess glided through an old forest. Something smooth and hot pulled her by the hand. Lush trees brushed against her arms until she reached a clearing where a winding lake was filled with crystal-clear water. The object in her hand pulled harder, and she heard herself call out, "I am the new guardian of Glademont, sent to free you!"

"Get dressed, quickly," Lady Matilde whispered, shaking Tess awake. A stout candlestick lit her mother's worried face.

"What? What time is it?" Tess grumbled.

"We have to get to the castle as quickly as possible. Wake Dahly and come downstairs." Lady Matilde disappeared down the hall.

Tess stumbled out of bed and pulled on a pair of riding boots. She touched her braid to make sure the *shenil* was still there. Dahly stirred in the bed across the room.

"I'm awake, and I'm not happy about it," she whispered hoarsely.

Still in their cotton nightgowns, Dahly and Tess shuffled downstairs. They followed muffled noises through the servants' corridor and to the kitchen. There, they found their mother and brother silently packing satchels made of painted leather. The cook and housekeeper must have retired to their cottages hours before. Only a few candles were lit, and cold starlight crept in from the kitchen window.

"Are we going to be picnicking at the castle tonight?" yawned Dahly.

"Girls, why aren't you dressed?" their mother whispered. "Oh, it's too late now. Get your cloaks and stay away from the windows."

Tess and Dahly fumbled in the dark to obey their mother. Beside the cloak hooks, the door that led out to the stables swung open, and in stepped Sir Brock, still in his velvet from the wedding festival. He peered out the window. "The horses are ready. Hurry, Matilde. I saw torches up the road."

Lady Matilde handed Tess a sack of walnuts and pointed at the satchels. Dahly dropped into a chair by Tess, still groggy from her rude awakening.

"Where's Reggie? Is he all right?" Tess asked as her mother handed her a bar of soap.

"The Colonel's on watch outside," Lady Matilde said. "Girls, the queen has ordered all noble families to take refuge in the castle—tonight."

"Refuge?" Tess's hands shook as she broke the bar of soap into pieces for each satchel.

"Is this about the assassin?" Dahly said.

"You there," called a familiar voice. "Show yourself, in the name of Queen Aideen!" Outside, Colonel Regency Thorn growled ominously, and a strange dog growled in reply. The three young Canyons dropped their tasks and rushed to the window.

In the starlight stood the Colonel, straight and strong. He raised his hackles as he faced the gloom of the apple orchard. A red bloodhound stepped out of the darkness, teeth bared. Even when crouching, the bloodhound was at least three times as large as the terrier. Unmoved, the Colonel barked again.

"I warn you, scum. Take your rabble off of this estate, or you will be shown no mercy."

The bloodhound snarled and began to cross the bridge. Half a dozen torches materialized, carried by strange men. Each wore a belted woolen tunic and loose trousers tucked into high boots. Against their thighs hung wide blades. Tess had never seen a dagger in person, only in old tapestries and murals. The sight of them kindled a rising panic in her throat.

"Atheonians," Sir Brock said over Tess's shoulder. "But they are too rough to be soldiers. What is this?"

A grizzly Atheonian in front pointed his torch at the Colonel.

"Calm down, Sarge. We ain't here t'loot. We're on a special errand," he said. "Smooth Crow wants t'speak with a lady."

A large crow swooped to the low branch of an apple tree. As it fluttered to steady itself, its black body gleamed almost purple in the torchlight.

"A needless war has already been set in motion," it said. "But I might be able to stop it if Lady Tessamine has what I think she has."

The men holding the other torches shifted restlessly.

The Colonel stood his ground. "Tell your friend, sir hound, that no man or creature may enter the manor. I shall not yield until you and this poorly manicured flock have vacated the grounds."

While the bloodhound advanced toward the Colonel with a menacing growl, the fourteen-inch salt-and-pepper governor nervously licked his nose.

Tess gripped her mother's arm. Couldn't she see those men were going to hurt Reggie? Why wasn't anyone doing anything? Lady Matilde squeezed Tess's wrist and put her finger to her lips.

Six torches lowered as the men started for the Colonel.

"No," Tess shouted. "Reggie, run!"

The men stopped to look at the house.

"Alive, gentlemen," the crow said from his branch. "I want her alive."

"May the oath protect her," the Colonel said, almost as though it were a prayer. Then, retreating two steps, the Colonel lowered his head to the ground. The bloodhound mirrored his stance. A colossal growl resounded from somewhere deep inside the Colonel's chest. Tess had never heard anything like it. The jars in the kitchen pantries rattled. Ryon and Dahly held on to each other with fright.

"Come on, gents, into the house," yelled the leader of the band. The men made a dash for the Canyon home. One dark-haired Atheonian had sprinted ahead of the rest, but suddenly halted, mesmerized.

"Oy, watch it!" he shouted, and pointed to the terrier.

The Colonel's breath had transformed into a glowing, fluid gas, swirling from his nostrils and surging toward the Atheonians—a stream of golden air. The stream crashed against the dark-haired man and wrapped around his legs. Then, as the Colonel raised his head and barked thunderously, the golden stream burst about its target and flung the man high into the air. Over the orchard he flew, crashing hard on Nobleman's Road. Even from inside the house, Tess could hear the man's anguished moans.

By this time, the other men had taken shelter in the shrubbery surrounding the front of the manor, looking on their miniature adversary with horror.

"Come, you slobbering tree-chaser," called the Colonel to the bloodhound. "You will answer next."

His enemy responded with a flash of red from his nostrils. It snaked its way along the ground before wrapping itself around the Colonel's neck. The governor rolled onto his back and struggled to breathe.

Tess gasped. "Red magic."

The Colonel managed to pry a paw under the gaseous rope that squeezed his neck. It provided just enough room for a quick breath, and thin golden strands streamed from his nostrils. They converged and wound themselves around the red rope, causing it to dissolve.

"Smooth Crow didn't say nothin' 'bout no golden magic," one of the bewildered Atheonians shouted.

"That's why we've got the dog, bug brains," another answered. "Let 'em fight it out. Into the house."

Tess saw another flash of gold, and then flashes of red as the men rushed up the stairs to Canyon Manor. One of the dogs yelped in pain—but which one?

Five men bearing torches tumbled through the front door. Tess clung to her sister as she heard them barreling through the parlor and down the stairs that led to the servants' corridor. Sir Brock met them in the narrow hallway, blocking their passage into the kitchen.

"We do not know violence in this home. If you wish to see my daughter, you will respect the law. Surrender your weapons." His face burned with determination.

The Atheonians crowded around the kitchen door, laughing. "Did you hear?" one said. "His ladyship says we should mind our manners." He lunged for Sir Brock's arm and threw the nobleman into the kitchen. Grasping a chair, Sir Brock retreated, shielding his family.

"Matilde, get them out of here," he said, straining to keep his composure. Sweat dripped from his nose. Tess moved to pick up a chair herself.

"Get back, Tessy," her father shouted.

"So," sneered an Atheonian, slowly entering the kitchen. "That's our gal?"

Sir Brock lunged, splintering the legs of his chair against the man. The Atheonian yelled and dropped his torch, and within seconds the cabinetry and wallpaper had ignited. The ensuing flames sent two men back through the hallway and outside as Sir Brock stood to contend with the three who remained. Matilde rushed to her husband's side, desperately brandishing an iron pan.

"Tessy, watch out," Ryon called.

A clanging sounded to Tess's right, and something heavy crashed into the kitchen table. Tess turned to find an unconscious man lying crumpled on the floor, a dagger in his hand. Ryon stood over him, holding a water jug.

"*What has gotten into you?*" Tess shouted over the chaos.

"I told you I could fight," he said. He tossed a red satchel at Tess.

"We have to get you out of here," Dahly yelled. "The stables."

Tess and Ryon stumbled to the door by the cloak hooks. As the house filled with smoke, it became more and more difficult for them to breathe.

"Mother," Tess called.

"Go," she heard Lady Matilde answer as an Atheonian howled in pain.

Dahly disappeared through the open door. Tess lingered, straining to see through the billowing smoke. Sir Brock fended someone off with the remnants of his chair. Tess could not see her mother. Ryon shoved her through the door.

Tess ran to the stable, clutching her red satchel. Her head buzzed from inhaling smoke, and her eyes stung. When Tess reached her stallion, Jesse, he was already saddled. She threw her arms around his neck and allowed herself one silent sob. Jesse's butterscotch body and creamy white mane quivered in the starlight. Like all noble horses, he never spoke, not with words. Tess loved him as her brother. She pulled a white-socked hoof toward her chest and hugged it. At a full gallop,

Jesse could outpace any horse in the dione, and that was what Tess was counting on.

"Ride for the castle." Dahly spoke in a tense whisper. Tess stole a glance back at her beloved home. Smoke twisted out of the windows. Jesse shook his head and snorted.

"Mother and Papa are still inside," Tess said.

"They want you, Tess," said Ryon, hoisting himself onto Jesse's saddle in front of his sister. "They're not after Mother and Papa. We have to get you out of here."

Jesse's accord was clear enough. His strong legs pounded out of the stable, leaping over the creek and onto Nobleman's Road alongside Dahly's chestnut mare.

Ahead, two more Atheonians on horseback pulled onto the road, their saddles gleaming with fine clothes and silver. Tess's stomach turned. The foreigners were looting Glademont's nobles. Behind, four more torches fast approached, and Tess recognized the voice of the pack leader who had struck her father.

"There, Counselor. I see them on the road," he called.

"Hey, Tess, can I get 'em with my sling?" Ryon said.

"What? Yes, you have it with you?"

"Of course," Ryon reached into his pockets, which were bulging with stones and pebbles.

"Vermin and . . ."

"The ones in front, first," Dahly called to Ryon, pointing at the Atheonians ahead, who were gulping from flasks as their horses trotted along.

While Ryon loaded his sling, Dahly galloped ahead, veering toward a tree and snapping a branch from its trunk. Then, leaning skillfully on her horse, she came upon an Atheonian by surprise and thrust the blunt end of the branch against his head. A metal flask clattered to the ground as the man collapsed.

The second man dismounted, shielding himself behind his own horse. He pointed a saber at Dahly as she circled back, daring her to try again. Ryon shouted for Tess to duck. She obeyed, her pulse racing as Ryon's sling whirled over them both in great, whooshing strokes. A moment later, a stone hit the second man squarely in the temple, and he reeled. Seeing her opportunity, Dahly rapped her branch on the back of the dazed man's neck. He fell and did not move.

The Atheonians from behind were almost upon them.

Dahly pulled her mare alongside. Her whole body was shaking. "We'll need to separate them."

Tess nodded. She was a strong rider; she had to be to handle Jesse's speed.

Two Canyon horses galloped wildly down Nobleman's Road. And though the Atheonians had gained ground, their glowing torches served as perfect targets for Ryon. He twisted underneath Tess's arm, clinging close to Jesse's body. Before long, Tess heard the agonized screams of two men. Still, with Tess and Dahly riding side by side, the remaining two Atheonians were only three lengths behind.

A frightening rush of feathers swooped over Tess's head, nearly throwing her off of Jesse's back. She screamed. The feathery shadow descended on her again, and this time Tess could clearly make out the outline of a crow. Its beak was open as it reached for her shoulder with its talons. For one paralyzing moment, Tess saw the bird's eyes. They were milky gray, unseeing.

"Get away." Ryon batted at the bird. It wavered, circled overhead, and dove again. Ryon swung his sling, leaving the rock inside and using it as a mace. It hit its mark just as the crow's beak was inches from Tess's neck. The bird dropped out of sight.

"I'll lead them off," Dahly cried.

Before Tess could protest, her sister pulled her mare into the thick brush that bordered Nobleman's Road. A moment passed. Tess dared not look behind her. Then, a shrill whinny sounded close behind—the Atheonians had stayed on the road.

Grasping Ryon's waist with one hand and Jesse's mane with the other, Tess leaned forward and spoke in Jesse's ear, "Let's get out of here."

Jesse stretched his solid legs across the ground with a new burst of speed, his hooves thundering smoothly against the road. The air swirled around Tess's face, roaring in her ears as Jesse bolted away from the last of the Atheonians.

Tess buried her head in the blond stallion's neck and concentrated on her breathing, trying not to let fear get the better of her. Every passing tree looked like an ambush. Every *snap* that echoed through the brush sounded like an approaching Atheonian.

As they fled into the dark, Tess thought of Reggie, who could throw a man twenty feet in the air with one growl. She thought of the copper orbs in her hair, which the crow had almost taken. She thought of her mother and father, and their home consumed by flames.

As Jesse, Tess, and Ryon sped into the night, the stars began to give way to the first creeping light of dawn. Navy clouds raced across the sky. Tess held Ryon tight. Just a little longer and they would reach a bend in the road leading to the castle. Soon they would be safe.

Eventually, the brush turned to shaggy trees. Tess saw neither the clouds nor the stars. It occurred to her they should have made it to the bend by then. Tess slowed her horse's gait. All was still and silent; not even an insect could be heard. The air hung close.

"Tessy, are we lost?" Ryon whispered.

Tess peered around her in the gloom of early dawn, searching for anything that might look familiar. Ahead, she could make out the silhouettes of dense, gnarled tree trunks. Beneath her horse's hooves, the ground was covered in soft moss.

They were most certainly lost.

Tess sat cross-legged beside a sputtering fire in her nightgown and riding boots. Next to her, Jesse whinnied softly, and Ryon lay curled up on the moss. Tess twisted the pearls around her finger, and they caught the first rays of the sun stretching between tangled forest branches. She glanced at Ryon to make sure he was asleep.

"Jesse, I've always told you my secrets. I know I'd go mad otherwise." She walked to his butterscotch head and touched his flat cheek. "But last night I acted so unforgivably. I don't know . . . will you see me differently?" He nuzzled her hand. Tess leaned against her friend's strong neck, clutching the braid Queen Aideen had woven. "Last night, Queen Aideen gave me something she claims has protected Glademont for generations." Tess buried her face in Jesse's ivory mane. "I was supposed to keep it hidden, that's all. One simple task. But I didn't. I was so angry with Prince Linden for making a fool of me, and I was confused and . . . and I met a man." The muscles in Jesse's neck tensed. "I don't know how it happened—I showed it to him. And suddenly those Atheonians appeared on our doorstep, knowing what I have. They will catch me, Jesse. And then Glademont will fall."

Tess stroked her horse's forelock and stared at his eyes. She knew he was listening. Would he really keep his vow of silence, even now? When everything was falling apart?

A log snapped in the fire, and orange sparks shot into the air. Startled, Tess wrapped her arms about Jesse's neck. He nickered.

"I am a coward," she said with her face against Jesse. "I am as weak as the prince believes me to be."

"Looks like you've gotta use that mystery object now, don'tcha think?" asked a baritone voice.

"What in the heavens—" Tess jumped and nearly fell into the fire.

A robust little towhee flitted to Jesse's haunches. His black head and wings stood out like an overcoat over a soft white breast and thick red stripes beneath the shoulders. "There, there, there." He twittered pleasantly. "Now, now, now. I'm in no need for all that huffle and puffle."

It was shocking that such a deep voice could come from such a small beak. Almost as shocking as the familiar way with which he addressed perfect strangers.

"Pardon me, but you are standing on my horse," Tess said.

"Ooooooh, I don't mind. A horse is worth a thousand branches in my book."

Tess blinked. This creature was possibly mad. Hadn't General Bud instructed the prince not to speak to the wild animals? Had she already betrayed the *shenil* for the second time? Tess adjusted her approach.

"If we have trespassed in any way . . ."

"Horses are noble creatures, you know. Most humans forget that, because they sit on chairs as often as they do horses. I say the only similarity is that they both have legs."

"Forgive me, but may I ask who you are?"

Shaking out his wings, the towhee clacked his beak twice. "Most just call me Profigliano" was his answer.

Tess blinked again at the small bird.

"Now, as to the object in your head feathers . . ."

"I do not wish to discuss the subject with you, if you don't mind." Tess's heart raced. "I meant only to confide in my horse."

Profigliano hopped sideways until he reached Jesse's shoulder. "There's nothing sneaky about a fellow hearing what's being said."

"I fail to see how my predicament is your concern," Tess murmured, still hoping not to wake Ryon. The sooner this bird was on his way, the better.

Profigliano looked at Tess, his expression grave.

"Listen here, old girl," he said. "If you are going to be adventuring about in this here Hinge Forest, you will need to use your best forest manners." Stunned by this scolding, Tess fell silent. Profigliano continued. "There are heaps and heaps of creatures in this cobwebby old wood, and most of them do not take kindly to visitors. From now on, you better do a little sifting before you dump your words all over the place."

"Are we really in the Hinge Forest?" Ryon sat up, wide awake. "Excuse me, I am Master Ryon Canyon." He stood to bow to the towhee. "And this is my elder sister, Lady Tessamine." Tess shot Ryon a deadly glare. Profigliano, on the other hand, seemed pleased.

"Well, well, well," he said, clacking his beak. "My, my, my. That's what I'm talkin' about." His white underbelly glowed in the morning sun as he swooped down to Tess's satchel. Turning to Ryon, he bowed reverently.

"My name is Profigliano Julius Towhee the Eleventh, and in the name of Queen Aideen, I pledge to assist you in your quest—until death!"

Ryon grinned from ear to ear. Tess, on the other hand, was not so taken in. She pondered the eager bird.

"Master Profigliano, you are mistaken," she said. "We pursue no quest. Our only concern is to rejoin our family at Glademont Castle."

"Tessamine," replied Profigliano. "You are most certainly and without a doubt on a quest. If it looks like pie and smells like pie, you might as well loosen your belt."

Ryon was still grinning, his hands shoved in his pockets.

"Skies help me," Tess said. "I have yet to see the quest in this."

"The object." Profigliano twittered. "You said it yourself; the thug bugs from the other kingdom know you've got it. You might as well learn how to use it. Then you can face 'em when they get ya."

It wasn't a bad point, even considering its source. Tess held her braid out, and an orb buzzed against her fingers. Was it communicating with her?

"What is it, Tessy?" Ryon approached, peering into her black strands.

She sighed. "It's the reason we were attacked, I think. Queen Aideen gave it to me for safekeeping. She said it had the power to protect Glademont from red magic."

"Like what the hound used against Reggie?" Ryon frowned.

Tess nodded. "Though it didn't seem so powerful then. There is a magician named Pider . . . he was willing to kill the queen to get this. Now he will be after me." Tess swallowed. She couldn't bring herself to tell Ryon of her treason. She couldn't bear to guess what he'd think of her.

"If we try to get to the castle now, we'll run right into those Atheonians," Ryon said.

"What else can we do?" Tess rubbed her forehead. "We have no idea whether the rest of the family made it to safety. They may still need us."

"I see, I gotcha, hold a second then." Profigliano scratched his head with a talon. "My bird-brain is tellin' me that Tessy and the young master have got to go into the jungle, and not back through the prairie, if ya know what I mean." He shook his feathers with an air of importance. "So I'll just have to slip over to the grand old mountain house and observe what I can see for myself."

"You know Glademont Castle? Have you been there before?" Tess looked incredulously at Profigliano. The bird hopped from one foot to the other, looking out of the corners of his eyes and rubbing his head with his wing.

"Thaaaaat's a whole lotta questioning for one human, if ya wanna know what I think. So a bird's got the itch to travel—why all the hoopla?"

"I'm sorry, it's just that you said the creatures in this forest weren't fond of—"

"Profigliano said this! Profigliano said that! We're gettin' real cheeky over here in this camp." The towhee's voice raised in pitch to a low tenor. "So what if I fly out to see the mountains every-so-now-and-again? So what if I'm the only Hinger that leaves these stuffy trees? Those moun-tain jays are a good bunch of chirpers."

"I see," Tess said. "And I thank you for your offer, but if you will just lead us out of the forest, Ryon and I will . . ."

She could not finish her sentence. What if Ryon was right and they were walking right into the hands of the Atheonians? Queen Aideen's words rang in Tess's head: *Keep it safe.*

"Aaaaall right, no need to be insulting." Profigliano flew in a circle about the trunk of a nearby hemlock. "All you have to worry about is that special thingy in your hair. I'm no expert, but it sounds like the safer you are, the safer is the Mont of Glades. Moreover and hitherto, it is my first order of duty, as your dedicated Hinge Guide and Quest Captain, to make sure you stay far away from those Fatheos fellows."

After another lap around the hemlock, Profigliano flitted back to Tess and alighted on her wrist. He met her puzzled look with a shrug of his wings.

"What do you have to lose?"

And with that, the baritone towhee disappeared through the trees. Tess sighed as she watched him go.

"I have everything to lose," she said.

The forest air was cool, and the sun's rays glowed faintly through ancient trees. Under different circumstances, Tess would have enjoyed reading a good love story in their branches. But the tainted experience of her first kiss might have killed her affinity for romance for good. She stared woefully at the web of swaying timber. No two trees in the forest were alike. Spruces, oaks, hollies, and pines were all arrayed together like a bed of wildflowers. Each trunk was as thick as six men, rising like pillars into a silent stand. Strangest of all was the silence. It gave her the distinct impression of being watched.

Neither Tess nor Ryon had slept more than a few hours, and the effects were evident. Ryon's jacket was hopelessly crumpled, and his cin-namon hair swirled defiantly upward on the left side of his head. Tess groaned and pulled her cloak around her thin nightgown. Stroking her braid, she felt the *shenil*. She followed the thin leather strap as it inter-laced with her hair, down to the copper balls that adorned each end.

"What do we do now?" Ryon said.

"I don't know." Reluctantly, she set to work pulling apart her hair. She held the *shenil* in her palm, with the long strap coiled in a pile. The spheres on either end of the strap ignited with a soft light, creating a warm buzzing against her skin.

"By the skies," Ryon whispered.

Tess carefully turned each orb in her hands. The surfaces were smooth; no inscriptions. The light from the orbs receded.

"Do you think it's a good sign when the glowing stops?" Ryon asked.

"I doubt it." Tess slowly uncoiled the strap, running her fingers along it until they caught on a small dangling item. "I found something."

It was an oval medal, no bigger than a thumbnail. Waving markings ran around its perimeter. Tess could not make out the symbols, but she distinctly observed a figure etched into the center of the medal.

"It's a woman's torso," she said. "See there? She has long hair, and these must be her hands in some sort of pose."

"What is that on her stomach?" Ryon said. "It looks like a flame."

Then Tess remembered. "Queen Aideen spoke of fire when she gave the *shenil* to me. She said if I listened to it, I would become fire." She shivered at the thought and moodily worked the *shenil* back into her hair. The braid was not so intricate as when the queen had spun it, but it would hold. "If we are going to stay here until I learn to use this, we may turn old and gray among these trees."

"I'm afraid that is out of the question," came a startling reply from above.

Tess looked upward and found, perched on the ancient branches of the surrounding trees, a host of several hundred birds of different size and color. Lack of sleep and a strong dislike for being surprised had made Tess bold. She stepped forward, directing her gaze somewhere between a violet canary and an orange chickadee.

"Can there be no privacy in this wood?" Tess demanded. "Or are its creatures unaccustomed to introductions?" Ryon tugged at Tess's cloak.

"Its creatures consider humans a special case," replied a large red owl. The creature spread a pair of grand wings and glided to the forest floor. "I suggest you quickly and politely tell us what you are doing in the Hinge Forest, girl."

CHAPTER 6

The trail along the foothills of the Zere Mountain stretched west from Glademont Castle toward the northernmost border of the Hinge Forest. Though it was nearing midnight, Linden's horse sauntered comfortably in the dark. She had borne him along this path almost every evening for months. Over an hour had passed since Linden had been sent away on this ludicrous errand, and he let his mare pick her way across the shale and weeds at her own pace. His hands took turns clenching the saddle horn. He was almost to the tree line, and he closed his eyes to concentrate on the familiar silence of those ancient branches.

The canopy covered Prince Linden and his mount like a thick quilt. He felt his confidence slowly returning. If delivering this absurd letter to King Nabal was what Queen Aideen requested of him, he would obey. But he would carry out his mission on his own terms—that meant weapons. He would not die a fool in a foreign country. He would arrive in Nabal's court a warrior, a true prince.

And he would leave alive.

Linden's mare halted and lowered her head to graze on a tuft of moss. The prince almost nudged her to continue on until he saw the beech tree. A shot of exhilaration stirred him from his gloomy thoughts, and he slipped from his saddle onto the brittle carpet of leaves. He scaled the tree, digging the toes of his boots into shallow notches along its trunk and steadying himself against the sloping branches. At the center of the beech, perhaps three men high, rested a small, thatched-roof hut. Its round sides fit snugly against the tree's creaking arms. Linden hoisted himself onto a branch and balanced along it to where a low door greeted him.

Until the first night of his cursed wedding festival, every evening Linden spent in the Armory was a good one. Six months ago he, Nory, and Rette built this hideaway to stash the weapons they made. Before their drills, the three of them would swagger around the small hut, testing the swords and arrows, making note as to how their next attempts would fare even better. Rette made regular journeys to Green Reed to consult with a blacksmith sworn to secrecy. Linden's covert visits down to the archive rooms revealed more and more of the art of weaponry. The thrill of possibility and power pulsed through their veins.

But the feeling that shivered through Linden's limbs now was a kind of dreadful anticipation. They were no longer preparing for a distant, romantically epic war. Instead they were scrambling to defend themselves against a possible horde of seasoned soldiers. Linden struck a match, lit the lantern, and scanned the carefully arranged bows, lances, knives, and shields within his Armory. He thought of Nory and Rette wrangling undisciplined, naive young Glademontians in the castle at that very moment. How long did they have before the assassin returned for the queen's life? How long before Nabal mobilized his own forces? Glademont's defenselessness haunted Linden like a dormant disease, ready to flare, poised to expose his weakness.

He set his jaw and strode to his longbow, savored the feel of the wood grain against his palm and plucked the string. Quickly, he strapped his quiver to his back and stashed a dagger in a thin sheath sewn inside his boot. It was one of the first ways he devised to conceal a weapon on his person. Every time he touched it, he thought of his father, and how things would be different if the king had had even a simple dagger in his boot when he last left Glademont. . . .

The prince tightened the leather vest across his chest and covered his shoulders again with his cloak. He could not live in the past. Glademont's future needed to be different. He would see to that. All he could do now was deliver the note quickly, cautiously, and then return to train his militia. Linden turned to leave his beloved Armory, perhaps for a long while, when he saw something lying on the worktable.

He laughed dryly and shook his head. A new sling he fashioned only a week before as a gift for little Ryon Canyon. It was more powerful than the first sling, and more elegant. Should he take it now? No, it would only upset Lady Tessamine the more. Though what living creature could avoid upsetting the lady? Linden hung the sling on a nail by the door and promised himself he'd take Ryon here in secret one day, wife or no wife.

He blew the lantern out and closed the door, careful not to break the tip of his longbow against the low frame. Laden with his weapons, Linden paused at the base of the broad branch to test his balance. But before stepping out, a shrill neigh pulled his attention to the forest floor. His mare shied from under the beech, and some flying creature glided over Linden's head. Its feathers rustled inches from the prince's ear. He dropped to his knees and froze, listening for where the creature went. But no more sounds came, except from his perturbed mare.

Only one other Hinge Forester had dared go near the prince in all the months they had hidden among these trees to train. And he didn't fly.

CHAPTER 7

Tess stared at the large red owl hooting at her feet. Surrounding them in the trees, an impressive array of smaller birds raised their high-pitched voices, apparently in support of the owl's chagrin. With great effort, Tess again recalled General Bud's instructions for journeying through the forest.

"We are foreigners to these lands . . . merchants," she stammered. "We are passing through this forest only to reach the lands west of here." Tess could feel Ryon's eyes on her. She prayed he would keep still.

"You and your party will follow us," the owl replied. Her words were clipped and on edge. It seemed the merchant story was no good. Tess wondered petulantly what reasons this nocturnal creature had for patrolling at this hour.

At once the trees swarmed with fluttering yellows, oranges, and blues. Most of the birds took to the sky and disappeared, but two dozen remained, flocking around the Canyons and their horse. Tess grimaced at the abundance of high-pitched chattering. To Tess's left, a row of birds sat expectantly on a pine branch. When she turned to discuss this strange occurrence with Ryon, she found that the same was also true to her right.

"This is absurd," Tess muttered.

"I don't believe we have a choice." Ryon took his sister's hand and began to walk.

Twenty paces later, the birds abandoned their branches with great commotion and assumed new ones along the path. Tess felt Ryon's hand squeeze hers. He nodded toward the braid down her back. Carefully, Tess pulled the *shenil* free of her hair and gathered it into her fist. It was only a precaution. Surely these wild animals knew nothing of the object. Then again, why would Prince Linden be instructed to hide his nationality from them?

"Excuse me," called Tess to the owl. The sentry birds near her shoulder tweeted and sang in admonishment. Tess winced but ignored their screeching. "Are we nearing the kingdom of Atheos? Or have we turned east to Glademont?" Tess hoped she was giving a convincing impression of mild interest. She squinted up at the treetops where she knew the owl was waiting impatiently for them to catch up.

The owl swooped nearer but not lower, forcing Tess to look into the sun. Tess heard a sharp suspicion in the bird's voice.

"Have you business in those lands?"

Tess cleared her throat as Ryon squeezed her hand again. "Only to sell our wares."

"You have no wares, girl," said the owl. "You have only two bags and a horse. Those who travel between the human lands know to go south through the hills. This land belongs to the wild, but it seems your kind have found reason to break that agreement."

"Whatever your dispute with Glademont, we are not a part of it—"

"Our dispute is with humankind." The owl hooted, and her many sentries fell upon Tess, pecking at her hair and temples. Clinging to the *shenil* in panic, Tess turned toward her brother. He reached for her hood and covered her head.

"You try to deceive me as Glademont deceived our ancestors," called the owl. "The cycle will not be repeated; the council is determined of that."

Tess curled in on herself, grasping the *shenil* until finally the owl called off the tiny attackers with another shrill hoot.

Ryon swatted at the last of the finches about his sister's covered head. "Where are we going?" he asked angrily.

"Close your beaks and do as you are told," came the owl's reply, and again she disappeared into the treetops.

Tess's hope grew dimmer at the passing of every hour. Even if they could escape these birds, how would Tess find her way back to the edge of the forest? How long would Profigliano wait with news of her family? Tess's sockless feet ached in her riding boots, and the red owl eyed her as she swooped to and fro between the trees. Finally, Tess's limbs and stomach could be ignored no longer. With no more than a few hours repose in two days, she chanced another exchange with the owl.

"Could we rest?" she called at the treetops once more. "We've been walking for so long, and my brother and I must eat."

She expected no more than a spiteful glance from their captor. But to Tess's surprise, the owl glided straight for her. Instinctively, Tess adjusted the *shenil* in her moist palm and rubbed her finger over one of its orbs. The object snapped into a quiet buzz. Then the owl's round eyes met Tess's, and something odd happened.

As Tess and the owl gazed at each other, all the world seemed to pause. The owl hung in the air with rays of sunlight glistening on her wings, so that some feathers even seemed to glow like precious metal. Somehow, Tess found solace in the gleam of the owl's wings, and she forgot the pain in her feet and the emptiness in her stomach. Then Tess heard a soft voice, sounding remarkably like her own.

Trust her.

But the words had not left Tess's lips; she had heard them only in her thoughts.

Trust her, rang again in Tess's ears, but not in the air.

It occurred to Tess that she might be half-dazed from exhaustion. Confused, Tess tore her gaze from the owl.

"*Keehee,*" screeched the owl as she tumbled into the brush. Rushing toward the fallen creature and shooing away the chickadees and finches to get a better look, Tess found the owl crumpled in the prickly leaves of a holly bush. The persistent birds swarmed about the owl, straightening her feathers with their beaks. But the owl paid no heed, staring up at Tess.

"If you are tired, you may ride on the horse," she said.

"What happened?" Ryon ran to Tess, despite the objections of the cardinals who stayed behind to watch him. Seeing the owl in the bush, Ryon couldn't help but grin. "Holy cider, did you knock her out, Tessy?"

The owl's feathers now in place, she returned to the air with two swift flaps of her wings. Then she circled overhead and addressed Jesse directly.

"Sir, I have given permission to ride on account of bodily fatigue. Nevertheless, you and your party are our prisoners. If you attempt escape, you will not get far in this part of the Hinge."

"Tessy," whispered Ryon, "do you think she knows about noble horses?" Jesse shifted nearer to his human companions. His soft lips moved briefly, but no words came.

"At this point," Tess said, "I am sure of nothing." She swung onto Jesse's back and waited for the chirping birds to resume their formation.

CHAPTER 8

J udging by the setting sun, Tess and Ryon had been traveling south and a little west through the Hinge Forest for much of the day. With only a few minutes of sunlight left, Tess wondered if they would continue on through the night. She had twice dipped into her satchel for some bread and a green apple. Ryon, who had joined Tess on Jesse's back, reclined against her shoulder.

As twilight settled in, they approached a cluster of enormous brick-red trees, their trunks riddled with holes large enough to fit a human fist. Each hole teemed with glowing fireflies. Tess couldn't help but admire the display.

"Come, the council is anxious to see you," the owl said.

"Our presence in the forest has offended you." Tess had to bring Jesse to a trot to keep up with the owl. "But I can assure you, bringing us here—wherever this is—is unnecessary. We are willing to take our leave."

"This forest has not seen humans for over two hundred years. Now they are appearing everywhere. Forgive us if we are inclined to investigate." As they drew near the red trees, the owl alighted on a low branch. "The creatures of the Hinge are accustomed to a certain degree of formality. I advise you watch what you say and do." The red owl turned to face the trees and hooted. "I will see you inside the nest," she said as her head swiveled. Great wings swooshed against the dusky air, and the owl disappeared.

Tess waited in the silence for several slow seconds. Their chattering sentries had left. It was too dusky to see much of anything except for the fireflies gathered inside the tree trunks. The scene was almost peaceful.

Finally, Ryon dismounted and tucked his soiled shirt into his trousers. Wanting to regain feeling in her numb toes, Tess landed beside her brother and pulled her cloak around her shoulders. Jesse tossed his white tail. They waited silently for what seemed another age. Nightfall was almost upon them.

From the nearest tree trunk, one of the glowing holes emptied itself of fireflies, which then floated delicately toward the three Glademontians. Two hovered in front of Tess's nose, two in front of Ryon's, and two on either side of Jesse's butterscotch head. Tess's eyes crossed as she tried to focus on the glowing insects.

"Does this steed call himself Jesse?" the sharp voice of a robin called out from the vacated hole.

"Yes . . . yes, my lord." Tess was not sure as to the proper way to address a bird. Did they hold rank like the governors back home? If so, she certainly didn't want to guess incorrectly.

"Silence, girl," the robin said, hopping slightly farther from Tess.

Counting on the fireflies that illuminated her face, Tess shot the bird a withering glare. The robin twittered and rephrased his question.

"Sir, are you Jesse? Rumored to be the swiftest steed on Diatonica?" he asked.

No one moved. Tess glanced at Ryon, who was looking at Jesse's glowing face expectantly.

"I am," Jesse replied. Tess heard Ryon gasp. She bit her lip and shook her head in disbelief. The pitch of the stallion's voice sounded like a young man's, but the quality was airy and quiet, as though he had just woken from a restful sleep. Tess never dreamed she would hear that voice. And despite the shock, she smiled inwardly; he sounded exactly as she imagined he might.

"I am Jesse of Glademont, beast of Lady Matilde Canyon. Yesterday, our household was attacked, and we fled into the forest."

So much for keeping their identities a secret.

"I see," the robin replied. "I assume the horse clan in your land does not normally communicate with humans?"

"Many choose the Way of Silence."

"A wise decision, no doubt. Although it is better to avoid humans altogether."

"We disagree" was the horse's reply. Tess smiled, outwardly this time.

"Yes, yes, I see." The robin hopped to the rim of his hollow. "Then you are indeed the one called 'The Rushing'?"

"The Rushing?" Ryon cut in, gazing at the stallion with a wide grin.

The robin ignored Ryon. "The council requests the Rushing act as ambassador for these prisoners," he announced. "Do you accept this proposal?"

"I do," Jesse said quietly.

"Good." The robin sighed and spread his wings. "This way, please."

The fireflies darted after the robin. Jesse moved forward deliberately, and his companions followed. A path was lit for them past the outstretched branches of the red trees. And as the brusque robin hopped impatiently from one trunk to another, Tess, Jesse, and Ryon carefully navigated the twisted branches of the trees.

"Come along, prisoners," chirped the robin.

Finally, they cleared the twisted ruddy trunks and came to what looked like an enormous upside-down basket reaching four stories high. The skeleton of the structure consisted of live trees, all arching toward the center. Brambles and leaves were carefully woven in the spaces between the trees, forming thick, curved walls. The result, in fact, was an enormous nest. Two openings punctured the structure: one at the top, and a much narrower one accessible from the forest floor. Although the latter threshold was easy enough for Tess and Ryon to pass, Jesse stepped through it with some difficulty.

Inside, they found the branch-lined walls covered with birds. There were ten times as many as that morning. A large, shallow pool sat still and silent on the floor of the nest. Moonlight glowed on the surface of the water, illuminating above it seven dignified-looking owls, each on its own perch extending from the walls of the nest.

A small, round owl on the right squinted at the three Glademontians before squawking, "The Fourth Council of the Nest, in this third session, requests the full cooperation of Jesse the Rushing, and Tessamine and Ryon Canyon of Glademont. Do you comply?"

"No," answered Jesse.

Tess thought this an unpromising start.

"You do not?" the owl replied. "I see no reason for noncompliance."

Jesse flicked his tail. "Like you, we prefer to be cautious. Considering this creature's courtesy"—Jesse nodded toward the red owl, who was perched among the seven—"we will match it."

The round owl blinked twice, which was a noticeable gesture for an owl. His head swiveled toward the other six owls, after which they all blinked significantly. The red owl, who was perched third from the left, hooted for their attention.

"Jesse the Rushing," she said. "I am Wyndeling the Red. These with me form the Seven Wise of the Fourth Council of the Nest. We have established this council due to disturbing events here in the Hinge Forest. Your presence in the wood has complicated matters." The round owl, who seemed to be the eldest, issued an ill-tempered squawk, but then was still.

"How did this council learn of our names?" Jesse said.

"Ho ho ho!" cried a familiar deep voice. "I-eee think I can take it from here, Chiefy." An enthusiastic bird with a bright white-and-red breast descended haphazardly from the wall of the nest and landed on his favorite perch: Jesse's haunches. "Did I promise a quest or did I promise a *quest*?"

CHAPTER 9

The prince's detour to the Armory cost him precious time. If he wanted to be back in Glademont Castle, training his militia within the fortnight, he would need to cross through the Hinge Forest at its center. Too far north and he risked the snow wolves, which he knew came down from the mountains when the weather started to change. Too far south and he'd never make up for lost time. He knew cutting through the heart of the Hinge could mean clashing with any number of hostile animals. But if he stayed close to the forest center on his way to Atheos, in case of grave danger, he could retreat to the realm where his friend lived. Linden would trust that creature with his life, though he hoped he wouldn't have to.

He spent half the day picking through the soft forest floor on horseback, heading south by southwest. By midday Linden reluctantly turned due west by his compass. Though he'd like to have gone farther south, he had run out of time. It would take him four days to reach the western border of the Hinge as it was. Then seven more leagues to the Atheonian citadel.

Empty, gnarled branches loomed over the prince. Not a single living thing seemed to crawl or flit around him. The silence unnerved him. He thought it was like this only on the forest edges, where animals avoided chance encounters with humankind. But if they did not dwell in the center of the forest, then where?

Hours passed without incident. Linden finally relaxed from straining his ears and eyes enough to notice the golden light filtering through thin tawny leaves. It splashed pleasantly across his shoulders, then spilled onto the brown leaves and ferns. His mare paused and nickered, resisting the prince's command to continue. They had reached a shallow brook. Linden stroked his mare's neck.

"We must develop more enduring constitutions, Casion." He dismounted and stretched his stiff legs. "And in short order, for I intend to pass through these trees in excellent time." Having chastised his mare to his satisfaction, Linden retrieved his waterskin and knelt by the brook.

"Maybe two more hours before sundown," he muttered. Casion the mare dipped her lips in the crisp water, ignoring him. He shook his head at her, wondering what real warhorses might have been like in the golden days of Glademont—in Old Glademont. Surely they were stout, fearless creatures. Records of cavalry marches told of some battalions that could travel a day and night without rest.

The forest stream ran cool and clear, with a few minnows nestling between stones for the evening. They reminded Linden of the scarce times his father took him fishing in the mountain streams north of the castle. Before dawn, they would hike up the face of Zere together, searching for the perfect hideaway to drop their lines. Then, as the early sun colored the mountain skies, they would sit together on slick boulders, watching their lines and talking low. Those precious mornings were some of the only moments Linden spent alone with his father. King Antony seemed to sense the importance of their retreats, and he'd fill the hours asking Linden about his studies at the academy or offering advice.

"You seem worried, my prince," he had said one morning as Linden fixed a grasshopper to his hook. "Surely at fourteen, life cannot be so burdensome?"

Linden dropped his line in the clear water. "I don't see why you must go to Atheos."

The king waved a hand dismissively. "I shall be gone but a month. Yuir admires our dione, my prince. It is a great compliment that he seeks my counsel. Relations with Atheos have not always been so cordial, you know. I cannot refuse his request."

"He is king. He should know how to rule his own people," Linden muttered.

King Antony raised an eyebrow. "How do you mean? All kings should know just what to do, is that it?"

Linden shrugged, embarrassed. He thought his father would be glad to know how much his son respected him.

"My responsibilities are light indeed," King Antony said. "At your mother's side, and in such a thriving land, where do my difficulties lie? Nowhere." He glanced at Linden, then rubbed his son's shoulder. "Except in pleasing you, it seems!"

The young prince hesitated. "You are king, but not like kings in other nations. You rule, but not absolutely. Mother says you reign in her heart, but I think that's nonsense." Linden stopped himself, fearing he had gone too far. His father smiled calmly.

"It's all very humbling, isn't it? But I'd not prefer another man's kingdom. I feel quite sorry for King Yuir and his new bride. There is no balance, no harmony in that country. He has all the power you speak of my lacking, and yet he keeps it by the thinnest of threads. Is there any peace in that?"

"Our history scholars are always talking of peace, and how grand it is," Linden said. Something tugged at his line. He let the fish nibble at his bait. "Sometimes I find it maddening."

"Don't say that, my prince." King Antony hoisted Linden's line in one strong, fluid motion. He pinned a speckled grayling to the boulder. "Never grow tired of peace."

That peace was surely in peril now, and Linden was in the uncertain position of trying to reclaim it, if only his mother's message hit true. But as unswerving as he was in his devotion to his dione, he and his horse were not indefatigable. To his right, Linden spotted an inviting fallen trunk. Vowing not to spend more than a few minutes to have his supper, he staggered to the trunk.

Linden chewed a cold potato from the castle kitchens and rubbed his sore legs. He wondered what his mother ate for supper, if at all. The last time he coaxed her to eat some corn cakes, trout, and greens, there were only a few gray strands at her temples. But since the assassin's curse, it was as though all the youth was draining from her body. All her desperate entreaties to marry Lady Tessamine quickly, to secure

Glademont's next queen—Linden couldn't stand to hear her talk of it. He agreed to it all only to see his mother rest, to watch her brow go smooth again with relief. How would he have gotten through the last few months otherwise? Urgency had colored his every decision. His mother's health, the nation's vulnerable state, secret pleas for a successor to the throne . . .

She shan't die. Glademont had a queen, the most honorable and wisest of any on the continent or indeed amid the continents. With the militia to defend Glademont's borders, she would have time to heal. Talk of marriage and new queens had exhausted her to a perilous point. But Linden would make her see that there was no need to rush. He would protect her. Eighteen was too young to talk of marriage, even for the royal family.

When Linden finally shook himself from worrying over his queen and dominion, the sun had begun to set.

"Zere's Peak, Casion." He cursed. "You've let me delay. I'll fetch my compass and perhaps we can walk another hour in the dusk. . . ." A rustle overhead set Linden's heart pounding against his ribs. "Who's there?" He retrieved an arrow and swung his back to his horse, searching the canopy. Something squawked to Linden's left, and he pointed his arrowhead at a gigantic vulture.

Casion squealed and bolted.

"No!" Linden started for his mare, but the vulture flew in his face, forcing him to retreat. The light chuckle of a man drifted in the air. Linden scrambled for his arrow again and fitted his bow.

"Is someone there?" he called.

"Oh, most definitely." Out of the dark trees came a young man—an Atheonian officer in full military uniform. His hair was light and he grinned at Linden, showing a deep dimple on his left cheek. "Lower your weapon, or Lady Tessamine dies."

CHAPTER 10

I believe you have met one of our clan: Profigliano," Wyndeling said. Several of the Seven Wise shook out their feathers at the towhee's name. The round owl on the end shifted warily along his perch. "Be still, Buchanan of Westbend," Wyndeling snapped.

Ryon and Tess exchanged looks. Since Profigliano had already perched comfortably on Jesse's back, it seemed unwise to deny their acquaintance.

"There is nothing like a reunion to put some gusto back into the ole lungs." Profigliano rocked to and fro on his little feet.

"By the skies," Tess whispered. "What kind of trouble have you gotten us into?"

"You see, Lady Tessamine," Profigliano said. "There is always a tale untold without me to tell it." Hopping onto Ryon's head, the towhee loudly cleared his throat.

"I found your big rocky castle without the slightest difficulty," began Profigliano. "'Ho ho ho!' say I, 'I found it!' And I'm bringing 'round the ole wings for a landing when I spy some vultures, which used to be pals of mine, but now they're running with the muckety-mucks. So I change the course and I say to myself, 'Let's change the course, shall we?' Now, I see a rocky castle window, and I fly to it with vim and vip. I'm not one to wax my own feathers, but my maneuvers elude all thug bugs, and I come in for a safe landing.

"'Anybody home?' say I. 'A messenger from Tessy Canyon calls!' But then I notice with gleaming intelligence that I'm sharing the window with two or three testy vultures! Off I go again before they know what's what, but as it seems to my keen eye, *every* window's got a gaggle of thug bugs on it."

"Vermin and vinegar," Tess said.

"Then I get to noticing the whole place is crawling with muckety-muck human men. All over the front lawn, they're setting up camp and stinking up the place. And not a peep from inside that mountain castle. No, sir, not a peep."

"Oh no," Ryon said.

"Don't interrupt, please," replied Profigliano. "Well, here I am, and it's a mighty fine miracle, because those old friends of mine sure got mean in a hurry. See there? I'm missing a flight feather." Profigliano proudly displayed a wing, which indeed lacked a feather. Then, looking around, he quickly folded the wing against his side. "Quit staring, you loons."

Tess massaged her forehead, evaluating the events recounted by Profigliano. So many things confused her already, and the way Profigliano told stories did not help. She turned to Jesse, her eyes pleading.

He shifted his weight toward Tess in his familiar, comforting way. "Are these vultures of your clan?" Jesse asked the Seven Wise.

Wyndeling the Red swiveled her head toward the rest of the Wise. "With the council's permission, I will recount the events that have brought us to our current predicament."

"Proceed," said the tall bluish owl.

"When the moon was last full," Wyndeling began, "a band of humans was spotted here in the wood. Their number grew by the day; some said dozens, others said hundreds. We feared humans would again bring violence to our forest."

"When have humans brought violence before?" Ryon interrupted.

All seven owls went stock-still.

Then Jesse spoke.

"No Hinge Forester has lived long enough to know the truth of such things." Jesse's soft nostrils expanded.

"Ha." Another of the seven unfolded a speckled pair of wings. "Fine and fit is the animal who flies and flits with brevity."

"Without the bond, I agree that a shorter life is preferred," Jesse retorted.

"I don't understand," Ryon said.

Tess was equally confused. Was Jesse much older than they? What bond was he talking about? When Jesse referred to Hinge Foresters not living long enough, the red owl's deep eyes had turned immediately to Tess. It was a conflicted gaze, but there was longing in it.

"If you can explain, Rushing," the speckled owl said, pulling Tess out of her musings. "I suggest you omit your superstitions."

Folding his ears against his head, Jesse continued. "Centuries ago, King Baasha of Atheos waged war against Glademont. Scholars call it the Forest War. Much was destroyed—even innocent animals."

"It was the last time a human set foot in the Hinge Forest," Buchanan, the prickly round owl, bellowed. His voice was rusty and sharp. "The creatures of this sacred wood expelled your greedy lot once and for all. None has since dared to enter the Hinge until that shabby horde of twig-burners came clambering through the tree line."

Wyndeling spoke next, tearing her eyes from Tess to speak to Jesse. "The humans who appeared in the Hinge Forest a moon cycle ago were all males, despite their dull colors. This fact led us to suspect that an army was forming in our wood. We decided to wait out the danger. But then, a stranger came to us—a blind crow claiming to be an ambassador from Atheos."

Tess swallowed, shifting the copper orbs in her palm. It had to be the same bird, the one who burned her home and tried to claim the *shenil* for himself. What had that Atheonian swine called him? Smooth Crow?

"The crow made a proposal," Wyndeling continued. "It would be in our interest, he said, to ally ourselves with the men already in our wood. In exchange for our cooperation in their war, these men would swear to leave the Hinge Forest in peace."

"Many were frightened," added one of the Wise with a thin hoot. "Frightened the two kingdoms would again make war in our midst. Others were seduced by the crow's promise of new powers for the wild."

"Red magic? Bah!" Buchanan laughed.

"He had a smooth way of talking," another said.

"Who joined the crow?" Jesse asked.

"Yes, I was getting to that." The feathers around Wyndeling's face quivered impatiently. "The raptors of our clan have mostly abandoned us—vultures, eagles, and hawks. But as you can see, the falcons of this wood have some sense." Wyndeling swept her wing gracefully to acknowledge the thirty or so falcons perched inside the Council Nest. Tess had failed to notice them amid the array of stunning colors.

"The crow and our kinsmen headed east not six days ago. It was then deemed necessary to establish the Fourth Council," concluded Wyndeling.

"May I venture a question?" Tess stepped forward.

Buchanan of Westbend went so far as to shake his round head vigorously. Wyndeling ignored him.

"You may," she said.

Tess smoothed her nightgown nervously. "What else do you know about this crow?"

"He called himself Pider," a snow-white owl replied. He clacked his beak with distaste.

Tess's mouth went dry. Pider, the assassin. Pider, the magician whose dark magic had reduced Queen Aideen to a dying ghost. Tess's knees buckled as she pictured his talons, inches from her face.

"We are eager to learn more," one of the Wise said while Tess vainly attempted to adjust to this revelation.

Wyndeling the Red heaved a sigh before saying, "This council is at a crossroads. An army of human men make camp in our forest, and many of our own kin have joined their ranks. We know little about the crow, nothing of the men, and we are forced to treat our own as the enemy."

Buchanan nodded wearily. "We want the lady's magic."

Tess felt her face flush. She looked at Jesse, whose dark eyes remained steady.

"Explain," he said.

A particularly distinguished-looking owl sat farthest to the left among the Seven Wise. Her perch was slightly lower than the rest, but her starry eyes and heart-shaped face gave the impression of a highly esteemed animal. Her voice, though like the lilt of a flute, was not inviting. "This girl has used magic that is neither red nor gold. Such magic has not been known since the Human War—or the 'Forest War,' as you call it. You humans are indebted to us for the innocent wild lives you took. We claim your ancient magic in payment of that debt." Her head tilted toward the roof of the nest, where the moon's light receded.

"You are mistaken." The arching walls of the nest seemed to swallow Tess's thin voice. "I have no such magic."

"There has been too much talk tonight," the owl sang out. "You, girl, possess the key to our survival. Aid us in defeating the human kingdoms and the crow, or you will not see your brother again." She raised her wings to the multitude of birds along the nest walls. "Never again will we tolerate the depravity of human ambition. This time, we will snuff it out."

The nest erupted with the sound of a host of agitated birds.

"Madame Theodora," called Wyndeling. "Must we inflame the members of the council? Speak words of tranquility to them." But the enraged owl paid Wyndeling no heed, and the din only grew stronger.

Tess turned to Profigliano, who was still perched on Ryon's head.

"Profigliano, what did you tell them?" she shouted frantically.

Profigliano tapped the end of his beak with a wing and shouted back, "Not a word, my lady! Don'tcha know I'd remember a solemn pledge before nosin' up to these feather bags?"

"What do we do?" Tess cried. The walls of the giant nest creaked and shifted from sheer noise. Terrified, Tess pulled Ryon to her.

Then Theodora left her perch and stretched her elegant wings over the members of the Fourth Council of the Nest. All the while, her great black eyes were fixed on Tess.

"The time has come," Theodora hooted, "for the council to prove the worth of the wild animals—animals whose lives are brief but whose hearts are free!" Cheers resounded throughout the leafy walls.

The moon had almost completely deserted the nest, leaving only a faint glimmer of light reflecting on the pool of water. As the din escalated, Tess clung all the more fiercely to Ryon. Theodora dropped straight for the boy like a rock. She cut through the air in a matter of seconds, and soon her talons were upon Ryon's arm. Ryon floundered for his sling, crying out in pain.

But as he swatted at the creature clinging to his arm, a flash of gold appeared. It splashed into Theodora's surprised face, knocking her backward and forcing her to release her grip. The flash became a stream, and the stream seemed to gurgle as it spread itself thin between Ryon and the fallen owl.

Tess looked on with amazement as a small golden barrier took shape. Quickly, quietly, the barrier curved upward then downward again, melting over an invisible curved roof, which hovered above their heads. Soon, a small golden dome had completely surrounded Tess, Ryon, and Jesse. The dome hung over them in perfect stillness, yet its surface shimmered and moved, like a transparent, golden planet buried halfway in the ground.

"Well smack my beak and call me a beaver," Profigliano said. The towhee landed on Jesse's haunches, with a light cloud of shimmering gold dust curling around his wings. Sticking his head between his feet, then inspecting his feather tips, Profigliano whistled in amazement. "If I had known I could do that, I would still have all my flight feathers," he said.

Bewildered, Theodora careened back to her perch among the Seven Wise.

"What is the meaning of this?" Buchanan squawked. His circular head swung left and right. "Profigliano, you slimy centipede, what is the meaning of this?"

"Now, now, now. There, there, Your Wiseness." Profigliano retreated down Jesse's broad back. "There's nothing to see here. Where were we? Miss Theodora was giving a rip-roarin' speech and we were all feelin' hunky-dory."

Tess and Ryon stood awkwardly inside the golden dome, observing the aggravated owls.

"You dare threaten our clan with your magic," Buchanan cried. And, with all the abandon of a bloodthirsty warrior, he exploded from his perch.

"Run," Wyndeling called to the Glademontians as she sailed toward Buchanan, brandishing her talons.

Tess and Ryon leapt onto Jesse's back, and the dome floated higher to adjust to their combined height. Jesse sped toward their exit. Although the nest opening was too small to fit a horse and rider, the magic dome cleared a way, folding branches and brambles backward as the prisoners of the council launched through.

Once in the open again, Tess chanced a look over her shoulder. Through the swirling wall of the magic dome, she could just make out Buchanan and Wyndeling locked in battle. A bundle of feathers and ferocious talons tumbled into the now-dark pool of water.

"This way," Profigliano sang. "Follow the magic bird."

Forgetting about the chaos behind her, Tess concentrated on Profigliano's white underbelly. He darted out of the magic dome, which slowly began to dissipate. Tess led Jesse through the low, gnarled branches of the red trees. Ryon wrapped his arms around Tess's waist and buried his head in her cloak. Aideen's words rang in Tess's ears.

Keep it safe.

Tess heard a sound to her left. Wyndeling had somehow broken from the nest and was gliding unsteadily nearby. Clumps of feathers were missing from her bloody, wet breast.

"Wait," Wyndeling cried, breathless.

"She'll lead them to us," said Jesse with a new burst of speed.

Wyndeling struggled to keep up. "They are too afraid to follow," she said, gasping.

Tess pulled Jesse sharply to the side of a fallen tree, barely missing its exposed roots. Wyndeling reeled over the tree, somehow managing to remain in the air. Ahead, Profigliano flitted between branches, oblivious to the owl's presence.

"I beg you. I cannot fly any farther."

There it was again: that look of longing in the owl's eyes. A memory flashed in Tess's mind—the moment she asked this same creature for rest. She pressed the *shenìl* against her chest.

Then it happened again. All around Tess, the world seemed to slow. Tess felt calm and clear-minded. Finally, she heard the words again:

Trust her.

"By the skies." Slowly, deliberately, Tess knotted the *shenìl* around her loose hair. Keeping her seat with her knees, Tess reached out and felt the soft feathers of the large, wet owl. As Tess grasped Wyndeling's body, the world began to move again.

Tess cradled Wyndeling's limp figure against her chest. Ryon pulled his hand away from his sling and settled back against Tess's cloak. Jesse thundered nimbly against the forest floor. Profigliano whistled to himself as he led the way. No one followed as the five companions fled deeper into the Hinge Forest.

CHAPTER 11

The strange young man stood before Linden, grinning. Casion the mare had disappeared into the darkening forest, leaving her master to fend for himself.

"I said, lower your weapon."

Linden froze. The bowstring pinched at his fingers. In the back of his mind, he checked his stance. He was perfectly balanced. This soldier could not make a move without Linden's arrow striking his chest first. And yet, was Tess in some danger?

"What is the meaning of this?"

The Atheonian glanced to Linden's right. His companion, the vulture, had landed clumsily on the forest floor. "You may return to your post."

The vulture bobbed its wrinkled head. "Right, sir." It flapped into the gloom.

"Lower your weapon, royal," insisted the Atheonian.

"Take another step and I shall strike you through the heart."

"Strike me through the heart and my men will proceed with the lady's execution, I'm afraid."

"I see no men, and I see no lady." Dusk was quickly shrouding the woods, but Linden trusted his eyes and ears well enough to guess they were alone. "I proffer your soul to the night sky, Atheonian." He stretched his string another inch. His target held up a patronizing hand.

"If you will accompany me to my camp," he said, "I can take you to her ladyship. We have orders to execute her, but you may be able to negotiate other terms—"

Linden relaxed his string but kept the arrow pointed at its target. Was it possible that Tess followed him into the Hinge and somehow got herself captured?

"She's here? In the Hinge?"

"Definitely." The light-haired Atheonian grinned. "She's wearing a crimson gown, rather becoming. And a sort of rustic leather tie with two beads in her hair." Linden let his jaw go slack. He felt the heat of fear rising under his vest. "Ah," continued the Atheonian. "I see I've convinced you. Now, the weapon? I shall have to bind your wrists before we embark on our little trek."

CHAPTER 12

For the second night in a row, Tess, Jesse, and Ryon had galloped blindly through the darkness of the Hinge Forest. This time, however, they had the advantage of a towhee.

"Oh boy," Profigliano sang. "Questing sure has its perks."

The bird finally stopped in the middle of a clearing, bookended by two fallen elm trees and covered with the broad leaves of a magnolia.

"Where are we?" Tess said.

"My lady, you are standing on my very favorite worming ground." Profigliano beamed.

"I'd rather not know what that means," Tess said.

"This is where the fattest of the chubbiest worms come to have a cup of mud tea and catch up on the latest gossip. And all I hafta do is tuck a napkin under my beak and dig in. Those wormies never know what hits 'em. Don't you worry about the council finding us here. This spot is secret as an elk's den."

"Thank you, Profigliano," Ryon said.

"There, there, Master Ryon. You can call me Fig."

As soon as Ryon had a fire going, Tess brought Wyndeling's damp body close to the crackling flames. Long gashes streaked across the red owl's chest, which Tess cleaned and bound with the cloth napkins from her satchel.

By the comfort of the fire and in the security of Tess's lap, Wyndeling was lulled to sleep. Watching her dreaming patient, Tess found she longed to sleep as well. Profigliano was pleased to hear it, as he relished the opportunity to take first watch. Needing no further encouragement, Tess slept.

Midmorning light peeked through the old trees of the Hinge Forest as Tess munched on a breakfast of bruised apple and bread. Ryon entertained himself by launching rocks clean through magnolia leaves, without separating them from the stem.

"Oh boy, oh boy," Profigliano said. "Master Ryon sure knows his way around that whirly string. But that wouldn't help him with the worming sport! A *real* wormer—the true sportsbird—he takes as few pecks as possible." Profigliano hopped along his branch, looking at it sideways and glancing behind him suspiciously. "He doesn't waste his time on muckety-muck dirt specks. He hops real quiet-like; he knows his target; he strikes only when it *counts*." Profigliano reached into a crevice in the branch and pulled forth a centipede. This flourish was so impressive, Ryon applauded.

"Fig, that was great."

"Every creature's got his livelihood," answered Fig, his mouth full.

Just then, Jesse stepped into the clearing, unsaddled and with his blond coat shining. "No birds for many lengths. Well done, Profigliano."

The towhee gave Jesse an elaborate bow.

"Well," Ryon said, stowing his sling. "What's our next move?"

All eyes landed on Tess.

Tess cleared her throat. The question recalled all the unsettled feelings of their situation, like waking up from a cozy nap in the middle of a thunderstorm. She rose and stepped to the center of the clearing. Wiping the wisps from her forehead, she looked around at her new companions.

"Before we move . . . ," Tess said to Wyndeling, "I should like to know why you helped us out of the nest."

Wyndeling bristled. "Very well. There was little time to explain. . . ." Her auburn feathers quivered around her bandages as she looked nervously about the clearing. "When the lady first cast an enchantment, I was . . . fearful. I conferred with the Seven Wise, who reminded me of a particular legend surrounding the Human War."

Ryon interrupted. "Does she mean the Forest War, Tessy?"

"I think so," Tess answered. "The last war Glademont ever fought? It was a kingdom, then. We lost the war, and those who survived fled to Zere Mountain and created a new dione—without weapons or military, so we would never pose a threat to others or ourselves." Tess thought of all she learned from her dying queen, not two days before. The history books were wrong. Glademont had endured so long without war not because the queens were protected by Zere Peak and blessed by Xandra's horn. If Aideen was right, the queens themselves had been doing the protecting. But Tess still didn't understand how that could be, or why Aideen felt so strongly that she should be next in line. "Wait, Wyndeling, did you say enchantment? I've never cast an enchantment. I wouldn't know how."

Wyndeling tried to convey her irritation with a wing, but the pain allowed for only a weak flap. She moaned. "I notice you were not educated about the slaughter of animals, which happened during said war. But that is not my point. At the time of the Human War, it is said the queen of Glademont wielded unseen magic more powerful than red and gold put together. But she could not master it, and so the kingdom fell."

"We never learned about the queen of Old Glademont," Ryon said. "Only that a king ruled, and that he was too eager to make war. King Wallis."

"I still don't understand," Tess said. "What enchantment of mine were you talking about?"

Wyndeling glanced at Jesse uneasily. Then her gaze returned to Tess. "Do you not know your own power?"

Tess concentrated to keep her expression neutral. She would not give herself away as easily as she had two nights before. Although it seemed the *shenil* trusted the owl, Tess was not convinced. "You still haven't told us why you helped us. A day ago you captured us, and hours ago you handed us over to your clan."

The owl looked to Jesse, as if for direction, but the stallion remained still.

"Well, it would have all seemed ridiculous if not for that Pider character. He reminded us of the old stories. He demonstrated red magic. . . ." Wyndeling shuddered. "But while in the nest, I thought again about the words I heard when you enchanted me: 'The time has come. Ye who now bless the creatures of Glademont shall yourselves find blessing.' And it struck me that we must have been in the wrong. That . . . that animals should honor Glademont. Like the Rushing has come to do."

Ryon cleared his throat. "When did Tess enchant you?"

"Before I fell. She held me spellbound and spoke those words in my head," Wyndeling whispered, focusing on the forest floor.

Tess spun the ring on her finger, finding it equally difficult to meet anyone's eye.

"I heard a voice, too. When the . . . when Wyndeling fell. But it didn't speak the verse; it told me to trust Wyndeling."

The red owl lifted her soft face and peered into Tess's eyes.

"I could not return to my perch now, my lady, even if I desired it. If you will allow me to stay in your company, I will help you as best I can," she said.

"If you genuinely wish to help us," Tess said, slowly, "then you and Profigliano will lead us back to Glademont. If my family made it to the castle—and I hope to the red star that they did—"

"We can't go back," Ryon said. He stooped at the edge of the clearing, his fingers gently prodding the ground.

"Of course we can," Tess said more confidently than she felt.

Her brother moved away from the clearing, still stooping and prodding. He searched between the ferns and observed the bark of a tree trunk, running his fingers over its rough surface. Tess pursued him a few paces.

"What are you doing?"

At first, he did not answer, covering more ground and moving from tree to tree. Finally, he straightened and walked back to the clearing, meeting Tess's exasperated glare with a frightened eye.

"At least one hundred men crossed through here . . . perhaps more. Two nights ago. There are tracks everywhere and scratches on the trees as far as I can see. That means they were loaded down with sharp objects . . . and I'd guess they weren't farming tools." Ryon sat on an arched root, his head low. "There are too many of them. Profigliano was right; we have only one choice." His gray eyes landed on Tess's braid.

A sickening pang of apprehension rose in Tess's throat. "I don't know *how*."

"Didn't Queen Aideen say it was our secret weapon?" Ryon asked.

"But I'm trying to tell you, I've no idea how to turn it into a weapon." Using that last forbidden word recalled Sir Brock to Tess's mind. Would her father approve of her using the *shenil*, even in defense of Glademont? He certainly had made his opinion of Prince Linden's militia known.

The owl shook her head. "My lady, whatever you possess, you have three times used its magic in my presence. Once when I heard your voice in my mind, again when the gold barrier appeared. It was not invisible, I grant you, but—"

"Weeeell, well, well. We all seem pretty mystified and confusified by this golden bubble, don't we?" Profigliano winked. "Seems like eeeverybody is wonderin' who baked the worm pie they're eating out of, if ya know what I mean."

"It was Profigliano who made the barrier inside the nest," Ryon said. "He saved us from that terrible owl."

"You mean to tell me that this troublesome chatter-beak can perform magic, too?" hooted Wyndeling.

"'Tweren't nothin'. All for the sake of the quest. Who knew I had magic bubbles in me?" Profigliano swooped to land on Tess's shoulder, proud as could be. Tess smiled despite herself.

Wyndeling gave Profigliano a look that, on a human, would surely be a scowl. "Well, one thing is clear: none of us has any idea how magic works." She turned to the butterscotch horse and said, "Unless you're not telling us something, Rushing?"

"There is a difference between selfish deception and patient wisdom. I do not claim to harbor either," Jesse answered, "but I strive toward the latter." Something about Jesse's twinkling eye made it seem to Tess that he was pleased.

Tess raised an eyebrow at Ryon, who grinned at Profigliano, who chirped a melody to himself.

"That sounds awful fancy for a whooole lotta not-so-much in the information region, if ya know what I mean. No disrespect, Mr. Horsey, sir. No disrespect meant from *this* bubble-bird!" Profigliano puffed his brilliant breast. "What we need is a nice, smart training spot. I'm thinking somewhere with a goodish number of bubbles. . . . How about a hot spring?"

"Profigliano, you clever bird," Tess said with a gasp.

"I? I mean. Who is? Little old me?" said the bird.

"Training! I've just remembered: Queen Aideen said she would *train* me when everything was safe again. She said she would take me to a place called the Thane's Hold."

"Then that's where we shall go," Ryon said, retrieving his satchel. "Surely that's the way."

Tess looked around at the creatures who had risked their lives for her, and who were now counting on her to set things right. They had no idea what she had done, revealing the object to Tynaiv. Pider had been waiting for the right moment to strike, and Tess gave it to him. If she didn't find a way to stand up to this invasion, she'd be no better than Prince Linden thought her to be.

"Right," Tess said with sudden determination. She reached for her braid and pulled it across her shoulder, taking the two copper spheres of the *shenil* and placing them in her palm. The other creatures watched in silence. She concentrated on her breathing and stared at the dull yellow reflections in the spheres. *Shenil,* she ventured, *where is the Thane's Hold?* She held her breath for what seemed like a century. Nothing happened. *Shenil*—her thoughts were more insistent this time—*please guide us.*

Still nothing.

"If I may," interjected Wyndeling, "I believe I know what that bauble would have us do next." The owl turned to Profigliano and said, "Do you know the way to the Ruins from here, chatter-beak?"

CHAPTER 13

Three Glademontians and two creatures of the Hinge trekked through the deep forest under a high autumn sun. The breeze pushed them along, swirling and whistling through the trees. Tess's feet felt better, as Profigliano had suggested she stuff moss into her riding boots. Those who were able either walked or flew, while Wyndeling reluctantly agreed to perch on Tess's shoulder.

"When you enchanted me," she said, "the leaves on the trees glimmered, and the sounds of the moles and the squirrels were hushed. Then your voice came." She thought a moment. "That is, the voice sounded like you, perhaps older. I realized I had seen that phrase written. It is inscribed on the walls of an abandoned castle. Weeks ago, I was lost and took shelter from the rain there, and I distinctly remember reading the words 'Ye who now bless the creatures of Glademont shall yourselves find blessing' on the walls. When I asked Buchanan about the place, he told me that it was referred to simply as 'the Ruins.'"

"How far until we get to the Ruins?" Ryon said.

Profigliano circled overhead. "I could sail over there in three blinks and be back by midnight-snack-time. But with the kind of weight we got in the hull . . . I'm bettin' two days."

"I hope we find the Thane's Hold there," Tess said.

Ryon squeezed Tess's arm. "The *shenil* said those words for a reason."

The rest of the day's march proved mercifully uneventful. Tess and Ryon walked in front of the caravan, while Jesse brought up the rear. Profigliano flitted off to hunt for worms, some of which returned in his beak as an offering to Wyndeling. Not surprisingly, the offer was rejected. Ryon came across a few good stones, which he stowed in his pockets. The only occasion for concern was when they came upon a family of goldfinches, who assured Profigliano that their lot had gotten out of the political circuit years ago.

Evening fell as they came to a wide creek. An inviting stretch of grass met the rushing blue-gray waters, and fallen autumn leaves surfed along its current.

"Ruby Creek, my comrades." Profigliano whistled. "All we gotta do is cross it, and we'll be almost to the Ruins."

Despite its beauty, Tess glared at Ruby Creek. From bank to bank, it was perhaps three men across. There were no stepping rocks save one solitary boulder, which protruded a few paces from the opposite bank at a slant. The current was too swift for Tess or Ryon to swim across.

"I—uh, suppose a little magic bubble trick wouldn't go amiss around here right about now. Eh, Red?" chimed Profigliano.

"By all means, chatter-beak," replied the red owl. "Conjure one up."

Profigliano hopped onto Tess's shoulder—the one not occupied by Wyndeling—and theatrically threw his wings straight in the air. Bobbing his shiny black head, Profigliano proceeded to hop from one talon to the other, his eyes shut tight.

"Grrrrreeat magic buuuuubble," he chanted, "come to meeee. Caaarrrry us, gentle-liiiiike, across this great sea."

"Oh, of all the . . ." Wyndeling groaned.

"Surround us, oh mighty bubble. Shimmer and shammer and creep on over this here group of noooble creatures." After a dramatic pause, Profigliano flung his wings toward the creek and shouted, "Ha."

The outcome disappointed.

"Keep at it, Fig." Ryon smiled.

"Indeed I *will*." Profigliano flitted to the bank to perfect his ritual.

The rest of the group continued to stare at the rushing waters. Many suggestions were offered, and just as many were rejected. Ryon said they should all climb onto Jesse's back and ride him across the creek. However, Tess pointed out that even Jesse couldn't swim in that kind of current, especially while carrying a load. Wyndeling suggested Jesse and Tess attempt to cross the creek together and allow Profigliano to lead them the rest of the way. But Tess was firmly against leaving her brother behind, especially with a creature they had only just met.

The evening waned, but Tess was determined that they cross Ruby Creek before nightfall. "I refuse to believe that this is the only way. And every minute we stand here wastes precious time. Atheos is bearing down on our family this very minute. Profigliano?"

While the rest had pondered the problem of the creek, Profigliano had persisted in rehearsing his magic bubble spell. He let his wings droop and turned to Tess.

"Profigliano, I want you to search upstream and see if there is anywhere narrow enough for us to cross safely."

"My lady," Wyndeling interjected, "Ruby Creek flows from the top of Zere Mountain. That must be more than a week's journey from here by foot. How can we be sure such a crossing exists nearby?"

"We can't," Tess said. "But what else would you suggest? Shall we build ourselves a bridge?"

Profigliano perched on Ryon's head, puffed out his chest, and gave Tess an emphatic salute. "I won't let you down, Miss Tessy. No indeed; that I won't." Chirping as he went, Profigliano darted up the bank and out of sight.

Tess focused her attention on Ryon. "Why don't you see if you can catch a few fish?"

An hour passed, and then another. The moon rose, and still Profigliano did not return. Tess's mood darkened, as it became clear they would have to spend the night on the wrong side of the water. She stared at a smoldering fire and allowed her mind to surrender to fear of imagined dangers. She saw visions of her sister and parents, bloodied and burnt. She saw Queen Aideen, receiving news that Tess had been found dead in the forest, and that the *shenil* was now Pider's.

After several more hours of overwrought imaginings, Tess finally yielded to an unsettled sleep.

Sleep was no better than waking for Tess, as visions of vultures, hawks, and glassy-eyed crows darted through her dreams. So many voices at once: Papa telling her to maintain the peace of Glademont, Mother reminding her to keep Ryon safe, Queen Aideen's worried entreaties to hide the *shenil*, Reggie barking out orders to stay alert, in case of Atheonians. All the while, Prince Linden laughed and joked with his friends, stealing quick glances at Tess as she stood in helpless fear. She hated him for his thoughtlessness. She felt her hands clench and her throat catch as she remembered his stinging words: *You don't understand the world, Lady Tessamine.*

Then, suddenly, Tess saw a silhouette of a woman, glittering in a tangerine hue, like a citrine crystal. It stood against the trunk of a tall gingko tree and seemed to reach behind its head to pull forward a braid of hair, just like Tess's. At the end of the silhouette's braid glowed the *shenil*, with its two small orbs burning like coals.

Whether this was her own shadow, Tess could not tell. But the figure felt so familiar and comforting that Tess began to concentrate on it. Mercifully, the voices of her friends and family faded away. The silhouette lifted to its toes and raised its arms like a demure ballerina. It bent a knee and bowed at the waist. Shimmering fingers fluttered at Tess. Confused, Tess looked down at her own nightgown and riding boots. Nothing seemed different about them. The silhouette fluttered its fingers again, this time higher, and Tess looked behind her.

The rushing waters of Ruby Creek looked even more menacing in the darkness of Tess's dream. Still jutting from its current was the solitary boulder, which now, mysteriously, bore the image of the shimmering silhouette. Reclining against the boulder, the silhouette beckoned Tess to cross the creek.

Obediently, Tess took a shaky step toward the bank.

"Be ye friend or foe?" bellowed a craggy voice.

Tess woke with a start.

CHAPTER 14

Two days after Linden had set out to deliver that cursed letter to Atheos, he found himself trudging through an open meadow some three leagues south of where he wanted to be.

The young officer of the Atheonian army prodded the prince's back with his own longbow. Sometimes the man would poke Linden's calves; sometimes he would twirl his hair with the tip of the bow. It was beyond humiliating. Linden set his jaw and fought the ropes that restrained his fists.

"If you think the stars are beautiful now," the officer said, "you should see them in the winter over the Seventh Cape." He nudged the prince's ankles with the weapon.

Linden did not answer. He had learned that conversation with this irritating worm only caused further humiliation. In fact, it was letting the Atheonian speak that put Linden in this mess in the first place. He wished he had been wiser, like the warrior princes of ancient Glademont.

He closed his eyes and tried to remember the tangy smell of old scroll cases—the smell of that first night he snuck past the royal scribes to explore the castle archives. He tried to picture the warm light of his candle as he inhaled scroll after scroll. He had felt his very soul would catch fire as he read about the days when Glademont not only had an army but boasted one of the most feared militaries on the entire continent of Diatonica. No history scholar at the academy had ever taught him of these things. Only that the past was gone, and good riddance.

What good was all his reading now?

The whistling Atheonian poked at Linden's elbow with the bow. "Almost there, Your Highness. You see that tower to the right? Your lovely bride-to-be is safe inside . . . for now."

"If she's been hurt, Atheonian, your blood is mine by rights," Linden said. According to *Epochs of the Hinge Forest*, this was the threat given by Prince Wallis before he slew a scoundrel attempting to kidnap his princess.

But Linden doubted whether his loyalty to Lady Tessamine was as pure and noble as that. The prospect of seeing her again filled him with a mix of relief and dread. He knew how furious she was with him. But he did not wish any harm to come to her, even if she was behaving like a vain child.

"You are so quiet, prince." The Atheonian plucked the tip of a blade of grass and mulled it over with his teeth. "Thinking of what you'll say to Tess?"

Linden chanced a look over his shoulder. "*Tess*, is it?"

"What do you call her? Lambie?"

Linden turned back, fists clenching. The tower was not far now. He could make out the pointed silhouette of its spire against the crowded stars. The rest of the ruins were camouflaged under the cloak of night and shadow, but Linden knew they were approaching the former location of Old Glademont Castle. Months of studying antique maps and exploring the forest had at least given him his bearings. He could make out the pointed silhouette of its spire against the stars. He could not help but feel a rush of exhilaration.

The prince closed his eyes a moment to remember. It was page twenty of *Continental Architecture Through the Ages*. He could see plainly the scratchy rendering by an architect's hand of the ground plan of the first floor of Old Glademont Castle, drawn with the entrance on the bottom of the page: north on the compass. A stout outer wall enveloped the castle in a long rectangle. The main entrance was a little to the left, and beyond it a grand foyer framed by columns. To the south were the kitchens and serving halls, and various staircases down to the cellar, armory, and secret rooms. To the far right, a tall tower with no windows.

Linden opened his eyes. They were very near now. "I see no camp. Perhaps your command has abandoned you."

"Nay, thoughtful prince. My troops love me like a father and fear me like the plague. They simply keep themselves hidden." He breathed an indulgent draft of air, swatting at the grass tops with Linden's longbow. "Have you thought about what you will say to your betrothed? This may be a good time to mend any torn sails."

Linden swallowed uncomfortably. How would the Atheonian know he and Lady Tessamine had quarreled? Perhaps they questioned her. Could she be trusted to keep his letter secret? Or Queen Aideen's trinket . . . whatever the value of *that* was.

A heavy sigh escaped the prince's lips. He glanced at the stars and asked them to protect Nory and Rette. They were probably training men at that very moment. Would Linden ever be able to return to help them?

"Mayhap the lady will not receive you warmly, considering your recent tiff," the Atheonian prodded.

Linden felt his stomach stiffen. "Watch your tongue, Atheonian. You might miss it one day." He gritted his teeth. If only he had used his weapon when he had the chance.

"That's the spirit, my man," replied the Atheonian.

Linden slowed his pace, trying to observe the landscape. They were almost upon the foundation of the old castle. The tower loomed over them to the right, and a once-magnificent staircase hoisted gloomily upward. Not even the buzz of nocturnal insects echoed off the stones. There was no smell of campfires, nor the sweat of men.

The prince stood stock-still, the realization finally upon him. There were no Atheonian troops hiding among these ruins. In all likelihood, there was no captive lady, either. He had been lured to this secluded place to die.

A disorienting crack rang in the prince's ears as the back of his head absorbed a heavy blow.

CHAPTER 15

After freeing herself from the fog of sleep, Tess found herself standing bolt upright on the shore of Ruby Creek. Above her glowed a congregation of stars. They seemed to be straining, intently watching the scene below.

"Bend yer ear," bellowed the craggy voice again. "Be ye friend or foe?"

The grayish-brown bear who spoke was so large, he could place his front paws on the boulder occupied in her dream by the silhouette and leave his back paws upon the far bank. His weathered, deep-set eyes flickered under thick brows, which grew like the stray boughs of long-forgotten hedges.

"Good sir, I am a friend to you, if you are an enemy to Atheos," Tess called. She hoped the bear chose to remain in the Hinge after refusing to join the Atheonian army. On the other hand, he might not like humans any more than the Council of the Nest—no matter which land they hailed from.

"That be good. But have ye the proof of yer worth?" the bear said.

"My worth?"

Without a doubt, this was the largest beast Tess had ever seen. He could cross the creek in a bound if he wished. What if she could not prove herself to him?

"What is happening?" Ryon loaded his sling before he was on his feet.

"Good sir," Tess ventured. "We mean only to cross the creek and journey beyond. We seek an inscription, nothing more."

After a frightful silence, the shaggy bear sighed deeply. The air shook with the force of it. "Whosoever crosses this here Creek of the Crown and enters the lands of King Wallis and Queen Miriam of Glademont be subject to her laws." He noisily resupplied his lungs. "King Wallis, whose honesty and strength do brighten our lands. And Queen Miriam, who rescues the weak and nurtures the sorrowful."

When describing the king, the great bear's weathered eyes revived, and his back straightened purposefully. And when he spoke of Queen Miriam, his voice lowered just above a whisper.

Tess twisted the pearls around her finger. Had he said King Wallis? As in, the long-dead king of Old Glademont?

"Most admirable . . . er . . . Master Bear," she stuttered.

"Osiris of Glademont, guardian of the castle and beast of . . ." Osiris faltered for a moment. "Beast of King Wallis."

"Most honorable Osiris of Glademont, guardian . . . and so forth," Tess began. It frightened her to think this may be some great ghost or vision from the past. On the other hand, she still had a chance to make an ally of this phantom—if she could keep her head. "I too am from Glademont, and desire to make peace, if you would only tell me how."

Again, Osiris sighed his trembling sigh and recited:

> *"Peace is found in faithful trust*
> *of fellow creature*
> *with fellow man.*
> *If trust be earned by thee or me,*
> *then the sacred bond must very near be.*
> *Show me the gift which yer fellow received*
> *when in ye both the fellowship was conceived!"*

"Oh dear," Tess muttered. "I wish Papa were here."

The night sky seemed to hold its breath as Tess looked frantically from Osiris to the surging waters. She could not think how to answer the riddle. After an uneasy moment, the air trembled again. This time, it was not from a sigh but from a tremendous growl.

"If ye be foe, prepare to cut me down or be cut down yerself," Osiris bellowed, the growl still emitting from his chest.

"Tess, get back," Ryon called.

The waters of Ruby Creek foamed and splashed at random as they changed color, like a giant pot of golden boiling water. The bear growled all the louder, and the Hinge Forest echoed with his powerful call.

"No, please," Tess cried as the shimmering waters crashed against her nightgown.

Losing her footing, Tess fell hard onto her back. Her head hit a root, and her left arm crumpled underneath her. The blow to her head sent black-and-white stars bursting across her vision. Every nerve from her neck to her left hand burned hot like sparked kindling. Through the pain of her fall, Tess tried desperately to reorient herself. She squinted at the night sky. A strong wind blew in the treetops, and Tess was strangely thrust into a memory.

She recalled how the breeze had blown over the pond in the royal gardens, easing her troubled heart. Tynaiv had said it would do her good. Tynaiv, who pretended to understand her.

Reminded of her thoughtless mistake and knowing her life might soon be taken, Tess felt true remorse. There was no excuse for it. She should never have trusted her feelings with a stranger. And she should have put her duty to the queen above her own silly, wounded heart. As her head, arm, and shoulder throbbed unbearably, Tess smiled sadly at how blind and proud she had been. Drops of blood fell into Tess's eyes and obscured her view of the moon as she remained in the memory of her mistake for one last moment.

Then Tess struggled to stand. She could hear her brother's muted cries, but they faded to the back of her mind as waves of screaming pain burst down her left side. Tess fought to keep her breath, planted one foot, then another, and straightened her quaking knees. With her right hand, she wiped blood and hair from her face. Her left arm hung burning and useless.

Across the rising waters, Osiris planted all four of his massive legs in the current, his head stretching forward gracefully. His nostrils flared. Golden magic flowed forth, pure and elusive as ever. It meandered through the waters of Ruby Creek, creeping toward Tess's feet.

As Tess's eyes locked with those of the great bear, she heard herself say, "I surrender."

Osiris sent the waters rushing up Tess's legs, catching her cloak. In the same instant, Tess felt the world slow down and could sense every reed bending to the creek, every strand of Osiris's fur and every inch of her own skin. It all seemed to sway and move along with her mind—like a familiar dance partner. Tess found herself holding the *shenil* in her good hand. It felt warm and friendly. She closed her eyes and calmly awaited the instructions she knew would come.

Rise and walk, whispered the voice.

Without hesitation, Tess lifted her right foot out of her riding boot and over the water that sought to engulf her. Placing her toes onto the churning liquid, Tess carefully trusted her weight on it. Up came the other foot, and something inside told Tess this could be no ordinary step. She thought of the silhouette, dancing in a light ballet. And with one more sweep of her leg, Tess alighted on the surface of Ruby Creek on her tiptoes, *shenil* in hand.

Though her eyes were closed, she sensed the waters had quieted themselves as she placed her left foot upon them. She could no longer hear the growl from Osiris, nor Ryon's desperate cries, only the calm rush of water under her strong feet. Even the pain had dulled enough for her to breathe one full breath. Then the voice came again.

Go to him.

Taking another breath, Tess moved forward. The *shenil* seemed to pull her now, gently, while the waters felt cold and tingly under her nimble toes. The object led Tess like a choreographer. She followed, keeping her back straight and her steps light. The *shenil* had left her braid for her good hand, and Tess's black tangles fell around her shoulders. The water made her wisps curl and tickle her cheeks. Then a faint whoosh sounded somewhere near Tess's hand: the sound of fire.

Although she felt she could be very near to Osiris now, the *shenil* did not stop leading, and so Tess kept dancing. That is, until a strong gust of warm breath lifted the curls from her face. Stunned, Tess opened her eyes and discovered she was inches from the gigantic bear's muzzle. She gasped and found herself sinking back into Ruby Creek. The water felt cold and ordinary again. Her left arm assaulted her with pain so sudden, so sharp, she began to lose her vision. A broad, furry arm scooped Tess out of the water and placed her on the bank, as easily as if she were a fallen leaf.

"By the trees," Osiris whispered to the nearly unconscious Tess. "That weren't the kind of magic I was asking for. But it'll do, young one."

PART II

CHAPTER 16

At the request of his new companions, Profigliano dutifully charged up Ruby Creek all evening. His strategy was simple: put the old eyes to work and find a safe crossing. Hours later, Profigliano had not lost hope, for he discovered that the farther north he flew, the more waterlogged pines lined the creek's bank. Finally, as the stars glimmered over the towhee, he observed several such trees that had fallen over the creek, forming a natural bridge.

"Do you see that, blinky stars? That's what I call a real easy crossing, if you catch my *drift*." Profigliano let out a deep chortle as he landed on a willow oak branch. "I wish you blinky stars knew my friend Tess. She just babbled and babbled about how she'd cross this creek." The chortle developed into chuckle, and the chuckle rolled into raucous laughter. "I gotta tell ya, the whole thing sounded pretty *fishy* to me."

At this point, Profigliano was leaning against the trunk of the willow oak, his wings grasping his belly and his eyes shut tight.

Unfortunately, the towhee's lack of subtlety proved costly. Just a few paces away, on the other side of a smattering of large river rocks, was the campsite of three Atheonian foot soldiers.

෪

"There ain't nothin' can rattle my chains worse 'an sittin' still when there's fightin' to be done, gents," growled Root, a sturdy middle-aged man with black eyebrows and a crooked mouth.

"Better bein' out 'ere in the woods than back home starvin' to death," replied young Grift. "All the aristocrats drinkin' their fine wine while the rest of us break our arms tillin' rock and sand. What grows in rock and sand, I'd like to know? Not a blessed thing." He threw a rock into the fire. Dark shadows danced on his thin face.

The third member of the party was a lieutenant named Pilt. His military cloth belt glowed a bright green across his muscular abdomen. He stood over his inferiors, reviewing an official-looking notebook.

"I've heard it said, 'Complaint is the mark of a coward,'" he remarked.

"I joined this outfit to get *human* blood on my hands, 'Tenant." Root grunted at the ground.

Pilt paused, then sighed at the old soldier. Slowly Pilt pulled a small hatchet from a holster on his leg. Root tried to get to his feet, but Pilt lunged and had him by the arm. He lifted the hatchet behind Root's ear.

"Human blood, you say?" He pressed the sharp edge against Root's skull. "I'd be happy to accommodate you."

A thin red stream rolled down Root's neck as he whimpered. "Don't cut me ear off, 'Tenant."

The lieutenant pressed his weapon another hairsbreadth, all the while staring at Grift, daring him to intervene. The younger soldier kept still, his temple twitching as Root moaned.

"Right then." Pilt removed the hatchet and wiped its blood onto Grift's sleeve. "We have our orders, and the sooner we complete them, the sooner we can return to the camp. Eh, Grift?"

"Right you are, Lieutenant Pilt." Grift gritted his teeth as the last of Root's blood was deposited on his shirt.

"Today was a poor shake. You two get lazier by the minute." Pilt drew his notebook again and slanted it so that it caught the fire-light. "Identified: five ducks, one black fox, and one buck. Ducks were exterminated according to Counselor Pider's orders. The fox is in our possession"—Pilt gestured casually to a sack leaning against a river rock—"and the buck escaped the power of soldier Grift."

"Hang on," Grift protested. "I'd like to see you or Root stay your ground with an eight-pointer about to gore you to shreds."

"It was an inexcusable blunder," Pilt said. "We are here to find out whether there will be any defiance from these woods, and that buck was as defiant as they come. Had you captured him, we might be heading back to the front lines right now with valuable information. We'd be spending the night on real cots with coffee in our bellies."

"What about the fox, 'Tenant? He said he had something for us," Root said hopefully.

"The fox will take more time. We can't trust a thing he says."

Deflated, Root tried to wipe the back of his still-bloody head on Grift's sleeve, which was met with a violent withdrawal.

"What do you think yer doin', old man?" hissed Grift. "Try that again and—"

"Quiet, gentlemen," Pilt said. "Do you hear that?"

The three Atheonians strained their ears as baritone laughter echoed nearby. Lieutenant Pilt grinned.

"Sounds like a big one," he said, and beckoned them toward the sound.

The three men crept over the tops of the river rocks, peeking through the cracks and keeping their heads low. Seeing movement in the low branches of a willow oak, Pilt motioned for his men to stop.

"Weeeeell, what's the harm in stoppin' for one little ole caterpillar? Miss Tessy will be sound asleep by now, and this red-breaster is starving," said a creature in the willow oak.

"Caterpillars, 'Tenant? Can't be nothin' but a bird, sir." Root looked to Pilt. "I don't see no point in killin' the birds, 'Tenant. They bein' so small."

"Perhaps it is a clever bear cub, or an eagle with a sensitive stomach. Either way, we will capture it," Pilt replied. "You'd hardly call Counselor Pider harmless, would you?"

Pilt nodded to Grift, who pulled from his back a peculiar device. At first glance, it looked like a traditional roughly hewn bow and arrow. But the soldier had no quiver—only the one arrow. Grift sifted through a satchel that was slung across his chest and pulled out a bundle of thin rope, which he attached to the shaft near the arrowhead. Readying his bow, Grift fixed the arrow into the drawstring and, crawling on his belly over the crest of the rocks, disappeared toward the bank of the creek.

"Gotcha, you shifty character." Profigliano spoke to a caterpillar recently snagged from the trunk of the oak. "I hope you told Mrs. Caterpillar you loved her today." Profigliano chortled, keeping the caterpillar between his claws. Then he paused thoughtfully and said, "Oh, that was a wee-bit heartless of me. I-ya didn't mean to make things uncomfortable for you, neighbor."

With a sudden *whrrr*, Grift's arrow shot past Profigliano's left wing, and the towhee was enveloped inside a sailing net. Profigliano lost hold of his snack as he was lifted from his perch. With a soft *thud* the arrow sank into the ground and Profigliano tumbled helplessly behind.

Grift was the first to arrive where Profigliano had fallen. Pilt and Root followed, while Grift leaned over the rustling net with a steely expression. He grunted. "State yer name and yer purpose in the Hinge, bird."

"Now, now, now, now," Profigliano replied, breathless. "Leeet's not forget that it is *you* thug bugs who've got some answerin' to do." Profigliano pressed a defiant eye against a hole in the mesh. "What makes you so sure I don't have a few golden bubbles up my sleeve? Eh, big boys?"

"'E's not right in the head, 'Tenant Pilt," Root observed.

"All the same, he's a bird in the forest, which means he did not join the counselor, and our orders are to exterminate him." Pilt leaned forward, peering over Profigliano's prostrate body. "Unless you somehow got lost, my friend?"

"In a manner of speaking," the towhee said with an audible gulp.

"Throw him in the creek." Pilt moved to return to the campsite.

"Pardon me, Lieutenant," Grift said. "But I made that net with my own hands. Takes a good week to get that kind of craftsmanship, by my buttons." Grift was looking at Profigliano with apprehension. "Couldn't we just snap the robin's neck so's I can keep my net?"

Several more gulps were heard from the neck in question before Profigliano commented quietly, "I'm a towhee, if it makes any difference to you, skinny-face."

"What did you call me?" Grift lifted up the net and shook it violently.

"Just a moment, now, comrades." Pilt was looking thoughtfully at Profigliano. "'Twas a towhee that flew through our ranks a few days ago. He was shouting something . . ." Pilt approached the net swinging in Grift's fist.

"A question for you, friend," Pilt said. "Do you, by any chance, know Lady Tessamine Canyon?"

Profigliano's eyes widened to an unnatural circumference.

"That's what I thought" was Pilt's chilling response. "Forget the buck, fellows. This bird is our ticket back to the front lines."

CHAPTER 17

Tess's arm ached as Osiris stood over her, steam rolling from his back, his trunk-like limbs soaked through.

"Be ye a gem dryad? Her Majesty told me to be kind to gems. Though I be havin' my doubts." He hummed distractedly.

"No," Tess gasped. The throbbing in her arm kept her from rising. "I am an advisor's daughter from the Dione of Glademont."

"Well, I do disagree." Osiris snorted. "Ye be a gem dryad, and a learned one at that."

Osiris lowered his massive head to sniff Tess's hair and then buried his nose in her sodden cloak. With difficulty, she attempted to be still. When he was finished, he pounded his paw on the sod.

"Bend yer ear, young one," he insisted. "Ye be a gem dryad. Yer magic be marked by naught but fire. Fire be the mark of the gem dryad. Ye spoke of Glademont, a kingdom in ruins just yonder past my trees." Osiris indicated northward, and then the eyebrows furrowed considerably. "Mmmmm . . . ," he murmured, "I be a mistaken bear." Osiris sniffed the air with his saucer-like nostrils. "I were saying," he rejoined, "that kingdom be restin' in ruins just yonder past my trees." This time, he indicated southwest.

Tess determined herself to be in the company of a ferocious scatterbrain.

"I can assure you I am not a dryad of any sort," she ventured. "Only recently have I been able to use magic because . . . because the queen of Glademont has passed it to me." It was partially true, anyway. Though Tess reasoned that Osiris was unlikely to react to the *shenil* as did the owls of the Council of the Nest, being more than capable of using magic himself.

Osiris plopped onto his hindquarters with curiosity. It was remarkable how harmless he now looked, considering he had nearly killed Tess moments earlier.

"Mmm-hmmm," he said.

Tess, propped herself up, her forehead wrinkling with pain. "I can assure you, Glademont exists still . . . though it is a dione," she said. "Its castle is on Zere Mountain, facing the valley. And it is ruled by Queen Aideen."

Osiris frowned at Tess. "We had better talk this out nice and thorough." Rising, Osiris began to saunter due west.

"Tessy, are you all right?" Ryon whispered loudly from across the creek. "Are you hurt?"

"I've hurt my arm, but I'm all right," Tess answered. "Oh, sir," she called after Osiris. "My friends still cannot cross the creek."

"Ah. Yes, yes. Ye came with a crow or some such creature?" A shadow passed over Osiris's face as he turned back.

"No, not at all," Tess assured him, fighting the memory of the blind crow. "My companions are a horse, an owl, a boy, and a . . . well, there is a towhee somewhere in these woods who also belongs with us."

"Yer lass the owl needs tendin' to," Osiris said, looking across the creek. "She may be needin' yer powers by end of the night, young one."

"What?" Tess looked across the creek, where Ryon was stooping over the small form of Wyndeling.

"She's feverish," Ryon called to his sister. "Her cuts must be infected. I can't wake her up."

An icy fear gripped Tess's already shivering shoulders.

"Here." Osiris lowered his head. "I've not had a rider for a bit, but if ye will hold on to my neck, we'll see about the rest, aye?"

With her good hand, Tess grasped a handful of dense, musky fur above Osiris's shoulder and hoisted herself onto his back. Gratefully, she pressed her body against his warmth.

"Right." Tremors from his voice rumbled under her body. "It's been many star shifts, young one. But by my tail there be something 'round here . . ."

The bear wandered near the bank of Ruby Creek, where a small statue lay buried in shrubbery and vines. Tess could barely make out a pair of delicate sculpted paws peeking from the tangle of leaves, until Osiris tore away the vegetation to reveal the impressive figure of a lynx in green marble. Even more remarkable was its unusual position, with the forelegs outstretched and head lowered, as if to enjoy a luxurious stretch.

"Mmmmm," Osiris hummed, approaching the statue. "A pretty likeness."

"What is it?" Tess said.

"Ye be meanin' *who* is it, aye? That there be Queen Miriam's beast, Rosemary. She were quick and clever and loyal as any creature Glademont's ever been privy to."

Tess strained to get a better look between Osiris's ears. Perhaps Queen Miriam was more than just a figment of the bear's imagination after all.

Facing the lynx's head, the shaggy bear lowered his front half, making Tess clutch tighter to stay astride. Then, mirroring the lynx's posture, Osiris addressed the statue.

"I pledge on my honor as a bondfellow that these creatures be posin' no threat to my king, nor to his kingdom. Up with the bridge."

Osiris spoke these words with such reverence that Tess half expected the statue to come to life. Instead, something within the statue triggered and the whole marble figure started to shift forward. After a few slow inches, the lynx stopped with a loud *click*. And then, much to Tess's amazement, a series of softer clicks echoed from beneath the nearby creek waters, causing the surface to ripple. Tess dug her knees deeper into the bear's ample fur.

In the next moment, the waters began to swell along a narrow strip running perpendicular to the flow of the current. After which, the boulder from Tess's dream did something peculiar—it tipped over.

Slowly, the boulder lowered itself sideways into the creek, and as soon as it disappeared underneath the surface, a thick and narrow slab of river rock running the width of the creek emerged. The rock bridge slid out of the water on its side at first, as though previously overturned. Within seconds, the ends of the bridge met the banks, and a thin sheet of creek water rolled gently over it. Tess stared at the simple structure. It fit so seamlessly into the landscape.

"Now then," Osiris said. "Let us fetch those friends of yers, madame gem. The night be terrible late and my den be cold as a stream by now, thanks to thee."

"I'm sorry," Tess said, her arm and shoulder throbbing afresh. "You see, we are on rather an urgent errand."

"It may take me quite a bit of time to find yon den again." The bear sauntered over the narrow bridge. "'Tis true in the past I've had to give up and make a new den instead, I must admit." He chuckled.

"Skies help us," Tess mumbled.

Dawn finally alighted on the Hinge Forest as Tess rode a shaggy bear between the silent trees. Profigliano had not returned. A timid blue light cast long misty arms through the forest ceiling and landed on her grim face, then on the muscular body of Jesse. Beside Jesse walked Ryon, who was gingerly carrying a small bundle of red feathers. Wyndeling had still not awoken, and Ryon was uncharacteristically solemn.

After a time, the party descended from a thick knoll of firs and cedars, which tumbled into a tidy grove of redbuds, whose heart-shaped leaves glimmered burgundy in the early morning sunshine. Osiris paused to draw a deep breath and sauntered cheerily between the redbuds.

"My happy wee trees. They be liking where they be planted, sure enough." The great bear patted a redbud fondly as they passed. "Here we be," he then announced as they reached a small fern-filled hill, the front of which was carved clean off and covered with stones. "Took me nigh on a decade to make yon den."

Except for its location at the center of the Hinge, one would never assume the rock facade before them could be in the least bit animal-made. Its round door stretched two men high, with each inlaid stone uniquely shaped, ranging from a palm's width to the size of a butter churn.

"This is *something*," Ryon said, despite himself.

"The young master be liking Den Five? I be pleased as a bee, being partial to it myself."

"How long have you lived here?" Ryon said.

"Nowhere near as long as in Den Two, but I reckon seventy-seven years ain't nothing to shake yer fur at, aye?"

"Did you really build it yourself, Osiris?" Tess was just as impressed as her brother.

"Of course, madame gem. What do ye be taking me for? One of these wild bears eating like hogs in the summer an' holing themselves up, first cave they find? I don't live like no insect, by the skies."

Tess nodded and smiled. Hardly a limb on her body had feeling anymore. "Might we go inside?"

"Yes, that were the plan, aye?" Osiris abruptly sat on his haunches, sending Tess sliding to the ground with painful *thump*. "Right then, there be a secret lever here, somewhere. I been known to forget where— having duties on the mind." Osiris growled to himself. "And the tunnel be long to yon den. And there's a fire to start. . . ."

"Shall we tend to the owl here, then?" Jesse suggested.

All eyes turned upon Wyndeling, who lay limp in Ryon's arms.

"She's barely breathing," the boy said.

"Tsk," grumbled the bear. "Whatever were she doing?"

"She was protecting us from an enemy," Tess said. An unpleasant tingling was starting to bloom in her left fingers. She dared not look at them. Her arm could wait.

The bear scoffed. "Ye must see the irony there. A wild animal, who thought she could be protecting you with only her natural power?"

Tess lowered herself to her knees and leaned toward her good side. Ryon joined her, placing Wyndeling gently on the ground.

"What do you mean?" Ryon said. "Why couldn't she protect us?"

"Don't tell me ye cannot see the difference between this wild creature and . . . say, yer steed, here?"

"Jesse is no bird . . . ," Tess replied, looking up at Osiris.

"That be not the sort of difference I mean. She be only a wild animal. This fellow here"—Osiris nodded respectfully to Jesse—"he be of the sacred oath. Our duties to our persons do grant us terrible privileges, young gem."

Tess nodded politely, but inwardly she burned with curiosity. Four months ago, she thought the academy had taught her everything she needed to know about Glademont. But if the past days had taught her anything, it was that she knew nothing.

"Please," Ryon pleaded. "Is there anything you can do for our friend?"

"Not I," Osiris said. "'Tisn't I who can heal this foolish creature." He glanced at Tess and tapped his moist nose with a massive paw. "The young dryad be yer best bet."

Tess reddened. She had been pondering wild animals and sacred oaths until that moment, and suddenly the conversation had turned to her again. The tingling in her hand had spread up her arm, as though it were submerged in a barrel of ice.

"I'm afraid I still haven't the hang of it," she said, biting her lip.

"In all my years never have I seen a woman dance on the water like a dragonfly," Osiris said gravely. "There be great power in thee, and no question."

Tess looked to Ryon, who nodded. "Show him," he said.

"What ye be showing me?" Osiris said.

"It is a secret," Tess said.

"Not just a secret," Ryon said. "A secret *weapon*. It must be kept hidden from our enemies, but Osiris is no enemy. Isn't that right?"

"Let us see this weapon of yers," the bear said.

Shaking, Tess pulled the *shenil* from her hair and held it in her right hand. In so doing, she realized her left arm had lost all feeling.

"Mmmmm . . . 'Tis magic, there be no question." His quick eyes focused on the curious medal that hung from the leather strap. In the center, Tess could still see the woman with long hair and what looked like flames emitting from her abdomen.

"Mmmmm . . . ," Osiris repeated. "That lady be holding this very trinket."

Tess's eyes widened. Floating above the etched palms of each upturned hand was a small circle, which must have represented the golden orbs of the *shenil*.

The *shenil* began to glow.

The great bear nodded. "Madame trinket be liking me."

"Is that the way I am supposed to hold it? I have just been holding it in my one hand or leaving it on my hair."

"The lady there be having long hair, madame gem, like yers."

"You don't suppose she *is* me, do you?"

"I wouldn't go that far, young one." The bear chuckled. "Ye be having a good fit of pride if ye think that trinket be made 'specially for thee."

Tess blushed. "I only thought . . ."

Jesse broke his silence. "It is in your charge now. You must become worthy of it." His eyes glinted kindly at her through his ivory forelock.

Tess nodded and knelt before an unconscious Wyndeling. An orb of the *shenil* glowed in her right hand. The other orb hung from her palm, the medal dangling halfway along the strap. Tess tried to reach for the swinging orb and gasped.

"Tessy." Ryon came to her side.

"I can't move my other arm." Tears streamed down Tess's face as she tried to keep her right hand in the proper position.

"I can help." Ryon pulled back Tess's cloak and choked down a gasp. Tess's limp arm was mottled with swollen purple bruises.

Ryon lifted the arm, and instantly a piercing pain lanced Tess's left side while dark splotches erupted across her vision. Desperately, Tess bit her lip, closed her eyes, and hoped against hope that the *shenil* would take over before she lost consciousness.

Ryon placed the other orb into Tess's left hand, so Tess now held a glowing copper orb in each upturned palm, the medal hanging between. Ten more seconds and Tess knew she would black out. She focused on Jesse's words. She wanted to be worthy.

"Fire," Ryon shouted. But Tess could only hear him faintly.

"Don't ye dare let go, young master," Osiris cried. Tess did not care what they were shouting about, determined to wait for the *shenil* to act. But the *shenil* had already taken its cue. The medal had burst into flames, and the orbs ignited into dazzling white lights—like diamonds in the sun, floating above Tess's trembling hands.

Then the pain in Tess's arm started to subside. She let out a tearful sigh.

Pick her up, said the now-familiar voice in Tess's head.

Before she could change her mind, Tess leaned forward and scooped Wyndeling up with her good arm. Soft feathers and rough bandages gave way under her fingers. A gust of wind swept over the flame in front of Tess. Its tongues extended and enveloped her left arm. Another gust blew upon the flame, which swirled around Wyndeling. Tess felt Wyndeling's sides expand with a deep inhale. The bandages fell. The fire faded from Tess's hands, though she longed for the warmth to stay. She lowered Wyndeling to the ground. The owl's wings and talons gently stirred. The wounds from Buchanan's attack looked as though they'd been healed for weeks.

"Mmmmm." Osiris nodded approvingly. "The proceedings be brief an' modest. Ye be a good dryad, aye?"

Ryon stared at Tess in disbelief. "By the skies," he breathed. "Your arm."

Tess held up her left hand, which was its natural freckled pink again.

"By the skies," she whispered.

"Ah, my wing seems to have finally healed. I should think I'll be able to eat now." Righting herself on the leaf-strewn ground, a perfectly fit Wyndeling busily smoothed her wayward feathers down with a curved beak, utterly unaware of the party surrounding her.

"Just like a wild animal to fuss o'er her feathers when her very life be saved," Osiris said.

Startled, Wyndeling fell backward and stared at Osiris's unkempt head. "Oh, my! This isn't that nutty bear, is it? I had hoped we would avoid you."

"Wyndeling," Tess rebuked.

"I beg your pardon, my lady. But if the rumors are true, this bear practices all sorts of unnatural nonsense."

Tess knew better than most that it was a mistake to agitate Osiris. An ominous growl had already begun to work itself in his throat.

"Wyndeling," she said hurriedly. "You were dying of fever, and Osiris helped us heal you. You owe him your life."

The growl subsided. "Now, madame gem, yer powers brought yon fool back to life. Though I'm not too pleased she be with us again."

"Behave yourself, Wyndeling," Tess said, setting the owl on her shoulder.

"Very well," replied the indignant owl. "I extend my gratitude to you both. I shall be glad to take to the skies again."

Tess rubbed her newly healed arm. If the *shenil* could perform such miracles, perhaps it really could save Glademont. But how could it be used as a weapon? She had to know more, and quickly. Yet, Profigliano was still nowhere to be found. "We must find the Ruins. But our guide has vanished."

Osiris snorted. "It be Old Glademont Castle ye be seeking, madame gem. Only two hours' walk."

"Do you really know the way? That's wonderful news. We will find the Thane's Hold in no time." Tess looked around at her friends. She had intended it as a reassuring declaration, but her heart trembled at the thought. Would she be able to reproduce the fire once they found this talisman training outpost? Or worse, had she misunderstood the queen, and there was no such place?

"I'm not going."

All eyes landed on Ryon, who already had his satchel strapped to his back. "Profigliano is out there somewhere, and either he can't find us, or he's in trouble."

"Ryon, what about Glademont? What about Mother and Papa and Dahly? We haven't any time to—"

"Fig promised to help us save our family, and he deserves help from us, too." Ryon hitched his trousers. "He's a loyal friend, and the whole Council of the Nest is looking for him and . . . well, vermin and vinegar! I just have to go."

Stunned, Tess looked on as Ryon checked the position of the sun.

"I will accompany you." Jesse shifted on his powerful legs.

"What?" Tess said.

Ryon smiled. "Good. We'll find him faster that way." He climbed onto Jesse's bare back. "Meet you here, at Den Five, within the week, I hope. Good luck, Tessy."

"What on the continent is happening?" Tess said, dazed.

From her perch on Tess's shoulder, Wyndeling clicked her tongue as Ryon and Jesse tore off through the redbud grove.

"Impetuous, that lad," Wyndeling said with an air of affected wisdom. "It will lead to untimely danger, I'll wager."

"Ho ho," Osiris cried. "If that ain't the heaviest helping o' irony been said today, then I be a caterpillar."

CHAPTER 18

It was well into morning when Linden woke. A glaring light flooded the small round room where he lay. Along with the pulsing in his head, his legs stung from various scrapes and cuts. Two enormous shackles, rusted and misshapen with age, surrounded his ankles.

He blinked through swollen lids until the room came into focus. A dilapidated wheat barrel stood in the corner against a wall of fragmented rock and sun-dried clay. The light came from an arched, barred window near the ceiling, too high to reach and too small to fit through. Opposite the window loomed a thick metal door. Above the door hung a tarnished silver plaque. The prince pushed himself to sit on the bench where he was lying. He squinted at the words. The style was cedarscript, a combination of illustration and verse used in official documents before the Forest War. It was some sort of patriotic poem:

> *Therefore, Glademontians, be sure*
> *While love of land confessing,*
> *Ye who now will bless its creatures*
> *Shall yourselves find blessing.*

Linden suddenly remembered something and fumbled through his pockets.

"His Highness is not too uncomfortable, I hope," the Atheonian's voice echoed from behind the door. The prince moaned as he caught sight of his jailer's eyes through a slit in the door. Then he heard the turn of a key and the piercing shriek of long-neglected hinges.

The Atheonian smirked, dropping the key into his blue sash. "I was as careful as I could be," he said. "But considering your very princely height, dragging you in here proved more of a challenge than anticipated." The man rolled his arms at the shoulders, making a show of his physical efforts.

Linden said nothing, but he made note of the blue sash—the liar was still wearing the mark of an Atheonian officer. The man followed Linden's gaze.

"Ah. You are wondering which rank I hold? This is the color of a general."

In his attempt to swallow, Linden felt a sting in his throat, and his eyes ached. "Where are your men, General?"

"No men at present." The Atheonian showed no embarrassment. "I travel alone, as my mission is of a confidential nature." He pulled a crumpled letter from his pocket and tapped it against his lips so Linden could see the half-torn forest-green seal of Glademont. "If I were a Glademontian, Your Highness, I'd feel great concern for your queen."

Although Linden's face flushed, he did not answer.

"I knew she was ill, but this . . ." He unfolded the letter to display the queen's plea for Nabal's cooperation. From the moment his mother had written that cursed letter, Linden had wanted to set it on fire. Now he wished he would burn along with it.

"Well"—the Atheonian shook his head reprovingly—"it seems the desperate entreaty of the dying, wouldn't you say?"

"Are you a scout?" Linden croaked, shaking the memory of his mother, of the horrible mark on her neck.

"A scout, Your Highness?"

"I know Nabal plans to attack. You were sent to study the lay of my dione, to form a strategy—"

"My dear prince." The Atheonian again shook his head with mock sympathy. "King Nabal's troops were dispatched weeks ago. They went south through the hills, while a rather rough band of hired muscle came through the forest. An attack was already launched on your castle. Didn't you know?" He crossed to the high barred window, ignoring Linden's moan.

"No, by the skies," Linden said hoarsely. He closed his eyes to subdue the aching. It was too late.

"Well," his tormentor continued with an air of business. "As I say, I am no scout; I am a general in the Atheonian army. An army that has already descended on your dione. An army that this pitiful note would not have delayed. I have ferreted you out, Your Highness, in connection with the confidential matter I mentioned."

"General what?" the prince spat.

"Hm?"

"What do they call you?"

The Atheonian paused. With quick tan fingers, he folded the queen's letter.

"General Tynaiv," he said.

Ignoring the inward pressure on his temples, Linden took a moment to study this man in the light. Too much sun on his face to have inherited such a high ranking. Too young to have fought in previous wars and climbed the ranks. His posture was loose and haughty; it lacked all discipline. The man didn't match the title. "Tynaiv, is it?" The prince fought the urge to slump. "You are no general. You are a deceiver, a foreigner, or both."

For a moment, Tynaiv's eyes brightened with rage. Then a thought seemed to come to him, and the anger dimmed. "A mischaracterization that, I may say, the Lady Tessamine did not herself make when we met."

Linden closed his eyes again and grinned, lowering himself on the bench. "You've played that hand, Tynaiv. You did not capture Lady Tessamine any more than you earned that sash."

Tynaiv shifted, but Linden did not lift his head to see where.

"I'd like to think I have captured her in a way," Tynaiv said.

Linden's stomach turned, but he willed it to be calm. It was a cheap tactic to throw the prince off balance. Linden told himself to focus. He needed to be free of this wretched man and on his way back to Glademont. There was a chance, a small chance, he could still save his dione. Or die defending it.

"Ahem." Tynaiv's self-satisfaction was almost deafening. "I brought you here, Your Highness, because conducting an inquiry in the open forest is hardly advisable." He strolled back toward the door and leaned against the wheat barrel, folding his arms and examining the prince. "You look unwell, Linden."

"Careful, pretender." Linden met Tynaiv's stare. He had found a weak spot.

But Tynaiv's angry glare vanished again before he yanked a pipe from his shirt pocket and rubbed the bowl against his pant leg. "If you wish to be released, Your Highness, I suggest you answer the following questions truthfully."

"As though truth were your trade."

"In a way, yes. I seek the bare facts." Tynaiv crossed his ankles, still leaning against the barrel. The bright late-morning sunlight reflected his long wheat-colored hair, pulled to a knot.

"The lovely Lady Tessamine has gone missing. She was last seen at your royal soiree—it was a wedding festival, wasn't it?"

Linden stared at the ceiling, feeling his face flush again. His many mistakes had culminated in that night. He should never have agreed to marry in the first place. He should never have left Glademont. . . .

"This same enchanting lady was given a trinket by your mother, the queen. Does this sound familiar?"

Linden sat up, focusing on the floor to keep his head from spinning. Learning how Tynaiv had gathered so much information was not as important as escaping his power. After a moment, Linden surveyed the man from beneath his eyelashes. If he could keep Tynaiv talking, perhaps he would cross the room again. Certainly Linden had enough strength left to bring the man down if they were close enough. He thanked the skies only his ankles were bound and not his wrists.

"What do foreigners to this continent consider trinkets? Scrap metal charms?" Linden said at last.

Tynaiv bit his pipe stem. "A thin leather strap, fastened on either end with a small copper ball."

"Glademont boasts of finer jewelry than that." The prince smiled weakly.

"Soon there will not be a Glademont," Tynaiv said without feeling. "You *have* seen the object. You were in the room when the queen handed it over."

"Were you skulking nearby, then?" Linden forced a soft chuckle. "Now that fits: Tynaiv the spy."

Tynaiv stood and approached. Linden gripped his own knees, checking Tynaiv's side for a weapon. There was none.

"What did Aideen say in that room?" Tynaiv said. "What properties does the trinket possess? What is Lady Tessamine's role? How do I find her?" Tynaiv paused a moment, then he bent to Linden's eye level. "It takes naught but a few days to die without water, Your Highness. And I can spare the time. Your dione, on the other hand . . ."

Linden lunged, wrapping a hand around Tynaiv's neck and knocking the pipe from his mouth. Quick as a cat, Tynaiv twisted his arm above Linden's and brought an elbow down hard on the prince's shoulder. Linden yelled in pain, lost his grip, and fell to the floor. His lip broke open against the filthy rock, and with a wave of shame he tasted his own blood. Months of training, and he would die with no more honor than his father did.

Tynaiv retreated, knocking over the barrel in the corner. It rolled against Linden's prostrate body. Tynaiv returned his pipe to his lips and let out a puff of air with mock surprise. "Your Highness, your conduct does not befit a gentleman." He retrieved the cell key from a fold in his sash. "Now I shall be forced to leave you here another day, to be sure there will be no more surprises. In the meantime, consider my offer: tell me what you know, and you shall go free."

The metal door shrieked open and clanged shut, and Linden was left alone again.

Linden rolled to his back, cursing the Atheonian spy and cursing his own weary body. Another day without water or food and he would hardly know himself. Then how would he best his captor? But to accept the man's offer would only bring him more disgrace. Though there was nothing to his mother's fevered ramblings, Atheos would surely execute Lady Tessamine if they knew of the legend. No, he could not have such a death on his conscience, nor would the queen ever forgive him. His only choice was to lie and hope to be believed. In the meantime, he would have to conserve his energy.

The prince's pounding head demanded he return to his bench. But as he sat up, he took notice of a yellowing, thick parchment just inside the barrel beside him. Linden reached for it and unrolled it—an old letter written in an awkward, inky cedarscript. The hand-drawn branches that bordered the words were twisted and smudged, and a solitary mountain jutted over the heading.

> *Sister Ember,*
> *I do avow, by a mother's bones bleached in the Dorian sun,*
> *I shall obtain the* shenìl, *no matter your designs.*
> *And you shall witness its destruction.*
> *—P.*

"By Luna," Linden said aloud. "What darkness is this?"

He was startled by the sound of shuffling leaves outside.

"Your Highness?" said a young woman from above.

Looking up, he saw the freckled forehead and black hair of Lady Tessamine Canyon.

CHAPTER 19

Tess watched as Ryon and Jesse disappeared into the forest. She had never seen Ryon that determined to do anything. Before that moment, Tess realized she had not paused to consider Ryon's feelings. Only twelve years old, and already so many terrifying dangers loomed over him. A pang of guilt struck her, and she mouthed a petition to Irgo, the mother star, to keep him safe.

"Before we go," Osiris said, "I just need to set the door lever, madame gem."

Tess tore her gaze from the empty trees and saw the bear rummaging around a pile of stones overgrown with ferns. Wyndeling and Tess glanced at each other dubiously. Tess was beginning to see Wyndeling's point about Osiris's eccentricity. The bear nudged a few more stones until there was an audible click behind the door.

Wyndeling shook her head. "Stones and doors and levers?"

"Yer ideas of what a creature be and what a creature be not?" Osiris said. "'Ha,' I say to that, little one. Ye be a young and forgetful lot."

Tess shouldered her ruby satchel. "No bickering, Wyndeling. Let's make for the Ruins."

Osiris snuffled and tapped his nose. "A fine day it be, don't it? And a nice walk through the meadows will do us good."

He lumbered a few paces to the left of his front door where the hill sloped to meet the lower level. He leapt onto the hill and cheerily sauntered over Den Five, disappearing behind the hill. Tess scrambled to follow her friend. Wyndeling groaned and took to the sky.

When Tess finally was atop the hill, she paused to catch her breath and blinked in the bright sunlight that she had only seen in dapples since entering the forest. Osiris's swaying back could just be made out above the tall golden grass of an enormous meadow, which stretched along small hills and under fallen tree trunks from the bordering woods. Sweet, dancing blades tickled Tess's elbows, reminding her of the yellow grass that grew behind Canyon Manor to the edge of Innkeeper Cliffs. A sad longing suddenly overtook her, and she glanced over her shoulder.

"Madame gem be thinking of her home?" Osiris called. "Even wild animals feel something toward their homes. Though, what, I don't know."

It occurred to Tess that this was the first moment she had been alone with the bear since they first met. There was so much that puzzled her about him, and without Wyndeling to provoke him . . . Tess hurried to catch up. "Osiris, I've been wondering about something you said today. About the difference in animals." She glanced at the sky to make sure Wyndeling was beyond earshot.

"Mm-hmm."

"You called yourself a 'bondfellow.' Are those the sort of animals who behave more like humans?"

"More like humans, y'say?" Osiris growled.

"Forgive me. I only meant that you and Jesse seem more civilized than wild animals."

"Be that a human trait? There be wild humans, same as animals. Bondfellows be civilized, 'tis true. What does civilized mean? When a creature's home be a sacred thing, an' when creatures be relying on one another to protect and nurture the home."

A lump lodged in Tess's throat. "My home was set afire by Atheonians."

"Young one"—Osiris paused to look at Tess—"be that the only home ye have?" He thumped a paw upon his furry chest and winked at her. "The first and last fortress for thee to protect: it be the home within."

They walked in silence for a time, until Tess could form her next question.

"Do you remember, when we first met, you said you were the beast of King Wallis? Jesse said something similar, when he introduced himself to the Council of the Nest. He said he was the beast of my mother."

"King Wallis died on this very meadow, though it weren't no mere meadow in those days." Osiris spoke with difficulty, squinting into the sky as if for assistance. Tess wondered what the bear could mean. Perhaps there were other King Wallises in Glademont's history, other than the famed last reigning king of the Forest War. He had died centuries before. But then, what was Osiris's king doing in the forest? Or was it all in the bear's foggy imagination? He certainly seemed sane in that moment, sad and silent at Tess's side.

"I'm sorry." Tess laid a hand on the bear's shoulder. "Do you miss him?"

"Even after so long, I still get the wind knocked from me, remembering he never be walking alongside me again. The bond be a strong thing, 'tis true."

"What is the bond, exactly?"

"When creatures make a sacred promise to a fellow—a human, I be meaning—they get themselves a witness and they make the vow. That's how come yers truly be using such magic up in yon creek, madame gem. It be in the service of the king."

"Even though he died?"

Osiris paused again. This time he sat heavily, sending a handful of butterflies fleeing to the sky.

"That be the question I been thinking on these lonely years. I wonder about my duty, now my king be gone and buried. But here lies the fact: I be alive yet, though my fellow be fallen. If I live still, without the oath to another fellow to keep me living, then my oath to Wallis be yet unfinished. 'Tis the only way of it."

"Osiris . . . how old are you?"

A rumbling chuckle vibrated from his chest.

"I be two hundred and forty-three now. The oldest creature I know, who be mortal."

Tess shook her head in disbelief. "But how? Because of the oath?"

"Aye, young one. An animal gets the gift of golden magic and long life so long as he be bonded to a fellow. 'Tis all for the service of the fellowship, mind thee. If a creature be thinking his power be for anything else, that's when the red magic lures him. Happens more oft to men and rarely to beast." Osiris drew a deep breath, then parted the grass with his exhale. "But the gifts still be with me. I be living still, and I be protecting the border still. If the oath expired, why be I not expired with it?"

"How bleak," Tess said. "To be waiting all these years for a danger that may never come? Doesn't it drive you mad?"

"Mad? Ha ha. Ye sound like yon little owl, little gem. They don't see the sense in it, while they be dying in a decade and have nothing to show for it. Ye never be knowing happiness till yer life be lived for another." Osiris sniffed and pawed an eye as he rose again. "No. There have been many questions in my life these long years, but never were I wishing to be wild."

Tess wanted to curse at the sun that gave her friend no answers. How lost and hopeless he must have felt, living on and on in a world that had forgotten him. Slipping her arm around Osiris's neck, Tess felt him lower his shoulders. Tears fell as she hoisted herself upon his soft back. She buried her wet face in his gray fur and clung to his neck like a weary child as he lumbered on toward the Ruins.

Tess had drifted into a light sleep astride Osiris, letting the sunlight warm her aching shoulders. But her rest was cut short as Wyndeling sailed into view and cried out, "My lady!" The owl landed in the tall grass at Osiris's paws. Tess lifted her heavy head. "My lady, there is an Atheonian man camping in the Ruins."

Sitting up, Tess felt for the *shenil* in her braid. It was still there.

"Aye." Osiris shook his gigantic head with distaste. "The little owl be right." He sniffed. "I know this man. I tracked him yesterday. Sea salt and tobacco be his scent."

Tess's heart skipped a beat, and she was pulled back to that night in the royal gardens. She could almost feel Tynaiv's breath on her skin.

"What should we do?" she said.

Osiris snuffled the air while Tess dismounted and Wyndeling alighted on the upturned branch of a fallen tree.

"Having himself a nice bit of cheese and a pipe, I wager. If Her Majesty were here now, she'd be putting Rosemary on that rat."

"All right, let's keep our heads," Tess said, more to herself than to the others. "If he is alone, I'm sure he can be easily handled with your magic, Osiris. But if he is not alone, we might be putting ourselves in more danger than we can handle."

"I saw no one but the Atheonian," Wyndeling said, a touch of hurt in her voice.

"Nothing to do but take a closer look." Osiris charged forward.

While Osiris had no trouble blending in with the tall grasses, Tess decided to remove her vivid green cloak, hoping her cream nightgown would help camouflage her. Although Wyndeling vehemently declared she could never be spotted in the sky, Tess insisted the owl ride in her satchel.

It was slow going through the last stretch of the meadow, especially for Tess. Every time her satchel bumped against her side, Wyndeling would nip her leg. Still, she concentrated to keep her wits about her for her next meeting with Tynaiv.

The grass grew thinner as they neared the bleached steep stairs, which skirted the Ruins like a temple's entrance. Osiris changed their course, and they took cover on the western corner of the structure, climbing the stairs where they met the foundation under a mammoth twisting pine. Tess peered over a weighty branch full of pine cones and tried to imagine herself in that spot two hundred years before.

Elaborate columns soared as tall as the trees in rows across the length of the ruins of Old Glademont Castle. Many archways still stood as well, with writings and symbols scrolling along the frames. A tower jutted from the westernmost corner closest to Tess, its roof still intact. The forward-facing walls of the castle were all but rubble, and some of their granite wore black char. But the rear walls remained untouched, clothed in vines and creeping brush. Tess would have observed a hushed reverence in that place if she were not bracing for an unpleasant encounter.

They paused against the foundation just before the stairs ran out. Osiris sniffed the air.

"There be another man . . . smelling of elk and leather."

"Only one other man?" Tess whispered.

"One other."

"Well, that's welcome news." Tess allowed herself a sigh and placed her satchel on the ground. Wyndeling hopped out as gracefully as she could. "But where did the Atheonian go?" Tess whispered. She placed her fingers on the top of the foundation and rose to her tiptoes. Her eyes were just level with the floor of the old castle.

Just beyond the charred rubble, under one of the narrower archways, lay a smoldering pipe upon a slab of granite. Beside it, a worn sack slumped by the remains of a campfire. Tess glanced around frantically, expecting Tynaiv to appear behind every dilapidated column.

"My lady," Wyndeling said, "the inscription I observed is located in a barred room in this tower. Shall I show you?"

"I think you had better."

"I'll be keeping watch for yon briny soldier. Ye be careful, little gem. Keep yer trinket close at hand." Osiris stared hard at Tess.

"I'll be careful." Tess draped her cloak around her shoulders. She climbed the remainder of the stairs behind Wyndeling. Now fairly in the open, Tess kept low while the owl hopped along the western edge of the ruins toward the tower. A few paces from its circular wall, Wyndeling stopped and nestled into some brush that had grown against a column. Tess crouched behind, listening. It wasn't long before she heard voices. Wyndeling's head swiveled for a sign of confirmation from Tess, then they moved slowly, carefully choosing the ground before them so as to avoid brittle sticks and dry leaves.

Cut from the northern side of the tower and sitting half-buried in the ground was a small barred window. Wyndeling glided over a patch of open ground and flattened herself against the tower wall. Tess followed suit with less finesse. From this position, they again heard the voices through the barred window.

"If you wish to be released, Your Highness, I suggest you answer the following questions truthfully."

Tess immediately recognized that inviting voice. Tynaiv was inside the tower. Tess almost spun her engagement band off of her finger as she listened.

"As though truth were your trade."

At the sound of this second voice, Tess's heart nearly leapt into her mouth.

CHAPTER 20

I say we snap his neck, 'Tenant. We been at this all morning, and he don't know nothing."

"I will take your suggestion under advisement, Root. Although I should mention I'd sooner snap your neck than that of this bird." Pilt wiped his face with a kerchief.

Profigliano lay helpless against a large stone, his wings pinned to his sides by a twisted river reed.

"Perhaps you think me a dishonest man, towhee." Pilt regarded his prisoner. "And that may be true at times." He grinned. "But when it comes to threats, I am ever so honest."

A burlap bundle convulsed to Profigliano's right.

"I am a believing kind of birdie, chappy," Profigliano said. "If you say there's a hungry fox in that mystery bag, then by my beak, there is."

"He has not eaten in over a day." Pilt bent over the bundle, brandishing a knife. "And I'm interested to know whether he might like a sniff of you."

Pilt slit one of the ropes that bound the sack, and from the loosened bundle, the black muzzle and glimmering teeth of a fox shoved itself in Profigliano's direction. The rest of the fox's head could not squeeze its way out, but Pilt held the sack just close enough for the fox to taste Profigliano's tail with his tongue.

"Hey now, ho now," the frightened bird cried. "This is not what we call a fair fight!"

"Where is the girl?"

"I'm no tattletale." Profigliano tried to rock out of reach. "And you thug bugs can shove off a cliff—yaaah!" Now inside the fox's mouth, the towhee squirmed desperately while the fox strained to chew.

"Spit him out!" Pilt dealt a swift kick to the bundle, which howled and released the bird.

Facing his small squad, Pilt stowed his knife in a holster attached to his forearm.

"Gentlemen," he called brightly, "a word?"

"Yes, sir, 'Tenant Pilt," answered the men (Root's reply being more enthusiastic than Grift's). They moved a few yards away, toward the shore of Ruby Creek. Pilt wiped his face with the kerchief.

"If there is anyone who knows the ins and outs of Glademont Castle, men, it is Tessamine Canyon. The little lamb was chosen to be the queen's successor and has been snuggling up to lords, ladies, dignitaries, and the like ever since. She is a flighty idiot, if the gossips are right . . . therefore, easy to break."

Root squinted with concentration at his superior. Grift fingered his own knife, the possibilities having dawned on him.

"If we wind up at Glademont with that girl, we'll be set for life," Grift said.

"Precisely." Pilt brightened. "Grift, your tracking skills are above average."

"Erm."

"Indeed. I propose that we keep the towhee for the rest of the day, then feign defeat. We'll release him come twilight, and track him through the night. I'll bet you ten to one that little codfish will lead us straight to the would-be princess. What say you?"

"Trackin' in the night, Lieutenant?" inquired Grift.

Pilt raised an eyebrow.

Grift hesitated. "It's just that we ain't been sleepin' lately, sir. And trackin' at night's trickier than trackin' in the day's all I'm sayin'."

"It's the best way to slow the bird down," Pilt replied. "And if you even think about losing sight of it, I'll empty your eye sockets." After a short sigh, Pilt smiled cheerfully. "Are we in agreement?"

Two long hours passed. Pilt's orders were to keep Profigliano from falling asleep. Of course, this meant Grift and Root had to decide who would keep watch. Grift won out in the end, citing that he had already done his duty by capturing the creature in the first place.

Sulkily, Root took up his post and hung Profigliano from a low branch so that he would be at eye level. Pilt filled his notebook with the daily report, and Grift curled up in the shade to nap. Eventually, the cool breeze and the warm midday sunshine overtook Pilt as well, and Root was left to fight drowsiness alone. His struggle was far from heroic, however, due to Profigliano's moaning. He lifted a grubby hand and whacked the captured towhee, sending him awhirl.

"Oy, stop your howlin', or I'll cut your feet off, eh? You wouldn't like to hop about on your twiggy li'l knees, would yeh?"

"Oooooh," replied Profigliano. "That sounds like wormy pudding compared to spinning around here for one more second. Ooooh. Why'd you have to mention pudding?"

"I didn't say nothin' about no pudding, you whiny little beetle."

"Oooooooh."

"I mean it. Shut up, or I'll slice yeh into slivers."

"Oh, please somebody make those trees take a break. They'll forget where they used to be standing if they keep it up. Oh, if only I knew how good I had it when I was lying still. Ooooh. Aaaah."

"That's it, you half-witted bag of feathers," Root hissed. He cut the line, sending Profigliano to the ground with a soft thud. "I don't care whether yeh live or die," he whispered. "I'm done pretending I care a grain of sand about any half-witted animal in this cursed forest. I'm going to the front lines to kill me a creature wot has a brain."

Snatching the line from the ground, he padded to the bank of Ruby Creek, grumbling to himself as he dragged the bird along. Reaching the bank, Root reeled in the line to get a better look at his victim. "Do yeh think I'm going to let those two stumps drag me 'round this endless forest, picking off doves and mice whilst a real battle is going on? *Do yeh?*"

"Oh," Profigliano replied, reorienting himself, "I should say not. No, no, no, no. Those animal-wallopers don't know real brains when they see it."

"That's the first thing you've said wot hasn't made me want to squeeze the life out of yeh."

"Don't mention it."

"They think you're so important? They can bloody well chase yeh down the creek if they like. And when the stupid idiots have pulled yeh from the water, I'll be long gone."

"Heeeeyyy now. This plan is lookin' a bit thin, don'tcha think? Don't get me wrong; it *is* brainy to the gills. Just a little tweaking is in order—"

"Now, don't start screechin' for a minute. I'll need a head start. . . ."

Root slipped the line from Profigliano's body, leaving the river reed that pinned his wings. Casting the line into the creek, Root observed its swift movement southward.

"Creek's nice and full, eh?" Root winked at the towhee. "Must have been a bit of snowmelt up in those mountains. Off yeh—"

"The most unimaginable thing has just occurred, comrade."

Root froze midtoss, with Profigliano hovering over the water. A little squawk of terror escaped the soldier's lips.

"'Tenant Pilt, sir."

His commanding officer leaned against a towering boulder by the creek bank, cracking his neck. "I happen to be a light sleeper, you see."

Root swallowed, but stayed his hand over the water.

"It's kept me alive. You wouldn't believe the sorts of things people do while a man is asleep."

"D-don't you come any closer, 'Tenant."

"For instance, the unimaginable matter to which I was referring." Pilt untied his green sash, folded it neatly, and tossed it upon the bank. "I distinctly thought I heard a man call me a . . . what was it?" Pilt pulled off his jacket, folding it as before.

"I swear on me pa's grave," came Root's shrill cry. "If you take one step closer, I'll drown your *precious* bird."

"It was 'stupid idiot,' Root. 'Stupid idiot.' Do you think I'm stupid, Root?" The lieutenant withdrew the miniature hatchet, which had threatened Root before. "I think I'll remove your vocal cords for that." He did not smile.

"Put it down," Root shouted. He dropped to one knee and dunked Profigliano up to his head in the creek waters. "Do y'see now? You so much as wink at me, and this little idiot will drown and you'll be knocking on mole hills for the rest of this bleedin' war." He submerged the bird.

A steady succession of bubbles burst on the creek's surface as Profigliano fought for his life. Root growled with determination, driving his arm deeper.

Pilt glanced at the creek, then at Root. Taking his kerchief, he wiped his face and neck. Root breathed heavily, his face screwed up like buckled dough.

"Very well," Pilt said at last as he rested his weapon against his shoulder.

Visibly relieved, Root withdrew his victim from the creek. The towhee sputtered and gasped as Root stated his terms.

"I'm leaving the bird right here on the bank, and you toss your weapon on the ground in front of me. Don't follow me or report me, or I'll tell them that I saw you take money from that fella Tynaiv for keeping your mouth shut, got me?"

Root had hit a nerve. The lieutenant's eyelids flickered. He readjusted his grip, but the hatchet remained on his shoulder.

"I don't think you know what you are talking about."

"Don't I? You and that boy think I'm such an ox, but I got ears just like anyone else, see? And I for *sure* got eyes."

Pilt stroked his face, squinted at the treetops, and spoke.

"That was a mistake, Root. Telling me you witnessed my exchange with General Tynaiv was a grave mistake."

Needing no further incentive, Root bolted, leaving the gasping towhee on the bank. He sprinted for the nearest boulder, covering his head with his hands. But Pilt had already loosed the hatchet with frightening power, and the weapon sank deep into Root's back. He howled in agony, colliding with the boulder and falling to the ground. His arms and legs twitched as blood spilled on the dirt beneath him. Ten gruesome seconds later, he was still.

Pilt reached for his sash on the creek bank and was just about to tie it on when the staccato thudding of hooves sounded in the distance. Agitated, Pilt started for his hatchet, still buried in Root's back.

"Stand aside," came a boy's cry amid the trees. Jesse burst from the shadows with Ryon astride, a stone poised in the boy's spinning sling. The stallion came to a jolting halt between Pilt and Root's body.

The lieutenant's eyes shifted toward the camp as he slowly raised his hands in surrender.

"Your friend back at the camp is unconscious," Ryon said, guessing the meaning behind Pilt's glance. "Either he thought he was quick, or"—the young boy lowered his sling a bit to grin at Pilt—"he thought I was slow."

Pilt smiled back with a wink. "Aren't you a sharp lad."

Ryon flicked hair from his forehead, keeping his sling at the ready. "We found you, Fig. Me and Jesse have been looking along the creek since morning."

"Oh, young master, this soggy red-breaster needs a three-day nap."

"Just as soon as we take care of this Atheonian." Ryon stared hard at the Atheonian. "Get on your stomach and put your nose in the dirt."

Pilt remained still.

"Do as the boy commands," Jesse said. He did not shout, but the sound startled Pilt. After a moment, the lieutenant lowered himself to the ground and placed his forehead in the grass. Ryon dismounted.

But the moment Ryon's feet touched the ground, Pilt rose to his knees, reached into his sleeve, and drew his knife.

"No, sir, Loo-tenant," came the towhee's throaty baritone just as Pilt let loose his blade. A burst of gold light crackled in the air. The bird's magic shattered Pilt's knife into harmless specks that fell to the ground like dust. Almost without thinking, Ryon aimed a stone at Pilt's throat and let it loose. His aim was true. Clutching his neck, Pilt flailed and fell backward with a gurgle.

Ryon stumbled to his friend to free the bird from his bondage. "Well done, Fig. I was half a breath away from death."

"Just doin' my duty, m'lad." Profigliano bowed unsteadily. Clearing his throat, he made a second attempt, then tipped over altogether.

Ryon stood, watching Pilt writhe. He made sure he could see the man's hands, in case there were any more surprises. But it was hard to look in Pilt's direction without seeing the poor fellow who died. The hatchet in the dead man's back made Ryon's insides feel out of sorts. A wave of guilt washed over him, as he wondered what his father would have to say about the sling in his hand. But then Ryon looked to his brave friend, and remembered where the little towhee would be if Ryon and Jesse had not come to rescue him.

"Why didn't you use magic when the Atheonian was holding you over the water?" Ryon said, distracting himself from his inner debate.

"Believe me, I concentrated all of my bird-brains on it. But it wouldn't take, ya know? Just like before when I couldn't get a good bubble going."

"That's odd. I wonder what the difference—"

"Hullo? Don't leave me here!"

"What was that?" Ryon brandished his sling. The voice had come from Pilt's camp. "Do you think that other Atheonian is awake already?"

"Now, Master Ryon, I think we've had enough chucking stones. It's sleep time. It's time to put on the old nightie and put out the candles."

"Hold on, Fig. Jesse, guard that one. I'll be right back." Pilt was now lying still, his hands cradling his throat. A thin and steady squeaking suggested he could now breathe.

Ryon led Profigliano back up the bank toward the camp, and keeping to the long shadows of the trees, he paused to listen.

"Is anyone there? For the love of life, don't leave me. I've got a mate and seven pups to feed."

Profigliano landed on Ryon's shoulder—not without teetering—and whispered in the boy's ear.

"That's not skinny-face talking; it's that gobbling fox. He was picking my feathers from his teeth, that rascal. If you'll take my advice, Master Ryon, you'll shoot a whole *bucketful* of rocks at him."

"Hush, Fig. I'm thinking."

While Ryon and Profigliano spoke, the burlap bundle holding the fox was still. Then it stirred.

"Forgive me, kind sirs," the fox from the bundle said. "But I could not help but overhear your exchange. Might I offer a suggestion?"

"No," Profigliano said.

"I suggest," the fox continued, "that you allow me to explain how I came to be bagged, tell my side of the story. If you still don't trust me then, you can put me back in this sack and leave me to die. I am a captive of the Atheonians, just like you were, sir bird."

Profigliano scoffed. "There'll be no *sir birdin'* from you. It's Julius the Eleventh, Duke of Magic to you. Do you know what I'll call you? I'll call you Sir Nasty Breath. Ha ha."

"Oh, Fig." Ryon rubbed his face.

"Do you even have seven pups?" Profigliano sneered.

There was an uncomfortable pause.

"My sister has two."

"Ha ha *ha*," bellowed the towhee triumphantly. "Your story will never soak."

Another uncomfortable silence.

"Oh, I'm going to let him out," Ryon said.

"Suit yourself. But if that fox starts rollin' you around in his mouth like a hard candy, don't count on old Figliano to save you."

Ryon stepped around the unconscious Grift and over to the bundle to untie the cords. A dusty, slender black fox crawled forth. His eyes were rich amber, and half of one ear was sliced away.

"Many thanks, good master." He blinked indulgently at the after-noon sun as a bushy tail curled about his paws. "My name is Evening."

CHAPTER 21

Tess pressed her back against the tower wall and waited to hear the cell door close. She had not dared look through the window during Linden's harrowing inquisition, but she could easily gather he was weak and in pain. This alone might not have inspired much sympathy in Tess's heart. But the prince had also not betrayed her secrets, despite caring so little for her and even less for the *shenil*. She had to admit: although Prince Linden was an arrogant, delusional heel, he didn't deserve to be left to starve.

Tess stooped to the cell window. "Your Highness?" she whispered.

Linden sat below with his back to her, bent over something in concentration. Wyndeling hopped to the window as well. Slowly, the prince looked into the light from over his shoulder.

"Lady Tessamine? But, how could you possibly—?"

"By accident, Your Highness. Is there no one else but you and . . . ?" She swallowed the name.

"No one," Linden answered, his expression dark.

"Then it won't be any trouble to free you. A friend of mine is dealing with the man."

"I—I can't believe this." Linden struggled to stand.

Tess lowered awkwardly to her knees to see better through the arched window. She saw Linden squinting at the owl next to her. "This is Wyndeling."

"Wyndeling the Red, Your Highness," the owl said with a slight bow. "Member of the Fourth Council of the Nest."

Linden bowed in kind, which seemed to please Wyndeling. But Tess noticed he could hardly open his swollen eyes, and his bare feet were shackled and bloody.

"I am grateful to you, Your Highness, for keeping my secrets." She managed a slight smile.

"That man knew a great deal about us." His voice dragged with dehydration. "He claimed to know you personally." He glanced at her through strands of dusty hair.

Tess opened her mouth to answer, but a tremor in the ground forced her to steady herself on the tower wall. She got to her feet, looking for the source. But then she caught Wyndeling's eye.

"The bear, my lady," the owl said.

Tess felt a wash of panic. If Osiris killed Tynaiv, how would she ever learn the truth about him, and who he told about the *shenil*?

"I must see to my friend," she called to Linden, trying to hide her anxiety. "I shall only be a moment."

She hurried from the western tower toward the center of the Ruins, with Wyndeling close behind. Pausing in the brambles surrounding a column, Tess caught sight of Tynaiv's camp. There she saw the foreigner on his knees, raising his hands in surrender before the towering figure of Osiris, who had lifted himself to his hind legs. The ground trembled again as golden magic poured from his snout.

"Stop." Tess rushed to the campfire.

Tynaiv turned, keeping his hands in the air. His eyes scanned Tess. A corner of his mouth lifted. "Well, hello," he said.

Tess tried to speak smoothly, though her heart thumped madly. "A moment, Osiris, before you finish this man."

Tynaiv stood and his head bounced in a casual bow. "My lady," he said. "Have you come to rescue me?"

Osiris snarled as he lowered his front paws. Thin clouds of gold expanded around him. "Naught but Luna herself can save thee, scoundrel."

Tess drew herself up, wrapping her cloak about her shoulders. "My friend has every right to punish you for your trespass. Though, crossing into his territory is far from your only crime."

"My *lady*." Tynaiv bowed low this time. "I mean no trespass. I sought only a safe place to stow my prisoner."

"The prince of Glademont?"

"Have you loyalties to the man, my lady?" Tynaiv relaxed his arms and turned his back on Osiris, giving Tess his full attention. "Has he no crimes of his own to pay for?"

Tess's pulse quickened. She knew this game, using her hurt against her. As she searched for the nerve to reply, Wyndeling came to her shoulder. She could feel the owl's head oscillating at Tynaiv with disapproval. She breathed in the cool air.

"Who are you?" she demanded.

"I never lied to you, Tess." Tynaiv met her eyes.

She took a step forward, not knowing how to respond to his audacity. But now anger surged through her limbs like wildfire.

"You will tell me who you really are and why you seek the *shenìl*."

"You know who I am. A seaman from Talon. And it is not I who seeks the *shenìl*."

"You sent Pider and those horrible men to my home."

"Counselor Pider and I are only temporarily allied. I assure you, my lady, I did not expect any harm to come to you—"

"You go to great lengths for this temporary alliance, do you not? Even so far as to starve the prince."

The usual confidence in Tynaiv's eyes flickered. He shifted under Tess's stare. "I was originally sent into the Hinge to find you, my lady."

"Knowing what Pider would do to me?"

"Hardly . . . Pider keeps much from me, and I was determined to learn the implications if I were to surrender you to him. When I came upon the prince, I saw a way to know more of the object and of your role in this."

Osiris growled. "The man be naught but a deceiver. Let us be done with him."

Tess searched Tynaiv's face for sincerity. He was impossible to read. He simply stood there, relaxed yet expectant.

"Wyndeling," she said, holding his gaze. "Please take the key from this man and free Prince Linden. He has waited long enough."

Tynaiv shook his head, reached into his sash, and tossed the key at Tess's feet. "You trust the royals far too easily, my lady."

Wyndeling fetched the key and sailed away. Tess could see that Osiris was getting restless. He tossed his weighty head behind Tynaiv's back.

Tynaiv took a step toward her. "I could protect you from Pider, you know," he said. "If you would confide in me, tell me what the object is for—"

"I will not betray myself to you again."

Tynaiv rested his hands on his hips, cocking his head at her. "You mean betray the *royals*, don't you? You think your actions or mine brought this war? No. It was the doing of your sainted queen and prince, my lady."

"Lady Tessamine," a familiar voice called out. Tess saw Linden striding toward her, still barefoot and weakened but eyeing Tynaiv with energy. "I beg you not to speak to this man. He is a spy and a villain."

"Your Highness." Tess curtsied, still feeling Tynaiv's eyes on her. "I was questioning him."

Linden knitted his eyebrows at her. Though his face was streaked with dirt, she saw his expression was as earnest as ever. He then caught sight of Osiris. The bear's sheer size gave him pause, but he recovered himself.

"You must be Lady Tessamine's new friend. I thank you. Glademont thanks you," he said.

"Who be this, madame gem?" Osiris said.

"This is Prince Linden of Glademont. Prince Linden, this is Osiris of . . . Glademont."

"Ho ho," Osiris bellowed. "Well, Prince Linden of Glademont, so you be saying, I was just about to finish this villain of yours."

Linden stepped into Tynaiv's camp and searched the items strewn there. "I'm afraid I must deprive you of that privilege, Osiris." He found his bow and quiver and, with relish, aimed an arrow at Tynaiv's heart. "For it will fall to me." He carefully backed toward Tess, out of striking range from Tynaiv.

"Forgive me." Tynaiv hooked his hands on his hips again. "But do we really believe the good prince would harm me? The spoiled pup of a weaponless country?" Tynaiv's dimple deepened with amusement. An arrow hummed past his head, nicking the flesh between his neck and shoulder. He shuddered and grasped his bloody shirt, while Linden drew another arrow.

"Killing you is currently my foremost desire. Explain your accusation that I had anything to do with this war, or I will indulge myself."

Tynaiv's eyes watered, but still he smiled through gritted teeth. "Yours was a plot for revenge gone awry."

"Whose revenge?" Tess said.

"Revenge for the royal family, my lady." Tynaiv stared meaningfully at her, working his jaw.

"He's no use, Your Highness." Tess returned his gaze fiercely.

"No such plot existed," Linden said. The arm holding his bowstring drooped with exhaustion.

"It seems," continued Tynaiv, pulling a handkerchief to stop the bleeding, "that Linden and his mother have a certain death to avenge." He looked at Linden, an eyebrow raised. "Isn't that right, good prince?"

Linden threw down his bow, picked up a rock, stepped forward, and struck Tynaiv on the side of the head.

"Your Highness," Tess cried.

"Osiris, if you would be so kind as to take this rodent down to his cell."

CHAPTER 22

Ryon bent over the sleek fox in the mottled afternoon rays. From the boy's shoulder, Profigliano eyed their new acquaintance ruefully. The soldier named Grift lay prone a few paces away. Ryon pointed to his limp body.

"Listen, Evening," he said. "We don't have a lot of time before that man wakes up. Profigliano claims you tried to eat him. What about it?"

The black fox batted amber eyes with apparent woe.

"A lamentable truth," he purred. "An event that occurred only a few hours ago, when I thought all was lost and I would starve to death."

"Ho ho ho," Profigliano cried. "You were savoring me like a sugar pie."

"The brutes kept me in that sack for so long," the fox insisted, "my stomach ached with hunger. Please forgive my eagerness to ingest you."

"Psha." The towhee crossed his wings and spun about on Ryon's shoulder.

"I think you had better start from the beginning, Evening," said the ever-patient Ryon.

"Of course," Evening said. "Two days ago, I happened to be napping in the groove of an old tree root, digesting a bellyful of . . . um, fish. Suddenly, a man stood before me. At first, I thought he was the prince of Glademont, for I had heard rumors he was back in the forest. But when the gentleman lifted me by the tail, I understood otherwise. He inquired as to my allegiance, and I knew him to be Atheonian. 'Speak or be executed,' said the man. Can you believe the nerve? Waltzing into the Hinge and holding creatures by their tails?

"Nevertheless, we foxes are skilled in the art of survival. 'I wish to serve the crow and King Nabal's army,' said I—a ruse, you understand. It took many reassurances on my part to convince him, but once I promised the locations of all the creatures in the Hinge who refused to follow the crow, he seemed to brighten up. Again, a ruse, I can assure you—'biding time and staying alive,' as my dear mother used to say. At any rate, they bagged me up and jostled me about and generally treated me harshly. When I tried to escape, the lieutenant took a souvenir, as you can see."

Evening proudly displayed what was left of his ear.

"There's something I don't understand," Ryon said. "How do you know Prince Linden?"

Evening shifted his weight. "Are you the leader of this company?"

"I wouldn't say that," Ryon said, surprised at the question. "My sister and I came here by accident—"

Evening gazed up at Ryon in a foxy sort of way. "What is her name?"

"Don't you tell him, Master Ryon." Profigliano turned about and hopped up onto Ryon's head. "He's a sneaky snake and he's up to no good. Put him back in the bag and let's get outta here."

Just then, Grift began to moan behind them. "Oy . . . oh-oh. I needs some cool water. . . ."

Jesse trotted into the camp, gracefully stepping over Grift.

"Time to go," he said.

The hoarse cursing of Lieutenant Pilt could be heard as he tromped through the trees. And Grift was beginning to get his bearings.

"Come on, Fig." Ryon raced for Jesse and leapt onto his back. He loaded his sling and caught Evening's glinting eyes. The fox lowered his head an inch, his light body tensed and at the ready.

"Master Ryon," Evening called. "You carry a weapon I know to be made by the prince of Glademont. He has been captured. But I can take you to the prince's allies here in the wood. Follow me." With astonishing speed, Evening whipped into the underbrush.

Jesse hesitated as Ryon's gaze followed the black fox.

"Did he say Prince Linden was in trouble?"

Profigliano circled Ryon's head. "We should never have opened that stinky bag."

"If Prince Linden isn't free, Glademont will never win this war," Ryon said, sweat dripping from his forehead. Jesse shifted unsteadily on his hooves as Grift got to his feet.

"Come on, Jesse," Ryon urged. He pressed his knees against the stallion's sides.

Pilt limped into view, holding the hatchet from Root's back. He yelled and drew his arm to throw.

"Jesse, come on." Ryon pulled at Jesse's mane until the powerful legs beneath him began to churn. The next moment, they were thundering after the fox.

Evening had waited for them just beyond the Atheonian campsite. Once in view, the fox shot off again, pattering over the forest floor, barely disturbing the ferns and dry leaves. Ryon clutched Jesse's white mane, keeping a watchful eye on the slender black figure ahead. The trees were thick and Jesse could not manage his full speed, but the shouting of the Atheonians soon grew faint.

"Evening," Ryon called out. "The Atheonians are gone. Tell us where are we going."

Ryon's eyes were tired, and his head was beginning to ache. From the time that Tess crossed Ruby Creek to the moment Evening crawled out of a burlap sack, there had not been a moment's rest. Had he eaten that day? He could not remember.

The fox leapt upon a limestone ledge and looked back to the boy. His velvet head cocked to the side as Jesse checked his pace alongside the ledge.

"We go to see a friend of your prince's."

"Prince Linden has friends in the Hinge?" Ryon said.

"Yes, and with Atheos taking the castle as well as the valley, these are the only friends he may have left."

"What do you mean? Has Atheos taken the villages in the valley?" Ryon hoped the fox could not see the frantic pulsing of his chest. Even if Tess had found the Thane's Hold, would she be too late?

The fox stared solemnly. Then his head turned to the lowering sun. "Come," he said, and leapt from the ledge.

Before Ryon could inquire further, the fox was speeding among the ferns again. Profigliano, who had been pursuing his rescuers from the air, landed upon Ryon's shoulder huffing and puffing.

"I gotta say . . . your Ryon-ness"—the towhee panted—"this kind of race is *not* for the birds. I've rapped my brains on more than one branch a-tryin' to keep an eye on you boys. I think I better take a break in your pocket, if ya don't mind?"

Ryon gently stowed his small friend, and Jesse charged onward.

The day aged, and the sun grew heavier. At one point, their path veered due south, and Ryon began to worry they would not find Ruby Creek again. His head felt so foggy from worry and sleeplessness, he distrusted his sense of direction.

When Evening finally slowed to a trot, the fox lifted his muzzle to smell the air. To their left and in front of them, the sky seemed much nearer than it had been. A broad ribbon of cobalt blue stood out from behind the old tree trunks of the Hinge, softened only by the orange-rimmed cotton clouds that drifted near eye level.

"We are almost upon the cliffs," Evening said quietly. "We must be cautious. Atheonians came this way not too long ago."

Ryon dismounted and followed Evening toward the tree line, keeping close to Jesse's neck. They descended into a small hollow shaded by a single poplar. Evening trotted through a thick mound of ivy to the very edge of the hollow. Ryon gazed out into an empty expanse. The spot overlooked the west side of Glademont Valley, where the cliffs plummeted before bending into a vast, lush valley, dotted by the four villages of the dione. Ryon glanced over his left shoulder and saw, above the cliffs, the Gull Mountains looming beyond. Glademont Castle was hidden from view by the tall pines of the Hinge, but Ryon knew it was there.

"They're camped in Redfoot now." Evening slanted his jeweled eyes toward the southwestern corner of the valley, where Glademont's great city sat. The bustling hub of the dione nestled against the southwestern border.

Ryon followed the fox's gaze. "Who is camped there?"

"The Atheonian army."

Ryon could hardly believe it. Redfoot was the most vibrant place he had ever known. He had grown up hearing of its color and excitement from his sisters while they attended the prestigious Redfoot Academy. Two months ago, it was finally his turn, and the city did not disappoint him. He met more interesting, more joyful people there than at any banquet in the stone halls of Glademont Castle. Were they all captive now? Or worse?

"Where in the city has Atheos camped?"

"At the center. Where I believe the market is held," Evening said.

Ryon focused his memory on the Market, the tallest building in the city, from which all streets radiated in a large web. The building was actually a self-contained collection of three smaller buildings. First, the great rotunda faced the Miri River to the east, and two long wings curled out from its sides, joining at the end by a gate and gatehouse. Ryon strained his eyes and saw smoke emitting from the city. Black billowing smoke.

Atheonian drums could be heard echoing against the cliffs: the low, quick monotone beat of a warring people.

"They have five hundred soldiers at least down there," Evening said. "They brought all kinds of things with them, including enough rope and chain to imprison most of the villagers in that rotunda."

"Have they taken any of the other villages?" Ryon scanned the rest of the valley.

"Well, they've taken Redfoot; that's clear enough. I heard when they came out of the southern woods, the Atheonians charged like men possessed. Most of the Redfooties had taken shelter in the Market, but the gate is split to pieces now. A battering ram. The Redfooties are even being forced to mend the ram. So they say."

"Why?" Ryon saw his hands were shaking.

"We think they're heading for Glademont Castle. There are only a few hundred Atheonian rabble up that way, and they can't get into the castle." Evening looked sideways at Jesse, who was eyeing the fox in a piercing fashion.

"Who escaped from Redfoot?" Jesse said.

"Oh, yes. That is . . . how did you know? Yes, some of the Redfooties resisted. We heard legends, but had never seen . . . Well, there were bursts of gold light that night—giant clouds of it. Some escaped north."

"And there were animals among them." Jesse looked to the center of the valley where the pony breeders of Foggy Plains lived.

"Yes. There were animals. Can you actually *see* them from here?"

As Evening glanced at Jesse with a degree of uneasiness, Ryon tried valiantly not to let the news of Redfoot's fall further the commotion in his aching head. That the Atheonians had not yet penetrated the castle was encouraging. On the other hand, what of his friends and professors at the academy? What of the tradesmen and their families?

"Now, my friends and rescuers," said Evening in a cordial but hurried manner, "we really must be going."

"Looks like stinky squelcher is up to his usual tricks," Profigliano said.

Ryon tore his eyes from the black smoke to the south. "What are we in such a hurry for? Who are these people you say will help Prince Linden?"

"You lot seem to think you are the only ones with reason to be suspicious," Evening said. "But the truth is, I am not inclined to trust you, either. There is something dangerous about this horse; it puts me on edge. Jesse, did you say?" Evening eyed Jesse as though his mane and tail were about to burst into flames.

"You are right," the steed answered. "I am dangerous, and I do not suffer deceivers. Tell us where you are taking us." Jesse lowered his head and took a slow step forward.

"Oh, my." Evening retreated, then sat with his velvety tail wrapped around his paws and smoothed out his shorn ear. "Well, if we are late, you've only yourselves to blame. We go to see a band of animals, not people, Master Ryon. They call themselves the Friends of the Militia. The FOM. Currant of the Birch Herd is their leader. I say *they* because I am not in the habit of joining rebel groups—or any groups for that matter—that do not afford much in the way of anonymity. Nevertheless, Currant is a friend of mine, and—"

"Friends of the Militia?" Ryon could not help but interject. "As in Glademont's militia? Why, that was only formed a few days ago. . . ."

"Oh, for Luna's sake, just come *on*. I'll never make it to the meeting at this rate."

The fox took a few paces before looking over his shoulder. Ryon glanced again at the smoke rising from Redfoot. A moment ago, it seemed Glademont was lost. But this band of animals—these Friends of the Militia—could they really help his people? He thought of Tess hoping to learn the ways of the *shenil*. She was trying to save her dione the best way she knew. Perhaps this was Ryon's chance to do the same.

With a determined nod to Evening, Ryon deposited Profigliano on his shoulder and followed the impatient fox southward into the heart of the Hinge. Jesse snorted briefly, but there was no further protest. Ryon walked a little taller. In time, he would show Tess and Papa he could fight for his dione. Perhaps he could even save it.

CHAPTER 23

Evening kept his eyes on the falling sun as he scurried through the auburn leaves and purple ferns of the Hinge. Behind him, Ryon trotted doggedly and Profigliano surveyed from atop Jesse's head. Since fleeing his home, Ryon had grown accustomed to walking amid the dead silence of the Hinge. But now that they were headed toward the southern wood, the hum of wildlife could be heard. Ryon flinched as a pair of ducks quacked overhead.

"Don't worry, Master Ryon," Evening called over his shoulder. "That was Cheekathistle and her mate, Thorestook. We haven't missed the meeting after all."

Ahead loomed a steep slope, climbing upward and decorated with roots and yellowing vines. A series of trails snaked back and forth along the surface of the slope, well used yet subtle. The climb seemed a trivial exercise for Evening and Jesse, whereas Ryon, the only two-footed animal on the trail, found it tough going. The ascent was steep, with nothing to hold on to but old roots. Several times, Ryon slid backward in his smooth-soled boots. Fig hopped nearby, calling out suggestions and unnecessary warnings.

"An excellent move, Master Ryon. You are so quick, so sharp. So very muscly are your muscles . . . oh, careful now, careful there. I-ya don't wanna squash your soufflé, but that left leg is gonna skate right off the side there. No use clawing up a hill with mangled legs, now is there?"

At last, all four creatures crested the slope as the day's parting sunbeams splashed across their faces. Relieved to be on solid ground again, Ryon leaned against a tree trunk and noticed it was considerably smaller than the house-like trees of the Hinge. Then, looking about, Ryon beheld with awe a vast expanse of silver birches. It was one of the last days when the leaves of the silver birches danced in their most dazzling hue of yellow. The pearly birch trunks glowed in the setting sun, and the ground was aflame with the scarlet leaves of blueberry bushes, thick and happy in the breeze. It was such a stunning sight, Ryon did not notice the sudden appearance of a tall and graceful elk stag cantering toward them.

"Well, well," Evening called. "Have I arrived in time, prince of the Birch Herd?"

The creature moved easily between thick berry bushes, his hooves making no sound. As Ryon admired the black twitching nostrils and young but sturdy antlers, he realized this creature must be Evening's friend, Currant.

"How on the continent are you still alive, Eve?" Currant said. "I *told* you not to nap in the open, and the very next hour I come across an Atheonian. I thought for sure he would catch you."

"I was indeed ambushed," Evening said. "Fortunately, fate intervened and brought me these three rescuers. I have news of Prince Linden, though I doubt you will like it."

Currant jerked his head to sudden attention.

"Is he alive?"

"Alive when last I saw him—or rather, when last I heard him. But you see we have been traveling. Will you not invite us in? I will tell all if you will lend me a fish or two. Or perhaps an egg?"

"You don't fool me; I know you'd prefer a chick or a mouse, but a fish is all you'll get. The meeting has been postponed until tomorrow—I couldn't get an audience with Father before then." Currant expanded his chest a few inches. Was it with pride or anxiety?

Then the elk nodded to Ryon and his friends. "As for these three, introductions are in order, I believe." Currant flicked his tufted tail. "I am Currant of the Birch Herd, and this is our home. Our herd has lived here for centuries, and by design, the Grove is difficult to find. Yet, here you are. I don't mind, of course, if you are friends of Evening."

Ryon glanced at Jesse, hoping that he would speak on their behalf. Jesse blinked, but said nothing. Ryon sighed, and an involuntary growl emitted from his stomach.

"Excuse me." He blushed. "Er . . . I am Master Ryon Canyon of the Dione of Glademont. This is Jesse of Glademont. He goes by 'The Rushing.' It's his legendary title, apparently—"

"The Rushing?" Currant interrupted. "The elders speak of you. Did you really leave the Foggy Plains breeders and live like a wild animal in the Hinge? I've heard Father call you 'a torch of freedom.' Though, I don't love how he uses that term. By 'free' he really means human hater. The elders will be surprised to see you here . . . and accompanied by a human." Currant nodded to Ryon, not unkindly.

Jesse snorted and pawed at the ground. "I was young and short-sighted when last I came to the Hinge."

Ryon half smiled with confusion. How much did he really know about his family's noble horse? It seemed not much. Leaning on Jesse's shoulder, he persevered in the introductions. "And this is Profigliano of the Hinge Forest."

"Profigliano Julius Towhee the Eleventh at your service, oh great elk prince." Profigliano bowed with much flourishing of wing and tail.

"Well," the young elk said, "twilight is closing in, Evening demands refreshment, and I am anxious to hear of Linden. I don't think the elders will mind the unexpected guests. Anyway, they'll be pleased to meet the Rushing. Follow me."

Where Currant directed them, Ryon did not see, for after a full day without food or rest, his body surrendered to exhaustion and he collapsed amid the fallen leaves of the Birch Grove.

CHAPTER 24

Ryon woke to the sound of Profigliano twittering in his ear. He waited for his eyes to adjust to the darkness. His hands stroked a bed of sweet moss and hay. Overhead gleamed a starry night sky. The branches of the silver birches bent and bowed in a strong wind, and Ryon could hear thunder in the distance. Though the night was cool, his jacket had been laid over him, and he thought how peaceful it was to lie with his head on his satchel, listening to Fig's sleepy whistles.

As Ryon closed his eyes again, his stomach gurgled. A hollow, sickening feeling crept into his abdomen. He rose and rummaged through his pack. Empty.

Tiptoeing from his elk bed so as not to wake Fig, Ryon slipped between the blueberry bushes into a clearing carpeted with thick, wild grasses. Pausing to don his jacket, Ryon noticed the grass was dotted with large depressions. Curious, he started for one and kicked a fallen branch. The slender head of an elk cow appeared, hovering delicately above the grass. Ryon straightened.

"I'm very sorry, but I was looking for something to eat."

"If you keep traipsing that way, you will wake the whole herd," the cow answered. Her voice was reedy and musical, like the frog pipe of a minstrel. She lifted herself onto her legs. Ryon picked his way forward and saw a fawn curled up on the flattened grass next to her.

"This way, Master Ryon." The cow yawned.

Ryon followed her away from the dreaming herd and back toward the blueberry shrubs. While the cow ambled easily between thorn and branch, Ryon constantly pulled his pant legs from snares and ducked beneath the twiggy arms of the birches. Eventually, Ryon saw Jesse's outline in the dark. He seemed to be in conversation with someone.

"Forgive me, Rushing, but I found your boy wandering for food."

"Thank you, Iris." Jesse's young-sounding, calm voice made Ryon homesick, even though he had never heard it before that night in the nest.

"Until morning, young master." Iris's shining muzzle quivered curiously as she turned away.

"I'm sorry, Jesse," Ryon said as Iris disappeared into the darkness. "Oh, Sir Currant . . ."

"Just Currant, Master Ryon." The stag's ears flapped amiably.

"The fox found pears for you." Jesse indicated to a small pile at the foot of a birch trunk.

Ryon sat with his back to the trunk and gratefully selected a soft yellow pear. He held the fruit to his nose and breathed in the faint sweetness. Jesse and Currant stared into the night sky. They stood at the edge of a small precipice. The Birch Grove seemed to grow on some sort of plateau—a high point in the southern woods. Before them, the landscape sloped toward the hills west of Redfoot.

"Everything depends on this audience tomorrow," Currant said to the Rushing. "Father is the most respected of all the elders in the wood. If he rejects our plan, few will join us."

Jesse snorted softly. "Fighting Atheos is the only way?"

"I cannot allow Linden's home to be destroyed. I didn't believe this could happen until the Atheonians came tearing through, not ten leagues from the Grove. I should have paid more attention. I should have started gathering animals before now."

"But how can you help against a whole army?" said Ryon shyly.

Jesse turned to look at Ryon so that half his long butterscotch face was in shadow. "We must think of what ought to be done before we think of what can be done."

"But, what about Tess? The only thing we can do is go back to her and help her learn to . . . to defeat Atheos." He felt he could trust

Currant with knowledge of the *shenil*, but he was afraid Jesse would think him rash.

"I can not neglect my oath as a bondfellow or as a citizen," Jesse answered. He stepped to the boy and stamped a hoof inches from Ryon's legs. Ryon forgot his pear and listened. "It is time you understood that you, too, have been bound by an oath, Master Ryon. When Profigliano swore to help you until death, he became your bondfellow. That is why his powers come when you are in danger. You are bound to each other, just as I am bound to your mother."

Ryon struggled to reply as he processed what this would mean.

"I've heard tell of the oath," Currant murmured. "But it is hated in the Hinge as captivity, a denial of an animal's rights."

"To some it may seem so."

"Not to me," Currant said. "And if you are right, and the oath bestows power to the animal, then we may have a better chance than I thought. A friend of mine—a falcon—managed to convince a few animals from the valley to join us. They live with human masters."

"But . . . but what about Tess? Shouldn't we go back for her?" Ryon said.

"It will depend"—Jesse turned again to stand beside Currant—"on the outcome of this audience."

"With Currant's father?" Ryon said. "What are we hoping he'll say?"

Jesse shook his mane. The moonlight was beginning to fade, and a chill was setting in.

"I loved the peace of Glademont." Jesse spoke slowly, deliberately. "These last years were the happiest of any. But, while loving its peace, Glademont grew blind to signs of evil." Jesse looked over the edge of the plateau. His narrow ears swiveled against his head. "Peace must be protected. That is why Currant assembled this meeting."

"I do not know your sister's plan," Currant said to Ryon. "But Linden has told me much of Glademont's history. And it is my belief that, in the last war, so many lives were lost not because of the strength of Atheos but because the animals refused to come to Glademont's aid."

Jesse lowered himself, tucking his creamy limbs beneath him. "May the skies grant me silence again, when this is all over. To bed, Master Ryon."

Ryon returned to his elk bed and curled up under his jacket, lying awake for some time. He thought of his family, trapped in the castle, worrying over him and Tess. He thought of Jesse, proud and wise, and forced to be away from Matilde in order to look after her children. But mostly Ryon thought of Fig. Watching the bird's soft belly expand and deflate in his makeshift nest near the boy's bed, Ryon wondered what he had done to deserve such a loyal friend.

CHAPTER 25

In the early evening, with Tynaiv safely stowed in the tower cell, Tess and her companions settled wearily around a fire. A stiff awkwardness had settled between Tess and Linden. She handed him a flask of water and could feel him studying her face. He swallowed and leaned back against a fallen column.

"I surrendered to that man," he said in a hushed voice, "because he told me he had you imprisoned here."

"Yes, Your Highness. Wyndeling and I overheard." Tess concentrated on rearranging her satchel, adding provisions from Tynaiv's camp. "I thank you for your concern."

"You are . . . most welcome." Linden swallowed another mouthful of water. "It was my duty to be concerned."

"Your duty, Your Highness?" Tess cringed. Was he so determined to hurt her, even now? "I am not aware of any duty you are obliged to show me."

"Lady Tessamine . . ." Linden forced himself to sit upright. He glanced at Osiris, who was making no effort to hide his curiosity. "My lady, I feel it also my duty to thank you for coming to my aid. You and your friends."

"Of course." Tess set down the flask, allowing her braid to hide her face. Was it so difficult for him to say anything from the heart?

"Tell me of your errand, here." Linden reached for his boots, which Wyndeling had recovered.

"It has to do with the *shenil*," Tess answered hotly. "Something you do not consider vital to our crisis."

"Perhaps I did not. But if you have a plan to rescue Glademont, then I beg you to tell me what it is." He said this with trembling brows, his hands forgetting his boot buckle. For a moment, Tess was tempted to think him sincere, as though he cared what she said next. Then she saw his ridiculous leather militia vest, and all the sting of the wedding festival came rushing back.

"It is not my place to refuse the crown prince of Glademont." She stood and brushed the leaves from her cloak. Linden opened his mouth, closed it, and bowed his head.

"Then I am indebted to you."

Tess's chest fluttered. The hurt between them kept expanding and deflating, like wind in sails. She didn't like it. Hating him was easier.

"We seek the place called the Thane's Hold," she said. "You remember Queen Aideen naming it? A location designated for magical training." He nodded.

"No such place 'round here, by my paw," Osiris said with a low rumble.

"You've never heard of the Thane's Hold?" Tess's eyebrows worked together.

"The first I ever be hearing of it. And I be an old bear."

"What of the inscription over the cell door?" Wyndeling said. "It was there, just as I said it would be. And the *shenil* specifically instructed me—"

"Then, you weren't looking for me?" Linden looked from creature to creature, his lips parted with confusion.

"No," Tess answered. "Perhaps the *shenil* meant us to rescue you."

"But, bear in mind, my lady, it was *I* who wished to be of service to *you*. . . ." Linden dusted off his cloak, perhaps with more fervor than he intended.

Wyndeling hooted irritably. "We must take another look at that cell. Perhaps if you stand in it, the *shenil* will speak to us again."

"By the skies, the *shenil*." Linden searched his trousers. "I found an old letter in that cell that actually mentioned it. I could hardly wrap my mind around the thing before I was . . . eh, liberated. Here." He handed the parchment to Tess.

The old letter's gray, ugly illustrations and chilling words gave Tess goose bumps. She imagined its author writing the threats on a night like that night, with dead leaves falling in the cold winds of a darkening forest.

"A mother's bones bleached in the Dorian sun?" She grimaced. "What sort of person wrote this?"

"Aha." Wyndeling flew to Tess's shoulder. "I'd wager a sturdy nest to a seed the *shenil* wanted us to find this—and rescue His Highness, of course. I dare say it's a good thing I have such a keen memory."

Linden traced circles over his knee and stared into the fire. "But what is the connection with the Thane's Hold? And how can any of this save our people?"

"There really be a new Glademont, aye, little gem?" Osiris seemed deep in thought.

"And it is days, maybe hours, away from ruin," Tess added, rubbing her aching neck.

Osiris's glistening eyes roamed around the Ruins. Tess tried to imagine Glademont as it was, to see what Osiris remembered. She followed his gaze to the topless columns, the weed-strewn foundation, the charred northern wall.

"Tell us of the Forest War, Osiris," Tess said. "You were there, weren't you?"

Linden's eyes widened. "Surely not. The Forest War was—"

"Two hundred and fourteen years ago t' the week. Two hundred and twenty-three since I pledged the oath to King Wallis."

Linden gaped, which Tess observed with a degree of pleasure. Perhaps he didn't know as much about Glademont as he thought.

"Go on." She smiled.

"It began with Queen Miriam's invisible magic, I'll wager," Osiris began. "The red magic of the enemy never entered these woods until Her Majesty were using her own magic. I ain't blaming her, but that's when the trouble started. Soon enough, we were trying to keep that scarlet poison out of the kingdom. But a scheming man in court started using it. That be the man in yon cell for nigh many weeks, even after the war were done with. He brought ruin to us all. He shared his knowledge of the evil magic to the tribes of Atheos, leading them right to the castle. Right on that there field, they came. Burning and killing."

Osiris's shaggy features hardened with grief. "'Twere fire took my king as he charged the monsters."

Tess's heart ached. She thought of her parents in their burning home, the Atheonians jeering at them.

"What of the traitor? He died in the cell?" Linden almost whispered, his awe unabated.

"I ain't proud of this. I did me best to guard yon scoundrel. But one day, I were coming to look in on him, and he had disappeared. No trace of him, only a woman I never seen. She was from a southern continent, with skin like clay, same as the traitor's. But she weren't no twisted courtier. She were glowing like a jewel." He grumbled at the memory. "She said, 'The man be flown, but your duties be not done for a little while yet.' By the skies, 'tis been a little while, aye?"

"How mysterious." Tess pulled her cloak around her goose-bumped arms. "Who do you think she was? Did she use magic, like the queen?"

"Hmm." Osiris nodded. "I wouldn't be surprised. She were disappearin' quick as she came."

Linden shook his head, still agog. "Now, wait." He waved an arm for attention. "You say it was not just the Atheonians who were using magic during the Forest War, as we were taught? In fact, you claim it was the queen of Glademont who first took up enchantments. Is that right?"

"Aye," the bear replied.

Linden looked to Tess. "You realize what that might mean, don't you, Lady Tess?"

She straightened. "Osiris, what kind of magic did Miriam use? Was it golden, as the bondfellows use?"

"Nay," Osiris said. "Golden magic she were teachin' to some in the palace, when we were hearin' about Atheonians comin' for us. But it were too late then. The trap be laid already."

"What kind of magic did she use, then? Was it like mine? Was it marked by fire?"

"No, indeed. She were human, born of human parents." The great bear scratched an ear with concentration. "Her Majesty were doin' her best with her enchantments, but she said 'twould take practice. She said 'twould be a long road, learning the magic of a dryad. Never did make fire, like you, young one." He leaned back on his haunches, clearly proud of this insider's knowledge.

Tess stared at her new friend, lounging large as a carriage between ancient columns.

"Osiris?" she said. "Are you saying there really are such things as gem dryads? Born out of wildfires, like Fyrian of Dorian? From the ballet?"

"Oh, ho ho," Osiris chortled. "'Tis a strange thing for a dryad to be asking about dryads." He shook his messy head as Tess eyed him sternly. "All right, young one. I never seen a gem dryad, but Queen Miriam were knowing a thing or two 'bout them." His warm breath blew audibly from his wet muzzle. "The gem dryads be comin' from deep under the earth. They be born from the ashes of a burnin', ancient tree. When royal tears fall on the ashes, they say, baby dryads pop up from the earth."

"Even if that were true," Tess said, "I couldn't be one. I have a human mother and father."

"Ah!" Osiris grumbled. "But that fire magic you be brewin' be the mark of a gem, no mistake. And yer enchantments be much stronger than any Her Majesty were making."

"A gem dryad's magic is marked by fire?" Tess asked.

"Aye." Osiris pointed at Tess with his impressive claw. "Fire does the gem dryad's bidding, and she never be burned by it."

Tess self-consciously ran a finger over the medal of the *shenil*.

Prince Linden took another swallow of water. His cheeks had returned to their normal color. "I was under the impression the ballet was a folk story," he said. "About good queens and rash kings. It never sat well with me. An excessively emotional king burns the land he is entrusted to rule, and the forgiving level-headed queen comes along and puts it all right?"

"She's helped by the gem dryad, remember," Tess said. "Fyrian gives her a new breath. The Breath of Life so she can heal the land. It is really the dryad who saves Dorian." She couldn't think why she was feeling so defensive.

"Yes, I remember," Linden admitted. "That's the part of the dance with the long orange scarf."

"Exactly," Tess said.

"You wore crystals in your hair," he said.

"Yes." Tess stared at Linden. One side of his mouth pulled to a half smile.

"I remember," he said.

Something stubborn in Tess kept her from returning his smile. Eons ago, when dance consumed Tess's life and all she worried about were costumes and keeping her balance, she would have given anything to know what the prince thought of her in that ballet. But now? Now she was just plain tired. And worried. And so confused.

"Your Royal Highness," she said, dropping her eyes. "Perhaps you wish to eat and rest a little while, before we decide on our next course of action?"

Linden cleared his throat. Out of the corner of her eye, Tess saw him dab the cut on his lip. "Perhaps that would be wise," he said. Tess reached for Tynaiv's satchel that had been left at his camp. She offered it to the prince.

"I hope you don't mind pillaging our prisoner's supplies? Sadly, mine are running low."

"It would be a pleasure," Linden said.

The company settled around Tynaiv's camp. Soon, all were dozing off, even Tess. The last thing she saw through heavy eyelids were the treetops rocking against a billowing wind, and the first, silver clouds of a storm.

CHAPTER 26

An echo of a voice drifted on the churning wind. Tess sat up. Above her, thunder boomed distantly, but the voice's clear pitch called urgently over the coming storm. There were no words—only a melodious humming. But Tess knew the voice was beckoning her.

Despite the ominous sky, the rest of Tess's party still slept. She looked around for the source of the voice and saw something move against an aged column. A delicate copper form disappeared from the edge of the stone—the silhouette of a woman.

Secure in the knowledge that she was only in a dream, Tess rose from the campsite to follow. The silhouette hummed to her as she walked through the bruised, towering ruins of the old castle. Every few breaths, Tess caught another glimpse of the silhouette, swaying against the surface of a crumbling archway. Finally, the glittering figure paused at the tower. She gestured to the door that led underground.

Tess hesitated. Since Tynaiv was now in the cell below, would he be in her dream, too? The memory of her first, painful encounter with Osiris sent fear through her veins. Perhaps dreams were not so harmless, after all. Perhaps she should wake herself up.

The silhouette waited. Tess blinked emphatically. She tried to become aware of her body—her real body—so she could tell it to wake up. But the dream was so lifelike; she could not seem to grab hold of any other consciousness. Winds rattled the leaves at her feet and thunder beat against her chest as she tried in vain to banish the vision of the silhouette. And still, it waited.

"Stars keep me," she whispered, and stepped into the tower.

The shining copper woman's form lit Tess's way. It descended a short staircase, then padded toward a door. When the silhouette arrived at the door, it did not wait or gesture. As Tess approached, the old metal swung open to reveal the cell where Prince Linden had been imprisoned only hours before.

Tess's heart leapt in her mouth. She expected to find Tynaiv waiting for her, cocky and remorseless as ever. Instead, she saw another man, sitting on a bed of straw, carefully drawing on a parchment. He was drenched in warm sunlight, streaming bright as midsummer through the high window.

After adjusting to the jarring light, Tess studied the man. He seemed completely oblivious to her presence. His clothes, though dusty and torn, seemed fitted for a nobleman. The sheen of silk on his sleeve still winked through the grime that covered it. A faded emerald collar rubbed against his long terra-cotta jawline. The quill in his hand scratched slowly against the parchment, spraying flecks of black ink across the page and over his fingers. Then the man fumbled to return the quill to its inkwell, sitting beside him on the straw bed. His movements made Tess feel as though he were sitting in a dark room, though the light shone so cheerily. He looked up with deep-set mahogany eyes. Tess started. The copper silhouette had disappeared.

"I . . . I'm sorry to intrude," she began. But the man did not seem to notice her. In fact, he seemed to be looking through her. The man rose, his eyes fixed just past Tess's right ear. His ink-stained hand held the parchment gingerly. Slowly, he shuffled forward, counting his steps in whispers. His face twisted with frustration as he approached. His feet ventured haltingly over the rough floor. Tess stepped aside as the man reached for the corner of the cell. His fingers brushed the barrel, which looked as new as if it had just been built. The man finally placed his parchment on top of the barrel.

"There is magic more powerful than you can fathom, Ember," he said. The voice sounded familiar, like a memory from a nightmare.

A soft flutter came from the window where Tess and Wyndeling had come to Linden's rescue. Now there sat on the sill a crow. It stepped between the bars, its beak full of vegetation. The bird carefully placed its harvest on the sill and cawed for the man's attention. Tess expected the sound to terrify her, but it was not the same sound that Pider had made when he had chased her into the forest. This crow called to the man with a single soft note. And its eyes were clear, bright, and black.

"Ah, Cedric," answered the man jovially. "What did you find for me today?"

"Wild onions, my lord," answered the crow. He scooped the onions into his beak and glided to the barrel. Like the prisoner, the crow, too, did not acknowledge Tess, though his vision seemed good enough. "You've finally written the letter, my lord? I am sorry I was not here to assist you. Where shall I deliver it? I'm sure whomever it is will have you freed—"

"Leave it there," the man said. "I will be free soon enough."

"Oh, my lord." The crow shook his shiny head. "If you mean the bear, it is no use. He has lost his mind. He thinks there is still a Glademont to serve. He swears—I am so sorry, my lord—he swears he will die before he sees you freed from this rubble. I cannot reason with him. We must find another way."

"You are a good friend, Cedric."

The crow puffed his chest. "Thank you, my lord, but a bondfellow is yet more than a friend. I am proud to have my soul bonded to yours. And now that Queen Miriam has blinded you—forgive me, my lord— you may rely on me. I will free you. We will leave this cursed forest and start anew."

"Thank you, Cedric. I believe you are right."

The crow bowed, pleased with his little speech.

The man sighed. "And I accept your invitation to rely upon you, my friend. After weeks of keeping me alive in here, while the stench of battle has wafted through that window, day in and day out, your wish for my freedom will be fulfilled. With an enchantment."

"No, my lord," the crow begged. "You promised me that we would never touch magic again."

"I cannot live out the rest of my days in this tower, Cedric."

"I will find another way!"

"May I rely on you, my bondfellow? Let us not contradict each other now. Not when I am so close to freedom."

The crow hopped about the barrel top, shaking his head. "I do not like it. I do not like it."

"There is no one left to be harmed here, is there? The kingdom is dead and gone. The animals avoid the field like a plague. The damage has been done. All I wish to do now is to start anew. Just as you say. Will you help me? Will you allow me one last spell? Look at me, Cedric." The man held a fistful of tattered silk and offered a grim smile. "I am nothing but a castaway. I have nothing, not even my sight. Do I seem like a danger to you?"

Cedric's ebony chest oscillated with nervous breaths. "I . . . I do not know. I am afraid."

The man raised a palm. "Fear has no place between us. Remember how bravely you defended me, when they came to arrest me?"

The crow shuddered. "That was the last time I saw you cast red magic."

"Come sit in my hand," the man cooed. Cedric paused, then obeyed. "This enchantment will work," the man continued, his thumb stroking the crow. "I promise. And no one will be harmed. Simply close your eyes, and keep them closed. The magic will be very bright."

Tess's heart raced. She wanted to burst into the scene, steal little Cedric away and hide him in safety. But she knew her presence in that cell was like that of a ghost. The silhouette had brought her to the past, the days after the Forest War. Something was about to happen in that cell that filled Tess with dread and sorrow. Something she could never change.

A gentle breeze swept into the cell. It swirled around the man and his crow, lifting black feathers and torn silk as it went. It developed a scarlet hue. The wind grew redder, its speed increasing. The window dimmed, and the room was enveloped in a dark, red swirling cloud.

"My lord!" Tess heard Cedric cry. But the man did not answer. His free hand slowly rose, and the wind with it. Tess pressed herself against the door to keep from being blown away. Finally, the man yelled and threw his hands down, including the one holding Cedric. The room exploded with red light. Tess covered her eyes and fell to the ground.

The winds had stopped. The room was dead silent. Only when Tess heard the distant twitter of insects outside did she venture to open her eyes. Before her, on the cell floor, the man and the crow lay motionless.

Tess crawled to the crow first. Had he survived? One wing covered his face. His feathers were coated in dust. She held her breath. Then the crow stirred.

"Cedric," he said, blinking. "Cedric, is the window covered?"

The voice coming from the beak was not Cedric's. It was the blind man's. It was the voice from Tess's nightmares.

Nearby, the man groaned but did not reply.

The crow hissed. "I still cannot see! I cannot see!" He cawed the raspy, hateful caw that had chased Tess from her burning house. "It can't be." The crow floundered on the floor, still cawing. Its wings beat the air wildly. Tess looked on with horror as the bird left the ground. It landed on the bed, panting. Its wings extended like ungainly arms feeling their way toward the pillow, which lay directly beneath the window. With another bout of desperate winging, the crow arrived at the windowsill. A final, bitter cry, and the crow disappeared from view.

Tess tried to go to the motionless figure of the man, the body that Pider had forced his bondfellow into. She wanted to tend to him, to comfort him. But the vision was pulling away from her. The more she tried to move forward, the farther the cell retreated, until soon she was kneeling on the other side of the door, staring at its rusted metal. Her surroundings continued to blacken, until she could no longer see the door, either. A crack of thunder pounded overhead, and Tess's body startled into wakefulness. Heavy rain rattled against the tower.

"My lady?" Tess heard from somewhere in the dark.

"Lady Tessamine, are you down there?" said Prince Linden.

"I . . . I'm here," she answered.

Lightning flooded the underbelly of the castle ruins with white light. Tess saw her companions descending the tower staircase, shaking rainwater from their heads. "Lady Tessamine, what are you doing down here? A moment," Linden said, clearly agitated.

He shuffled his way through the dark, and soon Tess saw the spark of a match. Linden had found a lantern, its candles still intact. He came to her. The roar of the heavy rain crescendoed on the tower walls.

"My lady, I instructed you not to speak to that spy," he said, touching her elbow.

"I was doing no such thing," Tess said. She got herself to her feet without Linden's arm. "Simply taking cover from the storm."

The prince did not respond, but he hovered near her, his eyes moving from the cell door to her face.

"What this company could use is nice big bowls of soup and a warm place to be curling up." Osiris lumbered into the candlelight. "'Tis the perfect time to be heading to good ole Den Five. Then we'll all be having a rest. The way to me back door be just over yonder, through Whisper Passage."

"Ugh." Wyndeling groaned from the stairs. "That infernal den. Do you mean to say we are to spend hours passing *under* the same terrain we passed *over* this morning? If this place really exists, it is the least convenient residence in the forest."

"Silence yer chattering beak, little owl," Osiris boomed. "Den Five be a mighty fine home, and no mistake. Stay here at the castle, if ye like. Peck and pick at the ground, and see what ye will be finding." With that, Osiris left the glow of the lantern, and his grumblings echoed down the corridor. "'Tis time for going home, aye."

"Osiris, come back," Tess called, trying to follow. But after a few paces, the lumbering noises had already grown faint. "Oh, Wyndeling." Tess moaned. She longed to lie in a bed again and feel the weight and safety of a proper blanket. Linden came forward, determination etched in his face.

"Wyndeling," he said. "Stay with Lady Tessamine while I get the prisoner." The red owl flew easily to Tess's shoulder.

"You may take the lantern, Your Highness," the owl said. "I can see perfectly well for both the lady and myself." Wyndeling shifted close to Tess's cheek with warm, soft feathers. Linden nodded and pulled an old length of rope from the lantern's ring. With the rope coiled in his hand, he retrieved a knife from his vest and headed for the cell.

"Are you sure we should take him?" Tess called out weakly as Linden bore the lantern away. He did not answer.

It was difficult to see anything but the flickering flames, though an eerie shaft of gray light shone onto the staircase from outside. Tess strained to hear some sign of Tynaiv as the key turned and the screech of the metal hinges rang out.

Another painful minute passed as Tess heard Prince Linden speaking roughly to his prisoner. A searing blast of white light flooded the tower and Tess saw Tynaiv emerge from the cell, Linden's dagger at his back, his hands tied in front.

They approached with Linden holding the lantern aloft.

"Good evening, Lady Tessamine," Tynaiv said. "Are we going exploring?"

Linden roughly spun Tynaiv about. "You will go where I tell you and you will not address the lady." In the dim light, Tess thought she saw Tynaiv's fingers flickering. But then they were still again.

"Certainly, Your Highness," he said, and the next instant he thrust his bound hands upward. Something jagged in Tynaiv's hands struck Linden in the palm, and Linden's dagger clattered to the floor. Encumbered by the lantern, Linden could not get to the dagger before Tynaiv kicked it away. Enraged, Linden swung the lantern at Tynaiv's head. But the seaman ducked and threw his shoulder against Linden. The lantern fell. The flames went out.

Tess heard the grunting of wrestling men. Panicked, she clutched the rough wall behind her with one hand and the *shenil* in the other. Then someone cried out—but who?

"My lady," Wyndeling said. "The Atheonian has found the dagger and is cutting the rope."

"For pity's sake," Tess said. "Help the prince."

"He ordered I stay with you—"

"Oh, *vermin and vinegar.*" Tess tore the owl from her shoulder and tossed her in the direction of the struggle.

Another minute of confusion followed. Tess could not tell from the sounds who had the upper hand. Then, a hoarse, pained yell echoed against the dark walls.

"Your Highness?" Tess shouted. "Wyndeling, what's happened?" Another blast of lightning lit the pantry, and Tess could see Prince Linden kneeling alone. His knife lay beside him. He saw it, too, and reached for it.

Darkness returned, and Tess heard hurried steps approach her. Before she could move, she felt a firm grasp on her upper arm. Just as she was about to scream, she was quieted by a hearty kiss. Warm breath remained at her ear for a moment before her arm was released. Then, by the dull light on the staircase, Tess watched Tynaiv slip out into the storm.

CHAPTER 27

Tess's heart thumped in her ears as she touched where Tynaiv's kiss had landed. She felt hot and dazed.

Wyndeling guided Linden back to Tess, warbling peevishly.

"Well, the scoundrel did not evade my talons," she boasted. "I was able to keep him from taking the dagger with him."

Grumbling, Linden placed the lantern at Tess's feet and relit it. "The blackguard had a wooden shard. He must have splintered that cursed barrel while we were out of earshot." He held his hand to the light. It was covered in blood, with a long gash from his wrist to his little finger.

"Your Highness." Tess knelt to look at his wound. "We must get you to Osiris's den. I have nothing to dress your hand with. Wyndeling almost died from infection—"

"I will do no such thing," Linden said. "I am going out in pursuit of that spy."

"You cannot possibly," Tess said. She felt shy of the light, and it seemed that Wyndeling was glaring at her. Perhaps it was just the gloom. "You are too weak, and how are you to secure him in the dark and rain with only one good hand?"

"I must try." Linden stood. "If he reaches his master, he will tell him where we are. He will tell him where *you* are, my lady."

Tess was glad the prince could not see her fingers go to her engagement pearls. Was it only his duty that made him so worried?

She pulled the flask of water from her satchel and gently poured it over his hand. "It is more than a day to Glademont on foot, Your Highness," she said. "We will have plenty of time to be gone from this place."

"Will we not search for the Thane's Hold?" asked Wyndeling.

"It can't be here." Linden panted and grimaced as Tess washed the blood from his hand. "If it is a place well known to my mother, Osiris would have seen her visit it. And he'd have known there was a new Glademont outside these woods."

Tess could not argue the point, nor did she want to. She wanted to get out of the dark and be somewhere warm and dry . . . and free of amorous sailors. "Let's follow Osiris, then? No good haunting this tower any longer," she said.

Together they started down the passage where Osiris had disappeared. Wyndeling sat on Tess's shoulder while Tess held the lantern. Still stinging from Tynaiv's escape, Linden followed. "How many times is that scum going to make a fool of me?" He righted his longbow across his shoulders with his good hand.

"I'm glad he's gone," Tess said, a little louder than she intended.

"I'd rather have my enemies on a short rope," Linden said.

Holding the lantern high, Tess illuminated a floor of solid, polished wood blanketed in thick dust. Giant paw marks created long drags in the dust. Linden stooped to investigate.

"Our friend Osiris has been through here a time or two. It should be easy to follow his trail," he said.

As time went on and the sound of rain grew distant, the passage expanded, and Tess observed large archways above them. The floors changed from polished wood to rough-hewn cobblestone as they apparently moved beyond the foundation of the old castle.

An hour passed. They followed Osiris's trail through various forks and side tunnels until finally Linden paused and signaled for Tess to wait.

"I hear water," he said. Tess heard it, too, and she saw the walls gleam with moisture. Her legs felt so stiff.

A blue-white haze beckoned them ahead, and the party came to one last, yawning archway overlooking a sleepy stream. The water's surface glinted in the thin light. The curved, stone ceiling was studded by narrow windows, through which roots and vines hung freely, dripping with rainwater. Tess had the unexpected urge to twirl and stretch her arms in this moonlit dream.

"We must not be very deep underground," Linden observed, insensitive as ever to romance. "We're just under the forest floor, somewhere east of the Ruins."

"And look." Tess's lips parted in a rejuvenated smile. "Osiris's back door."

Decorating the wall on the opposite side of the stream, there sat the welcome sight of a door, fashioned much like its counterpart by the redbud grove.

"There be the adventurers. I had been wondering to myself how much longer I would be staring at the stormy sky, sighing for the ole days when I were tramping around with a wild owl." Osiris emerged out of the gloom upstream to their left, pulling something in the water behind him. "I passed some time fishing out this raft for me guests," he said cheerfully.

The stream was shallow enough, for Osiris waded through it while keeping his back dry. Once Tess and Linden had boarded, Osiris pushed the watercraft toward his back door. Wyndeling shifted uncomfortably upon the post that secured the raft's poles. "Osiris, I spoke rashly in the tower. I am . . . unused to eccentricities."

"Ye be a stubborn, silly little owl," the bear replied. "Where be yon briny fellow and his tobacco, speaking of unusual creatures?" Osiris surveyed his companions from beneath his overgrown brows.

Tess was certainly not up to offering an explanation, and it seemed Linden could not find the words, either.

Wyndeling hooted softly. "He injured the prince and slipped away." For the second time, the red owl shot Tess a knowing look.

"Hmm. Bad tidings indeed, Glademontians. I have a feeling in me bear bones yon seaman ain't through with us."

Much to Tess's relief, Osiris pursued the subject no further. And even more to her liking, the door was finally opened.

CHAPTER 28

Morning broke on the Birch Grove as lavender clouds surged up from the valley and formed a fog over Ryon's resting place. His eyes fluttered heavy with sleep. Profigliano, on the other hand, swooped and twirled, singing notes of greeting.

"Oh, what a morning to be alive and flapping," the towhee announced. "I've got a nice long snooze and three juicy worms in me. Boy, am I glad you're awake, Master Ryon. I wanna know when this mysterious meeting starts. Don't tell the fox, but I'm hoping the first order of business is to put his moldy mouth on trial—"

"Ahem." Evening, who had silently slipped between the pair, sat with his tail wrapped about him. "It's time we moved on from that, don't you think? I was sent to fetch you. The meeting is about to commence."

Ryon pulled on his jacket and hunched against the thick fog as Evening led them deeper into the Birch Grove. They passed the grassy elk beds, then over a trickling, jade-colored creek. Eventually, Evening stopped in a place where the birches grew especially close, and the fog culminated upon a large mossy embankment.

"The bull is called the Oak Elder, especially by those who are not of the herd. His four mates are the other elders. Best just to call them Madame Elder to cover your hide." Evening hopped upon the embankment. "Try not to embarrass me," he whispered, and scurried aside.

Ryon followed and found the elders on the embankment. They formed a semicircle, with an imperial-looking elk bull lying at its head. The bull was dark, almost chestnut in color. His throne was an enormous mossy stump, whose years as a living oak must have numbered at least four hundred. His forelegs curled under his chest, while his back legs splayed comfortably to one side. To the left of the throne stood four lovely cows. To the right stood Iris, the young cow who helped Ryon find something to eat, and Currant, who trotted forward to escort Ryon closer to the bull.

"Father, here is Master Ryon Canyon of Glademont," Currant said.

The imperial-looking bull stared at Ryon, much the way Iris had stared at him the night before. It was a curious, frozen look, still and solemn.

"He is in the company of the Rushing." Currant nodded toward Jesse. Ryon moved to join his horse, who stood off to the left, facing the moss throne.

"This is the boy who was hungry in the night," the bull stated. His voice was old—much older than he looked. Ryon paused.

"I apologize for disturbing the lady Iris." He bowed to her.

"Ha. Hear how he addresses your sister, Currant?" the Oak Elder said. "He uses human titles for the wild." The explosive laugh made Ryon uneasy. It was not malicious, but neither was it friendly.

"I rather like it," Iris said. "It sounds sophisticated."

"You would feel differently if you knew what *sophistication* brings to free animals, daughter. Be still." The bull rose.

"Father," Currant said in a formal tone, "patriarch of the Grove and Oak Elder, will you allow this boy to join this audience?"

The bull swirled his tail and pounded a rear leg upon the moss. "We shall see how he behaves under the Rushing's care. Evening, bring in the rest." He nodded to the fox.

Ryon tried not to fidget as he stood by Jesse's shoulder. Evening disappeared through the trees, leaving them to stare at an open carpet of vibrant, springy moss. But soon a number of birds flitted to the ground before the throne: a falcon, a few bluebirds, a drake and his mate, and none other than Buchanan of Westbend from the Council of the Nest. Buchanan looked sharp and stern as ever. A fresh scar ran the width of his feathered breast. Ryon cringed as he remembered their last encounter.

"Welcome to the cotton moss, Councillor," the bull said to Buchanan.

"Thank you, Oak Elder." Buchanan gave a short bow. "I come seeking your advice. The forest is torn apart—"

"A moment, Councillor," the Oak Elder interjected. "With whom have you come?"

"I come alone," Buchanan answered with energy. "These birds are not authorized by the Council of the Nest, Oak Elder." He eyed the falcon to his right with venom.

"I have invited them," Currant said, his voice remaining calm. "This is Cantor"—he gestured to the falcon with his nose—"recently elected captain of the raptors who remain here in the Hinge." Cantor's round midnight eyes blinked several times, but he made no comment. "The bluebirds are the Stitchipeeps. Their family has dwelt in this forest even longer than we can trace the Birch Herd."

Ryon observed vigorous, colorful movement on the moss. Five brilliant bluebirds with fuchsia breasts issued small, polite bows in all directions, flapping their wings for balance.

"And Cheekathistle and Thorestook of the Northern Flock," Currant said.

Thorestook the drake sported iridescent, jewel-like bands of green and cream. His mate, though wearing more muted colors, rattled her bill energetically. Buchanan's raspy hoot made all the birds still.

"I represent the Five Wise in seeking your advice, Oak Elder. I do not know why these birds have come," he said, eyeing Cantor again.

"Only five?"

Buchanan grunted. His head swiveled on his short, round body. "Two have left their perches," he said with a severe clack of his beak. "Wyndeling disappeared, and Theodora was removed after putting the entire nest in jeopardy and causing a dangerous enchantment to be cast in our midst." Buchanan's head finally swiveled enough to catch sight of Ryon and Profigliano. "Hm. I heard tell *you* were here," he said so low and rough, Ryon thought he could feel the owl's voice in his toes.

"Rest assured, Master Ryon." Cantor the falcon hopped before Buchanan. "You have nothing further to fear from us. It is clear to the Nest that we should never have meddled with human magic."

Buchanan stared stonily at Ryon while the falcon spoke.

The Oak Elder swooshed his tail again. "Already, this is a strange morning come to the cotton moss."

Evening appeared again, and behind him followed two creatures Ryon never thought he would see in the Hinge Forest: a silver mountain goat and a snow-white dall ram.

"Oak Elder," Currant said, "these are Tartan and Pipe, cliffdwellers from the human village of Wallaton."

Sir Brock had always said that, other than the shepherds, these were the only creatures able to live on the sheer, rocky face of Innkeeper Cliffs. Ryon understood now how the cliffdwellers earned their reputation as a hard and severe people; Tartan and Pipe looked in no state to be trifled with.

Tartan the mountain goat measured as tall as Currant's shoulder, from hoof to horn. His silver woolly coat hung thick over a rock-solid frame. The horns were short and sharp, and he tossed them with agitation. Whereas Tartan looked hurriedly about with acute interest, Pipe was content to look upon the throne with serious, quick eyes. He was a dall ram with great, twirling horns—slighter in build than Tartan and lacking a beard.

"We thank you for your time, Oak Elder," Pipe said, lowering his head.

The bull stamped a hoof. "I was told there would be four domesticated animals," he said, his nose twitching. "Who are the other two?"

"Yes, Oak Elder," Currant said. Ryon could tell the young elk was making an effort to stick to formalities. "Cantor has brought four animals from Glademont, the same birth country as the Rushing. Here come the ponies from Foggy Plains."

The Oak Elder snorted as Tartan and Pipe moved aside, and two stocky horses approached from the trees.

"Shila and Abe of Foggy Plains," Currant said.

A smoky, speckled mare came forward. Her mane and tail were strewn with braids. A stout reddish stallion trotted beside.

The Oak Elder looked down his nose as the ponies bowed. "I have heard the horses and ponies of the Plains speak freely with humans." The bull made clear by his tone that he hoped this was merely a rumor.

"We adhere to the Way of Silence," Shila the mare answered, "when we leave the heather to serve elsewhere in the dione."

In response to the look of disapproval upon the bull's face, the one named Abe interjected, shaking a thick red mane. "Cannot you extend us the same courtesy as the boy, Oak Elder?"

"I extend courtesy to the Rushing, only. A most honored guest. A legend of the Hinge."

The female elders bobbed their heads and flicked their ears with excitement.

"Jesse of Glademont, now," Jesse answered. A swell of surprise moved through the elders. The bull stared at Jesse, then at Ryon. Without further comment, he turned to the collection of creatures before him.

"Let us hear why you all seek my audience." He lowered himself on his throne.

Ryon leaned against Jesse's butterscotch neck with relief. But then, flapping to Jesse's head, Profigliano drew a dramatic breath. "Ahem. Profigliano Julius Towhee the Eleventh, at your service, your most wisest of patriarchs, sir, Oak Elder, sir, most excellent smarty-elk." Profigliano must have been practicing his bow; it had become more embellished since Ryon had seen it last.

"Er . . . yes, very good." Currant twisted his muzzle curiously. "Oak Elder, with the exception of Councillor Buchanan, the creatures before you represent the FOM and seek your audience regarding an event that, I think, could alter the course of our history." Currant could not help but look pleased with this possibility. "Shila?"

The braided pony hesitated.

"I am listening," the bull said.

"Yes, Oak Elder." Her voice rang with sweet, alto tones. "Two days ago, Atheonians invaded Redfoot. Some of the Redfooties escaped in the night and fled to the Foggy Plains for refuge. One young woman barely escaped the city with her young. She stayed with my master, and spoke not only of the havoc wreaked by men but also of their hounds."

A murmur rippled through the animals present.

"A sort of dog, aren't they?" It was a beautiful, plump cow who spoke.

Shila hesitated. "The dogs of Glademont Valley are trustworthy, Madame Elder. But hounds are new to the valley, and they delight in the spilling of blood."

The plump cow shuddered. "I do not wish to see a hound in my lifetime. And you may call me Dove, my dear. I am Prince Currant's mother."

Shila lowered her head gratefully.

"Tell me," Dove continued, "why do the Atheonians partner with these hounds?"

"The hounds have learned red magic," Shila said. Another swell of murmuring animated the semicircle. "The woman said it was terrible, hearing the baying of the hounds tracking them in the night."

Then Abe stepped forward. "Another man spoke of how his dog defended them from the hounds in a battle of magic," he said. "He was surprised as a mole in a tree, if you get my meaning."

"The Glademontian dog used magic?" Thorestook the duck cocked his colorful head.

"Something different. Something yellow," Abe said.

Buchanan of Westbend growled. His round, piercing eyes shot across the cotton moss to Profigliano, who shrank behind one of Jesse's ears. "*He* might have something to share on that front, Oak Elder."

Profigliano nearly fell from his perch. "Oh, that's not . . . I mean, it sounds like that *dog* is who we ought to be raking over the coals here, am I right? That dog sounds miiiighty dodgy to me. . . ."

Buchanan hooted. "That bird—that disgrace of a Hinge Forester—used golden magic to destroy the nest." Buchanan's fearsome beak opened menacingly.

Ryon could not stand to see Profigliano so accused. He had resolved to remain quiet, but Jesse was right; he had his duty.

"Oak Elder"—his mouth went dry as the wise stag's inscrutable gaze fell on him—"it is true that Fig has the gift of golden magic, but the councillor should admit that he does not understand what he saw that night in the nest."

The semicircle erupted with hoots and neighs, some indignant, some triumphant. Profigliano straightened on Jesse's head, his black eyes fixed on Ryon.

"I might be human," Ryon insisted, "but I have reasons to want the Hinge's safety as well as my own dione's. This is my friend, my bondfellow." He beckoned Profigliano to his hand. "He uses golden magic only in my defense. His oath binds us until death."

At this, the Oak Elder grunted and stood. "The wild cannot enter into such an oath." And another series of outbursts filled the foggy air.

While the creatures on the cotton moss snorted and blustered, Profigliano peered at his companion in amazement. "Master Ryon," he whispered, "we are *bondfellows*? The word is unknown to me . . . and yet not." He adopted a chivalrous tone. "I desire to take flight and tear apart these cloudy skies with my magical wings. Nay—I'll golden bubble the next pokey-poke who thinks he can wisecrack *my* bondfellow."

Arguments over the issue of the bondfellowship had reached a boiling point. The cliffdwellers and ponies hotly defended themselves, while the animals of the Hinge accused them of being less than true beasts. Finally, Currant thrust himself into the debate, butting his antlers against Tartan's lethal horns, which had been inching ever closer to Buchanan.

"Enough," he bellowed. Currant's wide eyes flickered, and Ryon thought he looked like a real prince of the forest.

"It is this very debate over the human-beast bond that has put Glademont into such peril, my friends." Currant paced in the center of the cotton moss. "To say wild animals are free from servitude is to say the fallen tree is free from its roots. Man and animal were meant to defend and support one another. And look now how the neglect of our duties has put Glademont into the mountain lion's mouth."

The elders shifted nervously.

"The reason we have come to you, Oak Elder," Currant continued, "is not because we are undecided in this matter. We desire only your blessing."

Currant's father flicked his tail. "I wonder, is this decision worthy of a prince of the herd?" The bull stepped forward, his muscular chest heaving.

"We are the Friends of the Militia," Currant replied. "And we will gather what creatures will follow and go to war in defense of Glademont. We hope to honor ourselves and our clans through our service to men once again." Currant bowed to his father, who towered on his ancient, natural throne.

The plump cow, Dove, stepped gingerly between her son and his father. She looked upon the Oak Elder with a pleading eye.

"This matter cannot be dismissed lightly. You know Currant is a worthy, sure-footed elk. He has always served the herd with strength and skill." The Oak Elder did not move. "I believe Currant called these creatures together to honor a friendship. Our Currant and the prince of Glademont have come to understand each other."

"Mother, how on the continent did you—"

"Your movements are far from invisible to me, son," said Dove.

Currant chuckled and dipped his antlers toward his mother. "It is true," he said. "He knew nothing of the creatures of the Hinge, as I knew nothing of the Glademontians. But we have taught each other, and we have become as close as any animal can be to his own kind. But now there are rumors he has been taken captive. Meanwhile, Nabal himself and hundreds of men are camped outside the castle gates. Glademont has few weapons, no trained army save the few who support the prince."

"I can tell you this much," Thorestook the duck broke in, "those Atheonians have weapons. Murdered our ducklings, they did." As her mate spoke, Cheekathistle lowered her brown-gray head. Thorestook's voice shook. "Almost full-grown, they were. Five young ones. When we found them . . . it was too late." Cheekathistle buried her bill behind Thorestook's wing.

"These Atheonians must be stopped," Shila said. "They will surely burn through the rest of the valley the same way they burned through Redfoot. And if the Atheonians take the castle, no Glademontian will be safe."

"You valley folk are not the only ones with reason to fear," added Thorestook grimly. "If Glademont falls, the Atheonians will scour the Hinge for every last creature, making them swear allegiance to Nabal or killing them in cold blood."

Ryon's heart dropped. If Glademont fell, there would be nowhere to hide. He joined the rest of the animals in an anxious silence. The Oak Elder descended from his carpeted stump to meet the level gaze of Currant.

"I fear the elders must make a choice that cannot be undone," he said. "I must turn to one who has known both the wild of the Hinge and the confines of human civilization. Rushing, what say you?"

Next to Ryon, Jesse flung his creamy mane, his head rising and pitching. "In my youth," he said, "I sought freedom in these woods. Since then, I have learned the fellowship is the only thing worth living for. So, too, it is the only thing worth dying for. As for the Rushing, he goes to war."

The bull looked to the female elders. They stared tensely, uncertainly. But the Oak Elder pronounced, "So be it. The Friends of the Militia shall go to battle. And any animal of the Hinge who so chooses may freely join with this effort, with the blessings of the Birch Grove upon him."

Ryon closed his eyes and said a prayer to the red star. *Let this be the way,* he prayed. *Let us rescue our land from death.*

CHAPTER 29

Tess stepped into a cold, dark room about the size of a parlor. Toward the back, a simple kitchen reminded her of a butler's pantry she saw at Glademont Castle once, with dried and fresh fruits and vegetables neatly organized, and two deep consoles for preparing meals. To her right, flush to the wall, stood a thick tabletop balanced on a pedestal of stone. To her left, a cluster of upholstered chairs faced a sizable fireplace.

Osiris made a show of shivering. "Nothing worse than comin' home to a frigid state o' affairs. Quickly, madame gem."

Tess found her way to the firewood beside the hearth.

"Honestly, Osiris. A fire indoors?" Wyndeling lamented. "Have you no wild instinct left?"

"Ye never cease to amaze, little owl." The bear snorted good-naturedly and pricked his round ears forward. "Every home be needing a hearth. Ain't that so, little gem?"

"Oh, indeed," Tess said, still crouching by the fire.

The bear nodded and went about his duties as host. "Besides that, there be a library o' sorts in Den Five, as well there should be. Wouldn't be wanting the old scrolls destroyed by the wind and damp." He pulled potatoes and leeks from various baskets, which occupied the shelves along the far wall. "For the love of stars," he said, "take ye a chair, young folk."

Tess and Linden moved to the four large reading chairs covered in worn fabric. Several pillows occupied each, with scrolls strewn between the cushions.

Smiling, Tess plopped into a red rounded chair stocked with yellow pillows. Linden placed his weapons against the mantel and lowered himself into a tall-backed leather chair to her right. The fire caught Tess's well-placed kindling and expanded, tickling her nose with the familiar, soothing aroma of burning spruce.

Now that the fire had cast light upon it, Tess thought the den smaller than one might assume. The ceiling just touched Osiris's ears as he reached for a basket of radishes. Large sturdy shelves lined the dirt-packed wall to the right of the hearth, each full of root vegetables. Opposite these, the pedestaled table supported oversized cast-iron pans.

Linden was already engrossed in a scroll by the fire when another bolt of lightning beamed through a small round window where the ceiling met the pantry shelves. Tess frowned.

"Do you think Ryon has found Profigliano?"

"What's happened to Ryon?" Linden glanced up.

"That boy be right as rain," Osiris said. "Yon yellow horse be sharp as a thorn." Osiris's furry sides brushed Tess's face as he shoved his body between the chairs to set an enormous pot upon the fire, filled with fragrant herbs.

Linden dropped his scroll and winced as he remembered the gash on his palm. "What is all this about? Who is Profigliano?"

Tired as she was, Tess rose from her chair to boil a cup of water with vinegar. While she busied herself dressing Linden's wounds properly, she described everything that had happened to her, from Pider's attack until Osiris had taken her to the Ruins.

Linden listened with deep concentration, while Osiris tended to his soup and Wyndeling roosted on the back of a chair. Every so often, the prince would stop Tess to ask her to recount the Council of the Nest in further detail, or to describe the mysterious power of the *shenìl*. The more she talked, the farther he leaned toward her in his chair, rubbing his knee. She reminded herself his concern was not for her, but for the fate of Glademont. Still, it was a pleasant change to be listened to.

Linden shook his head. "It's a wonder either of us has made it this far."

"Possibly," Tess said. "But had we stayed home . . ."

They both fell silent.

"It is good you have come to the Hinge, my lady," Wyndeling said softly. "Think of how miraculously you healed me with that trinket. I believe there will come an hour when I will see you wield it against the Atheonians. Against Pider." Wyndeling's intense eyes reflected the firelight.

"Ye keep that up, little owl, and ye'll be finding yerself taking the oath." Osiris stooped over his pot and prodded a turnip with a gigantic wooden spoon.

When finally Tess held a warm bowl in her lap, she let her shoulders droop and savored her first mouthful of potatoes in what seemed like an age. She chanced a glance at Linden, who resorted to drinking straight from the bowl since his left fingers were bound stiff. Even injured, dirty, and exhausted, the prince looked regal. He sat at the edge of his chair, careful not to spill his dinner. Though he leaned on his knee, his back remained straight and strong.

The sight of him made Tess realize what a perfect stranger he was when they became engaged, and each revelation since then had brought new feelings. First she was grateful to him for choosing her, then she chastised him for neglecting her, then she cursed him for embarrassing her. Never before had she been sad that he did not love her. But sitting by the fire in Den Five, watching Prince Linden quietly drinking soup, Tess felt something new. A pulling sensation below her ribs told her there could be something wonderful about being loved by this man, but that she would never know it herself. He would never let her into his inner circle. His trust used to be something she felt entitled to. Now it was something she wished for.

"To bed, now, young ones," came Osiris's gentle rumble.

Linden laid his bowl down and rose from his chair, bowing to Tess. "Sleep well, my lady" was all he said. Tess nodded, trying to hide her disappointment. Certainly, he was easier around her than he was before, but not warm. Never warm.

Tess bade good night to Wyndeling as the owl nestled in a hanging basket, and Osiris escorted Tess through a rounded door to the left of the hearth. It led to a narrow unlit hall and a thick curtain to the right.

"Now, gem," Osiris said as he lumbered past her into the darkness, "there be the guest room. Sleep well."

Through the curtain in the hall, Tess found a spacious room with a wooden chair, a small writing desk, two candles, and a woven grass rug. Surely, she was the first human guest in Den Five. And yet, Osiris had built a guest room all the same. Not for the first time that day, Tess felt her eyes burn for Osiris's lonely life, and for the friendships that were torn from him so long ago. She wondered if she would ever be brave enough to persevere in her promises for decades—even centuries. And did she want to be that brave?

The floor refreshed Tess's bare feet with the smooth coolness of clean soil. She searched for a place to sleep, and instead found a series of ascending limestone slabs, protruding from the far wall. Curious, Tess climbed the slabs and found near the ceiling of the room a cozy nook. She crawled in on her stomach. Soft light covered her face from a circular window, sealed with green glass. Just the other side of the window, ferns and fallen leaves rustled on the forest floor. Tess ventured to sit up, and found, at the other end of the nook, a large folded quilt.

There may never have been a night when Tess felt so exhausted or so unsure of her future. And while the storm grumbled harmlessly through the little green window by Tess's head, she slipped into sleep, dreaming vaguely of dryads and queens.

Tess did not wake the next morning until three hours past sunrise. The sun penetrated her loft window, and she listened a moment to the swirling of leaves. She wrapped her quilt about her and scrambled down the perilous stairs in her bare feet.

In the main room of Den Five, Linden sat holding a bowl heaped with steaming oats, his hair awry. He bolted up to greet her, excitement in his eye, but an excitement she was sure she had not caused simply by walking in the room. Tess smiled bashfully and shuffled to the fire, upon which half a dozen roasted apples sizzled. Osiris busied himself about the pantry and table.

"Morning, madame gem. Won't be asking whether ye slept all right, as it be well into midmorning by now. Get a bowl and help yerself. Oh, ye'll be wanting a spoon. Now, where be the other spoon?"

Tess chose the smooth silvery chair beside Prince Linden, determined to speak with him about their next move. The mystery of Ryon's whereabouts was weighing heavy on her, and she could not concentrate on seeking the Thane's Hold until her brother was safe again. Tess was impatient to broach the subject, even as she helped herself to oats and apples.

"Your Highness, I'd like to—"

"Wait," Linden broke in. He swallowed and set his bowl by the hearth. "I want to tell you something. I didn't sleep much last night."

Tess felt her face flush. Perhaps, after a night of reflection, he realized he had not properly thanked her for rescuing him, or—more important—that he had not apologized for breaking their engagement. She let her spoon drop into her bowl and told herself to be gentle.

"I could not sit here, sleeping," Linden said, "with all these ancient scrolls around. I was thinking about the letter I found in the cell, and 'Sister Ember' who is threatened in it. Perhaps, I thought, there will be something about her, or even the *shenil* among these writings. So I stayed up half the night, reading."

Tess took a mouthful of oats and scolded herself while Linden rummaged through a pile of ancient scrolls. When would she learn?

"Well, it was all extremely interesting," he began. "These are much older than the ones we have at the castle. But I didn't find anything really useful until I came across this." He held up a small, tightly wound parchment.

"This is the personal log of one of Queen Miriam's attendants. An ordinary sort of woman, from what I can tell. But she gives a daily account of the queen's movements. And it's *this* day that caught my attention." He unraveled the scroll and ran a finger down it.

"She says that the queen went into the forest in search of a place called Crescent Cave, which was under a waterfall that poured into Crescent Lake, it seems. There were rumors of a mysterious woman who lived there, and the queen took a few attendants as well as the lynx, Rosemary, to the cave to see whether the rumors were true, for some claimed the woman knew evil magic. It's interesting for many reasons."

Linden pulled his chair closer to Tess's, and rested his bandaged hand on the arm of her chair. His fingers hovered over her knee. She held her breath, careful not to brush against him, yet wishing he would reach for her.

"First, I discovered that humans had forgotten how to use golden magic until this point. Only animals knew how, if they were bond-fellows, and the Atheonians had dabbled in red magic for years. You remember what Osiris said? He said Queen Miriam was teaching golden magic to her subjects. But where did *she* learn it from? Well, according to this scroll, Queen Miriam had never cast an enchantment before this day"—he jabbed a finger at the parchment—"when Miriam and her attendants went to Crescent Cave."

Tess could not help but be fascinated. She leaned forward, and her knee touched the prince's fingers. He left his hand. "Does the attendant say what happened at the cave?" she said. "Did they find the lady?"

Linden grinned and slid another inch toward her. "The queen went into the cave with only her lynx, apparently. Here . . ." He handed the scroll to Tess and pointed with his good hand.

> *The Good Lady did enter the cave from 'neath the falls,*
> *as Rosemary shewd the way. The maidens and yours*
> *did wait in angst for what seemed an age, then out com-*
> *eth Her Ladyship with a face so shining, it dazzled.*

"And look at this," he said, tracing a few lines further.

> *Within her palm I bespied some small thing, to which*
> *Her Ladyship clung with disquiet. But of this we have*
> *daren't spoken since.*

"The *shenil*," Tess said. "It must have been in the cave." Their faces were so close, Tess could not look up for fear of brushing his nose.

"I guessed the same thing," Linden said, "because in later parch-ments, the attendant writes that a few men and women who lived in the castle began to use golden magic. She doesn't appear to have used it herself, but she recounts a time her sister was healed with golden magic by the mother nurse of the infirmary."

"Her Majesty were teaching them," said Osiris, brooding over a bowl at the table. Tess and Linden jumped, pulling apart. Tess's knee felt cool where the prince's fingers once were. "His Majesty King Wallis were mighty nervous about it," continued Osiris. "But she were teaching them, just the same."

Tess leaned back in her chair to see Osiris, careful to keep her knee still. "She must have found the *shenìl*. Didn't you ever see her with it?"

Osiris murmured to himself. Then, abandoning his breakfast, he came to the fire and rolled into the red chair. It had no arms and could allow for his width.

"I never did see yon object until I met thee, little gem." Osiris sighed and poked a few of the roasting apples with his formidable claws. "Maybe His Highness were right," he said suddenly. "Maybe humans don't be having no business with magic. That's when the trouble begins."

Tess didn't care that her breakfast had gone cold. She stared at Osiris. "Do you really believe that?"

He continued poking the apples. "Some be good fellows with pure hearts. But all humans—even pure ones—they get tempted to wrong-doing far worse than any animal."

"But surely this sounds like the Thane's Hold," Linden interjected, his tone hurt. "The place where Miriam found the *shenìl*?"

Tess watched Osiris in the firelight. He looked tired. Tired, and hundreds of years old.

Tess's gaze dropped. "I don't know. If Miriam found the *shenìl* there, but could not use it well enough to defeat Atheos, perhaps the Hold is somewhere else. . . ."

Agitated, Linden straightened, the attendant's scroll still in his hand. "We must try. We must *try*, Tess."

Tess clasped her braid, hardly believing the prince had just called her by her nickname. She prickled, afraid he might be using her feelings for his own agenda.

Linden leaned toward her, placing his bandaged hand on her arm. "Don't you want to save your family?"

"That's precisely what I want to do," she replied. "And I will." She searched for a simpler solution. Something more certain. "I will return to the redbuds and wait for Ryon and Jesse. We'll hide in the forest. We'll—"

"Hide away when we are so close?" The disbelief on the prince's face made Tess ashamed of herself. But had she anything to be ashamed of? What was it he had said that night? She didn't understand the world . . .

"How close are we, Your Highness?" She pulled her arm away. "And if we finally find the Thane's Hold, and I have no notion of how to make use of it or the *shenil*, what then? What can we possibly do against a murderous magician and the entire Atheonian army?" The aching feeling of the first night of the wedding festival returned to Tess. She saw Aideen's dying look of hope, placing all her cares on Tess's shoulders. It was too much to ask of her; she was not even the princess, let alone the queen. How could she ever fulfill her duty to a talisman so hastily given to her, with so little thought to her own consent? Was she to be made responsible for an entire dione by a prince who did not want her on the throne, and a queen who warned her not to wield the very object she was forced to protect?

Linden clenched his good fist. His manner became stiff. "Madame, you confuse me. It was your errand, if you remember—not mine—to find the Thane's Hold. Now am I to understand our efforts are in vain?"

Tess stood and turned away, shaking all over. She had no answer. Failure leered at her from every corner. And her family's peril frightened her almost to the point of collapse.

"Young one," Osiris rumbled kindly. "Only evil comes of forgetting one's duty. Lend yer ear, now." She looked into his enormous, feeling eyes, filling her with more shame. But she knew she could never make Osiris proud the way King Wallis did.

"Duty," she whispered, holding her shaking arms. "I cannot tell you how tired I am of that word."

Linden shook his head and dropped the old parchment on Tess's chair. "This is more than a matter of duty, my lady," he said. "It is a matter of love."

Tess drew a sharp breath. "A matter of love for whom?"

"For your queen and country," he answered. "For your family."

They stared at each other.

A sudden flurry of activity at the open window by the pantry punctured the tension.

"Miss Tessamine Canyon?" came a chorus of exceedingly high voices.

"Who's there?" Tess said, startled.

In an untidy little line at the top of the back wall, a handful of bluebirds blinked and bowed and tilted their quick heads.

"We have come from the Birch Grove with a message for the sister of Master Ryon Canyon of the FOM." Their voices hummed against the warm walls of Den Five.

"Forgive me." Tess forced herself to concentrate on these visitors and walked past Linden toward the pantry. "The FOM?"

"Friends of the Militia." The bluebirds chirped with enthusiasm. "We are the Stitchipeeps, founding members, sent to inform you the FOM has permission to aid the Glademontians in their plight. Master Ryon has much to do in preparation. He sends his apologies."

"Oh." She stepped to the wall, baffled. "But what does he intend to do?"

The Stitchipeeps blinked and bowed and tilted their heads. "Master Ryon goes to battle with the FOM."

Tess tried to say something several times, but nothing came. So the Stitchipeeps continued with a postscript: "Jesse the Rushing also sends a message. 'Follow the path of the *shenil*, and remain in hope.'"

Tess frowned, keenly aware of Prince Linden's piercing gaze at her back. "Thank you. Please tell Master Ryon I am safe." Tess tried to sound more confident than she felt.

Linden stepped forward. "Friends," he said, color rushing to his cheeks. "Inform Prince Currant of the Birch Herd that Linden is here with Lady Tessamine, and that I will join him as quickly as I can."

The bluebirds bobbed while Tess stared at the prince with half bewilderment, half residual resentment.

"Farewell," the birds sang. And as quickly as they appeared, the Stitchipeeps zipped out of sight.

Tess felt a hollow anxiety in her chest as she stood in the awkward silence of Den Five. Just when she thought she had laid a course, the earth shifted beneath her again. Was there nowhere she could hide from this horrible mess? Her world had not stopped exploding into graver and graver plight since she had arrived at her wedding festival. And while everyone around her rose to the occasion with unlimited courage, Tess could hardly keep her head from swimming. It seemed that ultimately she was expected to rescue her home from ruin, and yet no one believed she could do it. Even her young brother was taking matters into his own hands.

"Excuse me," she murmured, and practically sprinted from the room.

CHAPTER 30

Tess pried open the green window of her loft and tossed her riding boots out. Pulling herself through the window, she breathed in the morning mist and stepped into her boots on the soggy forest floor. The Hinge was quiet and breezy. Its multitude of distinct, ancient trees stood at respectable distances from one another, reluctant to mingle.

She listened for a moment, wary of birds, then ventured underneath a sugar maple, where the rain had covered the ground with yellow-orange pointed leaves. Sunlight streamed through bare branches and landed on Tess's shoulders as she leaned against the maple's rippling trunk. With a sigh, Tess closed her eyes and brought her hands to her heart.

Red star of wisdom, point out my path, she prayed, already bitter at the silence that would follow.

A reluctant tear splashed onto her knuckles. Why couldn't things go back to the way they were? She wished the skies would speak to her as plainly as Wyndeling or Ryon did.

Some time passed like this, with Tess fingering her trinket, brooding against the sugar maple, and glaring at the indifferent sky. Finally, moving to return to Den Five, she heard a familiar voice that sent her heartbeat erupting into her ears.

"I'm not so sure those little birds can do much against Nabal's army," Tynaiv said, leaning against the maple's trunk.

Tess gaped. And just as she regained her breath, Tynaiv sprang forward and shoved the bowl of a warm pipe against her collarbone. He pressed a finger against his lips.

"Let me be," Tess threatened in a deep, confident register. "Or I will call my friends. You're lucky to have lived this long."

"A bear couldn't fit through that little hole, Tess. Neither would the good prince, I should think. He is *so* athletic, by the way." He grinned, released her, and took a few puffs from his pipe, this time smelling of licorice. "Excellent physical abilities. He had me bound for at least a full minute." He retreated to the maple trunk, eyes twinkling.

Tess tried to relax her shoulders. She was unarmed, but the *shenìl* lay in her left hand, prickling her skin. She wondered what that meant.

Tynaiv eyed her hand. "The most sensible choice for both of us is for you to come with me." Three cuts from Wyndeling's talons shone bright red on his cheek—the one without the dimple.

"I will not." Tess's black hair fell across her face as she spoke. For a moment, Tynaiv stared at the strands, leaning against the maple, and flicked ashes onto the marigold leaves. Clearing his throat, he finally roused himself.

"Nevertheless—" He moved toward her.

"I'll use it," Tess said, retreating, but showing him the *shenìl*. Tynaiv paused, his face darkening.

"You still believe you are doing the right thing? Helping Aideen dethrone Nabal and bringing war on your dione?"

"War is already upon Glademont." Tess fell back another step. "And it was in no way summoned by Queen Aideen."

"Ha." He advanced.

"You are a foreigner," Tess said. "You know nothing of Glademont."

"Oh, are your royals so different? Incapable of deception?" snapped Tynaiv. "Your queen feigns illness and smuggles her precious talisman out of the country using an innocent girl, while the prince prepares an army." He puffed, agitated.

Tess felt the *shenìl* prickle against her squeezing palm, crackling on her skin like kernels of popcorn in a pan.

"You cannot fool me again. You deal in deceit."

The seaman peered at Tess, smoke clouding his face. "Have I ever broken a promise to you, my lady? Have I paraded you before a crowd only to abandon you?"

A frightening wound burned in Tess's heart. It was too cruel, to put into words the hurt Prince Linden had caused.

"*That* is deceitful," he said. "That is the way of the royals. They are governed by gluttony and snobbery. Your parents have been filling your head with cute little lies to justify their worship of greedy infants. I watched you dance with that girl from Wallaton. Do you remember her?" Tess did not reply, afraid of what he would say next. He leaned toward her. "I asked around about that girl, Belle, and her mother. Do you know who they are? The mother is the niece of none other than Queen Aideen herself." He paused, searching for Tess's reaction. She struggled to deny him the pleasure. "Aideen abandoned her family in Wallaton when she became princess. She left them to their poverty, ordering they never speak of their connection, erasing all memory of her tainted ancestry."

"Your ignorance astounds me. Our queens are never of royal blood. The dione lauds her Commoner Queens."

"And yet, vain pride need not be inherited. She was ashamed, my lady. Your royals are not so egalitarian as you'd like to think. Why else would Prince Linden choose a noblewoman such as you?"

"You don't know that any of this is true." Tess strained to keep her voice steady. "They are nothing but vicious lies." But in her memory she saw that pleasant crease under Queen Aideen's lower lip, a mark that exactly matched the smile of Belle's mother. There was a chance—a small chance—he was telling the truth.

Tynaiv put a hand on a low branch and rested his head against his bicep. "I know the ways of royals far better than you think," he said. "I am a prince, Tess."

He looked away as droplets fell from the treetops in a quiet breeze. Tess's lips parted, but no words came. Tynaiv continued while Tess stared at his sandy knotted hair and large shoulders.

"My parents sold me to an enemy kingdom as part of a peace treaty. As security." He allowed the words to sink in. "I had two older brothers . . . and I was disposable. On the ship, en route to a life as a national trophy, I jumped overboard and swam to a pirate ship." Tess shook her head, wishing she could unhear these things. She didn't want to know him better. She felt herself becoming entangled, involved. He was inviting her into his inner circle, sharing in a way Prince Linden never had.

Tynaiv emptied his pipe. "Every new continent, every new kingdom or dione I've seen since . . . all the same. The people trust those who reign, and their lives go up in smoke."

Tess squeezed the *shenil* against her stomach. "If you truly believed that," she said, her voice cracking, "you would not serve Nabal."

"I serve no one, and no one serves me," Tynaiv said with surprising calm. "Nabal is a pawn in Pider's game, and I owe Pider a considerable favor. He can call Nabal off, convince him not to take Glademont if you give him what he wants." Confidently, he stepped over an exposed root and came to Tess. He reached around her neck, pushing her hair behind her shoulder with the back of his hand. He held her arm, just as he had done the night before. "Come with me to hand it over, and my debt will be paid. Your life will be your own again. No royals, no war, no duty except to your own heart."

At Tynaiv's touch, Tess felt her face and neck warm.

"I know you think me an insolent pirate, Tess. I speak my mind. But I refuse to watch you be used—by anyone. I haven't stopped searching for you since we met. I worry that—"

A gruff voice came from behind the prominent mound and small stacked chimney that marked Den Five.

"General? Are yeh there?" The sound of clinking metal and heavy boots could be heard approaching.

Tess stopped breathing. This was it. She would be taken and the *shenil* would be in Pider's possession by sunset. Tynaiv stared at the *shenil* in her hand, but he did not move. The boots and clinking grew closer.

"General, Counselor Pider sends for yeh. . . ." Horses nickered.

"Here, gentlemen," Tynaiv called out in an authoritative tone. Tynaiv looked at Tess, her green-orange eyes glossy with fear. "Will you come?" he whispered.

PART III

CHAPTER 31

On the fifth night since the wedding festival, Glademont Castle looked haggard. Pider's men had stripped its decorations from the gates, and only shredded garlands and tattered banners remained. Among the carefully tended hedges outside the castle stood a mass of tents, where several dozen rough men meandered under the shadow of the outer wall. They were mostly mercenaries—hired thieves and criminals released from Atheonian dungeons. Many had been in the employ of the bird they knew as Smooth Crow for some time. They loitered at the foot of the castle in the mountain, tossing half-eaten jerky in the shrubs and rolling their cigarettes.

Removed from this brood stood an elaborate tent tucked between three old pines. Inside, four esteemed Atheonians crowded around a smattering of drawings, weighted down by a fat candle. Lord Cojab and Lord Silverear waited for their sovereign, King Agthew Nabal, to speak first. A coal-black crow cawed on Nabal's shoulder. Finally, the king shook his head and stroked the beads braided into his coarse beard.

"We don't know how to get to her private room," he muttered. "This rendering is incomplete, Counselor."

"As I've said," the crow replied, "General Tynaiv was discovered before he could explore the entire castle." Pider's stony, sightless eyes reflected the candle's flame. "But your men can easily find their way to the royal chambers once they breach the interior gates."

"That Glademont vixen is setting another trap for me. I can *feel* it." Nabal hammered a hairy fist on the table, rattling the mail shirt on his bare chest. "But she can't outwit me. There isn't a scheme on this continent I can't sniff out. I sit on a throne I paid for with blood, and I'll spill more to keep it."

"My wise and lordly king"—the words oozed from Pider's beak— "Aideen deserves nothing less than a criminal's execution. But remember you have promised to keep her alive in order to be questioned. We must know the extent of her influence in Atheos. We must be wary of future rebellion at home."

"The people are calling for her death, Counselor," the king growled. "I want her head at my feet and her body left to the vultures." Nabal reached for the handle of a worn war axe. Its short, broad double blades glinted, revealing carefully chiseled grooves to channel the blood of its victims. Above these jutted a long spearhead. The weapon never left Nabal's reach, neither at the table nor in his bed.

"Your wrath inspires, my king," Pider said as he preened a waxy feather.

"My king," said the one called Cojab, "I must intervene." He wore no beaded beard, but rather an extraordinarily long mustache, which twisted and curled around an angular jaw. Slicked hair hugged his knobby head, ending in a long, thin braid. Several stains marred his yellow military sash, and he pulled at the lapel of his embroidered coat in an effort to hide them. He adjusted his legs in a chair far smaller than those to which he was accustomed.

"It has been weeks since we left Atheos on this . . . errand. You have taken my counsel in the past." Cojab shot a glance at the crow. "Hear me now, I beg you. Let us burn the castle and return home. This is no place for our kind. We are used to a higher form of civilization, are we not? The people here are simple, lazy. There is no order, no discipline. Peasants and farmers and merchants, able to come and go as they please—"

"I could not help but notice, Lord Cojab," Pider interrupted, "your disdain for simple folk. May I remind you of the origins of your own, rightful king?"

Cojab turned pale.

Nabal stood, the blade of his axe digging into the table. "The aristocracy exists to serve the people, you overeducated, fat worm." A web of threatening creases formed on Nabal's brow. Cojab and Silverear glanced at each other, fidgeting.

"Forget your place again," their king continued, "and no amount of reading or writing, lands or money, will save you from my axe." Nabal raised the tip of his weapon against Cojab's neck. "You aristocrats think you can wriggle your way off the battlefield? No, Cojab. You will fight. All you dainty old men will *fight*, by the skies. Atheos has slumbered long enough."

From Nabal's shoulder, Pider cocked his black head at the lords, his frosted gaze shifting. "Atheos will rise like a mighty storm, my king."

With weepy, sunken eyes, Silverear glared at the crow. His hair lay plastered to a sweaty brow, and his yellow sash barely stretched across his heaving midriff.

"A storm has been brewing in Atheos for some time," Silverear said in a thin tone. "And I fear it will destroy much more than Glademont."

Nabal looked hard at Lord Silverear. "Speak plainly, man. You would leave Aideen in her ivory tower to strike at us again? Whenever she wishes?"

Silverear swallowed, wiping his neck with his sleeve. "Much has changed in Atheos, Your Majesty." He looked meaningfully at Pider. "I simply hope our kingdom does not overreach itself."

"Out," Nabal bellowed. "You sniveling comfort seekers."

Cojab and Silverear rose, bowed stiffly, then hurried from the royal tent. As they left, another Atheonian strutted through the entrance, wearing a general's blue sash and carrying a pipe.

CHAPTER 32

By the time Tess tumbled back into Den Five through the nook window, her legs felt like they might give way. Taking deep breaths, she attempted to slow her thumping heart.

"My lady?" Linden came to the door. He started, seeing her high in her nook as she shakily replaced the green glass. "What are you doing?"

"Crescent Cave." Tess descended from her bed, gulping air.

Linden squinted with confusion. "When last we spoke, you were not so—"

"I've changed my mind." Tess strode unevenly past him. "I shall go to find it."

"A moment." Linden followed her into the main room. "Where have you been?"

The room was quiet and dim. Wyndeling, back from her morning hunt, snoozed in one of the pantry baskets.

"Where is Osiris?" Tess demanded.

"He's gone to patrol Old Glademont," Linden said, barely hiding his exasperation.

"Oh, for Xandra's sake." Tess had never wanted to ride Jesse more than at that moment. Faster than she had ever ridden. The room seemed to close in on her.

Firmly, Linden ushered Tess into one of Osiris's overstuffed chairs and fetched a mug of water. "Catch your breath," he said.

Tess sipped the cool stream water. Linden shifted beside her.

"I went out my window to think," Tess said, fingering her mug. "I thought I knew what I had to do, but it seems Ryon doesn't need me. That is, if those birds told the truth and he really has joined this . . . what was it? Friends of the Militia?"

"My lady, the FOM was founded by my greatest friend."

"What? What do you mean?"

"Currant hoped for an animal alliance with Glademont."

"And who is Currant?"

He smiled. "A prince among the elk of the southern woods. We became friends last winter." Then, with sudden realization, Linden fidgeted with his bandage. "I should have told you."

Tess shook her head. "I don't know what kind of a fighting force your elk prince has scrounged up," she said, her dark eyebrows wrinkling. "But it won't be enough against Pider and his men." Her heart skipped faster as she recalled Tynaiv leaning against the sugar maple, carrying his pipe.

Linden rubbed his chin. "I'll need some time to chart our course to the cave. . . ." He looked to the *shenil*, still clenched in Tess's hand. "But Currant may buy us enough time to unravel this mystery."

To help calm her nerves, Tess occupied her hands by braiding her hair again, weaving the orbs deep into the strands. "Tynaiv followed me in the woods," she said, avoiding Linden's eyes.

"You saw him?" He bolted upright. She nodded.

"He's convinced that you and Aideen intended to overthrow Nabal." She finished her braid and looked on his taut face. "What did he mean in the Ruins? When he said there was a death to avenge?"

Linden shuddered. "I could not say."

Tess clenched her jaw. Always a secret.

Glancing at her, Linden ran a hand through his hair. "You are displeased."

"You seem to be in the habit of keeping me in the dark," she said. "And I do think it an odd coincidence you should be training for war just months before it is upon us." She stood and turned her back to him. "It also seems strange for Queen Aideen to be attacked by a member of the Atheonian court when the dione has had no diplomatic relations with Atheos since Nabal took the throne."

"What did Tynaiv say to you?"

Tess gripped the back of her chair. "Whose death does the queen have to avenge?"

Linden stood, too. "My father's."

Tess searched the prince's face. His expression had darkened to bitterness. His eyelashes cast shadows on his cheeks. She shook her head. "King Antony? It was an accident. He was thrown from his horse. . . ."

"There was no accident. His murder was covered up to avoid malice toward Atheos. To *avoid war.*" He stifled a mirthless laugh. "When King Yuir was still on the Atheonian throne, Father went, as you say, for a diplomatic visit. Yuir was concerned his people were stirring up against him." He dug at his eyebrows with his knuckles. "He was too right, by the skies. My father came just in time for Nabal's coup. Nabal and his men killed Yuir and everyone in the castle, including Father."

Tess wrung her hands on her nightgown. He sounded so sincere, his emotional torment written on his face.

"I swore I'd never die like that," Linden said. "If evil comes for me, I will not be slain like a netted fish." He reached for his longbow and massaged the handle. "That is why I dreamed of forming a militia. I saw how weak we were, but I knew the queen and advisors would object. . . ."

All of Tynaiv's warnings crowded Tess's thoughts. Linden admitted to having a good reason to hate Nabal, and yet she was to believe he did not seek vengeance. How could she trust a man who never trusted her? Perhaps he and his mother did conspire against her, against the peace of Glademont. Aideen might have feigned that Tess was set apart from the rest, when really she thought Tess too vain and simple to do any harm—a decoy for Pider to chase. Perhaps, in reality, Tess was as disposable to Aideen as a shepherdess of Wallaton.

Tess's suspicion struggled against her conscience. None of it made sense, and she knew Tynaiv was a smooth talker. But Prince Linden had never been completely honest, either. In the end, the only thing Tess could place her hope in was the *shenil.* Regardless of the queen's true motivations for giving it to her, Tess knew in her bones she could wield it, if guided. There was only one way to save her family from King Antony's fate: find the Thane's Hold.

"Do you believe the *shenil* can save Glademont?" she said to Linden.

"I want to believe," he said quietly.

She stared at the cold hearth. "What of my role in all this? I am not queen, or even princess. And I would be disobeying your mother by seeking this training ground."

"Well, she isn't Irgo, you know. I never delivered that infernal letter as she instructed, did I? In any case, I believe we've crossed into a time of bending the rules."

They smiled at each other, though Tess's anxiety was hardly eased.

Wyndeling suddenly flew to her shoulder, apparently awake from her nap. "Just wait until you have seen the lady wield the object's magic, Your Highness. You will see that your queen was right to entrust it to Tessamine's care."

"Wyndeling." Tess stroked her friend's breast. "How long have you been listening?"

"Long enough to know that His Highness is wasting precious time. Did you not have a course to chart, Prince Linden?"

He chuckled. "Right away."

CHAPTER 33

Passing two overstuffed lords on his way into the royal tent, Tynaiv touched the cuts on his cheek. Pider would not see them, of course. But he hoped the king would not ask about them. He found King Nabal leaning over the plans of Glademont Castle. Plans Tynaiv might have completed had he not found the *shenil* hanging from Tess's hair in the royal gardens. He had hoped his deal with Pider would end that night. Pider would have his object and Tynaiv would be free. Free, perhaps to settle in Glademont . . .

"General Tynaiv," Nabal said, running the blade of his axe over the renderings of Glademont Castle. "First, you hand over this useless collection of half-finished drawings. Then, you barge into my tent without a summons?"

"Ah," Tynaiv replied. "Do forgive me, oh king." He yielded a short bow.

"Well?" asked Nabal. "What do you have to show for it?"

"Your Majesty?" Tynaiv folded his hands behind his back. It had never been difficult for him to play innocent, particularly in front of brutes like Nabal.

"Don't clown around with me, boy." Nabal drew himself up, towering over his table, his beaded beard dangling. "Pider tells me you've been hunting Glademont's last heir. Have you found him?"

This was a relief to hear. Pider's story actually coincided with Tynaiv's movements over the past few days. Of course, he had actually been sent to capture Tess and the *shenil*, but Nabal knew nothing of the *shenil*. He knew nothing of Pider's skill with red magic, either. The man was utterly superstitious about all magic, in fact. Brute force was the only thing he trusted.

"Prince Linden has been disposed of," Tynaiv said, mustering an easy tone. He needed Pider to hear the calm in his voice. He needed to be above suspicion so he could retrieve Tess on his own terms.

"Is that right?" the king said. "Got your salty hands stained with blood?" Nabal grinned.

Tynaiv burned inwardly. What did this barbarian know of him? When he was fifteen, he slew two men to escape his fate as peace treaty collateral. Until he was eighteen, he sailed the Stella Sea as a pirate, fighting alongside a crew that would eventually betray him.

But trying to prove his worth to the king of Atheos would be a waste of time. Soon Tynaiv would have his reward, and taking orders from a half-witted king would be a thing of his past. He just needed to deliver to Pider, and then he would be free. Tynaiv reached into his vest and produced the letter with a broken Glademontian seal. "The prince carried a letter addressed to you. A letter he would not have parted with had he lived."

Snatching the paper, Nabal sat at the table. His eyes roved over the words. Then he shoved the letter under Tynaiv's chin.

"Make yourself useful and read it to me, boy."

Illiterate oaf. Tynaiv smirked. "With pleasure, oh king. 'Sir, it is with great distress that I write to you in the wake of a brutal attack on myself, which I can only conclude was carried out without your knowledge. There is a magician in your midst.'"

Here Tynaiv paused. He felt the lifeless stare of Pider as the bird hopped onto the table, making a low hissing noise. Nabal did not notice; he hated magicians worse than aristocrats. He couldn't understand them. Tynaiv knew the king's interest was piqued. Too piqued.

"Well?" Nabal waved a sinewy arm at Tynaiv.

Tynaiv cleared his throat with difficulty. "'A powerful deceiver.'" He wiped a hand on his shirt, carefully avoiding Pider's dead eyes. "'His name—er, I do not know his name.'"

It was a poor cover-up, and the barbarian leaned over the table, his overwhelming perspiration crowding the air. Tynaiv did not flinch, only tensed. He began to run a finger over the lines of the letter, attempting to lend himself some credibility.

"'Certainly, we have no reason to be friends; my son and I have suffered much at the senselessness of my late king's death.'" Tynaiv forced a snicker and chanced a look at Nabal. But the king's suspicious glare remained. Could the man really think the queen's words to be genuine? Until that moment, it was clear enough to Tynaiv how pitiful this damsel in distress act was. But the tension in the room told him a seed of doubt had been planted. Pider would be displeased.

Tynaiv swallowed and continued, carefully avoiding what he could. "'Nevertheless, it is in both our interests that this magician be stopped' . . . uh, so on and so forth . . . 'As a token of my sincerity and confidence, I have sent this message with my son, whom I trust I will see again soon. Long live the Home of the Heart' . . . etcetera."

As Tynaiv neatly folded the letter and held it out, Nabal growled. "Written by Aideen?"

"There, you see the seal, Majesty," Tynaiv answered.

King Nabal thrust his fingers into his wiry beard. "There's no magic left in Atheos," he muttered. "We banished the magicians." The king pointed at his crow. "*You* saw to it yourself. Slithering lords and ladies, rolling in silver they conjured and wallowing in parties and wine. I know better than to keep the serpents around, waiting to pounce whenever they itch for the crown."

"My king," Pider said without a hint of distress. "It is likely Aideen knows of your feelings toward magic, and seeks to weaken your mind. She would have you looking over your shoulder for any enemy but herself."

"She is a spiteful cow," the king said. "She thinks she can take her revenge on me with a few pitiful men of my guard. Ha. I'll go back in time and kill her fool of a husband myself."

"He was a fool indeed," Pider said, "to think he could stop your glorious ascent to the throne, my king."

King Nabal's eyes darted between Pider and Tynaiv. "But what of this magician?"

"A diversion, my king," Pider said.

"Those hounds . . ."

"Are merely slaves to their masters. Their powers are limited only to the orders of the mercenaries."

"Plague's corpse," Nabal cried, throwing back the tent flap and scowling at the castle carved into Zere Mountain. "This is a land of lies and riddles. I hope for your sake, Counselor, that you speak the truth." Dust swirled behind as Nabal stormed out of the tent.

"Sort of a finicky fellow, isn't he?" said Tynaiv, retrieving his pipe. His secret was safe. Nabal trusted Pider so completely, a single letter wasn't going to sway him.

"You half-witted sea rat." Pider hopped along the table toward Tynaiv, his beak clicking. "You nearly cost me everything."

"Have I, Counselor?" Tynaiv mumbled around the pipe between his teeth.

"He will now be looking for a magician in his court." Pider thrust his shiny head up at Tynaiv, clenching his talons. "She *names* me in that letter."

"I skipped that part," Tynaiv said, finding a chair. "And even if he could read the full letter, it makes perfect sense that the royals would accuse you. They are suspicious of any animals that aren't household servants. Is there any food in here? I've had nothing but water and apples for a day."

"There will be no food or rest for you until you tell me exactly what happened in those woods." Pider flew to the back of Tynaiv's chair and pecked his neck with a sharp beak. His jabs pricked the wound from Prince Linden's arrow. Tynaiv suppressed a moan and stumbled to his feet.

"All right. I tracked the girl, as you asked. But then I came upon the prince. I questioned him regarding the *shen*—"

"Shut up, you fool." Pider's words slurred into a caw. "You are never to mention the object by name. Do you understand?"

"Of course." Tynaiv concentrated on his tone again. He didn't want the crow to know he was nervous, afraid, even. He had seen what Pider could do to an enemy. When Tynaiv's crew members sold him as a slave at Gull Port, it only took one spell for Pider to decimate the slave traders. One boiling-hot spell, and three bodies lay charred on the dock.

"As I say," continued the seaman, placing plenty of strength behind his words, "I questioned the prince, but he knew nothing. I locked him in a cell in the Ruins—"

"You returned to the Ruins?" Pider stared in Tynaiv's direction, slightly to the left. "Why?"

Tynaiv rolled his shoulders. "It was the only place I could detain him safely," he said. "I . . . I thought I might question him, considering how close he was with the girl."

Pider's sleek back hunched as he muttered, "That place is full of suffocating memory."

"Why did you show me the place all those months ago, then?" Tynaiv strode to the table, eager to deflect the subject away from himself.

"Clues, hints, rumors, changes in the wind—the object leaves a trail wherever it goes, if you know how to look."

Tynaiv turned his back to Pider, tracing his pipe over the charcoal renderings. He thought of the first time he saw Tess's face in the corridor, her cheeks stained with tears. He thought of holding her in the dark as a thunderstorm drenched the Ruins above them, and the way she leaned into his kiss. He saw her under the sugar maple, brandishing the *shenìl* at him. Standing in the bright leaves, telling her his life story, he was so close to holding her trust. Then he let her go. Again.

A long minute of silence passed, and the flames in the lanterns grew dimmer. Then the crow spoke.

"Did you find the girl?"

Tynaiv took a breath, then another. "I am afraid not. She must be deep in the forest by now." Tynaiv turned, hardly making out Pider's outline in the candlelight. He tried to keep his movements slow and relaxed. "What do you plan to do with the object?"

"What do you care? You shall have the peace you desire," Pider said dully. "You will be untouchable so long as you live. But"—Pider's talons scratched against the wooden chair and his voice lowered—"you must bring me the girl."

Tynaiv leaned forward, studying Pider's stony eyes. "What will you do with her?"

Pider cackled—a short, ruthless laugh. "After I rescued you from slavery and practically tied that general's sash around your ungrateful belly, you think you can tell me what to do with this girl?"

Tynaiv was no longer able to keep his muscles from tensing. "She was not part of our deal. The terms were retrieve the object and deliver it to you. I can still do that, without harming Tess."

"I will ask you in plain words." The crow hissed. "You have not even the slightest idea of what I am capable, so I advise you to answer well: Where is she?"

Tynaiv's shaking fingers found his pipe. He needed to remember what he set out to do when he leapt out of his father's ship. His pipe was a symbol of the future he craved: the free man's leisure, the pirate's indulgence.

"How would you like to be stripped of your rank and left to those cutthroats out there?" Pider said. "How long would you last, do you think? Perhaps they will hear of the price you would fetch."

"I can get you the object. Soon."

"Where is she now?"

"With that bear." Tynaiv paced. His voice was not doing what he told it to. It was oscillating too much. "They're hiding underground, somewhere east of the Ruins."

"And you left them there?"

Tynaiv gripped his pipe stem with his teeth.

"Well, now I quite understand why you bribed Lieutenant Pilt to keep quiet while you skulked about the forest, thinking yourself a hero."

Tynaiv went rigid. "Who told you that?"

"The lieutenant himself. He came groveling back to camp only this morning."

"I paid him off because I didn't want him revealing my real mission to Nabal."

"Is that it? I thought it was because you didn't want information to get back to *me*. After all, capturing Prince Linden and dragging him halfway through the Hinge was not my instruction."

"I needed the prince to get to the girl."

"Lies," the crow replied. "You wanted to eliminate the prince because of your ridiculous obsession with the girl. Your frail vanity has been a *waste* of my time."

"Listen," Tynaiv answered hotly. "I don't care what you plan to do with the object. I don't care that you staged that fake coup to over-throw Nabal, or that you lie daily to that illiterate idiot. All I want is to live as I please, with nothing and no one standing over me."

A cold wind swept into the tent, closing the flaps and filling the place with gusts Tynaiv could actually see, for they glowed red. The lanterns blew out, and Tynaiv was standing in the pitch dark with a bitter chill on his neck. Pider's words met his ears with steely precision.

"You are *nothing*, boy. You are the wilting flower of a tree. You have barely lived long enough to know your own name. I am the tree, and my roots reach the center of the earth, and my limbs pierce the clouds." To Tynaiv's horror, the obscured figure of a man came slowly toward him.

"I have searched for that object longer than you can comprehend," the shrouded man said. "No man can grasp it, or he will be blinded just as I was. You had your chance to cut the girl's hair, but you failed. Now that she has been allowed to escape, the deal has been altered. I require both the object and the girl."

Tynaiv dropped his pipe and retreated as the red wind swirled all the more violently within the tent. "But what then? You still cannot touch it, my lord."

The gusts gathered about the man, illuminating only his hazy, clasped hands. "Two centuries ago, I slipped past an enchantment that kept me in that wretched cell. And though my blindness remained with my spirit, I was given a great gift. In the form of an animal, the object cannot blind me again. But before I destroy it, the girl must use it to restore my sight. Now, you will bring me the girl and the object with her, or you will long for a time when the whip was your greatest fear."

"My lord," Tynaiv whispered, bowing low. He didn't know what to make of this horrifying vision. He had never heard of red magic so powerful it could manipulate a person's own spirit. And if Tess refused to cure Pider's blindness or give him the *shenil* to destroy . . . Tynaiv told himself not to think of what might happen to her.

"You will go to Redfoot," Pider said. "And you will lead our forces here in two days."

"What of the object?" For the first time in his memory, Tynaiv's knees trembled.

"The harder we crush her people, the swifter the girl will return home. And when she does, you will draw her to me. Fail, and you both will die."

Above Nabal's tent, the pines were filled with sleeping raptors of the Hinge. Vultures, eagles, kestrels, and hawks weighed down the needled branches, each carefully positioned so as not to touch his neighbor. On one such branch perched a vulture named Baggs, who quietly addressed his comrades.

"He would teach us red magic; that's what the crow said. Have you had a lesson, Curvyclaw?"

"Not me, Baggs. Not a blessed minute of instruction," Curvyclaw answered.

"Well, what does that tell you?" Baggs's naked head swung up and down the way a cobra follows a charmer's pipe.

"It tells me he hasn't gotten around to it," Wingmolt said. "Anyway, we haven't done our part of the deal yet, Baggs. When we've helped them take down these humans, then he'll teach us the red magic and we can be on our way."

"Supposing he decides he doesn't want us to learn red magic?" Baggs shot back. "Supposing he says, 'You're welcome for keeping a war out of your forest, now go away'? Eh? What then?"

"Then we go home," Wingmolt said. "And we leave the humans to deal with each other. Either way, there's no fighting in the Hinge."

"I'm with Baggs on this one," Curvyclaw said. "If we don't have the red magic, what's to keep these brutes from turning around and marching straight back into the Hinge? They may not offer an alliance next time, and we'll be defenseless."

"Exactly. That crow never intended to teach us red magic; he's afraid we'll *use* it." Baggs's head bobbed faster.

"He taught the dogs, Baggs," said Wingmolt. "He taught the dogs, and he'll teach us. Now shut up so I can get some shut-eye."

"Those dogs," Baggs said, "are as dumb as squirrels. They are *dumber* than squirrels. They spend half the day catching their own tails."

Wingmolt squawked broodily. "Well, what of it?"

"We aren't dogs; we've got some brains," Baggs said. "And it's brains you don't want in an enemy. Mark my words, lads, we're going to come out on the wrong end of this carcass."

The vultures looked at one another dubiously, but there was no time to debate the subject further, for a hawk came rocketing through the night, calling out an alarm.

"An escape. There's been an escape. Glademontians on the run." The piercing cry echoed through the camp. "Three of them headed for the Hinge."

CHAPTER 34

The waning moon shone bright enough for Ryon to see himself in the reflection of a shield propped against a several-hundred-year-old beech tree. In the shield's surface, Ryon examined the leather vest strapped to his chest, thick enough to stop an arrow. Clamped to each forearm was a metal vambrace, which Ryon hoped would deflect the blow of a sword in battle. His hair was slicked back with a salve of Ryon's own invention—a combination of mud and oils. Completing the look, Ryon bound his hair with a strap of green cloth across his forehead. He grinned with satisfaction, jumped to catch the lowest beech branch, and hoisted himself into the tree.

Amid the gently sloping limbs, Ryon approached the simple wooden tree house with a thatched roof, rounded walls, and four small windows. Prince Linden's militia called this place the Armory, and having pieced his armor together, Ryon entered once more in search of weaponry.

He lifted a lantern from its hook and took stock of all that Prince Linden, Nory, and Rette had crafted in the last months. In one corner leaned a bundle of spears with bronze tips, all twice Ryon's height. Almost as large as these were the few longbows hanging nearby, and much as Ryon wanted to emulate Linden, he knew his arms could not draw the tension needed to release a fatal arrow. At last, Ryon knelt to observe a row of swords, knives, and daggers, carefully arranged on a long woven runner. His eyes widened with excitement when he spotted a slender dagger in a polished sheath lined with velvet. The hilt was bound with comfortable, worn leather. When Ryon attached the sheath to a hook on his vest, the end of the dagger almost reached his knee.

Perfect.

No other weapon seemed suitable, but as Ryon headed for the door, a night breeze blew against an object swinging on the wall—a simple sling.

The sling boasted a superior design over Ryon's old weapon. The strap proved sturdier and longer, which would allow for increased power. The pouch felt soft and malleable to the touch, sure to secure any projectile before launch. Ryon stowed the sling, and replaced it with his outdated model. He smiled. He would make Prince Linden proud yet.

Just then, Profigliano came flitting into the Armory.

"Is this where you've been sneaking?" Profigliano whistled. "Your horsey was getting a touch on the nervy-side and I says to him, I says, 'Rushing, Your Hoofiness, you leave it to his fellow of the bondship. He's the bird for you.' And what do you know? My Ryon-y intuition led me straight to ya. How's that for magical connectedness, eh? Un-dee-niable."

Ryon chuckled. "Undeniable, Fig."

"We're so magical, we've got nothing to worry about. Worrying is what those moldy old Atheonians should be doing right about now." Profigliano puffed out his chest proudly.

"I don't know." Ryon tried not to sound nervous. He had been suppressing a growing dread of the realities of battle ever since that morning's meeting at the Birch Grove. "I'm not so sure the Birch Herd elders should have listened to us. What do we know of war?"

"Master Ryon." Profigliano solemnly hopped to Ryon's shoulder. "All those great horned-ed animals made us a promise. Now, I'm an expert on promises and pledges"—Profigliano covered his heart with his wing—"and if there's one thing I know, it's that promises and pledges don't work if one fellow chickens out." Profigliano pecked Ryon's ear sternly. "And we fellows of the bondship ain't no chickens."

"Ow. All right, Fig. I'm no chicken." Ryon rubbed his ear. The towhee was right. If Ryon was going to dress like a warrior, he had better start acting like one.

"I have an idea," he said, blowing out the lantern and hanging it on his hook. "If Evening is right, we are only a half hour's march to the edge of the Hinge. And we're pretty far north. I bet we'd run smack into the castle grounds, if we headed due east. How about, as our first official act as members of the FOM, we scout out the enemy? They may have made a move since you last visited."

Profigliano whistled. "Right you are, Captain." He gave a salute.

Ryon swallowed, glanced at the moon, and begged for a touch of luck as he tightened the green strap across his forehead.

"Let's go."

With boyish agility, Ryon descended from the branches of the old beech, snatched his shield, and raced eastward in the moonlight. They traveled more easily than when Ryon was in the southern wood, as there were fewer ferns and the trees grew farther apart. Every now and then, Profigliano would flit to the treetops to check their bearings. The minutes crawled by in the dark and silence, until Ryon felt sweat collecting under his leather vest.

From somewhere in the distance, Ryon heard the sudden cry of a hawk. He froze and strained to hear the words.

"Escape."

Profigliano landed on a low branch. "Sounds like those sassy-beaks over at the castle aren't as crafty as they thought," he whispered.

Suddenly they could hear, "I've got them—first watch, follow me."

Soon, Ryon could hear the answers of other raptors squawking in agitation.

Within moments, Ryon reached the edge of the forest. From behind a tangled shrub, he saw Glademont Castle nestled against the mountain. Only a few lights flickered in the towers' windows. He wondered whether his parents and sister were somewhere behind those walls.

Raptors cried out from somewhere south of his position. "Come on, lads. Move your carcasses. Keep those filthy humans out of the Hinge," he heard between their squawkings.

Then three figures appeared in the moonlight, sprinting full speed toward the Hinge. Above, six raptors flying in a precise formation dove for the fleeing figures. As the birds descended, the two taller, bipedal figures halted to a kneel. The third figure, a small four-legged creature, stood rigidly between them. When the birds reached their targets, the men drew swords and carved slicing arcs in the air. The first four raptors were cut down. Two, however, managed to evade the blades and raked the face of the larger man. His companion grabbed a bird by the throat and slammed it to the ground, giving the other man time to run his sword through the last raptor. With feathers and carnage at their feet, the three escapees resumed their flight.

"Come on, Fig," Ryon whispered, "let's see what we can do for them." Ryon darted northward along the forest edge. From his new vantage, Ryon felt he might be in range of the raptors still in the sky. But from their wingspans, he guessed only vultures remained and thanked the moon for his luck. Vultures were slower than hawks, and larger targets.

The vultures ceased their circling and came swooping down upon the escapees once again. Ryon leapt into the open, swinging his new sling over his head, and before the first vulture could reach his victim, Ryon propelled a stone. The missile cracked against the bird's head. Ryon's target went limp before careening to the ground. The next moment, a swirl of golden magic exploded from the Glademontian animal in the distance and blasted the next two birds. In the face of such unexpected retaliation, the remaining three vultures took to the sky again.

"Did you see that, Fig?"

"Master Ryon, you are the bringer of pain and justice. That smelly joker didn't stand a chance—look out!"

One of the vultures had spotted Ryon and was diving toward him with talons extended. Though foiled by the metal vambrace on Ryon's forearm, the vulture knocked the boy off his feet. Completely forgetting his new knife, Ryon threw his shield over his head. When the bird came down again, a brilliant flash of gold knocked it to the ground and sent it into a wild somersault. The vulture's two surviving companions looked on with horror.

"Baggs, what do we do?" cried one of the stupefied birds.

Profigliano hopped out into plain view, golden magic still streaming from his beak. "You go and tell your sneak-thief crow that you're lousy babysitters, you rotten traitors. And remember what happens when you cross beaks with Profigliano Julius Towhee the Eleventh." He glared jauntily at the night sky and gave a triumphant laugh as the two remaining vultures fled.

By now, the three escapees had reached the forest edge and ducked through the thickets beyond. Ryon raced after them, but they were swift and clearly familiar with the terrain. He could not call after them for fear the raptors would hear. So he and Profigliano sped between the trees, barely keeping up with the two men and their four-legged companion. Eventually, as Ryon forced his tired legs to jog on, he noticed they were passing the Armory just to the left. The escapees were headed straight for Prince Linden's training ground.

Then, a shrill neighing could be heard from somewhere among the trees. When Ryon finally hurtled into the clearing, he swerved just in time to avoid the two men, who were now kneeling before Jesse. The stallion snorted and reared wildly. His hot breath formed clouds in the night air.

"Who comes?" Jesse demanded.

"Beg pardon," one of the men said, holding his side to catch his breath, "but you are in our training ground."

"Nory Rootpine," Ryon said, gulping for air and leaning on his knees. "I don't believe it."

Evening appeared from the shadows, apparently having hidden at the first hint of danger. "I know these gentlemen." He sauntered forward and cocked his soft head. "They are acquaintances of Prince Linden."

"I'm Nory." The shorter, more muscular gentleman waved. "This towering fellow here is Rette. And the Colonel should be somewhere around here. I don't mind telling you, we've had a time of it." Nory looked more pleased than anything.

"Colonel who?" Evening said.

Just then, the third companion stepped into the mulched clearing, his salt-and-pepper beard quivering with indignant anger.

"Colonel Regency Thorn, you bedraggled forest cat. You'd do well to show some respect." The terrier was covered in dirt, and a few dead leaves clung to his furry skirt. Otherwise, he was just as stern and wonderful as Ryon remembered.

"Reggie," Ryon cried. He fell to his knees, scooped up his governor, and squeezed him with abandon.

"Master Ryon, thank the skies." The Colonel's warm sides pulsated under Ryon's arms as the terrier snuffled his ear. Ryon buried his face in the Colonel's silky fur. But he knew the Colonel's show of affection could not last forever. "Now, Master Ryon, compose yourself. This is no way to treat a ranking officer."

Ryon released the Colonel and pulled the leaves from his coat. Profigliano peered scrupulously at the Canyon's governor.

"Real good pallies, are we? Best friends for life and a how-dee-do? Must be hard to keep track of all your best animal friends." Profigliano petulantly scratched his head with a talon.

The Colonel gave Profigliano a withering stare and growled.

"Reggie, calm down." Ryon looked about anxiously. "If you start that barking, you'll lead those birds straight to us."

The Colonel continued to growl, but kept his temper in check. "This is Glademontian business, you spy. You and that squirrel-tailed black menace can show yourselves out."

Evening scoffed. "So says the mutt with no tail at all."

"Come." Nory struggled to his feet and, despite a nasty cut on his nose, positively beamed at the creatures before him. "Let's get to head-quarters before any more vultures spot us. We have a small stove there. Or have you already discovered that, Master Ryon?" Looking to the shield and blade at Ryon's side, Nory winked, sending an adventurous thrill through Ryon's heart. Rette, the shier of the two, simply smiled. Ryon tugged on a loose strap of his leather vest (which he was pleased to see matched those of the other young men) and smiled.

"I hope you don't mind."

Nory laughed. "It was for just such an occasion that we built the Armory in the first place. Now, Colonel," he continued, "to our head-quarters? It's not much, but it's better than staying out here in the open."

And with that, the company set out.

CHAPTER 35

Tess and Linden resolved to leave that night, as soon as Osiris returned. In the interim, Linden studied old maps of the Hinge Forest, wiggling the fingers of his bandaged hand. Tess packed fresh provisions for the journey, then took a basin to her room to wash her nightgown. It was so thin and shapeless in her arms, with a mar for each harrowing memory. Ash from her burning home, rips from her flight from the nest, blood from her fall at Ruby Creek . . . and the faint smell of licorice and tobacco.

Wyndeling hung the nightgown by the fire, and Tess passed the time in her room wearing nothing but a cloak, contemplating all the possible forms a place called the Thane's Hold could take. When Wyndeling finally returned with the dry nightgown, Tess sighed. The rusty blood stains remained, and Tynaiv's smell was gone.

As Tess entered the main room, Linden rose from his chair and cracked his neck, a map sliding from his lap.

"How far?" Tess said.

"Not far. We can be there before morning."

"Then we should hurry with supper," Tess said, rubbing the weariness from her eyes.

They ate leek and mushroom soup. Tess even found a bottle of blackberry cordial in the pantry, to raise their spirits. Wyndeling hooted softly from the back of Tess's chair.

"Will you come with us to Crescent Cave, Wyndeling?" Tess said.

"I'm certainly not going to take up residence with that addled bear, if that's what you are implying."

Tess smiled. At least someone she could trust would be with her.

With an abrupt thud, Osiris burst through the back door, his legs and belly dripping wet. "All me cubs be safe and sound in Den Five?" he bellowed, shaking out his shaggy fur. Cold water splattered against the walls and into the sizzling fire. "Ye best be giving ole Osiris a bowl of that sweet-smelling stew."

Osiris was exuberant about something. But rather than inquire, Tess obeyed and served him leeks and mushrooms. After a mouthful, the bear casually reported that four Atheonians and a hound had crossed Ruby Creek that morning.

Tess started. "You *let* them cross?"

The glint in the old bear's eye reminded Tess of a rascally mouse she was always chasing from Jesse's stall. "It were one hard decision. True, I be bending me oath a bit." Osiris abandoned his spoon and plunged his muzzle into the bowl. "Little gem be a marvelous cook, aye." He snorted and smacked.

"Osiris, tell us." Tess took a chair across from the giant bear, whose elbows just reached the table while he sat on the floor.

"I be learning a thing or two." Osiris winked proudly at Tess. "Following yon brutes. They walked with the salty villain, cool as y'like. While they went along, this ole bear lent his ear to their chatter." Osiris paused to lick his bowl clean. Satisfied there was no more soup, he leaned against the wall with a paw on his belly.

"Vagrants at the new castle be waiting on orders to storm the place. And a whole army has taken the town Redfoot." Osiris pounded the table, as if to say *ta-da*. "Well, me fine companions? How d'ye be liking that?"

"It's horrible," Tess said.

"No mistake, no mistake," the bear conceded. "But I also be seeing me friends the goldfinches." Linden and Tess exchanged looks. "They be a fine class of wild animals, and no mistake." The bear eyed Wyndeling. "And the Prince of the Birch Herd be on his way to Redfoot this very moment. And the whole Council of the Nest be gathering up north to be fighting for the castle. How d'ya like *that*?" He thumped the table again.

Linden rose and started gathering his gear. "Well done, Osiris." He radiated. "The forest is joining with Glademont once again. I'm afraid we must cut short our stay," Linden said as he left the table to strap his quiver to his back. "And we will need use of the raft."

"Ye be going to Crescent Cave by raft?" Osiris looked grave, though still leaning against the wall.

"If I'm right, the stream outside this door leads to the lake," Linden said. "It forks east and south about three leagues from here, and the southern tributary leads to Crescent Lake. We're going to find the Thane's Hold." Linden looked to Tess. She straightened and nodded.

Osiris furrowed his bushy brows. "Hrmmm . . . right, right." The great bear mobilized, pushing himself off the wall and lumbering toward the back door. He opened the door and looked back at his confused guests. "Well? Are ye to help save New Glademont or no?"

Tess hesitated, not knowing how to say goodbye. Osiris gave her an amused look.

"Ye ain't got rid of me yet, little gem. The tides o' time be changing, and ole Osiris has his part to be playing. Get thee onto yon raft and be good to yer prince, now."

"Thank you for everything." Tess smiled sadly and gathered her satchel and riding boots.

"Glademont's gratitude to you, sir." Linden solemnly shouldered his longbow. "You are a good and faithful servant to our dione."

"Truer words, young prince. Truer words." Osiris patted the man on the back with a giant damp paw. "I'll be off on my way, as well. My friends the finches might can guide me to your brave brother, young gem. Perhaps he'll be needing me in battle, aye?"

"Oh, Osiris." Tess embraced his gray head. "Would you look after him? I'd be so grateful."

He grumbled good-naturedly and nudged her to the door. "Now, now. All shall be well."

Tess and Linden left Den Five to board the raft. Wyndeling flew to perch on Tess's arm. She addressed the shaggy bear.

"Your ways are strange to me. However, the lady seems to like you. That must count for something."

"A mighty compliment indeed." Osiris untied the raft with his teeth and tossed the rope aboard. "And fare thee well, wild owl."

Osiris's raft buoyed its passengers southward. A dim lantern swayed on its hook and cast strange shadows on the cavern walls around them. Steering was rarely required, but Linden obliged with the pole when necessary. More often, he busied himself studying his maps. Tess sat cross-legged at the front of the raft, looking into the gloom. Wyndeling bobbed on Tess's shoulder.

"Did that man kiss you again?" the owl said.

Tess felt her lungs would shatter with guilt and surprise. Wyndeling had seen them after all.

"I ask because you still have the *shenil*," Wyndeling continued. "Your last encounter could not have been entirely unfriendly."

Tess looked to see whether Linden could hear. His face was buried in a map while one hand absently held the raft pole.

"Our last encounter baffled me," she said. "I cannot tell his reasons for behaving as he does."

"I do not know how humans choose their mates, my lady. In my clan, the males display their superior qualities, and the females make their decisions. It is a quick and straightforward business, for we birds are not disposed to fooling with romance. With perhaps the exception of the heron."

"With humans it is more complicated." Tess twisted her engagement pearls.

"I would never lay eggs for an owl that had threatened me or those I hold dear."

Tess groaned. "You are not helping." She risked another glance at Linden.

"I should like to see you marry the prince, my lady. He is more worthy of you."

"He doesn't want me, Wyndeling. He looks down on me for . . . for who I used to be." Tess's mouth pulled tight in the corners.

"But Tynaiv is the enemy of Glademont, my lady. It is dangerous to linger with him. For your country, but even more so for you."

Tess blushed. "I don't know what you are talking about. I've never 'lingered' with Tynaiv."

Wyndeling chastised her with her curved beak. "We have a saying in the Hinge, my lady: *a silver tongue betrays its fork.*"

"What does it mean?" Tess said.

"It means the smooth ones should not be trusted." Wyndeling pulled at Tess's braid. "Are you listening, my lady?"

Tess smiled reluctantly and stroked Wyndeling's soft chest. "You wouldn't *let* me ignore you, would you?"

Wyndeling inched closer to Tess's cheek, and when Tess sighed, she noticed her lungs felt sturdier. It was nice to have someone to talk to—even if she was a temperamental owl.

"Not far now," Linden called from the back of the raft.

Tess drew her knees up under her cloak as they glided downstream, contemplating Wyndeling's words: *a silver tongue betrays its fork.*

Half an hour passed, then another as Tess drifted underground on Osiris's raft. She was starting to fall asleep when Linden uttered a sound of apparent relief.

"Ah, the shortcut," he said, pointing in the distance. Tess squinted at the dark and thought she saw a wide fissure. "Steady yourselves."

The raft swerved to the right, and Tess flattened herself against the logs. Linden grunted and heaved, pushing against the stream bed to slow the vessel. The wood scraped against the dark rocks that bordered the stream to the right. Favoring his good hand, Linden thrust his pole into the fissure, bracing against the pull of the stream. The raft came to a bumpy halt, swerving directly into the rocks, barely staying adrift. The prince's narrow shoulders bent against the pole.

"Climb out."

Obediently, Tess scrambled to her feet and steadied herself on the pole hook. She leapt into the damp darkness and landed in the mouth of a narrow cave. She crouched under a dripping, hard surface. The sound of rushing water echoed against the close walls around her. Stalactites thrust downward from the low ceiling. Rising to meet them, stalagmites jutted from the cave's edges, but the ground beneath Tess's feet was smooth enough.

"Look out," Linden called as he tossed a rope near Tess's feet. She wrapped it securely around a stalagmite.

Breathless, Linden crawled into the mouth of the cave within a cave, holding his bow and quiver in one hand, lantern in the other. Tess could see the stain where the wound on his hand had reopened.

"Where are we?" she said.

"A shortcut I found on the map." Linden grinned.

Tess hardly thought it amusing. "A bit dangerous, wasn't it?"

Wyndeling cleared her throat with a hoot. "Well, I am for it. I've already been underground far longer than I ever dreamed. The sooner we find Crescent Cave, the better."

Tess did not like leaving the safety of the raft, but she did not protest. She followed Linden along a narrow path between the glistening stalagmites, crouching along in the darkness with only the lantern to keep them from dashing their limbs. Even without the lance-like rock, Tess would have been on edge. Each plopping droplet sounded like a footstep, and each *plunk* of falling water on her boots felt like the enemy bearing down. They walked for what seemed like hours.

"Do you still know where we are?" she whispered after a time.

Linden jumped at the sound of her voice. She was not the only nervous one.

"We are sloping toward the lake," he said. "Maybe another hour."

Before long, the path took a sharp left turn and widened enough to fit two people side by side. The path's slant grew steeper, and Tess had to grab on to the larger stalagmites to keep her footing. They were cold, smooth, and rippling in her palm. She wondered if she was the first to touch them in centuries.

When Tess next managed to look up from her feet, she saw a faint glowing in the distance.

"Put it out," she breathed, and Linden extinguished the lantern.

The light ahead glowed a sort of green, more like moonlight than candlelight. They approached with caution, and Tess saw that the glow came from many lights—some green and some blue—hanging from long silver threads. Dewdrops reflected on the threads, and the little lights on the ends swung like ornaments from their string. There must have been thousands of them.

"No," Wyndeling called out.

Tess felt Linden's arm across her waist as Wyndeling's wings flapped in her eyes. The three companions toppled backward and landed on the damp rock. Tess heard a faint scraping as several of Linden's arrows slipped from his quiver.

"What on the continent . . ." The floor in front of Tess completely disappeared, plummeting into a pitch-black abyss. The glowing lights formed a canopy over the vast pit, which had a primitive, spiraling staircase carved into its sides. She shuddered to think what would have happened if Linden hadn't pulled her back.

"Are you hurt?" Linden asked as they untangled themselves.

Tess wiped the hair from her face and rolled away from Linden, embarrassed. "I am all right, Your Highness."

"Some of my arrows didn't make it." Still splayed on his backside, Linden held up an arrow that was broken in three places.

Tess checked her braid for the *shenil*, then pulled herself to her knees. "It seems we have nowhere to go but down."

"I don't like the looks of those stairs." Linden frowned under the eerie light. "I don't see an end to them."

Wyndeling tsked at them. "What toil it is to be human." She shook her head. "I'd not trade my sight for your fingers, nor my flight for your limbs."

Tess smiled. "Wyndeling the Red," she asked, "would you see what's at the bottom?"

The owl stretched her red wings. "With pleasure." And she departed without a sound.

They waited. Linden inspected his quiver and disposed of the useless arrows. Tess watched him with interest, realizing once again how much she didn't know about Prince Linden. She thought of how precisely he had shot an arrow at Tynaiv's shoulder, not two days before.

"So, you learned to make arrows?" she said. Linden looked up from his handiwork, both brows pressing into the space above his nose. Then his gaze dropped again.

"You can't learn combat without real weapons, can you?" he murmured into an arrowhead.

"All this time, you were . . . ?" She nodded at the arrow.

"This, and studying histories from the archives. We were trying to give ourselves the kind of training no one in Glademont could provide."

Tess gazed up at the blue-and-green glow. "But, you say you didn't *expect* Glademont to go to war. You were just . . . ready for the possibility?"

He grimaced. "If I were preparing for a war I knew to be coming, my lady, I failed more fantastically than would an infant."

Tess slid off of her heels and let her shins stack beside her. She stared at her hands in the folds of her nightgown.

"You were right to revoke the marriage. . . ."

Linden started. "That is not what I said, Tess." The nickname jolted her. "That isn't what I intended."

Linden walked to her and crouched, reaching for one of her jittery hands. Tess's heartbeat quickened.

Silent and sudden, Wyndeling returned, swooshing to land at Tess's feet.

"There is another tunnel at the bottom of the stairs, my lady. I took the liberty of exploring it."

"Wyndeling." Tess avoided the prince's hand and pulled herself to standing. "What did you see?"

"A pool lies at the bottom of the pit, but there is a tunnel at the foot of the staircase that leads to the lake. And free air." Wyndeling sighed.

"Well done, Your Highness," Tess said, still avoiding Linden's stare.

He ran a hand through his caramel hair. "I'm glad I read those old maps correctly. At least I'm good for something. Thank you, Wyndeling."

"You are most welcome," the owl said. "I hope I'll soon have a nice fly through the moonlight."

"I hope so too, Wyndeling." Tess kindly patted her friend's feathery back.

The party prepared to descend the stairs.

CHAPTER 36

The militia's headquarters—a small cave cut into a rocky crater just north of the training ground—now contained five Glademontians and two Hinge Foresters. Ryon sat on a roughly carved stool, his open hands nearly touching a hissing black stove. Nory, Rette, and the Colonel also gathered around the heat, dressing their wounds. Jesse stood some distance away, grazing on stout forest grasses that Rette had kindly gathered. Evening, who volunteered to keep watch, padded thoughtfully at the mouth of the cave.

From Ryon's knee, Profigliano kept one eye squarely on the Colonel. Ryon attempted to sort out what had happened to Glademont since he left.

"How did you get out of the castle?" he said to the Colonel. "There were birds everywhere."

"The vagrants hardly know the castle as we do," the Colonel answered. "The honorable General Bud led us to a hidden hatch in the wine cellar."

"Why didn't more of you escape?" Ryon said.

Nory gingerly prodded his taped nose.

"We weren't running away," he said. "We were going to find help."

"You were coming to find us?" Ryon said.

The young man laughed, his bare chest clenching. "Redfoot," he said. "We'd be too exposed if we tried to get to Wallaton, so we decided to risk the Hinge and race to Redfoot for more men." His mirth dissolved. "Otherwise, we're cooked."

"But Redfoot was taken. Didn't you know?" Ryon gazed at the men, astonished.

"No one knows anything in there." Rette's strawberry blond hair shifted as he shrugged. "We're completely cut off. Redfoot is lost, is it?" He massaged his pale forehead.

"Not quite." Ryon suppressed a proud smile. "That's why we're here. There's a whole army forming: the Friends of the Militia."

"As in *our* militia?" Nory's eyes grew wide.

Ryon nodded. "Animals from the valley and from the forest. Half of them have gone south to liberate Redfoot and defeat Atheonian forces there. And we're here waiting for the other half. To attack Atheos at the castle."

Nory and Rette exchanged awed expressions, their bandages forgotten. Nory spoke first, straightening his stocky torso.

"I'll be a sea turtle."

"Until now, our only hope was the governors." Rette pressed his palms against the back of his long neck and closed his eyes, as though he hadn't relaxed in a century. Ryon was glad to see the tall, hopeful warrior looking as exhausted as the boy felt. Not everyone had to enjoy battle as much as Nory.

The Colonel snorted. "The guild is ready and able, Master Rette. But two dozen of us against a hundred hounds—"

"But remember how you fought that hound back home?" Ryon said. He had intended to bolster Reggie, but then he suddenly saw, in vivid color, the last night he spent in his own bed. He ordered his face not to fall, afraid to look weak in front of Nory and Rette.

Nory looked at Ryon. "He's been training the other governors in the castle. Golden magic." He shook his short-cropped head. "Incredible. But it isn't enough."

"So you're a bondfellow, like Jesse?" Ryon stared at the ground, desperate for distraction.

The Colonel looked sharply at the boy and searched his face. When Ryon met the terrier's black eyes, twinkling under silver eyebrows, he did not recognize the expression. It was a kind of surprised look, as though the Colonel were seeing Ryon for the first time.

"I beg your pardon?" the Colonel said.

"Fig and I are bondfellows, too." This time, Ryon allowed himself a timid grin.

"Is that right?" the Colonel said. "Well," he addressed Profigliano, whose chest was puffed to its maximum capacity, "I hope you appreciate the magnitude of the responsibility you have assumed."

"Well, well, well, well, well." Profigliano cocked his head this way and that as he repeated the word. "Looks like *some* animals thought they were the only nobles and dignifides around here, eh?"

Ryon chastised the towhee on his knee with a poke in the belly. "Who is your bondfellow, Reggie?"

"I am the beast of Brock Canyon, advisor to the queen," the Colonel recited.

Ryon's smile broadened into a satisfied grin. Something about those words tapped his soul like a well-digger's pick, ushering a clear, cool spring of hope.

"Why did no one tell me?"

"It has become a ritual." The Colonel sighed through his black wet nose. "Governors are appointed to families, and a routine ceremony follows. According to tradition, taking the oath endows animals with golden magic to be used in times of danger. But so many years have passed . . . we believed it a myth. Even I doubted my abilities the night that rabble came to the estate."

Fire, smoke, and foreign voices flooded Ryon's vision again, and he fought the urge to put his face in his hands. He swallowed.

"Did . . . did Mother and Papa . . . ?"

"All accounted for, Master Ryon. I fended off the attackers until Sir Brock and Lady Matilde were safe inside the castle. Lady Dahly joined us not long after."

Then Ryon *really* wanted to cry. He had been suppressing his anxiety for so long, a rush of exhilarated relief surged through his fingers and toes, and he stood to turn away from his companions. Profigliano flitted to his shoulder.

"Safe for now," Nory corrected, apparently oblivious to Ryon's emotion. "Those bandits and hounds aren't going to sit smoking and gambling forever. Who exactly are these animals we're waiting for?"

"And where is your other sister, Master Ryon?" said the Colonel.

"Do you need a minute, Master Ryon?" It was Rette who spoke, not paternally, but practically, which was exactly what Ryon needed.

He felt Profigliano's button eyes on him, remembered the hope of the fellowship, and faced the stove again. "I'll start from the night the bandits came."

He told the whole story, from Fig to the Nest to Osiris to the Birch Herd. The Colonel interrupted frequently with questions, especially when it came to the FOM. He wanted to know exactly who had attended their audience, their origins, family trees, and ranks. The gentlemen of the militia simply listened, their hands resting on their thighs.

When Ryon finished, the Colonel paced the headquarters. "Forest cat," he called.

Evening slowly turned in response, and Ryon reproached himself for having neglected him so long. It was clear the fox was in a mild temper. He approached the stove, moping.

"Evening, is it?" the Colonel said with authority.

"Not that it matters to anyone," the fox replied.

"Pull yourself together, sir. The fearless guide to the distinguished members of the Canyon family and the comrade of the prince of the Birch Grove must conduct himself with pride."

This had a transformative effect on Evening, who sprang upright. "Well, it's about time I was recognized for my heroism. All the sacrifices I have made for you creatures—"

"Speak of Prince Currant's plans," the Colonel said. "Why have you been sent to this military outpost?"

"Right," said the rejuvenated Evening. "We are to wait while Buchanan of Westbend raises reinforcements."

"Very good, sir fox." The Colonel paced once more. "When does the FOM plan to attack the Atheonian forces in Redfoot?"

"Tomorrow morning," Evening returned. "When they have the city, the Stitchipeeps will signal for us to attack the forces here."

"Seems a tenuous plan." The Colonel growled, deep in thought. "I see no way of knowing how many birds will assist us, nor how useful they shall be in battle. Moreover, I fear there is no way to estimate the abilities of our forces in the valley." The Colonel sniffed and turned to Jesse, who had finished his dinner and was calmly watching the scene. "Jesse, what do you say? Do we march into possible slaughter?"

Jesse shook his mane. "I have made my decision, Colonel, to fight for the survival of Glademont."

The rest of their conversation, Ryon did not hear. Instead, he focused on the splintered wood sizzling in the stove and the cold autumn wind whistling soulfully outside. It was really happening; Glademont was going to fight for its life. He held his elbows and rested them on his knees, feeling smaller than a leaf in a storm.

CHAPTER 37

Prince Linden was the first to lower himself onto the staircase. The decline was so dramatic, and its steps so narrow
and crumbling, Tess had to climb down backward to keep
her footing. Slowly, they descended into darkness, pressing
their sides against the slimy limestone for balance, until the canopy
of green and blue seemed only a hazy film above them. Several times,
Tess's boot slipped on the stone, and she would feel the prince's hand
around her ankle. Minutes passed like months, and when they finally
arrived at a narrow ledge, jutting out over an unsettlingly black pool,
they panted and shivered in the cool air.

"Oh—" Tess started, holding her braid aloft.

"What is it?" Linden said.

"The *shenil*—it was pricking me." Tess gingerly lowered her braid
over her shoulder again.

"Has it happened before?"

Tess thought of the *shenil* bristling against her hand when she last
saw Tynaiv. She bit her lip. "I think it is a kind of warning."

Linden handed Tess the lantern, retrieved his bow, and gestured
for her to remain close. Wyndeling, who had stayed behind to oversee
their descent, now flew ahead.

They advanced, crouching under a large slab of rock and into the
low tunnel. Inside, without the faint glow of the blue-and-green canopy, and the lantern in Tess's hand gone cold, all was completely dark.

Tess kept her free hand on the wall to her left as she followed the sound of Linden's footsteps. But eventually, a loud chorus of rushing water drowned out the echoing thumps of his boots. Tess reached into the darkness for Linden. She touched his back, and her fingers slid to his arm. She felt his bicep harden, then relax, and he pulled his arm against his side, securing Tess's hand.

The strength in Linden's arm reminded Tess of her father, of home and security. She longed to see her apple orchard again, or sleep next to Dahly and hear the sounds of Mama's clocks ticking away. She fought the urge to pull her body against the prince's and lay her head on his shoulder. He was the closest thing she had to home.

They spilled out of the tunnel into a high-ceilinged cavern. A faint light broke the spell between Tess and Linden, and she let her fingers fall from his arm. To her right, through a yawning portal to the outside world, she caught her first glimpse of the outdoors since Tynaiv left her at the sugar maple. Her view of the stars, however, was shrouded by the heavy, noisy curtain of a waterfall.

Crescent Cave.

They neared the falls with reverence, mouths open. Linden lowered his bow, and Tess allowed stray drops to cover her face like dew. She smiled and spun on her toes, arms outstretched.

"My lady." Wyndeling alighted on Tess's forearm and shook the water from her feathers. "Perhaps . . . perhaps someone should secure our location?"

Tess smiled a wide sympathetic smile. "Go on. I know you're desperate."

The owl hooted with energy. "I shall report back soon," she said. And away she flew, darting around the tumbling waters.

"Over here," Linden shouted. "Some kind of statue."

Tess followed him back into the gloom. Something stood at the center of the vast cavern, only as tall as Linden's shoulder. He stowed his arrow to examine it, and Tess stepped beside him.

It was a curious woman of green marble, naked but for a thin, fluid veil, blowing in an imagined wind. Tess placed her fingers along the edges of the veil, following its hard curved lines. But the veil flowed upward, as though blown from below. She suddenly understood: fire.

"She's beautiful," Tess said.

"Why does she hold out her hands? In welcome?" Linden rubbed his chin, apparently unable to appreciate the artistry.

Tess's lips parted with a gasp. "The medal." Tess pulled forward her braid and saw that, as she moved closer to the woman, the copper orbs buried in her hair glowed. Keeping his hands at his sides, Linden studied the medal.

"You're right, by the skies. Well, that means . . . do you think . . . ?"

They looked to each other with wide eyes, Linden smiling and Tess biting her cheek. Perhaps he wanted to hold her, but was afraid to touch the *shenil*. Or perhaps it didn't occur to him to touch her at all. Tess willed herself to focus.

"The only thing missing"—she pulled the object from her braid— "is the *shenil* itself." The shining orbs felt hot in her hands.

She hesitated, then placed each end of the *shenil* upon the hands of the fiery woman. Just as her own palms touched the statue, everything turned black.

"Who entrusts the Weapon unto mine hands?"

Tess saw nothing. She felt nothing—not even the ground beneath her feet. What had become of Linden?

"Speak," commanded a woman in a throaty, reverberating alto. Frightened, Tess tried to turn her head toward the source of the voice, but her body did not respond. She was weightless, suspended in blackness. She breathed in quick, shallow breaths.

"I am Lady Tessamine Canyon of Glademont. I cannot see. . . ."

"I am the spirit of Fyrian, Mother and Forger of the Weapon. How hast it come to thee?"

"Queen Aideen . . . passed it to me."

"So, the time has come for thy forming. The Weapon chooses its Thane. Art thou its Thane, Tessamine Canyon of Glademont?"

"I—I suppose so." Tess wished she had the *shenil* in her hair again. "But, I cannot see."

"Have you not the wisdom to see? All the better, for a Thane who lends innocence unto the Scarlet Poison's Enemy doth improve its potency. Mark you, Lady Tessamine, it is at the point of wisdom that the Thane must pass her mantle. Just as she has mastered the dryad's magic."

"Oh dear, I'm afraid I didn't understand any of that. . . ."

"Thy path to wisdom unwinds from this day hence. And yet . . . I sense . . . the Weapon hath lit its fire within you before."

"I'm sorry, my friend was dying—"

"Whither hast gone Aideen?"

"Oh." Tess hesitated. "Her Majesty has fallen ill. Our dione is under attack. We had hoped . . . I wish to use the *shenil* to save Glademont."

"Then it is time," the regal voice rang out, deep and solemn. A terrifying boom resounded. "Lady Tessamine Canyon, a choice lies before you, a choice no other reasoning soul hath the privilege to consider. For the mortal, the future broods in a darkness not unlike that which envelops thee now. But what sayest you to the illumination of such things? Have I not the power? Am I not a dryad of the deep earth?"

Tess did not know how to respond. She hardly understood. The voice continued.

"Two roads lie before thee. The first blesses thee with a crown of diamonds—queen and loved by thy people. Choose this path, and the cost shall be to abandon the Weapon here."

The words spilled into Tess's heart like oil in water. Was such a future possible? She pictured herself far away from her crumbling dione, free of the *shenil*, free to be loved.

"A second path beckons, which also blesses," the woman said. "Upon this road, thou shalt possess the greatest power on the continent, but few can know of it. Thou shalt be the unsung guardian of thy people. All this, if thou wilt keep the Weapon, and thine only cost be to deny thyself the crown."

Well, now Tess saw this plainly for what it was: a lot of nonsense. All this talk of diamond crowns and unsung guardians was some sort of trick. After all, Queen Aideen had clearly stated all thanes were queens. Even Osiris had linked a dryad's magic to Queen Miriam. Tess was not queen yet, but to promise never to be queen? It seemed a contradiction in terms. This was all wrong. She tried to take back the *shenil*, but she could not place her fingers. She tried to force her eyes open, but her lids seemed already ajar.

"Vermin and vinegar, get me out of here."

"Lady Tessamine Canyon of Glademont, a mighty yoke hast been put upon thee. Thou must choose, either to bear the yoke hence or cast it aside. Choose, and thou shalt take thy leave." The voice was unrelenting, and Tess began to fear this was no illusion.

"Her Majesty told me all thanes have been queens. They . . . they marry the crown prince." Her breath quickened with panic and embarrassment.

"Aye, each Thane until this day has been queen," said the woman. "Each Thane offers sacrifice according to her inmost desires. Never before has a Thane desired the queenship so eagerly as you desire it. Thine heart betrays thee, when standing before admirers. If thou art to be Thane, thine years shall be spent hidden from glory, apart from fame."

Tess felt a tide of shame cover her. Was this true? Was her only desire to be admired? At once she remembered the excitement of her leading role in the ballet, *The Ashes of Dorian Minor.* She danced as Fyrian, a dryad Tess thought never existed. Tess had reveled in the roaring applause of those nights. She thought she would never be happier.

Then, months later, she recalled the thrill of Linden's proposal, even then suspecting he did not care for her. She thought of her anger and embarrassment at having to arrive at her wedding festival with her family, and not with the prince. She saw the disappointed faces of the people when she stepped out of the carriage, the delighted expressions of the onlookers when she danced with Belle, and the devastation she felt when the prince cast her aside in front of the entire dione. Had she been deceiving herself all this time, thinking her bitterness toward the prince was justified? Perhaps she resented him not for using her heart, but for withholding the crown.

"Before you choose, Lady Tessamine, know this. The fate of Glademont is written in your stars."

A sudden jolt shot through Tess's heart. It was clear to her, now, how wrong she had been about herself, about the prince and the queen. It was not they who were selfish, but Tess. The queen was not hungry for power, but only wished to protect her people. Linden was not a heartless fiend, but a prudent prince who could see when a woman was not suited for royal life.

So, why did Aideen insist Tess was the chosen thane? Why was this spirit offering Tess the guardianship of the dione, while in the same breath telling her how unworthy she was? All signs pointed to someone else, someone who was not tempted by a life in the public eye. It would be better for Tess to leave the *shenil* in the cave. She could fly from Glademont, a dione she had only wounded through her own weakness.

To her surprise, Tess felt hot tears running down her cheeks. She wiped her eyes with fingers that she could now feel. Her senses were returning, but still she remained in darkness. A quiet sob gripped her throat.

"Why does this fall to me? Linden is right; I do not understand the world."

"The Weapon elects not the qualified. Rather, it qualifies the elect."

More tears wetted Tess's face, but she let them flow. Such a simple object. Two copper marbles and a strap of leather. But it had made her feel worthwhile. It had given her purpose.

"I choose the second road," Tess heard herself whisper. "I choose to be thane."

"Let it be done," the lady bellowed, and a golden light blinded Tess. Rubbing her eyes, she saw a luminous copper-skinned woman clothed in fire—fiercely beautiful, such that Tess felt compelled to look away.

The lady's voice came once more.

"Well done, dear one. Your life's adventure is yet to begin. Free mine worthy daughter held captive within yon grotto. Then, True Thane, get thee to the castle and rescue thy dione."

Tess fell backward, slowly, as the orange light dissolved to reveal the gloomy stone walls of the cave. The blinding orbs of the *shenil* pierced her vision, and she reached out for them while streaks of purple, red, and white swirled about her grasping fingers. Clutching the *shenil* to her chest, Tess soon felt the arms of the prince around her. She could hear him, distantly, calling her name as he held her. But all she could do was cry.

CHAPTER 38

Buchanan of Westbend did not enjoy sitting in caves. Ryon could tell by the way the owl shot suspicious looks at the ceiling, as though warning it not to try anything stupid. Before Buchanan stood Nory, Rette, and the Colonel. He addressed them as an official officer of the FOM.

"Nearly three-fourths of the Council of the Nest have come. The rest have agreed to join if the fighting breaches the borders of the Hinge."

Ryon sat against a boulder, staring absently at a pile of stones for his new sling.

The Colonel's beard had not stopped twitching since Buchanan arrived early that morning. Usually, that wouldn't bother Ryon; Reggie was always agitated about something. But today, it gave him a pit in his stomach.

"Are you quite satisfied, dog?" Buchanan hooted.

The Colonel growled. "That's Colonel Regency Thorn to you. Respect my rank, and I shall respect yours."

"I'll tell you plainly," Buchanan said, "I've never cared for domesticated animals. We'll see in battle whether you are as soft-beaked as I suspect."

"Gentle creatures," Rette interjected, much to Ryon's relief. "The first rule of war is to trust your allies and make yourself trustworthy in return." He palmed his ruddy hair behind his ear. "I believe

Commander Buchanan fully capable of an effective onslaught. The number of birds out there in the old quarry is, indeed, impressive. At least four hundred, I'd say."

The round owl nodded, eyes still narrowed.

Nory clamped a wide hand on Rette's shoulder. "My concern," he said, "is that our men and governors inside the castle will not know of our attack on Atheos. We will want them to be ready, especially those who wield magic."

Buchanan made a sour face but seemed unable to argue the point. The new councillors of war searched one another's faces.

Rette sighed. "With those raptors all over the place, there's no way we could send a message by air. . . ."

"Perhaps I can help," Evening said. He sat by Ryon's knee, his soft tail wrapped about his black paws. Only Ryon had noticed him pad into headquarters a few moments before. Buchanan hopped from the ground in astonishment, and the Colonel unwillingly let out a surprised yelp. Nory offered applause.

"Bravo, Evening. A master of stealth. You are just the man for the job."

"Remember, Master Rootpine," the Colonel said, "this is a matter of great importance. Perhaps a creature with some experience . . ."

Buchanan hooted his agreement. "Foxes are notoriously untrustworthy."

Ryon put a reassuring hand on the fox's back. "If it weren't for Evening, Jesse and I would never have met Prince Currant. And he's dealt with Atheonians before. I say we send him."

"Distinguished companions," Evening said, "I would be honored to perform such a task. Just give me the message and point the way."

Minutes later, equipped with his message and instructions, Evening pranced out of the cave, looking pleased with himself.

"We don't have much time," Buchanan said. "You. Human."

Nory pointed to himself. "Nory."

Buchanan nodded. "You wanted to show me your scribbles?"

"Er, a map," Nory said, his eyebrows twisting. "To pin down our positions—"

"Master Ryon, my fellow of bondship and warrior of the highest order, sir." Profigliano flew breathlessly into the headquarters.

"Please excuse him," Ryon said. "He didn't mean to interrupt."

"No time, no time," the towhee called. "Now is the time, now is the time."

"What are you chattering about?" Buchanan erupted.

"The Stitchipeeps, buddy-boy. The little ole Stitchipeeps are a-flappin' this way. You know what that means. It's go-time; it's fight-time. It's time to show those muckety-mucks who's boss. Boy-o-boy, are my feetsies itchin' for some *face*."

Ryon readied himself for battle, glancing at Nory and Rette to watch them do the same. Nory buckled a unique pack equipped with two full quivers around his torso, then checked the string to his stout longbow. Rette cleaned and sharpened a slender sword and several throwing knives, and the tip of a lightweight bow peeked over his head.

"Did you check your weapons, Master Ryon?" Nory called.

"Is your dagger clean and dry?" Rette said, his head almost touching the craggy ceiling of the headquarters.

Ryon nodded and rubbed his hands together, hoping it might help with his nerves.

"You'll be just fine." Rette ruffled the boy's cinnamon hair. "We've never been in a real battle, either. No Glademontian has for hundreds of years." He smiled kindly. "If you focus on your shortcomings, you'll never make it. You've got to think about why you are called to battle. Let the rest take care of itself."

"Cherrywater, you are a wise scholar," Nory hailed as he hoisted straw sleeping mats in a messy pile. "He's right, of course. We go to battle only because Glademont needs defending."

"Ryon, my magical buddy." Profigliano suddenly swooped into the headquarters. He had taken the role of camp crier, which was both useful and irritating for all. "A big old bear just got here. And me-oh-my is he ever having a top-secret-gab-fest with the Rushing out there. I'm downright offended, if you want to know."

"Osiris? What's he doing here?" Ryon hurriedly stowed his weapons and sprinted out of the cave. Wasn't Osiris supposed to be looking after Tess?

Standing out of the mouth of the headquarters with Profigliano close beside him, Ryon scanned the noisy crater for his sister's stallion. All around him, four hundred birds of the Hinge made themselves busy loading a dozen sprawling nets, all braided by the founding members of the militia. The larger birds—such as the herons, falcons, and owls—filled nets with heavy rocks, while the smaller birds—wrens and larks and the like—tied and secured the nets with their nimble beaks.

Circling overhead, the five members of the Wise directed their clan with relish, while sporting intimidating costumes for battle. They wore necklaces made of brilliant leaves and the bones of rodents. Bright blues and yellows were stained around their already alarming eyes. Buchanan of Westbend looked the most imposing of all. Upon his striped head sat a headdress, made of rabbit pelt and crowned with the skull of a carnivorous fish. He and his fellow councillors screeched out their orders. Word had come that Currant and the FOM were marching on occupied Redfoot. The Nest Battalion was to attack Glademont Castle within the hour.

Of course, the Colonel did his share of ordering, too. While acknowledging Buchanan as his commander, he had appointed himself "Captain of Land Movement." This meant that, as soon as any bird landed on the ground, the Colonel assumed jurisdiction. Every so often, a peal of irate barking could be heard, presumably when a bird had incorrectly considered the Colonel's orders to be optional.

From his high vantage, Ryon scanned the trees of the Hinge on the far side of the crater, where he spotted Jesse's butterscotch figure standing with a gigantic shaggy bear. The animals' heads were close, and Ryon could see Jesse's tail gently swishing.

"What do you think is going on over there? And where is Tess?" Ryon said to Profigliano.

"Beats me, fellow of the bond. Your illustrious steed shooed me away for the crime of curiosity. Some creatures are starting to think a lot of themselves around here." Profigliano clacked his beak.

"Wait, there goes Jesse. What on the continent . . ." As Ryon watched Jesse disappear between the trees of the Hinge, the mammoth bear descended into the crater.

"The bear character from that shifty Ruby Creek, eh?" Profigliano said as Osiris caught sight of them and waved a shaggy paw. "You seem pre-tty fam-il-i-ar if you ask me."

"Oh, Fig."

Soon, Osiris had crossed the crater and was ambling up the rocky exterior toward the cave.

"There he be now," he called jovially. "The brave brother o' the little gem."

"What is it, Osiris?" Ryon said. "Is Tess in trouble?"

"She be looked after, little boy. Don't ye be fretting." Osiris surveyed the bustle of war preparations. "It be shaping up t'look like a real fight, aye?"

"Where did Jesse go? Is he coming back?"

"Yon steed be going on his own journey, young one. He had a message to thee: 'Be confident in yer ability, and I'll be seeing thee.' Interesting fella, that steed of yers."

"But—"

"Nest Battalion," Buchanan screeched from somewhere overhead. "Move out."

A host of birdcalls answered the order, and suddenly the crater was emptied and the sky filled with birds and nets.

"Come on," Nory called as he and Rette came jogging out of headquarters. "We've got to get a move on—whoa." Nory stumbled back at the sight of Osiris.

"Pleased to be meeting ye both," the bear said. "I be Osiris, Guardian of Glademont and beast of King Wallis. Jesse be sending me as a poor substitute. I hope it be fine with ye?"

Both Nory and Rette sputtered something in the affirmative.

Ryon wanted to ask a million more questions, but the Nest Battalion was already on the move. After a quick recovery, Nory and Rette strode alongside Osiris, their weapons glinting in the sun. Ryon watched them with admiration as he stroked Fig's white-and-red breast. The towhee cleared his throat.

"A house-sized bear plus two fit-and-firm young chappies sure makes us look like a couple of freshly hatched chickies, eh, fellow bonder?" he said.

"You heard what Jesse said. We've just got to be confident in our abilities. The rest will take care of itself." He wasn't at all sure of this, but Fig needed the extra boost.

CHAPTER 39

Tess lay against Linden's shoulder. Her sobs had turned to quiet murmurs.

"I want to go home. Please take me home."

He pulled her closer. "Not yet. A little longer . . ."

A minute passed with Tess against Linden, both of them sitting on the cold floor surrounded by the roar of the waterfall. Tess lifted her wet face and breathed. "I heard a woman's voice," she said.

"It looked as though you were in a trance."

"I suppose I was. The voice was the spirit of Fyrian . . . like in the legend. She said that she made the *shenil*. She gave me a choice. . . ."

"Yes?"

"To either abandon the *shenil* or be its thane." Tess felt like crying again, but she managed to control herself.

"Well, you have it here. Did you choose to be the thane?" Linden lifted her hand to show her.

Tess didn't know what to say. She wanted to disappear, or soar out over the lake like Wyndeling.

"Let's get you on your feet." Linden lifted Tess and steadied her as she stared at the cool inanimate object in her hands. She had found the Thane's Hold, and it wasn't anything like she imagined. Instead of magic lessons, she was given two tasks: free someone trapped in Crescent Cave, and save Glademont. She couldn't think about the consequences of her choice any longer. It was time to act. She glanced at the quiver strapped to Linden's back.

"May I have a bit of that twine?"

With a puzzled look, Linden pulled off his quiver and uncoiled some of the twine that wound about the cylinder, cutting it with his knife. Tess tied the twine about the waist of her nightgown. She pulled one orb through the rope and left it hanging from her belt.

Linden grinned. "You look like a scholar. Older and wiser."

"Skies help me," Tess said. She felt older, but not wiser. She pinched the *shenil* for luck. "Do something for me?"

"Name it."

"Stay here." She had spotted the grotto, to the right of the tunnel where they had entered the cave. It was dark, much darker than the cave. And a strange gray vapor swirled within.

"Absolutely not." Linden shouldered his quiver and held his bow at the ready, his eyebrows meeting over his nose.

"If you don't stay here, Wyndeling will worry." Tess moved for the grotto before she could change her mind.

"Nonsense. She's always going on about how well she can see in the dark. Let her find us." He was at her side, his arm touching hers.

"Your Highness—"

They had entered the grotto, and Tess was suddenly freezing. She could feel droplets of icy water form on her arms and eyelashes. Tess drew her hood over her head, feeling as though they were walking through a frosty black fog. Her hands reached out for a wall or some stalagmite, but there was nothing.

"Hello?" Tess said after a while. "Is there anyone here?" A small pause followed, and Tess had the urge to turn back.

"I am here," someone answered. It was a woman.

A burst of blinding red gas ripped open the blackness and lassoed Tess's waist. She toppled and her shoulder collided with rock.

"Tess—" Linden grasped her arm and held on. The red magic pulled at her body, but Linden wrapped a leg about her, pinning her against the ground.

An echoing growl rumbled in the black fog, and Linden let go of Tess's arm to reach for an arrow. Tess frantically felt for the *shenil*. But without Linden holding on, the magic reeled Tess from under him.

The fastening on her cloak nearly choked her as she slid along the rock. Gaseous ropes around her glowed red as poison.

"Linden," she tried to scream, but her throat was pushed against the back of her neck. She could hardly breathe.

The prince bellowed, "I've got him." Tess heard the creaking of a taut string, then saw an arrow fly to the point where the red rope dissolved into darkness.

The arrow clattered against rock.

Tess gave up trying to reach the *shenìl* and dug her fingers under the fastening of her cloak. She yanked at it, and just as she was able to draw a breath, she crashed into a wet, warm, furry body. It growled.

"Skies . . . ," she choked. The body snarled, and Tess rolled from it. With a piercing bark, it lunged and caught her hood.

"I've got him," Linden yelled again, this time much closer. The hound threw the hood from his mouth and stepped over Tess's legs, lowering his head to the floor.

"Look out," Tess called. But instead of a menacing swirl of red creeping from the hound's nose, all went black again. The animal had made the ropes around Tess disappear, and they were enveloped in the pitch-dark.

Tess's heart felt colder than the fog. A wet nose inspected the mute orbs against her thighs. Then another growl. The hound barked again, and Tess braced for his teeth. He struck her forearm as she shielded her face. She cried out as his hot mouth tightened against her bone.

Then, somewhere close, there was fire. Not the *shenìl*'s fire, for it was as tall as a sapling. A shrill whining reverberated in the fog, and the iron jaws released Tess's arm. By the light of the enormous tongue of fire, Tess could see an arrow quivering in the hound's ribs.

Tess stooped over him, her body shaking from the shock and the cold. Blood spilled onto her nightgown.

The singular flame receded, changing color and taking shape. It went from yellow to orange, orange to red, then red to a dark apricot. Some live creature emerged, still full of light but no longer difficult to look at directly. Tess stepped toward a lovely petite woman with shining copper skin and deep violet waves of hair reaching to her waist. A billowing robe of reflective, charcoal fabric moved with her arms. She seemed to be standing, but with great difficulty. Her shoulders slanted, her dark lips hung slack. It was like looking at the stained glass image of a tired star spirit.

The woman smiled with soft cheeks. "I am *very* glad to see you, Tess."

"Madame." Tess curtsied, shivering and holding her bleeding arm. "I am sent to rescue Fyrian's daughter here."

The woman's large eyes twinkled. "Quite so."

Linden stumbled into the light the lady cast. His stare went to Tess, and then to the woman.

"Did he hurt you, my lady?" He straightened uncertainly.

"Thank you, Your Highness." Tess tried for a smile, but it failed to arrive. This was not how she imagined she'd complete her first mission as the true thane.

"Prince Linden," the woman said, "I am Ember. An arrow well shot, sir."

"I—thank you." He bowed with his head still inclined toward Tess. He had spotted her arm.

"You honor your mother in helping Tess safely to the Hold. You honor her well. She was wise to send you both to the cave, dangerous though it was."

"I was to hide the *shenil*." Tess was shivering so violently, she gave up all formality. "But I . . . well, it was no good. Pider found me anyway. So we had to come here. I had to learn to use it."

"You've done much more than that," Ember said. "You've become the thane. You are marked with its fire."

Tess looked down, expecting to see a flame tattooed to her palm, or some mystical aura hovering over her skin. But all she saw was the *shenil*, dark and silent.

"You have chosen your sacrifice?" Ember said.

Tess took a sharp breath and looked at Linden. His eyebrows knitted together.

"Whatever the loss, it was a worthy act," Ember continued. Her shoulders tipped farther, and the curls quivered. "Everything in our power must be done to keep Pider from obtaining the weapon."

"Forgive me." Linden bowed again. "You are Ember? The sister who was threatened in that letter we found at the Ruins?"

"That," Ember said with a sigh, "is a lengthy tale."

"Madame, please, I must know what plagues my dione." Linden took a step forward. "I must know how Glademont came to be hated by this magician. I have no other purpose on this continent but to protect her." He looked to Tess, again focusing on her bleeding arm.

Tess's shivering subsided a degree as a thrill ran through her veins. Did he speak of his home or of Tess?

"It is a story that begins on a continent much older than this one," the illumined woman began. "In the early ages of this world, when men could not resist the allure of red magic, entire civilizations crumbled into chaos. The animals fled to the farthest corners of their lands, for they were not safe with men.

"Then, on the continent of Dorian Minor, a sacred forest was burned by a heartbroken king. From its ashes, a new creature was born: Fyrian, the First Gem Dryad of Dorian. She taught good men to use golden magic, so they might redeem their lands and conquer the scarlet poison.

"Dorian Minor grew in goodness. And peace reigned so long that Fyrian settled among them, and fell in love with a mortal man. To him, she bore twins: a boy and a girl. My brother was born mortal. But the spirit and powers of a gem dryad were passed to me. Jealous of my gifts, my twin learned to manipulate the scarlet poison. He was cunning, and his skill threatened the peace of Dorian Minor. So Mother forged a weapon that harnesses a dryad's magic. In the right hands, it could defeat even the darkest of magicians. The weapon was intended for mortal use, beginning with the empress of Dorian Minor, as an everlasting defense against the wickedness wrought by red magic. In forging the weapon, Fyrian sacrificed the whole of her powers.

"But my brother, Pider, discovered the weapon had been forged and raised an army against the empress. Though too late to save its first, courageous thane, I recovered the weapon. In desperation, Fyrian bade me flee from Dorian, hide the weapon, and watch over it until another mortal could be taught to use it well."

Tess saw Ember's eyes shine with tears.

"I never saw my mother again. My brother destroyed Fyrian soon afterward. Her immortal spirit remains in the world, a shadow of what she once was. But her body was annihilated by my brother's powers. Pider searched the world to complete his destruction of dryads and their magic—for centuries he searched, until I made a disastrous mistake."

Tess felt an immense sense of smallness as she listened. It was the story of the ballet, but darker. The empress did not save her people, she was killed for the *shenìl*, as was Fyrian. All would have been lost except for one young dryad. Fyrian's daughter. Ember.

Linden sniffed against the fog. "Then Pider is your twin? He wrote that letter to you in the cell, two hundred and fifty years ago, swearing to destroy the *shenìl*. He's been hunting it. . . ." He looked to Tess and caught her grimacing against the pain in her bleeding forearm.

"I'm all right," she said. "The cold is numbing the wound." Linden wrapped an arm around her shoulders. He addressed the shining woman.

"Is Tess somehow a dryad? Now that she carries the weapon, as you call it?"

"One cannot become a dryad, any more than a pebble can become a jewel. The weapon channels my mother's powers to protect creatures of good will. The Hold channels her spirit to guide and bless each thane. I built and enchanted this cave myself, to instruct Queen Miriam as my mother had once done for the empress."

"You are the mysterious woman," Linden breathed. "The woman in Crescent Cave. The woman who spoke to Osiris, told him to keep his post."

Ember smiled sadly. "A powerful enchantment held Pider in that cell as long as possible. But in the end, he found a way . . ."

They stood in silence. The cold of the fog bit at Tess's lips and nose.

"After the war, I was careful. The queens never entered the Hinge but through the southern hills, never stayed longer than three days, never came but once a generation . . ." Ember's hands gripped her chest. "But Aideen's connection with the weapon was dimming, dimming . . . she came to see me. She stayed too long. Pider found us. I was afraid he killed her."

Tess's heart raced. "But if Pider could overpower Aideen, who has used the *shenìl* for years, how can I . . . ? Ember, I have not been trained."

Ember's tired mouth widened in a smile. First at Linden, then at Tess. "Only one thing to know. Simple, yet challenging. By the three modes of surrender, the thane wields the weapon's power."

Tess didn't like the sound of that. The throbbing in her forearm sent jabs of pain into her shoulder and neck. "What are the three modes?"

"For a mortal human, the dryad's magic requires a wisdom difficult to attain. But, with the help of the weapon, you can become fire."

Tess nodded and looked to Linden, whose arm was still around her. His damp hair lay flattened against his brow. He seemed restless.

"The first mode of surrender," Ember continued, "is confident obedience to the *shenil*. When she speaks, act as you are bidden without doubt or skepticism.

"The second is selflessness. You must concentrate on those whom you serve.

"The final mode of surrender is acceptance of the future. Do not force your desired outcome, but calmly welcome whatever lies ahead." Ember turned up a palm. "Of course, you can achieve many small things by submitting to one mode. But, abandon yourself to all three, and the weapon will work miracles for the sake of your people. And now"—Ember closed her eyes—"you must return to Glademont and wield the *shenil* against my brother." A pained expression flashed across her face.

"But you must come with us," Tess pleaded.

Ember opened her eyes and lifted her heavy, charcoal robes. "See what keeps me here."

Underneath the iridescent fabric, a pair of distorted-looking bare feet appeared. Tess left Linden's arms, stooped, and discovered the feet were encased in a solid block of black ice.

Linden knelt beside Tess. "Can your magic not melt the ice?"

Ember chuckled. "Outside this fog, yes. But Pider's curse has suppressed my powers. I ignite a flame, the mist becomes heavier and colder. These many weeks, I have become a soaked and soggy dryad." Her eyes glittered with mirth.

"How have you not frozen to death?" Tess could not help herself.

"It will take more than ice to kill me. But, for the moment, I am trapped. The weapon is the only way to dispel Pider's curse."

"Xandra's horn," Tess murmured.

"Just remember to surrender, and the weapon will do the rest."

Trying to ignore the blood on her hands and the aching in her forearm, Tess took up the *shenil* and held out the orbs. At first, all she could do was try to *not* think about things—things like the hound, the black fog, Fyrian, Linden, and the promise she made . . .

All of that would have to wait. She took in a deep breath through her nose. The air felt tingly and bitterly cold inside her nostrils—just the thing to clear her mind.

The *shenil* began to feel warm in her palms. Tess focused on the warmth. It spread to the tips of her fingers and the points of her elbows. She began to listen and heard a kind of scratching echo within the grotto. Still, she did not open her eyes. The warmth felt nice, and even the scratching sounded friendly. Every so often, the sounds would culminate in a *pop* from somewhere near Tess's hands. An intense heat emanated from between her arms, and a bright red light shone on her face. Still, she did not open her eyes. A voice sounded from Fyrian, the gem dryad of Dorian Minor.

Knowest thou the ways of the Great Weapon? Get thee away, then, Thane, and stow upon thy bosom the whole of thy people.

Whatever it meant, it made Tess feel proud. For the first time, she was sure of the object in her hands. It had chosen her, and it belonged with her. The heat between her arms increased, and she tossed her head so that her hood fell onto her back. Then she heard another voice.

Touch the ice, it said.

It was the same voice Tess had obeyed before, when she danced on Ruby Creek, and when Wyndeling lay unconscious in the redbud grove. It was undoubtedly Tess's own voice, though it sounded different somehow—a bit like her mother.

Tess opened her eyes.

Tall orange tongues of flame burned between her forearms, emitting from the medal as before. Tess found she had the ability to see through the fire, and she observed the orbs of the *shenil* shining diamond white above her palms. Calmly, Tess bounced on the balls of her feet and curtsied low. Her hands extended from her chest in a movement she learned as a child when she danced as an ocean wave. Her fingers swept over Ember's feet and touched the block of ice.

Flames formed tendrils that wound about Tess's arms and swirled downward, wiping the congealed blood from Tess's skin and enveloping Ember's feet. The curse resisted the flames, and cold mist blew into Tess's eyes as the ice began to melt. Tess closed her eyelids, but kept her hands firmly on the ice. Soon, the mist became a frigid downpour. Tess felt her drenched nightgown cling to her body and water collect in her boots, but she did not move.

The fire went out. Tess dropped the orbs. All was dark again.

"Come," Ember shouted, and was suddenly ablaze. Her charcoal robes cracked and moved like melting rock in boiling magma. Her chest and arms flared under the robes, twinkling and shimmering, unaffected by the sheets of freezing water now gathering around them.

With astonishing agility, the dryad sprinted for the main cave.

Tess attempted to follow, but her feet were numb within sloshing boots, and she fell. Linden had her in his arms in an instant. Above the howling of the wind sounded a deep and ominous rumbling.

"Hurry," Ember called.

With a deafening crack, the ground beneath the prince's feet began to collapse. He squeezed Tess's legs and ribs, leapt into the air, and landed hard on the stone floor of Crescent Cave. Tess tumbled from his arms, a drenched bundle of skin and cloak.

Eying the raw, red teeth marks on her arm, Tess pulled herself upright and tried to control her shivering. Ember stood before her, bright as a meteor, facing the tunnel that led to the winding staircase. Panting and shivering himself, Linden crawled to Tess and took her face in his hands.

"I'm so sorry I doubted you," he began. But the sentence died with the moment. An eerie chill descended on the party—not from the air, but from something far worse.

Tess and Linden looked along the tunnel and beheld an army of tiny glowing lights inching toward them. Rather than hanging innocently overhead as before, the lights crawled like droves of worms, slinking silently toward them along the walls of the tunnel. Linden took Tess's good arm and they knelt behind Ember's reassuring light.

The lights formed a rapidly approaching tide, oozing and taking shape—the shape of a man. Ember advanced, her volcanic cloak folds rippling against the cave floor.

"You cannot corner me now, brother. Not with an old sentry curse."

The figure before them stopped and grinned while blue and green strings wiggled about its body, which towered a full torso taller than the tallest man.

"What astonishing arrogance," the figure mouthed, and an echoing voice radiated from the rock around them. "You have served your purpose, sister. I've no further designs for you. Has she come to rescue you? Where is she?" It was Pider's voice, and yet many voices, all tumbling over one another.

A hard lump bobbed in Tess's dry throat, but she stepped from behind Ember, closing her sodden cloak around her waist and the *shenil*.

"Ah," Pider said through green-and-blue lips. "Now I know what I am dealing with. Fifteen? Sixteen? No sleep, beaten by the forest . . . had a talk with the little statue, perhaps but . . . yes, that is very helpful. Thank you, Ember."

"Yes, she is nothing. *I* am nothing," the dryad taunted. "Come back to the Hold yourself and see how easily we can be taken." Ember's cloak swept into a puddle, and the steam hissed around her.

"I propose an alternative course," answered Pider's curse. "I remain in Glademont to destroy everything the girl loves. She is welcome to try to stop me. You must stay in the cave, afraid as you are to leave your precious memorial to dryads gone by—"

"You couldn't destroy it before."

The glowing figure regarded Ember, its surface still squirming. "Oh, sister, I could turn the Hold to dust. You can be sure of that." It focused on Tess and folded its blue-and-green pulsating hands. "If you hurry, little mouse, you might heal Aideen yet."

Tess looked to Linden and could see from his shoulders he was breathing heavily. The pain in his eyes made Tess's heart ache.

"Goodbye, all," Pider's curse called out.

Before Tess could move, the lights dispersed, crawling up and up against the walls of Crescent Cave.

"Run," Ember cried.

A mighty wall of water came ripping down the tunnel. It gathered the glowing worms and spun into the cavern, knocking Tess to her knees. Linden grasped her around the waist and pulled her toward Crescent Lake, but she resisted. Tess grabbed the spheres of the *shenil* and stood her ground. Linden kept his arms around her, his chest pressed against her back. She raised her arms, closed her eyes, and tried to let go of all her selfishness, all her plans, all her fear.

The water crashed against her legs, and the glowing blue and green worms stuck to her boots, her nightgown, and her cloak. She could feel them inching upward toward her waist. Tess wavered, horrified. She opened her eyes and saw no flame had appeared between her hands. Linden batted against the worms as the water rose to their knees. The worms reached Tess's arms and crawled toward the *shenil* in her hands. She screamed.

Ember stood before the marble statue, which contained her mother's spirit, ablaze from head to foot, her cloak swirling. She plunged her hands into the waters, and a hot blast exploded along the surface, blowing the worms from Tess's arms.

"Come." Linden pulled Tess away from the curse. They stumbled to the cave's edge, and Tess looked over her shoulder for Ember. She could just barely make out a pillar of fire and smoke before Linden took her by the hand. They leapt from the mouth of Crescent Cave and into the waterfall.

CHAPTER 40

The sun hung high overhead as Ryon lay flat among the ferns of the northeastern edge of the Hinge. Though unnecessary, Profigliano flattened his little white belly against the ground, too. Nory and Rette crouched nearby, and the Colonel stood behind Ryon, looking out between the ferns. Overhead, Buchanan and his clan sat motionless in the high branches of the ancient trees. From where he lay, Ryon could see the castle gates and the bandit camp in front. At least, he saw where the camp *used* to be. The tents had been taken down and the area cleared away. The bandits themselves were nowhere to be seen. All was still, and it seemed the Nest Battalion had arrived just as Atheos had given up their siege.

The call of an eagle issued from somewhere south of Glademont Castle, and Ryon's body jolted. More than four dozen fierce-eyed predators sailed into view, their course set for the eastern towers. Ryon and his companions watched as the raptors glided over the castle walls and crashed through the tower windows. Then another flock glided into view—this time vultures. They peppered the windows of the lower towers. The Colonel growled.

"First Company, ready your nets," Buchanan hooted from somewhere above. Looking up, Ryon watched elm and poplar branches sway as three rock-filled nets launched from the canopy.

Meanwhile, a mass of hawks sped toward the western corner of the castle for another barrage.

"Company, attack," the commander of the Nest Battalion called out.

The hawks must have heard Buchanan's order. Before they reached the castle wall, the mass split, and several dozen circled back to face their unexpected enemies. Ryon smiled. Even the sharp eyes of a hawk cannot see into the sun. Buchanan's company had flown into the open toward the castle, so high the midday light shielded them. The hawks scattered, defenseless as a torrent of rocks tumbled upon them.

"Second Company, ready," came Buchanan's cry.

But Ryon could not afford to watch the Second Company take off into the sky. The bandits and their hounds had finally emerged on the castle lawn. Arranged into three regiments, the bandits advanced on the castle with speed. Ryon dared not loose his sling until the order, but he feared the Colonel was wasting precious time. Whatever the bandits were doing, it could not be good.

When the left flank reached a stone's throw from the outer wall, two scouts darted out and stooped at a divot in the rock.

Nory cursed. "The wine cellar. They're going in same the way we got out."

"I should say not, soldier," the Colonel said. "Ready your long-range weapons, Land Company."

Ryon fumbled with his sling as Nory and Rette took out their bows.

"Aim for the creatures closest to the cellar door," the Colonel ordered. "Down as many of those foul men as you can."

Nory and Rette drew their arrows toward the sky, while Profigliano flitted to a low branch and wiggled his black tail.

"Fire at will."

The *ping* of their arrows made Ryon drop his stone. He scrambled to fit another in his sling as Nory and Rette picked off more Atheonians. Once half a dozen of the bandits had fallen, the most exposed men took a knee and searched for the archers. Spotting Ryon and his companions at the edge of the forest, they shouted orders to their hounds.

A dozen hounds barreled toward the Hinge. Their snarls and massive paws sent a chill down Ryon's back. He swung his sling, missing the leader by inches.

"Come on, Ryon," he growled to himself. The hounds were fewer than thirty yards away. The boy stood and used all his body weight to send the next stone rocketing. This time, he hit his mark. The foremost hound yelped in pain and collapsed, which tripped up two more behind him.

"Archers, stay on those bandits," the Colonel called. "We can handle these slobbering excuses for dogs." With that, the Colonel bounded out into the open in front of Ryon. He lowered his head to the ground, and the earth began to shake.

"Don't you forget about me." Profigliano hopped out next to the Colonel and wiggled his tail again. "You ain't seen *nothin'* till you've seen a red-breaster on the battlefield. I been doing beak exercises for three straight mornings."

The hounds reached within ten yards of the forest edge when the Colonel and Profigliano released their spells. The Colonel's magic swirled elegantly from his mouth and nostrils, a mix of gas and liquid. It enveloped four of the hounds in a slow-moving carousel. Profigliano conjured a golden defense bubble around himself, and from it sent a stream of smaller bubbles, which burst against the hounds' forelegs. The gold skins adhered, binding their legs together like glue. As Profigliano's victims collapsed, Ryon pelted another hound between the eyes.

But then, one of the Colonel's victims blasted a red, ragged rip through the golden carousel. Now free of the Colonel's spell, the hounds vaulted straight for him, teeth bared. With an ominously amplified growl, the Colonel threw up a golden shield. Two hounds, unable to stop in time, hit the shield full force, and Ryon heard the crunching of bones. Another managed to leap over the shield, snapping onto the Colonel's throat. The hound shook the Colonel's body with his powerful jaws. Ryon reached for his dagger and leapt into the open. He rammed his shoulder against the hound to knock it on its side, and drove his dagger between the ribs. The Colonel whined, pulling himself away from his dying attacker.

Ryon cleaned his dagger with a shaking hand, returned it to its sheath, and moved to examine the Colonel.

"Very good, soldiers, very good." The Colonel panted, ignoring the blood streaming from the wounds along the back of his neck. "Resume the attack on the bandits at the cellar."

"They're already in," Nory said, wiping sweat from his forehead. "Close to fifty of them, Colonel."

"Look, the governors," Ryon said.

A volley of golden magic rained down from the castle wall walks onto the attacking bandits. High above the lawn, drainage holes near the top of the outer wall were filled with the heads of formidable terriers, barking and catapulting streaks of gold. A slew of red blasts from below pummeled the wall in retaliation. Meanwhile, the brunt of the bandit forces worked frantically with club and sword to pry open the outer gate.

"Colonel." Buchanan was suddenly by Ryon's side. "Our nets are emptied. We must do what we can with beak and talon. Where is that bear?"

"I be here, impatient one." Osiris appeared, shuffling through the leaves. When Ryon saw him, he gasped aloud.

Osiris was armored from head to tail with leather and metal. Numerous cuffs big enough to fit a human thigh surrounded his limbs. A man-sized shield covered his back, and yet another decorated his chest. Around his shaggy neck, he wore a studded collar made of two spiked straps, and a three-headed mace jutted from between his teeth. Ryon couldn't wait to see the looks on those bandits' faces.

The bear removed the mace from his mouth. "I be sniffing out the ole Armory yer boys be hiding in yon tree. This be nothing like the old armor of Glademont, but I don't be the complaining sort."

"Boy-o-boy." Profigliano shook out a few drops of golden magic left over from his skirmish. "This mountain bear is coming in handy."

"Get yerself on me back, Master Ryon," Osiris ordered, his large muzzle twisting into what might have been a grin. Ryon still shook from his first kill at close range, but he grasped Osiris's studded collar and hoisted himself onto the bear's shoulders.

A chorus of screeching and squawking echoed from the castle, where bandits slashed at diving birds. Many of the Hinge Foresters were dying, and the raptors continued to enter the castle through the windows. But the outer gate remained secure. The sheer volume of the battle overwhelmed Ryon, with the terriers on the wall, the hounds on the ground, the calling birds, and the yelling bandits. Too many of Glademont's allies were dying in the open.

"Reggie, we must fight from the inside, see if we can't push Atheos out again," Ryon yelled over the din.

"A fine idea, soldier. Charge," barked the Colonel, and they sprinted for the western corner of the castle, where one hundred more bandits stood between them and their friends inside.

CHAPTER 41

Tess regained consciousness on a pebbly bank, wiping dark, greasy hair from her forehead. The bite wound on her arm was sore, but not too swollen. A few sticks smoldered within reach, and Tess realized her head was resting on Linden's folded leather vest. It was late morning.

Across the campfire sat Linden, his untucked shirt almost dry. One elbow rested on his bent knee.

"Where is Ember?" Tess said, and began to cough. Her stomach sloshed with what she could only assume was lake water.

"Gone." Linden ran a hand over his matted head. "There were flashes and booms, but I couldn't see what was happening from where we washed up. After the noise stopped, I built a fire and returned to the cave."

"That was foolish. Pider's curse could have been waiting for you."

He shrugged. "I found nothing but a few inches of water and the Thane's Hold, still there, just as it was."

Tess sat up to look. The lake was not wide, more like the dammed end of a slow river. It formed a lazy horseshoe, with the cave and waterfall at the opposite tip from where they were. She could still hear the rush of the falls, and see the forest edge where Ruby Creek poured over the rocks. Around their little camp, there were no ancient trees or swaying ferns. Only sparse shrubs, low grasses, and scattered rock.

They were on the edge of the southern hills. Facing east, Tess let the sun warm her eyelids.

Ember was gone.

Wyndeling swooped to meet them. "Thank the skies. She's awake." She landed on Tess's knee.

"Where have you been?" Tess said.

"My lady," Wyndeling said. "I returned to the cave just in time to watch you and His Highness throw yourselves into the falls. I reproach myself for leaving you too long, but I think you'll be pleased with who I found." Wyndeling puffed out her soft chest and pointed a wing at an approaching butterscotch figure.

"I don't believe it." Tess stumbled to her feet and rushed to embrace Jesse. His glossy body was wet with perspiration. Heavy breath blew through his muzzle.

Linden stood and bowed in greeting. "Broken your silence, I see, Jesse Canyon?"

"Highness"—Jesse bent a foreleg—"I come from the Friends of the Militia who gather at the castle. They go to battle against Atheonian mercenaries this very morning."

"I see." Linden stomped the fire out with vigor. "Then we shall join them."

"It is to Redfoot that I will take you, Your Royal Highness," Jesse said.

"Redfoot?" He strapped Tess's former pillow to his chest. "No. My mother is dying."

"Prince Currant sends for you from Redfoot. He has reclaimed the city, and asks that you help lead his forces against Atheonian soldiers advancing toward the castle."

"Is Ryon all right?" Tess asked Jesse.

"In the bear's care," he answered. "Osiris told me where you were."

"So . . ." Tess looked to Crescent Lake where dappled light fell on green water. "Ryon got his wish. He is a part of the militia after all." Her shoulders drooped from the weight of worry for her brother.

"I don't like it," Linden murmured.

Tess remembered she had a mission of her own: to save Glademont. "It won't matter if we heal Queen Aideen only to be slaughtered by the Atheonians from the valley," she reasoned. "If they could take Redfoot so easily, think how they'll topple the castle. But, if we come from behind, make them fight on both sides . . . Currant will need us, Your Highness. He will need your knowledge of battle, your familiarity with the terrain." She couldn't help but grasp the *shenil* around her waist. He looked at her hands. Was he remembering how she failed to defeat Pider's curse?

Linden pondered another moment. "Glademont comes first," he said with restraint. "And we are closer to Redfoot than the castle. I hope these forces of Currant's can move quick." He mounted Jesse and offered a hand to Tess. "And are up to the task of harboring Glademont's secret weapon."

He almost smiled at her, the lines at the corners of his eyes deepening. Tess bit her lip as she took his hand. She clasped her arms about his waist and touched her forehead between his shoulders.

They soon left Crescent Lake behind, tearing east across the fine dust and gray rock of the rippling southern hills. Even after covering half the Hinge Forest in a single morning, Jesse shot across the bare land like an arrow through fog. The severe winds made Tess's hair cut into her mouth and eyes. She shielded her face in the folds of Linden's coat. Wyndeling sailed alongside, surfing an invisible current.

They raced until midday, when before them rose the thrusting silhouette of the city of Redfoot. The city's familiar market rotunda loomed to the left, and directly ahead glinted the white clock tower that marked the city's center, sporting its black piping and copper statues. Tess had never seen the city from the west before. Then again, she had never seen it so marred by billowing black smoke, either.

As they neared, Jesse slowed to a trot, breathing heavily. His riders dismounted, and the company made their way into the city. It was like entering a vague dream, where chairs and tables lay upside down in the street, and buildings gaped like empty lanterns. Redfooties wandered the cobblestones, crying or foraging. Tess gripped the *shenil* and held her breath. Eventually, Linden nudged her elbow and they followed Jesse through the massive, unhinged wrought iron doors that marked the entrance of the market square.

The burning smell overwhelmed Tess—wood, yes, but also metal and fish, fabric, paper, and oils. Common marketplace wares were strewn in charred heaps throughout the square. Rows of grimy stone columns stretched on either side of them, joining on the other end at the rotunda, which looked mercifully unscathed except for the three dozen deceased Atheonian soldiers marring its once elegant staircase.

At the center of the square, the obelisk in King Antony's memory towered over them. Tess's insides twisted as she remembered Linden in Den Five, swearing he would never die the way his father did. When she saw what awaited them at the foot of the obelisk, she hoped Linden felt reassured.

Over two hundred determined-looking creatures of Glademont shuffled into a loose formation at the center of the square. Breeders from Foggy Plains patted their ponies' shaggy manes. They wore the traditional high-waisted trousers of horse breeders and carried an assortment of farm tools as makeshift weapons. Mountain goats and sheep from Wallaton stood loyally by their men. The shepherds carried knotted staffs, and their hardened muscles showed through thin garments. All these stood amid the destruction, looking to an eight-point buck for instruction.

"Well, well." Currant bounced forward. "Friends of the Militia, I give you your commander, Prince Linden of Glademont."

The ponies, goats, and their human bondfellows gave cheer in their own way, the fire of battle in their eyes.

Linden released Tess's arm to pat the neck of his forest friend. "I was worried," he said simply.

"I'm all right. Your dione on the other hand—" The elk noticed Tess. "Prince Currant of the Birch Herd, at your service." Currant lowered his head.

"Lady Tessamine Canyon. How do you do?"

"Surely they were here with a larger force." Linden pointed to the bloodied Atheonians at the foot of the rotunda. Currant wiggled his ears in discomfort.

"We were too late for the army. They left those fellows in charge, with most of the Redfooties locked in the rotunda."

"No hounds?" Linden said.

"None," Currant said, clearly grateful. "Took all the red magic with them. Along with a battering ram as big as a redwood. They're headed straight for the castle, Your Highness."

"Right." Linden surveyed the scene. Both his and Tess's eyes watered from the smell and smoke. "None from Green Reed have joined us?"

Currant shook his dark, smooth head. "I'm afraid not. So far, the enemy does not march that far east. I'm told the river folk won't leave their skiffs and nets just yet. Waiting to see if the fight comes to them."

"I see," replied Linden. "If we live through this, I shall have something to say about that." He turned his attention again to the conquered Atheonians. "How many now approach Glademont Castle?"

A ginger pony trotted forward. "We'll need a closer look to know for sure, sire." He lowered his head to Tess and Linden. "I am Abe. Glademont evermore."

Then a mighty mountain goat cantered forward, eyeing the humans with horizontal pupils. "Are we going to stand around here all afternoon?" he bleated.

Currant laughed, but his round brown eyes remained serious. "This is Tartan the Terrible. I suppose he's right, Linden. We haven't got a lot of time."

"Right." Linden blew through his nose and gripped his bow. He addressed the creatures before him. "Creatures of Glademont, your valley and cliffs, your families and friends, stand in danger of this same decimation. The time has come for you to prove your love of home, of peace. Will your children and offspring know the dione that welcomed you into the world? Or will they grow under the fist of foreign rule, their lands occupied by a murderous king? And what will you tell them if you do not fight today? The fate of our great dione rests with you."

The members of the FOM tossed their heads and pawed at the ground with anticipation while their humans raised staff and pitchfork, calling out, "Home of the Heart!"

In the midst of this, an old goatherd stepped forward. He sported a short, wiry chinstrap beard. "You royals couldn't lace up your own boots if yeh tried, Highness." He might have winked, but Tess didn't catch it.

A snow-white mountain sheep with curling horns sidled alongside the old man. "May I introduce my shepherd, Asher Candlestock. I am Pipe."

"Pleased to know you both," Linden said.

The old man grunted as he gave Linden a hard, inscrutable look. He regarded them both with an upturned palm. "We Wallaton folk don't get along much with none but the herd. Never thought I'd leave the cliffs in my lifetime. Partic'larly not for some squirmer from the castle."

"I can assure you," Linden said, "those of us who live on Zere Mountain desperately need you at this moment."

"Pipe and me, we're not here for you, Highness," Asher answered with a wry smile. "We're here to see Wallaton don't end up like this city." Asher grimaced, deepening the lines along his thick brown cheekbones. "Ain't got no excuse to sit around, jawing on the grass. We're with yeh, young man. Wallaton and Foggy Plains've suffered enough."

Mournful as she was for the ruined city, Tess was glad to be leaving Redfoot. The Friends of the Militia and its human allies picked their way to the northern gates of the city, where the main road began.

Linden led the force, walking beside the prince of the Birch Herd. Tess rode Jesse while Wyndeling circled overhead. Mountain goats marched behind the leaders, followed by ewes and rams. Wallatonian men flanked the herds, and behind these, the men of Foggy Plains rode on their ponies, farm tools in hand.

As marigold sunshine warmed Tess's cheek, she gazed over Glademont Valley. Purple heather, mounds of ruffling grass, and the soft black rock in between all called to Tess, reminding her of her years at the academy. How many times had she ridden through these fields, relishing their humble beauty? Grouses flapped into the air from the underbrush. Dragonflies perched on blades of grass. To her right, somewhere beyond the plains, Miri River flowed from the cliffs down into the valley. Before her, mountains rose into shifting clouds. There was nothing Glademont lacked, nothing her lands could not grow, nowhere her people could not thrive. This land was a paradise, given to Glademont's people by the stars themselves. They had a right to defend it. What was it Osiris had said? To be civilized is to protect the home as a sacred thing.

At the far end of the plains loomed Innkeeper Cliffs, the only place where Nabal's army might be stopped by so small a force. Beyond that waited the last stand of the Dione of Glademont: a dying queen and her trapped nobles, praying to the skies for a miracle. Tess was praying, too. Praying Irgo the mother star would strengthen her, so she could be that miracle.

CHAPTER 42

It was already afternoon when Currant's forces set a hard pace northward on the main road, along the western outskirts of the plains. By the time the sun disappeared beneath the Hinge treetops, they had covered a lot of ground—more than the Atheonians could, lugging their cargo. Within an hour from the northern edge of the valley, Tess could just make out the flames that dotted the road that wound along the face of Innkeeper Cliffs.

"Campfires," Linden said. "They've stopped for the night. Must not have seen us yet. Or else, they don't think we're a threat."

"We need rest, sire," Asher grunted. "Traveled hard over this ways not one day ago, and fought into the morning. Wallaton's as good a spot as any."

"We can make camp at Wallaton"—Linden frowned at the fires above them—"but sleep may be out of the question."

Asher dismissed him with his staff. "Already taken care of, sire. Our people are hiding in them cliffs, and we've got methods for slowing down enemies."

Linden and Tess exchanged looks.

"If we can take them on the cliffs," Currant said, "they'll still be twice our number, plus stars know how many hounds."

"We have our bondfellows," Tess said.

"But do these animals *know* they can use golden magic?" Pipe asked as he kept pace with Currant. "I'm not sure most of them even believe in it." The snow-white ram glanced about and lowered his voice. "Truthfully, I am nervous myself as to whether I'll be able to use it, when the time comes."

Tess looked behind her at the throng of loyal animals. There was so much potential among them, so much power to be unleashed. It occurred to her that these creatures needed a teacher, someone familiar with the fellowship, who could prove to them that their oaths really *meant* something. She looked down at the coarse white mane in her hands.

"Jesse," she said softly. "You could teach them to use golden magic, couldn't you?"

"I have wielded it once, my lady, when your mother and I were young ones," Jesse said.

"A good idea," Pipe said. "The Rushing gave us a few pointers back at the Birch Grove. Won't you teach us properly, Rushing? Even the horns of a dall ram can't fend off an arrow."

The Rushing's tail brushed Tess's back as he thought a moment. "When we make camp at Wallaton, I will prepare the animals, as you request."

"Thank you, Jesse," Linden and Tess said at once.

The town of Wallaton stretched among the firs and up onto the lower ledges of the cliffs in a diagonal line. Its villagers had abandoned their huts, boarding up the doors and windows. The only cabin lit from within stood atop a hill at the foot of the village, which Asher claimed as his own.

The footsore Glademontians set up camp just before the main road snaked onto the rock of the cliff face. Atheonian fires winked above them, a constant reminder of their task. Currant volunteered to aid Jesse in training the bondfellows, which left Tess and Linden to follow Asher across the pine needles to his home.

Asher's long cabin on the hill seemed like many others Tess had seen along the main road. Its low roof was made of thatch and steeply pitched. A small covered pen had been built to protect a goat herd from predators, though not a goat was left in it now. They had either joined the FOM or been taken somewhere safe from the invaders. Tess climbed the stone path that led to the cabin's deep-set door. A little girl appeared and rushed to squeeze Asher's legs. Her blond curls were greasier now, and she sported a long red line from her temple to her neck, but Tess knew her immediately.

"All right." Asher grunted as he patted her yellow head. "This is my granddaughter, Belle. Been with me ever since the bandits come."

Tess knelt in front of the girl.

"Do you remember me?" she whispered, pained. The last time she had seen Belle, she was holding her mother's hand. They were walking back to Wallaton on the night of the first attacks. Tess swallowed, remembering how in her thoughtlessness she had stepped on Belle while they were dancing.

Belle's lip quivered. "Fyrian, the dryad." Her small fluty voice struck Tess clean through.

Asher's hand grasped Belle's shoulder and he sucked air through his teeth.

"Yer the one," he said. "Lady Tessamine, the dancer that Belle . . . she went to see yeh that night, my daughter and her." His coarse beard lifted as his mouth twisted in anger. "She was killed, you know. My girl was killed on her way home. Belle left to hide in the thickets until I come for her."

"I assure you, I . . . I didn't know. . . ." The breath left Tess's lungs. Linden stepped forward.

"Mister Candlestock, we've all had an abyss of a week. Atheos is to blame, not this lady."

Asher snarled and stepped into his cabin, holding Belle's hand. "No, the royals are never to blame," he muttered.

A speechless Tess followed, with Wyndeling on her shoulder. Inside, Asher threw off his coat. It fell onto a scarlet-and-mustard rug at the center of the square cabin. He lowered himself to a bench, facing the fire and a pot of hot water. A worktable with baskets of unspun wool sat in the left-hand corner, adjacent to a large old loom. To the right, Tess spotted a washroom and bedroom. Though she longed to lock herself in the washroom and out of Asher's sight, she went to sit at the loom and look out the window at the creaking pines.

Linden accepted a cup of hot tea from Belle and ran a hand over his forehead.

"How many did you count? Four hundred?" he said.

Asher nodded, staring into the fire. "Thereabouts."

"Our forces make up less than half of that," Linden said.

"Our odds'll improve when those soldiers breathe in the cliff laurel. They'll be needing to tend to their sick." His tone was still unfriendly.

"Cliff laurel?" Linden asked.

Asher pointed above their heads, where an assortment of herbs hung on hooks from the ceiling. Tess recognized all of them except one—a thick tangle of a vine with small rounded leaves and bright white flowers in bunches.

"Our women brew a toxin yeh set on the wind. We use it to fend off mountain lions. A couple whiffs's enough to have yeh on your knees for hours." Asher clasped his hands over his staff and scowled, his dark lips pushing out.

"It won't make the women sick?" Linden said.

"Wallaton women ain't never been sick," Asher snapped. "But even the best of them can't stop a knife—" He cut off, looking at his granddaughter settling by the fire with Pipe. Then Asher's hooded eyes hovered on Tess.

"She is not to blame, Candlestock," Linden said.

"Oh?" Asher stood and approached Linden, talking low. "Does the lady know what price there is to pay to be princess? My Belle surely don't, though the lady makes it look so easy."

"I do not understand you," Linden said. Tess saw his hands clench then relax. He was wondering the same thing she was: Did he know about the *shenil*?

"I had a sister once," Asher said. "She knew nothing of the royal life, loved to be a shepherdess with all her heart. But then they come calling, and it seemed the prince wanted her hand. She didn't want to go, sire. She cried and cried, thinkin' if she didn't accept, she'd put herself to shame. She left us and went up the cliffs to live in the castle. I never saw her again."

"Speak plainly, Mister Candlestock."

"All right, Highness; I will. You weren't never told about yer Uncle Clove? Clove Asher Candlestock?"

Linden sputtered. "My mother's brother . . . ?"

"Never said we was from Wallaton, did she?"

"Yes, but . . . well, she never spoke of you." Linden's astonishment seemed only to embitter the goatherd all the more.

"I never set foot in that castle," Asher said. "All this nonsense about our starlit Commoner Queens? What was the point of ripping my sister away from me? We were happy here, because we kept to ourselves. But then, Belle went to see the lady's dancing . . . first in Redfoot, then—" He couldn't go on. He marched away from Linden, consoling himself by the stone hearth again. He rubbed his jaw and looked over to Belle, who had fallen asleep in the crook of Pipe's woolly neck.

Then he turned to Linden with glistening eyes. He swept a disdainful hand at Tess. "My sister, gone, so some prince could have his way. My daughter, gone, paying her respects to the next generation of the heartless Crown. By the skies, I thought I could stomach it to take down those Atheonians. But I can't stand to have you two loomin' in my house."

Linden glowered. "Mister Candlestock, you are wrong to group all royalty together into some kind of compassionless brood. My father loved my mother more than any man has loved his bride. If my mother gave up a life in Wallaton to serve as queen, it was surely her free choice. Moreover, though I mourn for your losses, *this* lady"— he pointed at Tess—"cannot be blamed for your misfortunes. That I cannot allow." He ran a hand over his matted hair. "Right," he said, seemingly surprised to have the attention of the room. "This war with Atheos depends entirely on Tess, and our support of her."

"Your Highness—" Tess stood, eyes wide. What was he doing?

"She carries the key to our victory, and her safety *happens* to be in the interest of those who reside in Glademont Castle, but also to you, sir. And all creatures of the valley."

"Your Highness, you must not—"

"What—what does she carry?" Asher's eyes darted to Tess, anxiety covering his face.

Tess felt a rush of panic and involuntarily scooped the *shenil* into her hands. Fyrian's voice sprang to her mind, telling her to remain Glademont's unseen guardian. How could she know when to share her burden and when to conceal it?

It was the burden itself that answered Tess's doubts. It warmed in her hands, its light barely visible inside her palm. The tips of Tess's fingers tingled as she pulled her cloak around her, wondering where to begin.

"There is a magician," she said, "who started this war, because he desires this object." Tess unthreaded the *shenil* from her twine belt and held it for Asher to see.

Asher eyed it scrupulously. He lowered himself onto the bench.

"It's the only thing that can stop him." Tess swallowed. Asher stared in bewilderment as she pressed the ends of the *shenil* into her palm. "It was forged so there would always be someone to overcome red magic."

Asher looked from Linden to Tess, his forearms pressing against his thighs. "If it's as powerful as that, how do we know this isn't more evil magic?"

Tess took a deep breath and stepped around the bench to where Belle lay on Pipe, an arm span from the fire. Slowly, she held out her hands in imitation of the Thane's Hold. The golden orbs snapped into a bright glow, hovering above her palms. With a loud *crack*, the flames from the hearth began to twist and swirl before her, their orange color turning more and more to white. The shape of a slender hand appeared amid the white tongues and reached toward little Belle.

"No." Asher lunged for his granddaughter.

But the white hand was already stroking her face, tracing the long wound that marred it. Then, in the blink of an eye, the hearth fire glowed its familiar orange again, the white hand was gone, and Tess threaded the *shenil* about her waist.

"What sorcery is this?" Asher rocked Belle against his chest.

"She's all right, she is perfect. Look," Tess said.

When the shepherd finally unfolded his arms to see the girl, she was wide awake and smiling.

"Your face," he whispered.

Belle covered her cheek with her hands and tried to wriggle out of Asher's arms.

"No, no. It is perfect. Just as the lady says."

Tess knelt beside Asher and stroked Belle's curls. "I don't know what would happen if Pider ever came to possess the *shenil*, but if he is as powerful as I think he is, not even the bondfellowship could protect us then."

From the corner of her eye, Tess saw Linden watching her. She could tell from the stillness of his body that he was thinking seriously on something. When she ventured to look, she could not read his eyes. He breathed through his nose, looking her all over. What was he deciding?

Then, Currant's antlered head appeared at the door. "Your Highness, if I could borrow you a moment . . . ?" He looked around the tense room.

"Excuse me, please." Hoisting his longbow, Linden bowed and followed his friend outside. As Tess listened to the thudding of his footsteps, something told her to follow.

Tess smoothed the wisps of her hair around her face as she excused herself from Asher's cabin.

Wyndeling glided behind her and perched on a pine branch.

"My lady," she said, "hadn't you better sleep?"

"I don't think I could." Tess touched her engagement pearls. "I'll see how Jesse is doing. Don't worry about me." She hurried down the straw-covered hill.

At the foot of the hill, Tess avoided the murmuring valley creatures, none of whom seemed able to sleep themselves. She veered left, away from the road, and noticed some gathering taking place under a gigantic, wide-reaching cedar. Its exposed roots snaked from the ground to its trunk like dark noodles from a giant's pot. Catching sight of Linden and Currant walking toward the cedar, Tess retreated to the shadows, watching from a short distance.

"Prince Linden," came the young, comforting voice of Jesse the Rushing, "your friend has something to ask of you." The horse's white mane and tail seemed to glow in the moonlight as he faced an excited knot of men and animals.

"Er, yes." Currant faced the prince of Glademont. "Well, I've decided . . . it's just that I think I had better be your bondfellow."

Linden stared at Currant, and then at Jesse. Then a bashful grin crept across his face.

"No polite way to refuse, I should think." He clapped Currant's neck. "I'd be honored."

Currant led Linden to a row of hooved and horned animals standing in front of their corresponding shepherds and breeders. They joined the ranks, and all eyes fell on Jesse.

"Creatures who enter into the fellowship commit their lives." Jesse's voice rang out in the night wind. "Person and animal must protect the good of the other, and keep the other from harm and from corruption. Creatures who wish to make such an oath, step forward."

Goats, sheep, ponies, and Currant all stepped forward.

"Untamed: Do you pledge to assist your persons, in whatever goodly quest, until death?" Jesse boomed.

Tess shivered with anticipation as the ancient words echoed against the cliffs.

"I do," many voices called out, some more confidently than others.

"Then persons step forward, seal the oath with the bondfellow's consent."

Some of the older men came forward first. They turned their backs to the cedar so that they faced the untamed, and the younger men—including Linden—followed suit. Once all were in place, one of the experienced men bowed to his animal. Tess held her breath as his mountain goat gracefully lowered her head and forelegs in turn. Then the entire row of animals joined in the humble pose.

An image suddenly surfaced in Tess's memory. She thought of the statue of Rosemary the lynx, which had raised the bridge over Ruby Creek. She, too, was depicted in this pose—the bondfellow's consent.

"May the gift of goodly powers and long life be bestowed on each of you. You are now members of the bondfellowship."

The men and animals paused in disbelief, looking from Jesse to each other. It was so simple, so brief, some of the men started laughing. A lifetime of self-giving, and all it took was a word and a bow. Tess understood now how people had forgotten the sacredness of the oath since Osiris's time. Then again, she knew that night was different. That night, every creature who walked from under that cedar knew his oath would soon be put to the test.

Another hour remained before the prescribed time of departure, and the members of the FOM, each according to his way, prepared themselves for the steep journey ahead.

Tess wandered the camp, watching bondfellows practicing their positions and concentrating their efforts. Without real danger, none of them would know how the golden magic would respond, not until the battle was upon them. Their human counterparts watched with amusement and shouted out words of encouragement, while many of the older men and animals slept.

Eventually, Tess returned to Asher's cabin, pondering why the *shenil* had not chosen someone like her elder sister, Dahly, as the thane. Dahly never let fear get the better of her, never wavered in her convictions. And when she set her mind to do something, nothing could stop her. Tess, on the other hand, couldn't get through a single day without questioning everything.

She shuffled to Asher's loom, lonely and pensive.

Asher appeared from the bedroom. "I thought yeh might be wanting these." The hardened shepherd held a bundle of clothes. He passed a hand over his thin hair. "They were my daughter's, years ago."

Tess looked down at her thin cotton nightgown, covered in blood, dirt, and horsehair.

"Belle's gone to find some proper boots for yeh, too."

"Thank you. For everything." Tess curtsied and took her new clothes into the washroom. She rinsed the dust and sweat from her body. The icy water sent goose bumps down her limbs. She bound a clean strip of linen around the bite marks on her forearm.

Their lives depend on you, she told the flushed face and wild black hair in the glass. It was hard to believe that a week ago, she believed herself worthy of Linden, worthy of ruling. She smoothed her thick eyebrows with a moistened thumb, but it didn't make any difference. Tess's time in the forest had beaten all the polish out of her. The young woman in the mirror looked more like the untamed animals of the Hinge than the guardian of Glademont. Tess pulled her chafed, blistered feet from her riding boots and she suddenly felt very small. What could she do against a magician? Against an army?

Tess untied the bundle of clothes. The creamy long-sleeved shirt fit perfectly, and when she fastened the ankle-length skirt around her waist, she felt warmer than she had been in days. She sat on the floor, pulled the thick stockings over her feet, and hugged her arms while quiet tears landed on her knees.

Belle knocked meekly on the door and handed Tess thick leather shoes that laced over the ankles. Tess smiled gratefully. The shoes made her feel sturdier. She requested a belt as well, and in her own little ritual, she kissed the golden orbs of the *shenil*, pinched the medal with her forefinger and thumb, and wrapped the strap around the belt at her hip.

When Linden returned to the cabin, Asher excused himself to tuck Belle in before departing. Tess sat alone in her fresh clothes, pretending to stoke the fire.

"Well, look who makes a fine Wallaton woman," Linden said.

Tess prodded at the charred wood. Linden joined her on the bench, took the stoker from her hand, and laid it against the hearth.

"May I . . . may I speak with you?" he said.

"Of course," Tess whispered, afraid her voice would shake if she spoke any louder.

"You've been keeping something from me. I don't know for how long. But, if we are to . . . *should* we keep secrets from each other?"

Tess's lips parted, not knowing what to say or how to begin. He took her hands firmly in his.

"Don't you trust me, Tess?" Linden's eyes searched her face. Tess could feel her palms moisten, and she fought the urge to run.

Asher's sudden, heavy footsteps startled them apart. He coughed unnecessarily.

"We'd better be off now."

"Right," Linden said.

They stood, and Tess's green-orange eyes glistened at Linden's profile. He turned, catching her glance.

"I pray you will confide in me," he said softly. "I wish to earn back your trust, my lady."

Tess forced a smile, unable to keep herself from twisting her engagement pearls around her finger. If the prince saw, he did not show it.

At the foot of the hill, Currant had already begun to assemble the company. Forty-five Wallatonian men and thirty woolly animals waited for Asher as he descended from his cabin with Tess and Linden. Beside these stood sixty-five horsemen and breeders, accompanied by forty-five of their prized ponies, with Shila and Abe at the head.

"Friends of the Militia, it is time to overtake the battering ram upon the cliffs," Linden commanded. "Foggy Plains, with me."

"Aye," Asher added. "And Wallaton folk, into the cliffs with me." He raised his staff and began to skirt the hill toward the cliffs, away from the main road. "Come now, Miss Tessamine," he called.

"Keep safe, my lady," Linden said before joining Currant. The creatures of Foggy Plains followed, marching toward the main road. Tess looked about and found Jesse cantering toward her.

"Jesse, don't leave me again." Tess tucked her hand under Jesse's mane and rested her forehead against his neck.

"Remain in hope. I will see you soon." Jesse's whipped his tail.

"Hurry, miss," Asher called out. "The dawn won't wait for us."

Jesse nuzzled her neck, then joined the ponies out of the old firs and onto the road.

As Tess mechanically followed Asher and the cliffdwellers, she wondered how she would bear what was to come without anyone she knew from home. Even more frightening was the realization that if she ever wanted to see them safe again, Pider had to be stopped.

Then Wyndeling swooped to her shoulder. The unexpected weight set Tess off balance.

"Apologies, my lady. I took the liberty of a quick hunt." Wyndeling paused, and Tess could feel the owl studying her. "Are you well, my lady?"

"It's up to me to stop this war," Tess said. "And I'm afraid I will fail." She looked over her shoulder for a glimpse of Linden.

"Perhaps you would fail if you were on your own, my lady," Wyndeling said soberly. "But, if I may say so, you will always have me."

CHAPTER 43

"This way," Asher beckoned his charges to the sheer face of the cliffs where the fir trees ended and rock began. "Into the tunnel yeh go. Keep your voices low; the echoes carry."

"Oh, for mercy's sake; more tunnels," Wyndeling groaned as Tess followed the rest of the Wallatonians into a narrow fissure dug out of the rock.

Pipe sauntered cheerily alongside them. "Some of these have been around since before Glademont's time. There've been cliffdwellers living here since, well, since the beginning of Diatonica."

"It must have taken years to build," Tess said, gazing at the dense rock.

"Patience runs in a cliffdweller's blood—that is, for most of us." Pipe cocked his head toward the fearsome mountain goat to his right.

"Hah," Tartan cried. "I'll tell you what impatient means. To the cowardly, it means young and stupid. To the courageous, it means hungry for justice."

Pipe slipped Tess a knowing wink.

The tunnel took a sharp turn, and the Wallaton warriors padded along just inside the face of the cliffs. Long slivers cut into the outer wall allowed the starlight in.

Half an hour passed, and the men and animals ahead stopped. Before them rose a pile of rubble, blocking the way forward. To Tess's surprise, rams and ewes leapt up the jumble of fallen rock as easily as one ambles through a garden path. More surprising than this was the ease with which their shepherds scaled the same rocks. Even Asher scampered up the blockage like a squirrel on a trunk.

"Here," said gentle Pipe to Tess. "Grab hold of my horns."

Tess obeyed, grasping each of Pipe's sturdy, curling horns. Slowly, the ram pulled Tess up the shifting rocks. More than once she slipped and had to place all of her weight on Pipe's head and neck. But the young ram proved solid as an oak. The pair reached the peak of the rubble, and as Pipe lifted his head, Tess was forced to stand up straight. Blinking, she found herself eye level with the worn leather boots of several Wallatonian shepherds. Asher's strong arms lifted her out of the hole she was peering out of, and soon Tess stood in another tunnel.

They scaled four more mounds of loose rock. Each time, Tess felt she would twist an ankle if not for her sturdy boots. When the company finally reached the fifth tier of the tunnels, the glow of predawn crept through the slits in the rock. Tess was beginning to sweat under her cotton shirt, and the cold snap of the morning felt good on her face.

A hush came over the shepherds and their bondfellows, and Tess noticed the men crouching to avoid the slivered openings in the tunnel wall. The distinctive western accent of an Atheonian soldier suddenly cut the stillness.

"Had to get out of there. That foul smell will stay with me till my dying days, mark you."

Tess and the cliffdwellers froze.

"My throat'll feel like sand for a month," answered another voice.

The footsteps of the two men faded into the distance, and Tess tiptoed to an opening in the rock. She could just make out the men as they headed back to a cluster of Atheonian soldiers, packed tight along the main road. Many bent over with compresses to their heads. Because of the sharp bend in the road, Tess couldn't tell how many men there were, but she heard the baying of hounds.

"We're close." Asher handed Tess a strip of burlap. "It'll keep yeh from gettin' ill."

Tess tied the rough cloth across her mouth and nose.

"No, thank you very much," Wyndeling hissed as she watched Tess tie her makeshift breathing mask.

"Oh, for pity's sake. This is no time to be vain." Tess tied it about the red owl's beak.

The first shafts of soft pink sunlight streaked across the tunnel. Tess felt the golden ends of the *shenil* gently bumping against her side as she waited for their next move. Then a dozen women appeared, threading between the men and animals and carrying heavy buckets. Their long hair, twisted in cloth, wound about their necks like scarves. They grinned to themselves as they snaked between the creatures of the FOM.

Even through her burlap mask, the smell of the cliff laurel seeped into Tess's nostrils. It tasted thick and sour on the back of her tongue, and she felt her knees go weak. A passing woman forced Tess's chin down to her chest and pressed a thumb hard against the base of her skull. When Tess's legs felt solid again, she whispered her thanks. The woman winked and continued on.

The buckets of cliff laurel were soon gone and Tess untied the burlap from her face. Wyndeling had tumbled to the floor and was swaying precariously on her talons.

Ahead, the sheep and goats gathered to one side of a large opening in the rock, through which a ghostly sky was visible. Behind the animals, shepherds gripped their staffs. Tess slipped to another window, and through it saw more Atheonians. The soldiers differed from bandits—clean-shaven and dressed in smart military uniforms. Those who had sashes around their waists also carried elegant swords.

A goatherd spotted Tess. "Get down."

Tess tiptoed back to the far wall and waited in silence.

"Lieutenant, are we ready to proceed?" The voice from outside the tunnel wall was unmistakable—Tynaiv. Tess's knees felt weak again. "Fall in, men. If I see you slacking, I'm not above kicking you off this cliff."

The blast of a shepherd's horn reverberated throughout the tunnel, jarring as a rooster's crow. Asher leapt into the tunnel opening, his staff resting upon the great slab of stone. In his other hand, he blew through a hollowed-out ram's horn, while the mighty herd of bondfellows thundered past, spilling onto the main road.

"Bondfellows first," Asher shouted as his kinsmen passed. "Separate men from hounds. Isolate the battering ram. Move, Wallaton."

Tess watched, her leather boots pasted to the stone floor, her limbs unresponsive.

"Well, for pity's sake," Wyndeling cried. "What are we waiting for?"

"Linden, he . . . he told me to keep safe."

"Yes, well, my mother told me never to talk to humans, and look where we are. Come, Lady Tessamine. I could never face Buchanan again if he learned I hid in a tunnel while domesticated animals fought in my stead."

With that, Wyndeling darted out and sank her long talons into the visage of an Atheonian soldier. Tess inched forward, watching with fearful admiration as Pipe evaded the thrust of an officer's sword, spun about, and kicked the man clear over the edge of the cliffs.

But the shepherds struggled to make headway. Despite the Atheonians' night of nausea, they carried real weapons. Their swords and knives splintered Wallatonian staffs, and the battering ram was out of reach, high on the road and surrounded by a wall of men.

The mountain animals began to separate from their men, pushing down the road where a dense pack of hounds waited behind a team of bandits. The goats and sheep had not yet tried golden magic, their imposing muscles and rock-hard skulls being sufficient for twenty untrained bandits. The hounds watched, barking and howling with anticipation. But when the bandits had been scattered, and the Wallatonian animals found themselves face to face with the hounds of Atheos, a new kind of battle began.

Fat strands of glowing red streaked from the foremost hounds' jowls. A dozen mountain sheep struggled to breathe as the magical ropes constricted their necks. A bandit ran his blade through a suffocating ewe. Sneering, more bandits moved to do the same.

Tartan gathered himself first, planting his hooves in the ground, snorting, and sending a rippling stream of gold toward an unsuspecting hound. The stream rose up into a pair of straight, ribbed horns. The hound stared mutely at the shimmering horns as they thrust into him like lances.

The hound's blood spilled onto the main road, and one of the sheep cried out in relief, for the red rope had disappeared from her neck. With fire in their bones, the cliffdwellers planted their hooves and lowered their powerful heads.

While the bondfellows flexed their golden muscles, the Atheonian soldiers faced off with the men of Wallaton. The shepherds joined in circular formations, facing outward so no soldier could come close without a staff's crack to the head. Forty shepherds spun and batted at soldiers, trying everything they could to get to the battering ram.

Still hiding in the Wallatonian tunnel, Tess strained to see the great instrument of war. It looked to her like a colossal parade float, but instead of festive colors and confetti, it sported long strips of thick leather. The weapon rode on rough wooden wheels the height of two men. At its far end glinted the bronze head of a rhinoceros, haughty and wrathful. Tess's chest tightened as she thought of her beloved Redfoot, smoldering and desolate. She thought of the peace that was lost, and her blood boiled.

Tess discovered the *shenìl* was already in her hands, and a sizzling flame burned between them. To her left, golden magic clashed with red as rams fought snarling hounds. To her right, shepherds wielded their staffs against a constant tide of Atheonian soldiers. Beyond this, Tess spotted a team of archers stationed all over the battering ram, sending arrows amid the Wallatonians, and the fighting circles of shepherds shrank by the second.

Tess stood on the edge of it all, her black hair swirling and her face glowing in the light of her own flame.

Leap out.

Tess heard that familiar voice. She took a step backward and sprang into the air, her long legs stretching in a graceful jeté.

Time slowed almost to a halt, and Tess saw arrows spinning in place all around her. Then she was rising, passing the arrows, gliding in midair. Her feet swept over the heads of hundreds of frozen soldiers, ascending up over the main road. She reached the battering ram and landed on the road with a shudder. Invisible rings radiated from her toes like ripples in water.

The rings expanded in an instant, overthrowing every Atheonian foot and paw, from the archers on the ram to the hounds below.

"To the battering ram," Tartan cried.

Some animals formed a wide golden shield, blocking the hounds. The rest charged behind Tartan, and the shepherds tore through the ranks of fallen Atheonians. Reaching the battering ram, the mountain goats and rams squared their horned heads against the frame and lunged with all their strength.

"Send it to the valley, cliffdwellers," Pipe called.

The solid wood creaked. The rhinoceros head swayed reluctantly. But the structure would not yield.

The fallen Atheonians began to recover their footing.

"We'll never tip it this way," Asher cried as he sidestepped the blade of an Atheonian officer, bringing his staff down between the man's shoulders.

Tess's heart pounded against her chest as she grasped the ends of her trinket with each hand. Obeying the promptings of the voice only she could hear, she raised her hands so the medal of the *shenil* dangled above her forehead. A funnel of shimmering air began to twirl about the battering ram, scattering Atheonians and cliffdwellers alike. The mighty battering ram began to turn.

A man's hand clamped around Tess's throat, his arm pinned against her chest.

"Put it back," Tynaiv purred in Tess's ear.

Tess fell to her knees as she tried to wriggle free, and the magic whirlwind thinned. His hand stayed about her throat. She felt the prick of a blade against her lower back, and she froze.

Asher lunged forward. "Not another step, good citizen," Tynaiv said. He was kneeling behind her. He spoke in her ear again. "Tess, the battering ram. Put it back."

"I can't," she said, gasping.

"Do it, please." She heard his breath quicken.

Tess did her best to keep calm as she felt the trickle of warm blood seep into her cotton shirt. "I do what *it* tells *me*. Not the other way around."

"All this for a toy that won't let you play with it," Tynaiv muttered. "Lower your hands, then," He forced Tess to arch her back with his cold blade.

She lowered her arms, hanging the *shenil* on her belt. The winds vanished.

"Your attention, please." Tynaiv pulled Tess to her feet, his knife never leaving her back. "I assume this lady is important to you all, as she is to me. Allow my men to pass, and she will live. Harm one more of my company, and her life is forfeit."

Asher squeezed his shepherd's staff with trembling hands. "Let her go, and we will let you and your company retreat unharmed."

"No such luck." Tess could hear the flippant smile on the sailor's lips. "We have spotted your comrades coming up the road."

Asher's face contorted. Nearby, Tartan bobbed his head with a threatening grunt.

"No," Tynaiv continued, "you cease fighting while we carry on up the cliffs. Rebel, and your most powerful weapon will perish." He nudged the knife farther, and Tess cried out in pain.

Tartan pawed at the earth. His horizontal eyes were wild. "Don't let him take another step."

But Asher did not move. He gazed with agony on Tess's face. She tried to hide the pain caused by Tynaiv's unrelenting hand.

"Very good." Tynaiv slowly led Tess away, his back to the rocks. "Sands Tribe, with the battering ram, if you please. Horns, you're with me as well. Javas, escort our guests to the hounds and wait for their friends from Foggy Plains. Let's use the red stuff only for the ram, nothing else. Keep things civil, now."

Those who belonged to the Sands Tribe assumed positions around the battering ram and ordered their hounds to reorient it. Bundle after bundle of glowing red ropes slung across the body of the ram. It dug small craters in the dust as it righted itself on the road. The weapon lurched forward, and more men took up the rear, including a few archers who padded backward, their arrows notched and ready.

"You've done your best," Tynaiv called, forcing Tess to walk with the archers. "Go home now. After all, whom do you defend but the royals safe in their castle? Where were they when we stormed on Redfoot? Eh?"

Madly, Tess searched the skies for Wyndeling. Tynaiv's knife found a new spot to pierce, and fresh blood soaked her shirt. She watched her friends disappear behind a bend in the road, and then she was alone with Tynaiv.

CHAPTER 44

Tess clutched her *shenil* while a mass of Atheonian soldiers and a handful of bandits kicked up the fine dirt around her. They had been marching all morning up the cliffs, leaving Tess's friends farther and farther behind.

Come on, concentrate, she urged herself. Tynaiv had let her walk freely, the end of his officer's sword always within striking distance, and she had tried in vain to communicate with the *shenil*. Each time she strove to surrender as Ember had taught her, nothing happened. Now she marched to Glademont Castle not as a guardian, but as a prisoner.

"It wasn't too long ago I became acquainted with your betrothed in a manner such as this." Tynaiv thrust his sword in the air. "I regret to say, my opinion of him did not improve."

Tess closed her eyes and took a deep breath. The first mode of surrender: confident obedience to the *shenil*.

"Incidentally, what did he think of our rendezvous in the forest? Jealous, I'll wager," he mocked.

The second mode of surrender: forgetfulness of self. Oh, why wouldn't he shut up?

"I'd guess the prince is a very good *reader*," Tynaiv said, amusing himself. "Top notch at recitations, hmm?"

"Yes," she answered. "Just last night he read me a poem. What was it, 'The Tale of the Rat from Talon'?"

Tynaiv stepped in front of her and put his sword to her collar. "I gave you a chance to come willingly, remember? To surrender that wretched thing so there would be no war. You chose this for yourself."

She searched his face, unbelieving. "How do you change so easily? You allowed my escape. You made me . . ." Tess paused. "You made me believe you cared for me."

Tynaiv lowered his sword. The skin beneath his eyes reflected a dull, dark purple. "And yet, you made no sign you cared for me," he said sharply.

Tess found it suddenly difficult to breathe. He lowered his gaze.

Tynaiv softened. "Remember the first time I saw you, at the festival?"

The third mode of surrender—Tess gritted her teeth and started to walk again—let go of what you want to happen in the future.

"You were so proud and fine, already drinking in the privileges of your position," Tynaiv said, following closely. "But you aren't the same girl now. Dressed like a common villager and joining up with goatherds."

Tess heard Tynaiv pause. She turned, and he pointed at her with the sword. "You remind me . . . you look like the village girls from Talon dressed like that. If I didn't know any better, I'd say you've had a healthy dose of reality down with the little people, Tess." The dimple in his scruff appeared, and he looked her up and down.

"The only little person I have ever met is you," Tess snapped. "Men like Asher are courageous and loyal. You are courageous only in the dark, and loyal only to yourself."

Suddenly, violently, Tynaiv pulled Tess toward him by her arm. "You want me to prove myself to you? You want some kind of grand gesture?"

By now, Tynaiv and his army had reached the top of the cliffs, where Nobleman's Road intersected with the main road. Glademont Castle lay visible in the distance. And while the men came to an uneasy halt, Tynaiv stood among them, gripping Tess's arm.

"Lieutenant Pilt," Tynaiv called to one of his soldiers. The lieutenant trotted up from among the Sands. Tess didn't like his guarded expression.

"For King Nabal, till death, General," he muttered with a half-hearted salute.

Tynaiv patted the lieutenant's shoulder. "This lady will give you a very valuable bauble. I want you to keep it safe, and when you present it to Nabal, he will reward you handsomely."

"*This* is your grand gesture?" Tess tried to shove Tynaiv away, but his hand clasped fast about her arm.

"Give it to him, Tess, and I'll let you go. I swear it," he whispered inches from her face. "I'll meet you. Back in the Hinge. Under the sugar maple . . ." He held her there, blue eyes watering and sun-tanned arms flinching.

"You're afraid of it, aren't you?" she shot back. "You should be."

"Gladly, General." Pilt pulled a deadly hatchet from a holster. He grinned at Tess.

"Stand down, Lieutenant." Tynaiv pointed a finger at Pilt.

"You're nothing but a cowardly barnacle," Pilt said. "Leaching wherever you land. I know your game, friend. You want me to do the dirty work, and you'll take credit." He twirled the hatchet. "You never come right out and say what you're doing, do you, General? Come now, Lady Tresseme. Let us see this bauble." Pilt gathered Tess's loose hair in his fist. She pressed the *shenil* against her stomach, pulling away from him. Tynaiv retreated.

"You don't know what you are doing, Atheonian," she cried.

Pilt yanked her head backward, and Tess felt her neck might break. He pushed a knee into the small of her back, forcing her to the ground. From behind, he slid the blade of his hatchet under her hands so the orbs of the *shenil* rested on the shining metal. The surrounding men cheered, calling for her blood. Pilt released Tess's hair to reach for the object in her hands.

"No," she screamed.

Pilt's fingers grasped the copper orbs, and Tess felt a jolt of heat surge through her body and into her hands. The *shenil* remained cold and dull. But Pilt stumbled backward, yelling in fear.

"Argh . . ." He groaned and swung his arms. "My eyes!"

Tess kicked the inside of the lieutenant's knee, laying him flat. Then, an earsplitting cry of anguish tore through the air. Terrified,

Tess scrambled to her feet and saw an Atheonian soldier lying in the road next to Pilt, a painted arrow through his heart.

"We're under attack," cried Tynaiv's men.

Tess scanned the ranks behind her and thought she saw a flash of gold.

"They've come up the cliffs," said an officer as he drew his sword.

In an instant, heavy arms encircled Tess and tossed her in the air. Tynaiv threw Tess over his broad shoulder and ran between his own men, away from the cliffs.

"Formation around the battering ram. Archers, make for those boulders and bring the animals down first. No prisoners." He continued sprinting through the ranks, away from the fray.

Tess tried to scream for help, but his shoulder jabbed so violently into her stomach, she could hardly keep from vomiting. Atheonians scattered all around Tess as she fought for one breath, then another. She heard a beautiful sound in the distance—the shrieking whinnies of ponies and the rowdy cries of horse breeders. With every ounce of her strength, Tess fought against Tynaiv's grip to watch the battle behind her.

Then Tess saw them.

A magnificent cantering elk stag carrying a rider with a longbow emerged from the dust. They took the road, passing Atheonians on both sides. The elk blasted archers with spells from his nose and mouth while the rider kept his next arrow fixed on one target alone: Tynaiv.

"Halt, foreigner," Linden commanded when they finally gained on Tess and her captor.

Tynaiv swung around, flinging Tess to the ground. She rolled in the dirt and landed on her back. The clear sky seemed to spin, and Tess couldn't find her voice to call out to Linden.

"I warned you, General." Linden leapt from Currant's back. "I said if you hurt her, your blood would be mine by rights."

"Who, this lady?" Tynaiv studied the prone Tess like a botanist with a bloom. "She looks all right to me," he said, drawing his sword from his waist. "A little soap, maybe . . ."

With fists clenched and face flushed, Linden charged at Tynaiv, who nimbly stepped aside. Linden stumbled but managed to pivot. He swung on Tynaiv, his fist landing squarely on the sailor's ear. Tynaiv fell and his sword flew from his hand.

Linden stood over him, waiting.

"Oh, I see." Tynaiv spat the soil from his mouth. "An honor code? Bad manners to kick a man on all fours?"

"Maybe." Linden flexed his bruised hand. "Or maybe I'd like to watch you fall again."

He stooped to grab Tynaiv's shirt, and Tynaiv kicked Linden in the ribs with surprising speed. Two blows to the side, and Tess could hear the crack of bones. Linden doubled over, gasping.

"Now would be a fair time to inform you"—Tynaiv got to his feet—"I adhere to no such code." He drove a knee against Linden's chest and sent him sprawling.

Currant leapt forward, planting himself between the rivals.

"I could kill you just as easily as I did those hounds on the cliffs," he warned.

Tynaiv kept his eyes locked on Currant as he took a cautious step toward Linden. "I've made a living of being underestimated, my friend."

Tess finally found her breath again. She managed to pluck Tynaiv's sword from the ground.

"You are surrounded, Tynaiv." Tess dug Tynaiv's sword none too gently into his back. Tynaiv did not move.

Then, out of the midday sky came the humming of arrows. Dozens of them sank into the ground all around Tess's feet, and one arrow glanced against Currant's antlers and slashed Tess's side. Crying out, she dropped the sword.

Linden rose to his feet and dove for the sword. "Get back to the FOM, Currant," he commanded with difficulty, grasping the Atheonian weapon. "Stop the battering ram."

Currant paused as another volley of arrows shot over their heads. The clamor of battle had reached them. Despite the efforts of the FOM, the battering ram was advancing.

"Go," Linden repeated.

Currant turned back to the battle, formed a spherical golden shield, and repelled a fresh barrage of Atheonian arrows.

Meanwhile, Linden brandished Tynaiv's sword with a drooping arm. The seaman drew his dagger. They locked eyes.

Tess was so transfixed on the duel, she did not see the skinny, stooping Atheonian bandit until he was upon her. "'Ere, you wouldn't blind me, would yeh, m'dear?" He snaked an arm about Tess's waist. She threw her elbow across his nose and spun out of his grasp. Even at a full sprint, she knew she couldn't outrun the whole Atheonian army. She fumbled for the *shenil*, but it was useless. She was too distraught over the battle between Linden and Tynaiv to concentrate on anything else.

"My lady." Jesse emerged from a bundle of braided ponies, all sending ferocious streams of golden magic toward the ever-advancing battering ram. Above him sailed Wyndeling.

Tess scrambled onto Jesse's back. "I am glad to find you safe," he said.

"Indeed," said the red owl as she landed upon Tess's forearm. "So am I."

"Wyndeling, thank Irgo you're still alive."

"I knew the archers would have me if I tried to free you myself. Or worse, Tynaiv would finish you. So, I flew for Currant and the prince," she said. "I am glad to be at your side once more, my lady."

Tess risked a look back into the battle and saw Tynaiv on his knees. Linden brandished the point of a sword under the foreigner's chin.

Tynaiv smiled. The expression reminded Tess of their meeting in the royal garden, when he knew she was taken with him. Linden stepped forward and hammered the butt of his sword against Tynaiv's skull, and the Atheonian general crumpled at Linden's feet.

A cold sensation sprang in Tess's insides.

All around them, scores of soldiers and a few dozen bloodhounds battled the ponies of Foggy Plains, whose sturdy hooves delivered blow after blow. But the herds had been severely cut down, leaving only a few skilled enough in golden magic to combat the hounds. Currant protected the remaining bondfellows, sending a glittering pair of antlers into the Atheonian throng.

Jesse shook his mane. "We must reach the castle before the battering ram, Lady Tessamine."

Tess peered through the melee and saw Linden inspecting Tynaiv's body. But a soldier assailed him from behind, and Linden disappeared from view.

"Linden!"

Atheonians covered the road ahead of the rolling battering ram. They were almost upon her. Jesse reared, bringing his hooves down on a soldier. His forelegs hit the ground again, and Tess knew there was no more time. Her heart struggled to beat under the weight of fear. She drew her head against Jesse's neck. The stallion bolted for the castle and Wyndeling took flight. They raced northward, and Tess begged the skies for deliverance.

CHAPTER 45

King Nabal brooded on a stool in his tent, his battle-axe spinning slowly between his palms. He felt the revolting presence of that weasel Cojab quivering just inside the tent flap.

"Tell me you have broken through," he said through his beaded beard.

Lord Cojab froze. Did he really think himself that inconspicuous?

"My king," he began.

"Tell me you have gotten through that damned barrier, or I will shave that mustache off of your face—and your nose along with it." It was something he'd been meaning to do, anyway.

"M-my lord, please understand; we have never dealt with this before. None of us knows magic, and the hounds are afraid to go near it. We lost so many when the bear—"

The king stood, lowering his axe to his side as he approached Cojab. The silk-wearing rooster stared in disbelief, as though no one had ever expected him to do anything before. Probably no one had, with King Yuir relying solely on his high ancestry to run a starving kingdom. Nabal's broad hand caught Cojab by the shirt. "Glademont's reinforcements are on their way here, right now." He shook the man. "If we can't get past that damned magic moat, we'll be sitting ducks. They'll have us cornered. This is our last chance, fool. With the goods from these lands, we can feed the people of Atheos. We will flourish again. Do you not *see*?" The aristocrat turned purple with fear. His fingers fumbled helplessly at Nabal's hand.

In swooped the crow, landing impassively on Nabal's shoulder. "Do not be troubled, my king. Your soldiers march from the crossroads as we speak, battering ram in tow. The rabble from the valley delayed us only a little."

Nabal tossed Cojab to the ground. Of course he did not see. He wanted nothing more than to live in luxury as he always had, no matter how much the rest of his countrymen wasted away. Spineless. All of them. "Take reinforcements to the battering ram," Nabal barked. "Go."

Cojab mumbled a word of compliance before exiting the tent.

"That bear's moat . . . ," Nabal said to his counselor. A day before, he watched it pull the mercenaries down into the earth, as soon as they were within reach. Their deaths marked the beginning of the end of that battle. Nabal would not be so cavalier with the lives of his soldiers, some of whom helped him bring down Yuir.

"We will use the battering ram as a bridge," the crow said. "The hounds will push the ram over it using their powers. Our men will cross over and pull the battering ram to safety."

"Leaving what's left of the rabble trapped behind that moat." A smile of understanding crept across the king's face.

"Precisely."

Nabal pulled back the tent flap and looked out toward Glademont Castle. All around the royal tent, hounds and mercenaries nursed their wounds or cleaned their weapons, while raptors from the Hinge sulked on the branches of the pine trees above.

Nabal's eyes settled on the glowing obstacle that surged in a wide circle around the castle. He gritted his teeth as he remembered the sight of the great bear splitting the earth open and filling the wide crevice with swirling golden water. Nabal was a great warrior, traveling all over the continent on Yuir's orders. He and his men raided remote villages just to keep half of Atheos alive. It was never enough. Nabal's skill as a hardened soldier eventually won him the throne. But in Atheos, things were easier; one could overtake a spoiled monarch with the strength of an axe. This place was different; it was bewitched.

"Counselor," he said, "what do you know of this golden magic?"

"My king?" The crow flitted his tail.

Relying on magic was like playing with fire, that much Nabal knew. He rarely raided villages where animals were treated like people. The stars never worked in his favor, then. Nevertheless, he'd agreed to the hounds, against his better judgment. Here they were, reaping the reward for that foolish decision. King Nabal made a point never to meet an enemy blind, and he didn't intend to be caught unawares again. "They say it was you who taught the dogs red magic." He felt the crow on his shoulder stiffen.

"Idle gossip, my liege," the crow replied calmly. "The hounds came to me already skilled in the art. That is what makes them so valuable to us."

"You know nothing of sorcery, then? You could not take this moat down without the battering ram?"

"I am a simple creature, my lord. Feathers, mind, and beak are my tools."

"I wonder." The king fingered his axe.

"Sire—" A mercenary tumbled toward the tent. "A lady on a horse is comin' straight at us. Can we shoot her, m'lord, or do you want her? She looks like that girl you wus lookin' for, Smooth Crow—"

"Mind your tongue," the crow burst out. "You stand before the king."

Nabal narrowed his eyes and started to say something, but the counselor did not give him the opportunity. "The girl, is her hair black? Does she ride a horse with a white mane and tail?"

"Yes, Counselor. Like I—"

"That scampering little mouse. I'll break her neck myself—"

"What's all this, Counselor?" Nabal demanded.

"My lord, this is that spoiled girl betrothed to Prince Linden. Capture her, and you will have Glademont on its knees. You could take the castle and not lose a single soldier."

"I do not barter," the king said. "I threaten, and then I make good on my threats."

"Naturally, my lord." Talons dug into the king's shoulder like a cat's kneading claws. "But the Glademontians don't know that about you. They've grown so anemic, they do not recognize strength when they see it. You remember that pitiful letter? Keep the girl alive just long enough to get close to the scheming Aideen, then *cut them all down*." His rasp thickened.

The thought of taunting the queen of Glademont appealed to Nabal. He pictured Aideen holding her arms out for the girl. Then he saw himself telling her that the prince was dead and she would have no heir. And with a stroke of his axe . . . the soldiers would love him for it. Atheos, in time, would honor him for it.

The king grasped his weapon. "Take down the horse and bring the girl here," he shouted at the bandit, who scuttled away. "She may even know a thing or two about golden magic. Eh, Counselor?"

"One can only hope, my liege." The talons relaxed.

Suddenly, the king felt beneath his feet the unmistakable pounding of hooves.

"Plague's corpse, is that the princess brat? I thought I told you insects to shoot that horse down."

A stallion hurtled toward them, soil flying in small arcs behind his legs. The white hairs of his mane streamed in the wind and obscured the face of the girl on his back. Nabal squinted at her.

"That's no princess, Counselor. She's a peasant. Shoot them both down."

"No." Black feathers thrashed in the face of an archer who was fitting his bow. "The horse. Only the horse." The archer stared at the blind bird, bewildered. Nabal stammered.

"How dare you—"

"She is in disguise, my lord," he cawed wildly. "She can be questioned. She may know the extent of the conspiracy against you."

Nabal hesitated, his sharp eyes flitting from the girl to his counselor. His rocklike arms shook with anticipation.

"Don't you dare lie, bird."

"Keep the girl alive, my lord, and I will question her myself." Pider's black wings twitched as the girl and her horse charged into the camp. "You will see that I am right."

"M'lord, your orders?" called one of the bandits.

"Oy. They're gettin' away. By my hat, that horse is flyin'," said another.

"Bring the horse down, keep the girl alive," the king ordered. But by the time Nabal made his decision, the horse and the girl had already torn through the camp and were galloping away. The bandits did not have time even to throw a dagger.

"Get on your own horses, you lazy rats," Nabal bellowed, pulling the mercenaries by their coats and shoving their backs with his axe. Criminals, all of them. And criminals only respected those they feared.

"Ain't no use, sire," said one man chewing on a straw. "That horse'll be halfway to the sea in another half second. I ain't never seen nothing fly like that 'cept an eagle."

Nabal hoisted his axe and struck down a wooden support of his tent. The fabric billowed and fell inward, covering the lanterns within. As the fabric charred, then caught fire, Nabal faced his men, smoke curling behind him.

"To arms, men," he screamed, spittle frothing at the corners of his mouth. "And when the battering ram arrives, take it to the moat. Crash against those castle gates until your backs are broken and your arms have fallen off."

A sharp whistle brought his large red horse trotting toward him. Nabal mounted the animal in one bound and spurred his steed after the girl.

They pounded toward the castle, the glowing moat growing bigger every second. A streaming white tail and a cloud of dust could be seen before him, and Nabal whipped his horse's side with all his strength. The red stallion sped faster than he had ever galloped. They were closing the gap.

Then a small black figure fell out of the sky, streaking toward the Glademont girl, and Nabal saw her arms flail. A larger auburn shape shot toward the black one, and the two seemed locked together in midair until the black figure freed itself and took to the sky again.

Counselor Pider?

That was when Nabal saw a blast of thick red light, like lava. It spilled from the sky over the girl and her horse, but the horse, with all his speed, passed under it just in time.

"What on the—" the king sputtered in disbelief. He whipped his horse with the broad side of his axe. "Get there, you worthless animal."

The girl reached the moat, where swirling golden water rose to meet them. Nabal watched as she extended her arms toward the enchanted water, and an orange fire poured forth. Girl, stallion, and auburn bird soared through a giant cloud of steam.

The king of Atheos pulled his horse to a sudden halt and tumbled onto the lawn. He approached the moat with caution, just out of reach. Through the swirling, rising golden waves, he watched as the brat slipped behind the castle gate, and his counselor disappeared over the outer wall.

CHAPTER 46

Shaking, Tess searched the sky as she galloped toward Glademont Castle's outer gates. She couldn't see where Pider had gone since they crossed the moat.

"Open the gates," a governor barked from somewhere above. "Lady Tessamine approaches. Open the gates." Dozens of terriers howled with delight as Jesse slowed his pace. The giant, solid doors of the outer wall were scratched and bruised, but without rupture. One slowly creaked open and Jesse slipped inside, with Wyndeling flitting behind. The owl landed unsteadily on Tess's arm as the castle servants shut the gate and lowered its massive wrought iron locking bar.

"I was just starting to grow feathers on that shoulder," complained the owl. Tess could tell she was hiding her shock.

"We are both fortunate to be alive," she said.

Tess urged Jesse across the courtyard and up the royal staircase to the carved stone castle. A young woman's head appeared at the grand doors.

"The skies really *have* been smiling on us lately. Hurry in. Hurry in."

"Dahly." Tess tumbled off of Jesse's back to embrace her sister.

"Come on, come on. It's not safe to stand out here." Dahly ushered Tess and her friends through the grand doors, which once were so richly adorned for Tess's wedding. It felt like a century ago.

"My, you *are* looking casual." Dahly stood back to survey Tess in her shepherdess apparel. "But you've still got your Canyon cloak." She pulled Tess's hood playfully. "Ryon will be so happy to see you."

"Ryon is here? Thank the skies."

Dahly nodded.

"My girl." Tess couldn't remember the last time she saw her father run, but run he did into the entrance hall of Glademont Castle, rushing to take her face in his hands. "My darling girl," he said.

"I'm all right, Papa." Tess kissed his hands. "But I must see the queen. It's urgent."

"No, no." Sir Brock waved a hand. "She won't see anyone. She rests in the gardens, and we try not to disturb her. It's General Bud you'll want to see. And Masters Rootpine and Cherrywater."

"But—"

Dahly took Tess's arm and smiled with tired cheeks. "I can't imagine how hard it's been for you."

Relenting, Tess rested her forehead against Dahly's. "I wish you had been with me." An abrupt clinking of metal on metal interrupted them, and Tess glanced about her.

Glademont Castle had completely transformed since the wedding festival. To her right and left, disheveled servants swept shattered stained glass from the halls. At the far end of the entrance hall, where half a dozen archways led to half a dozen corridors, various noblemen and women brought armfuls of household tools to a set of long tables. There, groups of young men sorted and sharpened the tools.

"My lord." Wyndeling issued a curt bow from Tess's shoulder. "Wyndeling the Red of the Seven Wise, at your service. Can you direct me to where my clan is stationed?"

"Seven?" Sir Brock answered. "I thought there were five . . . the Nest Battalion has gathered in the glasshouses. Any of the servants can show you the way."

Excusing themselves to join up with the Hinge Foresters, Jesse and a rather nettled Wyndeling followed a servant out of the hall.

Soon, Sir Brock, Tess, and Dahly were passing through the chaos into a left-hand corridor. Sir Brock hurried through the cold, wide passage, his short yet steady figure stooped in focus. Tess thought of Linden's tall, narrow silhouette padding toward Crescent Cave in the dark, and her hand tucked under his arm. What if she had left the *shenìl* in the cave that morning? Would she have one day walked this corridor as queen, on Linden's arm?

Sir Brock pivoted to a wooden door, and from there they climbed a winding staircase in the western tower of Glademont Castle. Tess had so many questions, she didn't know where to begin.

"Papa . . . what has happened here?"

"More in the last week than in my lifetime," Sir Brock said heavily. "You remember Her Majesty called the advisors, the first night of the festival? We agreed to offer sanctuary to the wedding guests. These walls have withstood many more winters than enemy onslaughts, still . . ." He brooded over a pile of glass shards that had fallen into the stair-well. "But it was too late. Those bandits were upon us."

"Papa, Mother, and I all made it to the castle that night," Dahly said, "but then we were holed in. The next morning, there was a huge encampment of those evil men out on the castle lawns."

"Everyone in the castle fell on one of two sides: those against the militia and those for it." Sir Brock swallowed and looked at Tess. "Some of us thought we could still negotiate, try to understand what Atheos wanted . . ." He paused on the stairs to look out a shattered window. "I didn't even know Master Rootpine had gone for recruits until Atheos attacked. Until those vultures came pouring in through the windows . . ." He shook the memory away, and his round nose and light blue eyes pointed back at Tess. "I'm so sorry I couldn't defend you at the manor. I . . . I could never have imagined all this." He kissed her hair, then Dahly's.

"It isn't your fault, Papa," Tess said. "The queen entrusted me with a secret that night, and I betrayed it. I'm the reason Atheos has come."

"Nonsense." Sir Brock frowned at Tess reproachfully. "They planned this attack long before that night." It was obvious to Tess he didn't want to hear about it. To him, she was still a little girl. What harm could she possibly do? But Tess knew the truth. Her selfishness killed Belle's mother, and others besides. Who knew how long Pider might have waited to attack, had he not known the exact location of the *shenìl*?

The Canyons were almost to a Glademont-green door at the top of the tower.

"If we get through this, Tess, you'll make a wonderful queen." Sir Brock squeezed Tess's shoulder.

Swallowing through a dry throat, Tess nodded.

At the top of the western tower, in a round room covered in tapestries, Ryon leaned against a broken window and manipulated a flat stone across his knuckles. Profigliano wiggled his tail feathers on the windowsill.

"I still don't see how it will be enough." Nory stood behind a broad desk in the center of the room. Before him towered Osiris, decked in an array of armor. "Even if every man in the castle is wielding something that resembles a weapon," he continued, "he isn't properly trained to use it. We're outnumbered, and eventually those soldiers will cross that moat."

"Aye," the bear replied, "but yon miscreants weren't expecting no fight, until yesterday morn', young master. They were bested both inside the castle and on the field."

"We can't replicate that." Rette groaned softly as he crossed his feet on the desk and leaned against a bookshelf in his chair.

Without warning, the door swung open. Sir Brock, Dahly, and Tess stepped through. Ryon dropped his stone and sprang from the windowsill.

"Ah." Osiris's booming voice filled the room. "The little gem'll be leading us to vict'ry then? Glad as a rainbow, I be. Mark ye, this brother of yers be gladder."

"Well, if it isn't Miss Tessy, quester extraordinaire," twittered Profigliano.

Ryon grinned as Tess crossed to him.

"Hi, Tess," he said, taking in her Wallaton skirt and a bloodied cotton shirt.

Ryon knew she was looking at his combat vest and muddied hair. He hoped he looked as tall as he felt after fighting his first battle.

"What's happened to you?" Tess said with awe.

Ryon glanced at Nory, who winked. He shrugged at Tess with feigned nonchalance. "Well, you know how we joined up with the FOM?"

Tess nodded. "I wouldn't have believed it, except that I've seen them with my own eyes."

"Well, the Hinge birds joined up with us here at the castle. We attacked the bandits and hounds just as they were trying to get into the castle. The hounds were really pounding on us, even with the governors using their magic from the parapet. Some bandits were getting in through the cellar and killing the servants and everything. . . ."

Ryon noted the panic on Tess's face.

"Well, I made it out okay. Evening was there with—oh, you haven't met Evening. Well anyway, Osiris came out and made that moat. That separated us from most of the bandits and hounds, and the Nest Battalion really started thrashing into the raptors. That's when we got into the castle and Nory and Rette, Reggie and me, we found the bandits in the cellar and finished them off. Atheos fell back after that. I guess you could say Glademont has won her first battle in two hundred or so years."

Ryon couldn't help but beam a little as he finished his recounting. After all, he left out the part about there being twenty bandits in the cellar, and only the four of them fighting for Glademont.

"The spell only buys us a little time," Osiris broke in.

"We're getting ready for the next battle," Ryon said. He lifted his foot onto a nearby chair and leaned on his knee as he had seen Nory do before. The impression, he hoped, would be one of seasoned confidence.

Nory stepped around the desk, grinning modestly.

"It seems I underestimated you Canyons," he said, bowing to Tess and holding out his hand.

Ryon looked to Tess, hoping she would accept the peace offering. She raised an eyebrow, then extended a hand. Ryon smiled at her. Even with a gash in her side and mud on her boots, she looked regal.

"I can only imagine how on the continent you are so well tolerated by Master Cherrywater and the prince, sir," she said playfully.

"Lady Tessamine." He kissed her fingers. "What news from the prince?"

"He is close," Tess said with a flash of anxiety in her eyes. "We met with Currant's forces and marched from Redfoot to the cliffs. We have been trying to destroy the battering ram. Men and creatures from the valley are battling soldiers at the crossroads now, but . . ." There was a moment's silence as Nory palmed his forehead thoughtfully. He looked to Sir Brock.

"One hundred and fifty servants, maids, cooks, and footmen, doing their best to arm themselves as we speak. Added to that are the noblemen and their wives, numbering about fifty altogether. Our best assets have been the few dozen governors, some of whom have already fallen."

"And there are the birds," Sir Brock reminded them. "We have allies who can defend us in the air."

Rette leaned forward to press his elbows against the desk and hold the back of his neck. "Linden and Currant have got to pull through."

"Currant and the rest of them can destroy that battering ram," Ryon said. "Right, Tess?"

Tess stammered. "I—well, I hope so. We are outnumbered there, too. That's why I've got to get to the queen—"

"Master Rootpine." A servant appeared at the door.

Nory's deep brown eyes darted to the man. "What's happened?"

"They've crossed it," the servant cried shrilly. "The Atheonians have crossed the moat, and they're at the main gate. Three hundred soldiers at least. Hounds, too. The governors can't stop them."

Ryon and Tess rushed to a southern-facing window, and Profigliano hopped from the sill to Ryon's shoulder. They peered down from the high tower and saw the great battering ram making its way toward the outer wall, surrounded by Atheonian forces. A series of shimmering red ropes enveloped the ram, while a host of hounds crouched behind it. The terriers sent golden spells through the drainage holes in the wall walks, but the battering ram pommeled against the main gates unhampered.

"Alert the Nest Battalion," Nory said to the servant. "Come on, Cherrywater." Taking up his quiver and a short sword, Nory flew down the tower stairs, and the rest followed suit.

When Nory and the rest reached the bottom of the tower, Ryon caught familiar faces just outside the door. General Bud, the Colonel, and Evening skidded to a halt in the corridor.

"Master Rootpine," General Bud barked. "The Atheonians are through the main gates. They'll be at the castle doors any moment."

"But the stairs may delay them some," Nory said. "To the entrance hall." They raced toward their last defense.

"Hullo, Evening." Ryon jogged alongside the fox, who now had a notch missing from his other ear. Ryon pulled out his sling as they went.

"Master Ryon," the fox said.

"I hope you still have a taste for hound's blood?"

"Was it not I in the cellar with you?"

"I haven't forgotten," Ryon said with a grin. The rush of coming danger washed over him like a cold bath. He could already hear the pounding and shouting of man and beast. He smoothed the straps of his sling in his palm as he ran, flanked by his sisters, father, and flying bondfellow.

Rounding the last corner, Ryon and his companions entered a troubling scene. In the entrance hall, the great wooden doors to the castle groaned and separated along the seam as the Atheonians on the other side thrust the battering ram against them. The noblemen waited closest to peril, brandishing their fire stokers and kitchen knives while watching the doors nervously. Behind them, governors trotted back and forth, barking contradictory orders and generally raising the anxiety level. The Nest Battalion, apparently, had not yet arrived.

Nory grasped Rette's arm. "We need a barricade. The Atheonians have good archers. As soon as they break through the doors, they'll send arrows through. Without a barricade, we're sitting ducks."

Rette nodded. "General Bud, we need tables, clocks, sofas . . . all of it. Form a semicircle, facing the doors. Quickly."

"Yes, sir." General Bud and the Colonel sprinted toward the rest of the governors, barking their orders.

"Where is the queen?" Nory said. His animated face reddened with exhilaration.

"In the royal gardens," Sir Brock said.

"We mustn't let them find her. Ryon—" Nory clasped a paternal hand around Ryon's head.

"You'll be needing the young one in battle." Osiris stepped forward, looking determined. "I'll not be letting yon fools past me, ye can be sure of that." Ryon couldn't help but retreat a step. A bloodstained mace dangled from the corner of Osiris's mouth.

"Well, if it isn't the human girl upstart." Buchanan of Westbend floated down from the vaulted ceiling, which now teemed with a host of colorful companions. Ryon moved toward Tess.

"Watch what you say about her." He felt Tess's hand squeeze his shoulder.

Profigliano offered support as well. "Looks like Mr. Bossybird Snootybeak needs help eating his humble worm pie."

"Buchanan," Nory interjected, oblivious to the tension, "I'll need your battalion stationed at all the windows in this entrance hall, and also those in the banquet hall to protect the women and the wounded."

"First a summons from a servant, now an order to babysit—"

"Do it, Buchanan." Wyndeling swooped to join them, apparently reinstated as one of the Wise. She shifted on Tess's shoulder. "What are *you* looking at?" said the owl to Osiris.

"I be eyeing a surprising wild owl."

General Bud and his company returned to the cavernous entrance hall, each sustaining above his head a collection of heavy furniture in swirling golden clouds and funnels. They stacked the tables, chairs, and bookshelves in a semicircle, and the noblemen stationed themselves behind, armed with their household weapons. The castle servants stood on the peripheries.

Ryon did his best to help carry out Nory and Rette's orders as the large wooden doors continued to tremble, and the shouts of the Atheonian soldiers grew more desperate. He darted down the western hall toward the banquet hall, checking every nook and room for solid furniture. After a few minutes, he saw there was nothing else to be used for the barricade and turned back for the entrance hall. Suddenly a hand gripped his arm.

"Tessy, you scared me." Ryon nursed his bicep.

"I'm sorry." Tess wrung her hands. "I've got to go."

"What?"

"Aideen is dying, and . . . I need to speak with her. I need her, Ryon. I don't think I can defeat Pider without the queen."

Ryon looked around to see whether anyone could hear them. Twenty paces down the corridor, women hurriedly moved about the

banquet hall, some caring for the wounded, others shushing their children. He could hear Dahly's and his mother's voices echoing against
the walls, directing the women to stay calm and ready themselves.

Men and terriers began to yell from the entrance hall. Ryon could
hear Rette shouting for them to stay low. Then, a terrifying *crash* reso-
nated throughout the castle.

"Go." Ryon pulled a rock from his pocket. "We can manage."

"Don't you dare get killed." Tess shook Ryon by both shoulders.
Wyndeling circled overhead.

He gently pulled himself free. "Love you, Tessy." He flashed a smile
before sprinting down the corridor.

CHAPTER 47

Tess's boots made no sound as she hurried through the northward hallway of the west wing. Wyndeling hovered overhead, like an auburn winged spirit. They soon reached the plain door to the gardens—the same gardens where Tess had betrayed her dione just one week before. She felt heat against her palm and saw that the orbs of the *shenil* glowed a fierce orange.

Tess suddenly felt nauseated. What if she failed again to concentrate on the modes of surrender?

"I'm here, my lady," Wyndeling said, settling on Tess's shoulder. Tess nodded and pushed open the door and stepped onto the rosebush path.

Searching for the queen, Tess rushed to the end of the path, where the stones spilled into a wide patio bordering the pond. Aideen was nowhere in sight—not among the roses, nor by the shrine where Ola, the constellation of the future, stooped with her ladle. Quickening her pace, Tess ran along the edge of the pond, calling for the queen. Finally, just on the other side of a weeping willow, she came upon a woman so slender and listless, Tess thought she was looking at an empty cloak. Queen Aideen drooped on a carved stone bench, her hair blowing loose on her shoulders. She lifted her head and, seeing Tess, smiled with dim eyes.

"Is it still with you, princess?" she said. Her stiff fingers opened and closed in her lap.

Tess knelt, trying to hide the desperation in her voice. "Yes, Your Majesty. Just a moment; I can heal you." Tess threw back her cloak and took up the hot glowing orbs.

"I am beyond help." Aideen gathered a bundle of undone hair and tilted her head, revealing on her neck a small black wound. "How foolish I was to return to the Hold. But look"—the queen's dry lips stretched thin in a delighted gasp—"you have been imprinted, already?"

Tess let a tear trickle onto her nose. "I've been to the Hold, Your Majesty. Ember is free again."

The queen allowed her heavy lids to close and she took a shallow breath. "Good girl. The dione is safe now."

Biting her frowning lip, Tess focused on where Pider's curse had entered Aideen. The open wound revealed cracked, ash-like flesh, with blue veins snaking along the queen's paper-white neck. Tess thought of the worms from Crescent Cave, spreading silently across the walls. Catching herself, she breathed and concentrated on the modes of surrender. A low bluish fire grew between her hands.

"We need you, Your Majesty. Don't leave me. Don't leave me." As Tess held her breath to listen, she heard the soothing voice of the *shenil*, but the words were muddled, like someone trying to speak through her hand. She opened her eyes. "Something is wrong."

Wyndeling must have felt it, too. She flew to the uppermost branch of a young water oak and scanned the horizon. Tess sat still and tried again to listen for the *shenil*. The wind grew stronger, carrying the faint sounds of governors howling from within the castle. Tess thought of the wind the night of the wedding festival. She remembered how it pulled strands of Tynaiv's sandy hair across his forehead. . . .

"My lady," Wyndeling called from the tree. "Perhaps we should take the queen inside."

There was a note in Wyndeling's voice that pricked the back of Tess's neck. The owl had seen something, and she was trying not to let on.

"Inside?" Tess called out hesitantly. The queen's purple lids were still closed, and her head was beginning to droop.

"Above you," the owl screeched.

Tess sprang to her feet, shielding her head as an agitated squawk sounded in the garden. Terrified, Tess stumbled backward toward the pond. Fiery globs of lava crashed against the willow, and Tess looked up into the glazed eyes of Pider as he dove headlong from the treetops. Chunks of melted rock sizzled as they landed, splashing onto Aideen's bench and barely missing the fading queen. Then they were at Tess's feet, surrounding her, searing Tess's clothes with unbearable waves of heat. She had no other option—she threw herself into the pond's cold green water.

Tess swam deeper and deeper into the frigid dark, her cloak pulling at her neck. Dark, glowing masses shot in the water around her, with lines of fiery lava quickly cooling along their surfaces. The last of the air dissipated from her lungs, and Tess became aware that she was choosing her course of death—to drown or to burn. A pounding sounded in her ears. Her chest felt like an empty wine flask, wrung for every last drop, as she sank farther toward the muddy floor. She reached for the *shenil*, and her fingers brushed the medal with the last of her strength.

A voice called.

"Tessamine, Tessamine."

Tess was standing on a mountaintop. Clouds crawled at her feet. Rich forests blanketed the landscape far below. The emerald mountain where she stood was sliced on two sides by streams, which flowed into a pair of massive rivers. The rivers cut through the forests and flowed into two oceans—one to her left, and one to her right.

"Tessamine," the voice called again.

"I am Tessamine," she answered.

A tangerine-colored cloud rolled before Tess, and on it stood Ember. She wore nothing but starlight, arranged around her like the fine feathers of a bird's wing. Her lustrous purple waves lifted, almost weightless when she tipped her head.

"Tessamine," Ember said. "The skies formed you, and the skies wish to see you return."

"Am I . . . have I died?" Tess said the words with mild surprise, but also with relief.

"Irgo protects you, but Ola is not finished pouring your ladle."

Tess wanted to cry. If she threw herself from the mountain, then would the constellations take her into their company? "What else can I possibly do? I have given my life trying to do what is right."

"Surrender your past. Trust that every trial is for your good."

Ember's cloud floated farther away, toward the ocean to the left. Tess wondered if she could jump on the next cloud, follow Ember's apparition to the water. Anything to never go back to her messy, cruel life. She spotted the next one, and without thinking, leapt for the cloud, her legs split in a ballerina's flight.

Perhaps it was moments later, or perhaps an age had passed, but when Tess suddenly regained consciousness, she felt water surging out of her lungs and throat. She was still submerged, yet gently floating upward. Her limbs warmed. Her vision focused again. Her head and shoulders rose above the water's surface and into the air. The flame of the *shenil* erupted with an intensity she had never felt before as she continued to rise, dripping wet. Peering through her flames, Tess saw she was standing on the surface of the pond as easily as if it were a marble floor. Hot air blew through her hair and clothes.

Around her, the sun seemed to have set all at once, and the atmosphere was filled with a sickening red haze. From within the red haze, the shadow of a man appeared. He stood on the bank of the pond, his hands at his sides.

"Tessamine," Pider said, his looming shadow flickering in the gloom. This figure was slight, with uneven, angular shoulders.

The fire between Tess's hands licked at her arms reassuringly. *Irgo protects you.*

"I have only two requests." The shadow shifted impatiently.

"I know what can happen when you make requests, Pider. There is nothing—"

"Oh, Lady Tessamine. You have been fed so many lies, you think there is no greater good than the weapon," Pider cooed. His words spread thick in the air, and as he spoke, the red haze seemed to expand from him like a strong perfume.

"First, restore my sight. Then surrender the object, which has only caused you pain and sorrow. In return, I will erase all your past mistakes."

His words struck Tess's heart like a mallet. All the selfishness and vanity of her life flooded her mind. Could Pider know how ashamed she felt?

"I have the power to put you back in time, beginning whenever you wish. I can erase all that has happened in your life from the moment you choose until this moment. You can start again."

The possibilities whirled in Tess's imagination. She could refuse to marry Linden and preserve her heart against his neglect. The *shenil* would not be in her possession, and Tynaiv would have no reason to seduce her. The bandits would never reach her home. Little Belle's mother would see her grow up to be a good and kind shepherdess . . . but most especially, she would never have discovered the Thane's Hold, and been burdened with her promise.

"But . . . but you would still have the *shenil*," she said thinly. The red haze inched toward her over the surface of the pond.

"You have seen what horrors the object attracts," Pider said soothingly. "I will destroy it and have no further reason to bother your dione. I will sail away from Diatonica, and you will live in peace."

Tess didn't know what to say. It was the most wonderful gift anyone could offer to her: the chance to erase her mistakes. And since Glademont would still be safe, there was no reason not to at least consider it.

The shroud stretched across the pond and gathered at Tess's feet, and she began to sink into the water. The fire between her hands reduced to a low blue flame.

"You would put me back home with my family, and I would never see you again?" Tess said.

"Not quite. You would trace back time, but as someone else. Lady Tessamine Canyon, as everyone knew her, would be dead. But *you*"— Pider's voice softened to a whisper—"you would start over, avoid that other girl's mistakes, and earn all the love she threw away."

Tess pouted. "I thought red magic could do anything you wanted it to."

"No," Pider answered as a patient teacher to his pupil. "Rather, red magic requires an exchange."

The red haze surrounded Tess and lifted her slowly off her feet. Her limbs felt heavy and weak, and she hardly noticed that her fire had snuffed out. It felt comfortable, resting in the red haze. Before, she had to be brave, to try to recall all the sage advice so many women had doled out to her. But now she could just lay still. Her lips began to tingle.

"Imagine who you'd like to be," Pider said as his enchantment pulled Tess toward him. "I'll make you as lovely as you like, as captivating as you like."

Tess wanted to drown in the haze and feel the tingling on her lips forever. She let her head fall back, and all of her muscles melted into the red.

"Well done, well done." A shadowy face advanced out of the gloom, brown and smooth with hooded eyes. "Now, command it to give me sight."

From somewhere above her, a silent flying figure came into focus, disturbing the fog. Tess wanted to tell it to go away, but she felt too groggy even to open her mouth. Why wouldn't it just leave them alone?

Wyndeling the Red dove for the *shenil*, her talons snatching the leather strap and whisking it out of Tess's hands. To her distress, Tess's fingers closed too slowly to keep the object from flying away with the owl. Tess despised Wyndeling for making her break her promise to Pider, but a distant voice told her to be afraid.

"You still have not learned, owl?" Pider hissed. "I may be blind, but there are other ways to see."

The red haze flashed like a thousand bolts of lightning, and Tess collapsed on the bank. Pider's manlike figure dissolved to the ground as the haze swirled upward and disappeared. The enchantment lifted, and slowly the pond and the weeping willow reappeared by the glow of a low tangerine sun.

Pider was again a crow. He cawed savagely, cocking his head one way, then another. The next moment he was flying after Wyndeling, who still held the *shenil* in her talons. At first, the owl flew away from Tess, toward the garden wall. But the wall was barred by a stand of pear trees. Her wings disturbed the leaves as she climbed upward. A blast of magma slung against the branches above Wyndeling, and she faltered, dropping to the rosebushes, her wings badly singed.

Beads of lava sputtered from Pider's beak as he pursued, following the sounds of her gasping hoots. Another shower of fiery rock cascaded over the rosebushes, and Wyndeling rolled onto the garden path, burnt and blackened. Hooting desperately, Wyndeling hopped away from the smoke, dragging the *shenil* in her talons. Pider circled overhead, cocking his black head, following the wounded owl as she made her way across the gravel. She reached the bank beside Tess.

"Wyndeling—"

Struggling to shirk the effects of the red haze, Tess covered Wyndeling with her cloak and closed her throbbing fingers around the *shenil*. She breathed. Her head began to clear.

Tess pulled herself to her feet, still protecting Wyndeling with her cloak. Copper orbs floated over her palms, and the familiar flame resurrected in front of her.

Pider dove for the object, but the flame formed a fireball so large, Tess had to close her eyes against its brightness. It expanded, roaring as every tree buckled under the force of its heat. Confused, Pider spewed lava. But Tess's small sun absorbed his enchantment.

Surrender your past, said the voice of the *shenil*.

Despite the fierce heat, Tess felt tears wet her face. She could not erase her mistakes any more than she could abandon the *shenil*. They shaped her. They were reasons to grow in courage, not thorns to be plucked and forgotten.

Tess forced herself to open her watering eyes. The mass of white-and-orange flames before her spun in place, its surface constantly morphing into different hues and shining shapes. Tess took hold of it. Trusting the *shenil* would remain in the air between her hands, she stretched her arms around the fireball and bent her legs. Its boiling surface slid like weightless water under her unburned, graceful fingertips. She found her balance on the balls of her feet and turned her head, pulling the fireball into a tight circle before flinging it at the crow.

Pider retreated, flapping toward the garden wall and the smoking stand of pear trees. The fireball expanded, and Pider was catapulted through the branches to the wall. His feathers plastered against the stone. The fireball lurched forward, and the crow scrambled over the garden wall just as the flames exploded against the stone.

Suspended in shock, Tess stared at the cooling *shenil* in her hands. The light hiss of scorched hairs tickled her ears, and the wood of the garden trees popped and groaned.

"I still have it."

Her temples throbbed as she hooked her trinket back through her belt and scooped up the broken owl. A tangy smell stung her nostrils.

"Wyndeling, you were wonderful. Braver than all the Council of the Nest put together."

"My lady . . ." Soot and dirt covered Wyndeling's face. One eye was swollen shut. "I wish to take the oath."

"Shush, Wyndeling. I need to heal you. I need to . . ." The lifeless queen caught Tess's eye, and she released a sob.

As the receding rays of the sun bounced on the brown leaves of the water oak, Tess held her friend and knelt at Aideen's feet. The queen's head rested on her chest, her hands already cold. The rumbling, echoing cry of an animal sounded in the distance. Tess recognized it immediately, but she did not move.

"My lady—" Wyndeling said weakly.

"Another moment," Tess said. "I don't want to leave her like this."

"Allow me to stay with the queen. You are needed in battle."

"All this time, I believed I could save Aideen. She could guide me, she could . . ." Tess fought the despair. She needed a few minutes, time to recover her strength.

"The object draws hardship and betrayal," Wyndeling said. "It has changed your life. But anyone can see it is meant to be yours—it *has* to be yours. The queen would never have taken it back, had she lived." Wyndeling blinked at the sky. "She died trusting you to do what she could not. And if you don't put any stake in what a human thinks, know that I agree with her. You can save your kind and mine."

Tess gazed at the tattered bird in her arms. How long ago it seemed since Wyndeling confronted Tess in the woods, angry and fearful. But the *shenil* knew what lay behind the red owl's scrupulous eyes. *Trust her* were the first words Tess ever heard the object say. Trust Wyndeling, whose loyalty would grow so fierce, she would take on the most powerful magician on the continent to rescue Tess.

Again, a desperate roar drifted to their ears. Wyndeling pulled at Tess's shirt with her beak. "Go. I'm all right."

Tess kissed her queen's hand. She lowered Wyndeling into Aideen's cold lap and leaned on the bench to stand. Then, with utmost effort, Tess turned back to the castle.

"Your little gem is coming, my friend," she said, stumbling over the cooled lava along the rosebush path.

CHAPTER 48

Ryon sprinted behind Profigliano into the entrance hall, his sling loaded. An enormous hunk of wood burst from the castle doors, splintering against the barricades. The horrible bronze rhinoceros head of the Atheonian battering ram barely protruded through the castle doors, sending an electric wave of fear through Ryon's limbs. The battering ram rolled back again, and a score of archers knelt along the edges of the tattered hole it created.

"Governors, the shields," Nory called from behind a barricade. Together, the terriers formed enormous golden shields just in time to shatter a drove of whistling arrows. The archers retreated, and the ram resumed its slow rhythm against what remained of the castle doors.

"They'll do it," Rette said as Ryon joined him behind a barricade. "They'll get through."

"Governors, lower your shields," Nory ordered, his bow and arrow poised. "Men, stay behind the barricades until I give the signal. Ready yourselves, Glademont!" The noblemen and servants adjusted their makeshift weapons with sweaty palms.

Nory signaled to Ryon, and they sprinted to one side of the castle doors, while Rette moved to the other. Arrow and stone rocketed through the ragged doors. Furious, the Atheonian archers returned, but only a few of their arrows escaped before the governors rallied from the barricades with golden flurries, blowing the archers backward.

"Protect the bondfellows, Ry," Nory said as he eyed the battering ram. "They're our best shot at winning this thing."

Ryon's throat tightened. He checked his shoulder for Fig's familiar feathers.

A bloodcurdling war cry erupted from somewhere outside the doors. Ryon set his jaw and fingered his sling. The governors all broke out in a chorus of barking and howling, while Osiris rattled his mace in his paw and roared. The battering ram continued to pound its way through a foot of solid oak, and Atheos took up a chilling anthem.

> Glory for the kingdom, vic'try for the king.
> Our enemies' fat carcasses will stiffen as we sing.
> Glory for the kingdom, vic'try for the king.
> The wretched cling to weaknesses, but soldiers
>   mourn for no-thing!

Over and over, the rhinoceros rapped on the door. Each time the ram struck, the doors gave a little more.

"They'll kill us all," Ryon said while sticky sweat collected on his neck.

"No, sir," Nory answered. "The stars favor Glademont."

Ryon took a deep breath and repeated Rette's words. "You can't think about how things might go bad. You just have to remember why you're fighting."

"Most expertly said, distinguished fellow of the bond," Profigliano put in. "Let's give them a little bit of *this*, and spice it up with a little bit of *that*, and garnish it with something I like to call *this*—" Hopping to Ryon's head, the towhee sent flashes of gold at the hole in the castle doors. Some went over his shoulder, others between his legs.

Suddenly, the pounding stopped. The door was still. The governors stopped their wailing, and the Glademontians held their breath.

"*Eeeeee-aaaaaa-laaa-laaa!*" the war cry came again.

All at once, vultures, hawks, eagles, and kestrels streamed through the shattered windows high above. At the same time, the piercing calls of the Nest Battalion echoed into the entrance hall, and out of the corridors swarmed hundreds of wild birds. Ryon ducked under a storm of beating wings and fleeting shadows. The highest spaces between the buttresses came alive as talon and beak mingled in midair.

Above Ryon's barricade, the Stitchipeeps stayed together, pestering one enemy at a time from all angles. Above the bluebirds, the members of the Wise swooped in silent circles like flying wolves. Their enormous wings blocked the raptors from reaching the Glademontians below, and thwarted birds careened in all directions.

"You brainless, heartless cowards," Ryon heard Thorestook yell. The drake tore a bill full of feathers from a passing vulture's wing. "You dare betray us for these murderers."

"You mindless excuse for a bird," called his mate, Cheekathistle, her bill coming down hard on the head of an eagle. "You are responsible. *You* killed my ducklings."

At the castle doors, Ryon heard Atheonians groan in one final heave, and the wood surrendered to the ram's bronze head.

"Abandon the barricades," Nory called as he and Rette drew swords. Soldiers flooded the entrance hall while Glademontian noblemen advanced, meeting their enemies with irons and silver-plated candlesticks. Many noblemen were easily felled, while other Glademontians watched in horror, too frightened to leave the barricades. Hounds came bounding through the doors and immediately set to work tearing the tables and chairs apart. Those who still cowered behind the barricades were forced to scatter out into the fray, brandishing their ladles and brooms.

In a matter of minutes, the barricades lay in shreds amid red smoke. Baying and snarling, the hounds turned their attention to the Nest Battalion. Glowing red ropes and bright bursts rocketed from the hounds' mouths, enveloping the wild birds of the Hinge. One after the other, owls, falcons, and woodpeckers dropped to the floor.

"Governors, the hounds," Rette shouted as he dueled with an Atheonian officer.

The Colonel, General Bud, and their comrades engaged in one-to-one combat, gold against scarlet spells. They succeeded in driving the hounds back, but left their Glademontian bondfellows unprotected.

Amid the chaos, Ryon could see the light of battle in Nory's and Rette's eyes. The militia men fought with vim, in brotherhood with every gallant Glademontian who defended his country in the old days.

"Footwork, Master Ryon," Nory shouted as he whipped his longbow against the temple of an enemy soldier. "Don't forget your footwork."

"He's doing fine without your help, Master Nory," called Rette, pausing to admire Ryon's courage as the boy slashed and lunged with his dagger.

Taking advantage of Rette's distraction, an Atheonian brought his curved sword across the back of the young man's knee. Rette fell gasping, but not before swiveling in time to pierce the soldier in the stomach. His blood splashed onto white marble.

"Back-to-back," Nory called, helping Rette to his feet. And the three friends resumed combat in earnest.

Nearby, Osiris tore into the enemy like a barracuda. One Atheonian officer, who was nearly crushed by a ragged body Osiris had flung his way, turned and shouted an order that caused Ryon's heart to pound against his ribs.

"All Holts to me. Bring down the bear." Spittle fell on the officer's red beard.

A battalion of soldiers advanced toward Osiris. The bear laughed as he clenched his three-pronged mace between his teeth. Gripping their javelins, the soldiers jostled into a formation, while the red-bearded officer barked orders from behind. Osiris pulled back his powerful head and swept it in a deadly arc, ripping through Atheonians with his mace, tearing the flesh from their bodies. One soldier managed to duck and thrust his weapon under the shield that protected the bear's ribs. With a roar that brought tears to Ryon's eyes, Osiris dropped his mace and turned upon the terrified soldier. The bear clenched his teeth around the javelin, wrenched it from his own side, and plunged it into the hapless Atheonian, pinning his chest to the floor.

Atheos was gaining ground. Ryon trembled when he realized how many fellow citizens had fallen already. Nory, Rette, and Ryon seemed to be the only humans who could hold their own, and soldiers grew thick around them.

"Eeeeee-aaaaaa-hooo! Eee-hoo!"

The sound was so frightening, Ryon faltered as he parried an Atheonian's attack. The cold steel of a curved sword sliced a shallow wound across his forehead, and he fell to the floor. As Ryon tried desperately to regain his footing, he found the Atheonians surrounding him were dispersing. Through the blood trickling into his eyes, Ryon saw the giant snarling head of the battering ram entering the hall. He scrambled to one side just as an enormous wheel threatened to crush him. Atop the battering ram, looking out between the rhinoceros's ears like a lion before the kill, appeared a broad barbaric man wearing little more than a black chain mail shirt. He lifted a massive battle-axe over his head.

"I am King Nabal, ruler of Atheos and conqueror of Glademont," the barbarian king bellowed, swinging his axe. "Your queen dared send conspirers into my kingdom. I have come to repay the debt." Nabal leapt from the battering ram. "Atheos, find the queen."

Behind Nabal, the rest of the Atheonian army poured into the castle, no longer blocked by the battering ram. They were too many for the remaining Glademontian men gathering with Nory and Rette. Sir Brock stumbled to Ryon, unscathed but breathless. His right hand clutched an ornate cane, while the left awkwardly brandished a platter as a shield. He said something to Ryon, but the boy did not hear; he was searching the throng for Osiris. Soon he spotted the beast, backing into a corner of the entrance hall and the raging king of Atheos barreling toward the same corner. Ryon bolted toward his friend.

Several hounds pinned the bear in with a barrage of red spells as Nabal tore through the fray, waving his axe. Ryon watched in terror, dashing between men to reach Osiris. Nabal was working quickly toward the same goal until a single man appeared in his path—a man with no weapon but a cane.

"Papa," cried Ryon as Nabal brought down his blade. The axe missed Sir Brock's chest by inches and sliced open his arm. He went sprawling as blood gushed onto the floor.

"Glademont evermore," Ryon heard his father shout, touching his heart with a closed fist.

Enraged, Ryon changed his course, leaping onto the remnants of a barricade. He loaded his sling. With all his strength, he flung his stone. It struck Nabal at the base of his neck. Nabal turned, his cold eyes landing on the boy atop the barricade.

"Kill that boy."

Ryon sprinted for his father, crumpled at Nabal's feet. He drew his dagger and shielded Sir Brock, challenging the king himself. Osiris had heard the order, too, and suddenly he was charging through the hounds like a bull. Golden magic sprayed from his snout. It traveled across the hall, over the heads of fighting Atheonians. Then it converged on its mark: Nabal's face. The king staggered backward just as he raised his axe for Ryon's head. The magic stuck to Nabal's skin like honey and obscured his vision, shooting relentlessly from Osiris's jaws and spraying across the floor. Osiris finally reached Ryon and his father and stood between them and his victim.

Spitting, Nabal lunged for the bear, and the magic momentarily ceased as Nabal grasped Osiris's ear. Nabal wiped his face, the beads in his beard shuddering with his rage. He was a man possessed, bent on the destruction of all that Glademont cherished. Osiris opened his mouth to cast another spell, but before the magic could strike true, Nabal brought down the flat side of his axe against Osiris's snout. Stunned, Osiris dropped to the floor. Nabal pinned the bear's head down with the edge of his axe.

"You have to use your witchcraft to take me down, eh, bear?" He laughed as his sweat dripped into Osiris's eyes. "Even the beasts of the forest cannot defeat me, muscle for muscle. I am Nabal, the new king of Glademont." Keeping his axe on Osiris's temple, Nabal pressed a heel against the bear's throat. "Cast a little spell now, beast," he taunted, then commanded his soldiers: "Crush him under the ram."

Men scrambled to do Nabal's bidding, and Ryon, small as he was, found himself forgotten underfoot. He struggled to stay beside his father, but someone kicked him, and he was flung against an overturned table.

In the confusion, Osiris swiped Nabal's feet with a mighty paw, and the barbarian king tumbled to the ground. Osiris searched the throng. There was no air left in Ryon's lungs to call to his friend. He struggled on his hands and knees, and the next moment, he heard a familiar baritone voice.

"Master Ryon!" Profigliano landed by Ryon's side. "I'm not one to get peevish but that was one dirty trick, scooting away from me. I tell ya, it's hard to find a chum in all this—Hey, you don't look so good."

"Papa," Ryon's thin voice squeaked. "Osiris."

"I gotcha, don't you say another word." And with that, Profigliano was in the air again, circling about his bondfellow and whistling shrilly. "Over here! We got a situation, mountain bear."

Spotting them, Osiris barreled headlong toward Ryon. Atheonians scattered out of his way. He slid to a halt on the marble.

"Don't ye be moving, young one." Osiris panted over the dazed boy. Hot blood from his javelin wound dripped onto Ryon's leg. "I needs to be finishing with yon filthy warrior."

The bear faced Nabal, who stood in the path Osiris had opened between his soldiers. The king arched his back, threw his arms over his head, and coiled forward again, hurtling his axe with all his strength. It whistled over the marble, striking Osiris between his shoulder and neck—and it struck deep.

Ryon cried out as his friend crashed to the floor. Several hounds leapt upon the bear, baying with delight. Nabal strode forward, placed a muddied foot on Osiris's gray fur, and withdrew his axe. Ryon could barely make out Osiris's shallow, ragged breaths as Nabal waved his dripping axe before the Atheonian men, who cheered uproariously.

> "Glory for the kingdom, vic'try for the king.
> The wretched cling to weaknesses, but soldiers
> mourn for no-thing!"

"I pledge . . ." Ryon pressed his ear to the floor to hear Osiris's gruff words. "I pledge to assist my person, in whatever goodly quest, until death."

Ryon lifted his head with tears in his eyes.

Don't go. We still need you, he yearned to tell him. Profigliano trembled against Ryon's hand.

Osiris, too, was crying. From beneath those unruly eyebrows, tears fell and formed a puddle between his paws, mingling with his blood. The puddle quietly flashed bright gold—like a polished ring in the sun. It expanded, glinting and gliding across the floor toward Ryon's beaten body.

Oblivious, the barbarian king spun his axe triumphantly, drinking his fill of the lauding mob. He tore off his chain mail and displayed a bare chest, streaked with sweat and bear's blood.

"Glademont's king died as I rose. He withered before my reign. His son, too, is gone, and his greatest warrior lies bleeding under my feet." Nabal ripped the shield from Osiris's back. The rich green seal of Glademont glinted on its surface. "This dione yields to me, belongs to *our* people."

The men bellowed their acclaim.

"It be up to thee now." Osiris's soft words reached Ryon's ear through the floor.

Ryon refused to understand. Every nerve shrieked with pain and despair. Profigliano was calling for him to lay still, saying he would protect them. But what good would it do, now that Osiris had been defeated? Ryon yearned for the swift blow of Nabal's axe, for an end to his vain efforts. He had failed as a warrior for Glademont.

Then, a memory sprang into his vision, crowding out the sweat and noise of battle. Jesse the Rushing stood in the calm comfort of the Birch Grove, looking out over Glademont Valley. *Peace must be protected,* he said, smelling the breeze with his soft muzzle.

A cool, tangy liquid touched Ryon's lips and woke him from his reverie. He lay against the floor, bewildered. Could it be blood? The liquid flowed against his mouth again, as though reading Ryon's thoughts. Not just blood, but bear's blood, mingled with tears and enchanted by the gift of an oath.

Ryon pulled his cracked lips together and tasted the thick, smooth enchantment against the back of his tongue. It shot like a tidal wave through his veins, igniting every muscle.

Peace must be protected.

With a guttural cry, Ryon rose to his feet and drew his slender dagger. He bounded toward King Nabal, who stood lording over his subjects, his arms spread wide.

"Glademont evermore!" Ryon leapt, lifted high into the air by Osiris's last enchantment. Clearing over the heads of man and beast, Ryon then crashed against Nabal, and plunged his blade into the king's heart. His knuckles felt the wet of blood on Nabal's skin. He let go the dagger and fell at Nabal's feet. The barbarian king swayed, his throat and mouth working to draw air. A shocked gasp radiated from the Atheonian forces. Then king, shield, and axe clattered to the floor.

A moment of brilliant adrenaline, and Ryon stood over Nabal, gazing at the leather-bound handle of his dagger lodged in the king's bare chest. Then he felt a queasy pulling in his stomach. Dozens of Atheonian faces swirled in his vision. The slow, distant clapping of hooves vibrated in his ears. Then, all was dark.

CHAPTER 49

Moving unsteadily through the tomb-like corridor, Tess listened for another roar from her shaggy friend, but none came. She swallowed through a dry throat, and began to run.

Reaching the banquet hall, she saw a long line of noblewomen at the opposite end, barring the way in with makeshift weapons. Atheonian soldiers gathered behind the wide columns, apparently preferring to goad the women than to fight.

Tess cautiously crossed the floor, passing rows of cots where the injured were laid. The servants tried to stop Tess from nearing the fight, but she pulled her arms from them, searching for Osiris. Soon, she spotted Dahly and her mother leading the small brigade from the center of the line. They swung short spades at any nearing soldier while the men teased and sneered. Then, a flock of vultures swooped through the ornate archway to the banquet hall. They sailed over the Atheonians and stretched their talons to tear into the women of Glademont.

Tess sprinted forward, scrambling for her *shenil*. The vultures were already upon her sister and mother, ripping their hair and clothes. Soldiers cheered and advanced as the women ran for cover. Dahly was caught between two vultures, each gripping an arm. Lady Matilde called for help, her head under constant attack.

"Hold on," Tess yelled as she tried to calm down enough to use the *shenil* properly. The screams of the women and the screeches of the vultures completely clouded her mind, so much so that she scooped up an empty washbasin and prepared to use brute force. But then another sound rang in Tess's ears: hooves clapping on marble. Jesse the Rushing trotted before her, tossing his creamy mane.

"Get down," he demanded.

The stallion lowered his soft nose and issued one forceful exhale. The marble at his hooves cracked and ran in opposite directions as sparkling golden gas puffed over the fissures. The cracks ran from the floor to two columns. The columns burst, and the fragments went flying.

One by one, vultures were struck in midair by hunks of marble, beginning with Dahly's captors. Half-dazed, Lady Matilde and Dahly supported each other and stumbled to safety. By the time Jesse was finished, not a vulture in the room was left alive.

But the remaining Atheonian soldiers did not give up. Arrows and javelins flew all around them as Tess leapt onto Jesse's back. With her stallion's familiar, sturdy muscles flexing against Tess's legs, Tess regained her courage. She took up her *shenil* and summoned a flame. She fluidly traced a curving path with her hands. A fireball shot from somewhere near her navel and slung in a wide arc for the Atheonians, blinding them as it passed. The fireball returned to Tess's hands, and she readied herself for the *shenil* to speak again.

But the soldiers did not recover their sight. They groped at the air, moaning in fear. Tess allowed herself to exhale. The women and the wounded were out of danger. For now. She called to her mother and sister to get the wounded out of the open and urged Jesse to a canter.

Jesse's hooves echoed down the hall where Tess had last seen Ryon. She heard shouting and the shuffling of hundreds of feet, but not the clanging of metal or the cries of the wounded. Tess slowed Jesse to a quieter gait. She peered ahead and saw masses of shifting men, but their movements were not urgent.

Finally, tentatively, Tess and her stallion came upon the entrance hall. Bodies littered the floor, and to Tess's horror, the majority of them were Glademontian men. The surviving men and governors were being rounded up by disorderly, sporadic pockets of Atheonians. Among the prisoners were Nory, Rette, and a very pale Sir Brock.

"Sands and Yuniparos, to me," shouted an aristocratic-looking officer with a long twisted mustache. "Holts, report to Silverear," he roared over the hubbub, pointing to a fat gentleman with a flushed neck.

Searching the cavernous hall, Tess observed a small black figure with amber eyes hiding behind a tapestry by Jesse's left flank. She struggled to remember the forest creature's name.

"Evening," she whispered finally.

"My lady . . ." Evening slinked sheepishly out.

"Where is Osiris?" Tess felt the panic rising in her throat.

"Oh, my lady," the fox moaned. "I fear it may be too late."

"Where?" Tess insisted, no longer caring whether the Atheonians noticed her.

"The towhee protects his body, my lady. But we are all lost." Evening streaked out of sight again.

"Let's go, Jesse."

They charged through the tangled crowd. Soldiers shouted after them, leaping out of the way and brandishing their weapons. Several javelins spun through the air, but Tess spread her arms open and a dancing fire consumed each weapon as quickly as it flew. The din in the entrance hall reached an unbearable pitch as soldiers and prisoners jostled one another, but all Tess could see was a magic shield, and the motionless furry mass beyond it.

Jesse cast an enchantment that opened a way through the skin of Profigliano's massive bubble. As the shield closed behind them, Tess tumbled off of her steed, throwing herself onto Osiris. Blood soaked his fur, but he was still breathing. Tess held up the orbs of the *shenil* with shaking hands, but the *shenil* would not respond. The voice was silent, and the fire had died out.

Dropping the object, Tess tenderly took the gray bear's heavy head in her lap.

"It won't work," she sobbed. "It won't let me heal you."

"Now, now," Osiris answered with a breathy chuckle. "Don't ye dare be healing me, little gem. How long have I been waiting to see King Wallis again? Ye wouldn't be taking that away from me now, would ye?"

"Please don't leave me." Tess laid her face on his cheek.

"Two hundred and forty-three years . . . It were worth it just to be knowing thee. Now, with the help o' yer mighty brother, I be finishing me oath. Glademont be safe with thee now."

The last breath of Osiris the Defender curled gently from his soft nose in dim, golden strands. Tess shook her head and clutched at his matted gray-brown fur. She wept knowing she would never hear his thundering brogue again, telling her to protect her heart, to know her duty, to be good to her friends. She wept for a cold, empty den waiting in the heart of the Hinge. She wept for the death of Old Glademont.

Outside, the muted jeers of Atheonian soldiers could be heard.

"Tessy, deary," Profigliano said through a mouthful of magic. "We've got lots more problems." While the small bird endeavored to sustain a golden bubble of significant size, the Atheonians without had finally gathered enough hounds to begin an assault. The bubble reverberated as various bouts of red magic slammed against its surface.

Reverently, Tess kissed Osiris's closed eyes. She rose, wiping her cheeks, and saw the other ill-fated occupants of Profigliano's little fortress.

"By the skies, is that . . . King Nabal? Profigliano, tell me Ryon—"

"Alive," mumbled Profigliano, straining under the weight of the onslaught. "But let's tackle one worm at a time, don't ya think?"

The bubble started to thin, developing worrisome splotches. Tess ran to Ryon and checked for a pulse. There was blood on his right hand, but no wound. His pulse was slow but strong. Breathing a sigh of relief and kissing his forehead, she pulled forth the *shenil* and forced herself, once again, to focus on the modes of surrender.

A hound leapt atop the wavering bubble, baying and sending massive flashes of magic between his feet. The bubble groaned and swayed, and Profigliano's black tail drooped.

"Hold steady," Tess said. A flame burned high and white between her hands, tickling the top of the golden bubble. As it touched the dome's surface, a bright film melted over the dome, from the apex to the floor. Profigliano's newly fortified bubble flashed like a mirror at the Atheonians and hounds, who shielded their eyes.

"Rest, Fig," Tess said, keeping her hands firmly in the position of the Thane's Hold.

The towhee collapsed. His wings sprawled out on the marble and his little red-and-white breast heaved. Tess chanced another glance at Ryon. How on the continent was she going to get him out of this mess? She had failed to keep Aideen alive, then Osiris. Would she fail at saving him, too?

Commotion outside the gleaming bubble distracted Tess from her fears, and she saw through her spell the distorted image of an aristocratic man, who seemed to be arguing with the one called Silverear.

"—must make sure that he is dead, Cojab," Silverear said, "or he'll return to Atheos and he'll have our heads."

"Exactly how do you propose we get to him?"

"I don't know, Cojab. . . . Negotiate with her! We used to be a *civilized* people."

"Don't lecture *me* on civilized people. I've been saying all along—"

Then, the shadow of a dark bird materialized on the shoulder of the one called Cojab, and the orbs of the *shenìl* crackled frantically over Tess's palms. Her frightened heart sent out a single booming throb from her chest to her fingertips.

"My lords, I believe I can be of service," Pider said.

Tess bit her lip and closed her eyes. Pider had returned. Tess knew this time he would not bargain. This time, he was out for her blood.

"On one condition," the crow continued. "That no Atheonian come near the young woman, whatever his reason. I must be allowed to deal with her in my own way."

"Up to his tricks," Tess heard Silverear say as he nervously smoothed his hair against his head. But Tess knew only too well how persuasive Pider could be. She took a deep breath and waited.

"Profigliano, are you still with me?"

"Aye . . . Captain." The towhee, still flat on his back, held up a sagging wing.

"I need you to look after Ryon for just a bit longer. Can you do that?"

"Until death, Captain. We'll rage against the stormy seas." Profigliano wobbled to his little feet.

A grating, screeching sound filled their magical fortress, and Tess could not help but put her hands to her ears, relinquishing her flame. The bubble started to cave. It gave like molten glass and smelled like scorched metal. The sound subsided, and Tess mounted Jesse, slowing her breathing. She waited for the bubble to dissolve, her eyes fixed on Pider.

The crow circled high overhead, red magic erupting from his beak and falling onto the last remnants of Profigliano's shield. Jesse pawed at the floor and shook his mane. His ears flattened against his head. Atheonians and Glademontians alike looked on with horror. Lord Cojab visibly shook, calling shrilly for the army to fall back.

When the bubble was no more, Pider swung low over the heads of the Atheonian army and called out, "Remember your orders, Atheos. The girl belongs to me."

Tess lifted her chin at the magician in disguise. She was not afraid. He could not bribe her, and he could not deceive her. His puppet king was dead, his smooth-talking sailor gone. Pider had no more tricks to hide behind. And Tess had no more doubts as to her charge. If there was going to be one thing in her life that she would do right, it was this.

For several frozen seconds, the crow's *caws* echoed in the great hall as he glided high between the dark buttresses. But the next second he was dropping from the heights toward Tess, propelled by a stream of red gas.

Tess summoned her flame, but Pider was coming so fast, she did not wait for the voice to tell her what to do. Instead, she threw her hands forward to conjure a fireball. The fire flickered and turned orange, but nothing came. Pider opened his beak, and from it sprang a lightning bolt hot enough to slice through rock. Jesse reared, and the bolt struck Tess in the leg. The pain nearly blinded her, and the smell of burnt skin made her sick to her stomach. She pressed her forehead against Jesse's neck, struggling to breathe. But the *shenil* remained in her hands.

As Pider circled for a second attack, Jesse stepped backward, lowering his head. Before the crow could open his beak to cast another spell, magic from Jesse's nostrils sent a jagged hunk of earth surging up from beneath the marble. Soldiers flew in all directions, and the crow swerved, throwing another lightning bolt, which blasted Jesse's mound to dust.

The pain of Tess's injury was paralyzing. She almost welcomed the darkness of unconsciousness. For the second time that night,

Tess realized she might die fighting Pider. Perhaps her ladle had been poured after all.

At once, the *shenil* ignited, and the flame pushed Tess back from Jesse's neck, coaxing her to sit up. Covering her wounded leg with her cloak, Tess closed her eyes and pictured Ember's joyful, reassuring face.

The fire sprang even higher between Tess's hands, and she waited for her instructions. When the voice of the *shenil* came, Tess kept her eyes closed and made a fluid pushing motion with her hands and torso. It was the same motion she had danced when she played Fyrian, bequeathing new breath to a bygone empress. A hot, silent wind flowed from her palms, barely palpable even to Tess. When the voice of the *shenil* told her to open her eyes, Tess saw a divide blown through the crowded soldiers. A path appeared between Tess and the splintered castle doors. Squeezing her knees into Jesse's sides, Tess raced on her stallion toward the doors. Pider reeled. Jesse and Tess passed under him and shot out of the castle.

The free air felt heavenly on Tess's face, and she made no move to pull Jesse back. She kept her mind open to the bidding of the *shenil*, and did her best not to think of what was about to happen. Jesse descended the stairs, passed through the outer wall, and crossed over the tattered lawn. The *shenil* guided them through the bandits' trodden camp, right up to the gaping crevice of Osiris's moat.

Just on the castle side of the extinguished moat, Prince Linden and the valley creatures of the FOM formed a long, glorious silhouette against the horizon. By the purple light of sunset, Tess saw their horns and pitchforks, bloodied by battle. Their bodies stood ready as the hour they gathered at Redfoot.

Then Pider appeared. Searing lava cascaded over Linden, whose face was barely protected by a hasty spell from Currant's mouth. The FOM divided and flanked Jesse as several sheep used their magic to counterattack the crow.

Tess held her flame high in the air. The *shenil* responded immediately, and a terrible funnel of fire exploded from her hands, chasing Pider high into the twilight.

Ahead, a shepherd's horn blew reedy and clear. In response, the Atheonians poured out of the castle, crying, *"Eee-aaa-hoo!"* Within minutes, the battle was raging again. Mountain rams and ewes wasted no time in bowling over soldiers, crushing weapon and bone with their impervious skulls. Ponies reared on their sturdy hooves and slung golden magic from their muzzles, ripping into a pack of hounds. Shepherd and breeder joined together and fought their way through the mob, hardened by the havoc Atheos had inflicted on their kind. Nory, Rette, and the remaining noblemen managed to free themselves in the chaos and doggedly aided the FOM, fighting with their bare fists.

None of this affected Pider. He remained focused on Tess. Lava and lightning rained down on her and Jesse. Gasping, Tess did her best to stay true to the *shenil*'s direction. Whenever Pider flew near enough, Jesse would sling the rock beneath him. But nothing would abate the crow. Tess's leg radiated pain.

Then Tess heard the distinctive barking of Colonel Regency Thorn, fast approaching.

"Guild, to me! To me!" he commanded.

Over a dozen governors bounded after the Colonel, barking and growling in his wake. Exuberantly, they formed an arc in front of Jesse's forelegs.

"Ready your defenses," the Colonel called.

Pider sent crackling lightning streaking into the terriers, illuminating the battle in one terrifying moment. Three were struck down before they could raise a shield.

"Cliffdwellers!" Tartan the Terrible strode into view, tossing his sharp horns in the air. "We are needed here!"

Tess felt vibrations through Jesse's body as dozens of heavy hooves hurried to flank her. Pider circled overhead, spilling lava in torrents. A small army of shimmering golden horns, straight and curved, leapt into the navy sky at once. The spells chased Pider, like tongues of fire nipping at a moth. But many of the bondfellows below could not avoid the lava, and their wool was set ablaze as soon as it touched their fur. The governors hurried to save who they could. Tess's own fire wavered as she heard the desperate bleats of her suffering friends.

"Atheos, take down these animals," she heard Pider yell over the battle. But no man neared Tess's stronghold. Nabal's army stumbled in the dark, defenseless against the power of the bondfellows' magic.

"Ponies of the plains, rise with me." Young Abe leapt before Jesse, his long mane matted and muddied. The rest of his clan appeared with pricked ears. Overhead, Buchanan of Westbend and Cantor the falcon called to their kind, flapping in restless circles. Tess heard her heart thumping against her ribs. The *shenil* told her to wait.

Down came Pider, wild and wrathful, slinging lightning, lava, and swirling red smoke. The governors snarled while the Wallatonians pawed at the earth. The ponies reared, and Tess closed her eyes. She heard the pained cries of her defenders, calls for help, and the barking of her own governor. But still she did not act.

"I surrender to your designs, Fyrian. I surrender to the *shenil*," she said. She knew Pider was almost to her. But she knew with even more certainty that the *shenil* should be trusted. Her upturned hands drifted farther apart, and she opened her chest to the stars, like a dancer before her final bow.

Lava spewed from Pider's beak, landing on Tess's chest and spilling onto her arms.

The Colonel howled and Jesse spun about in shock. But when Tess opened her eyes and breathed, she was amazed to find she was unharmed. The lava on her chest sizzled and cooled, but she neither felt pain nor smelled the burning of flesh as before. Suddenly, something Osiris said flashed in her mind.

Fire be doing the dryad's bidding, and she never be burned by it.

The *shenil* held a gem dryad's magic, and as long as Tess gave herself completely to the modes of surrender, she was in perfect union with Fyrian's essence. Tess almost laughed as she peeled a smoldering piece of lava from her chest. She tossed the lava at the circling Pider. Its heat ignited the feathers on his back. He cawed and tumbled to the ground, rolling in the dust.

Tess dropped from Jesse's back and limped to Pider. She peeled more lava from her arms. It held together like burning gelatin in her enchanted hands. She stood over the squirming crow, her velvet cloak gathering in the dusky wind.

"This is the home of my heart," she said to him. "And you cannot have it."

Tess's arm extended over Pider's unseeing face, she bent her wrist and let the lava spill from her opening fingers. Pider screamed—the wail of a human man. His small black crow's body writhed under the thick puddle of lava. Red droplets formed on the surface of the molten pool, like livid dew. Pider's screams faded and the droplets spread over the burning mass. Soon the body of a bird was no longer discernible, and the puddle burst into a scarlet fire. It burned only for an instant, then withdrew into a pile of ash. Tess recoiled at the smell of charred feathers and bone. Colonel Thorn approached, sniffing. But the next moment, a howling wind surged across the sleeping moat and scattered the ashes to nothing. Tess turned her shoulder as the wind drove against her. She thought she heard a man's voice whistling with the air:

No home stands forever.

She shivered.

"Retreat, Atheos," Lord Cojab shrieked.

With apparent relief, the remaining soldiers lowered their weapons, slinking backward until out of range. The animals did not stop them as the Atheonians finally fled westward to the Hinge. The hounds scurried behind, baying woefully.

Tess heard Linden summon the captain of the raptors. "Cantor, follow them, and be sure they don't lose their way."

"Highness," answered the falcon as he called his clan to him. They floated silently after the Atheonians and disappeared among the trees.

Wrapped in the ecstatic, bleary cheers that followed, Tess pressed her face against Jesse's butterscotch neck and stroked his powerful head. Her knees trembled under her shepherdess's uniform, and she felt the steady arm of Sir Brock Canyon catch her before she fell.

CHAPTER 50

Would you dance with me?" Linden said. His brilliant green coat glowed in the firelight. Tess smelled oil and citrus on his slicked hair, kept in place by his circlet. She liked it better the old way.

A month had passed since the war with Atheos, and despite the chill of early winter, Glademont seemed rejuvenated. War-torn Redfoot was in the midst of its first Feast of Bondfellows. Chains the Atheonians used to enslave Redfooties had been melted down, painted, and hung as crests on the colonnade. Crests of Wallaton, Foggy Plains, Redfoot, Green Reed, and the royal insignia decorated the outskirts of the square. Friends of the Militia were especially honored. With Linden's help, Prince Currant of the Birch Herd designed his family's first crest—a large acorn centered in a stand of white trees. The Council of the Nest displayed its colors, too, with a crescent moon hovering over tangled branches and bordered by two curved feathers.

The new judge of Redfoot had ordered that the markers of the fallen be decorated with highest honors, not the least of which was fashioned in memory of Judge Glasmilk, who died at the storming of Redfoot. Just inside the colonnade, where brick walkways stretched along two arms from the rotunda to the Eastern Gate, long rows of plaques were set and engraved in memory of man and beast. Multicolored lanterns swayed along the walkways, and little bells dangled over each plaque, so that even the wind itself helped to commemorate those who had passed.

Baked treats and warm cider flowed at every turn. Artisans sold commemorative stones etched with, WAR WITH ATHEOS, AUTUMNTIDE, 315TH YEAR. Others set up collections for the rebuilding of the academy and the repairing of various homes or shops. Boys sprinted between the legs of their elders, donning paper circlets, sticks fashioned into antlers, or papier-mâché goat horns. Some had muddied their hair, tied a strip of cloth across their foreheads, and busied themselves reenacting the famous courage of Master Ryon Canyon, who slew the Barbarian King.

Amid all this, Tess went unnoticed. The noblemen who had seen her wield the *shenil's* power could not explain it. And no one who heard tell of her fire could recall a time when humans wielded magic alongside bondfellows. In fact, they had hardly believed in the gift of bondfellows before the war. The elders were afraid of her, and the young people were mystified by her. She was not praised as was Ryon, or Linden. Few knew the real enemy had been a sightless crow.

Linden offered Tess his hand in the middle of the square between the roaring fires. There was no orchestra tonight, only the mingled music of those who had brought their own instruments. A nearby band of Wallaton boys with fiddles and flutes began a rendition of "Mother Zere." Linden bowed.

"I believe I've owed you a dance for some time." The corner of his mouth tilted. It was the first time Tess had seen him smile since before his mother died.

Tess said nothing, but took his hand. It was warm. Linden pulled her in, slipped his other hand under her fur-lined cloak and around her waist. Tess gasped and leaned against him, bending her wounded leg. He hoisted her against his ribs, lifting her to her toes, and swayed.

"I've missed you," Linden said.

Tess closed her eyes and touched his cheek with hers.

"I'm sorry I haven't come to see you," he said. "There is so much to be done, now that Mother . . . now that we must start again."

"We are rebuilding, too. Rebuilding the manor, Papa's work . . . Ryon's formation is delayed a year, with the academy so damaged."

"And Osiris's burial?" Linden asked. "The Governor's Guild carried him safely to the redbuds?"

Tess hummed and sighed. "I wish you had been there."

They danced in silence and let the lilting words of "Mother Zere" soften their hearts.

> She cradles the cliffs on her bosom
> Shielding the flocks from the winds of the sea.
> Her snowy veil waters the blossom,
> Her rocky shoulder bends o'er the trees.

"I'm ashamed of my proposal," he began. "How I dismissed you."

Tess tried to keep her hand relaxed in his, but she couldn't help but breathe faster.

"I thought that marrying was a waste of precious time. I was always thinking of the castle archives, making weapons, training . . . keeping my mother alive."

Tess nodded, but kept her eyes on Linden's shoulder.

"I'm trying to say . . . I don't know when it happened. But, when you came to the Ruins, looking so determined, and when I saw how another man looked at you . . . Every day, your face appears when I close my eyes. I keep wanting to touch your hair, to watch you fuss over Ryon, to hear you say my name." Tess realized there was a lull in the music, and Linden gently lowered her, putting her fingers to his lips.

"Linden," she said.

He smiled. "There, you said it."

Tess swallowed and discovered she wanted to cry. But she daren't. "Once, I begged the red star every night for you to see me as more than a vain, silly dancer. But our world has changed since then." She lifted her orange-green eyes to meet his, and saw that they were moist. "My world has changed." Oh, *why* did this have to happen? "Asher has found me a cottage—"

"Tess, I'm asking you to marry me. Not because my mother chose you, but because I could not be a good king without you."

Tess pulled away, and her leg twinged. Her chest felt hot under her gown as she stared at the ground.

"I promised," she said with a quivering voice.

Linden stared. His styled hair had gone slightly askew when Tess pulled away.

"What did you promise?" he said. The fires crackled behind them and the cheers of happy citizens echoed distantly.

If Tess told him of her promise to never be queen, would Linden ask why Fyrian chose it as her sacrifice? Tess cringed at the thought of revealing her secret temptation, of her desire to be adored. And what if, after knowing Tess's promise, he felt obligated still to marry her? Would he renounce the throne and leave Glademont to flounder, when it was already so fragile? That was no way to begin her new life as the dione's guardian.

"Are you to marry another?" Linden asked, his voice quiet and steady.

She took his hands, shaking her head.

"Tess," he said slowly. "I should have seen from the beginning, you were my only one. You could rule the way my mother did. And you could make me happy the way my father was. But I won't force you. I won't speak of it until you are ready."

Tess heard someone calling her name. Linden reached out and pushed her wisps behind her ear. His hand lingered.

"I'll beg the red star every night until then," he said with a low voice. Tess could see his jaw clenching ever so slightly. Without realizing what she was doing, she moved her hand to her engagement band. She pulled the smooth pearl circle from her finger. Her skin where the band had lain felt icy and exposed.

"No, please—"

Tess forced the ring into his hand.

Ryon was suddenly at Tess's side, tugging on her arm.

"Tessy, remember Scholar Holly?" he said. Profigliano whistled from his shoulder.

"What?" said Tess. "Of course, I remember—Oh, Headmaster Holly."

A small redheaded man in his late sixties peered over his tiny spectacles at Tess.

"I-it's wonderful to see you," she stuttered. Headmaster Holly would always be imposing, no matter how long it had been since Tess's first day of class. She was especially surprised that he would speak to her in public, since most of his contemporaries had taken to eyeing her warily as she passed. The dione's abrupt transformation from a peaceful land to a place teeming with magic still did not sit well with the older generation, and they suspected Tess to be at the center of it. "I'm so sorry about the academy," she began.

"Naturally," the curt headmaster replied. He bowed to the prince.

"Wouldn't it be great?" Ryon breathed. "If we could all be together at the academy?"

Profigliano bounced his black-and-white striped shoulders. "All of us fancy-pants heroes, struttin' our magical stuff in the house of smarties." He threw his beak in the air.

"I don't understand. . . ."

The headmaster frowned. "Master Ryon, I sincerely hope you will have learned discretion by the time you return to the academy." Ryon shrugged. He had gained considerable confidence since holding his own in two full-fledged battles.

"Miss Tessamine, Your Highness," the headmaster said. "Perhaps you have not yet met the Venerable Judge Lucille Cedar?"

They shook their heads.

"I was unable to attend the robes ceremony," the prince said apologetically.

"Naturally," the headmaster replied. "My point: We at the academy work closely with the city's officials. We strive to accommodate Redfoot's needs as well as the needs of the dione."

Tess smiled and nodded politely, but wondered how any of this applied to her.

"My point *is*," continued Headmaster Holly, "Judge Cedar requests new departments be added to the academy's staff, in light of the recent turn of events." He waved a stubby hand around his head, as if to say, *You know, the battling and so on.*

"You"—he pointed emphatically at Tess—"have acquired a special skill set that, Prince Linden tells me, can be taught." Tess shot the prince a dark look. "And, since I happen to have instructed you myself, I know you are worth your salt." The headmaster pursed his lips with satisfaction.

"I still don't understand," Tess said timidly. The cottage in Wallaton called her name louder every second she remained in the square.

"My point"—Headmaster Holly adjusted his tiny frames—"I need new scholars for my new departments. Miss Tessamine, I'll need you to head the Magic Department. Of course, I'd prefer His Highness in our Combat Department, but since he must succeed as king . . ." He widened his eyes to nudge the spectacles down his nose, as if to say, *What's done is done, but it's a terrible inconvenience.* "At any rate, Master Cherrywater has agreed."

Both Tess and the prince offered their protests.

"Lady Tessamine may not be available. . . ."

"I'm afraid I will reside in Wallaton for some time. . . ."

Headmaster Holly showed a palm.

"Tut, tut, tut, tut, young ones," he said with extended eyebrows. "Details can be discussed at a later time. We will need at least until next autumntide to get back on our feet. You have until the spring to make your decision, Miss Tessamine. Bear in mind, however"—his watery eyes narrowed even further over his spectacles—"that we have few persons from which to choose. The academy desperately needs you. For that matter—though it is an unpopular idea at the moment—the dione needs you. If these animals had not come out of the woodwork to save our skins, Glademont would be under Atheonian rule as we speak. Hundreds more would be dead. You just ponder *that*." He jerked a stubby finger under their noses. Then, acknowledging Ryon with a nod, he briskly made his way to a cider table.

"So, what do you think?" Ryon beamed and stroked Profigliano's chest with a knuckle.

Linden ran a hand through his hair, realized that it was full of styling oil, then pulled out a handkerchief to wipe his fingers. "I'll need to talk to the advisors on this. The academy years seem young to be training in combat. I'll need Rette for the militia, and Tess . . . Well, Redfoot is no small journey to the castle." He glanced at Tess shyly.

"We've all been making plans, Ry," Tess said firmly. "Don't get your hopes up." She gave Linden a meaningful look.

"Wouldn't you rather be in the city than all alone up on the cliffs?" Ryon reasoned. "Scholastics could be your vocation, since you never had a chance to . . ." He stopped himself, seeing the panic in Tess's expression.

Linden, gentleman that he was, took his cue.

"I see your father has arrived. He's worked so vigilantly since the attacks, you'll be wanting to enjoy the celebration together." Linden bowed; threw Tess a final, furtive look; and strode away.

As Sir Brock waved from behind the Wallatonian minstrels, Tess thought he looked tired but relieved. He and the other royal advisors had been hearing trials for three weeks—mostly deciding the fates of captured Atheonians who fought for Nabal. Tess sucked in a draft of cold air, pulling her cloak tight around her shoulders. The last trial was Tynaiv's.

"Hello, my bright-eyed children," her father called in his usual warm way. His injured arm was bound against his chest, leaving an empty coat sleeve to hang by his side.

"Papa." Ryon shook his father's good hand. He no longer tolerated hugs.

Tess felt just the opposite, and she welcomed Sir Brock's shoulder against her cheek.

"How's my heroine holding up?" he said.

Though he did not know of the *shenil*, Sir Brock had watched Tess defeat Pider on the castle lawn. Unlike the other noblemen, he had no doubt the fire had come from Tess. Since then, he never pressed her to speak of it. He only kissed her more often and called her his heroine.

"We heard a bandit the other day," he said. "He described you riding through their camp like lightning out of the sky. Those were his words." He smiled and kissed Tess's thick black hair.

"Who did you hear today?" Tess tried to sound only mildly interested.

"Strange business." Sir Brock sniffed the night air and searched the clear winter sky. Tess wondered if he was second-guessing his verdict. "It was that fellow who kidnapped you on the cliffs. I was afraid I couldn't judge him objectively. But when he was brought out . . . well, he just looked like a troubled boy to me. A boy who probably imagined all this would go very differently."

Tess was surprised to feel thumping in her chest.

"Still, the fact is, he's guilty of quite a few crimes against the dione. Trespassing at the wedding festival, spying on the royal family, holding the prince hostage, the list goes on." Sir Brock rubbed his eyes. "He'll be held here in the rotunda until we can arrange for his banishment.

Matter of fact, the only way I was able to make it tonight was to volunteer to escort him myself. There he goes now."

With a jerk of his exaggerated chin, Sir Brock indicated the western end of the square, where the grand stairs led up to the Market's rotunda. Three men climbed the stairs, and the one in the middle had his hands tied at the back of his neck. The pounding in Tess's chest grew louder. Tynaiv still managed to strut, even to his own imprisonment.

"We're lucky the prince caught up with him. Just a boy, of course, but a dangerous one," Sir Brock said.

When Ryon dragged his father away to watch the blacksmiths demonstrate their new techniques for shield making, Tess smiled and waved, but inside she felt tired and dismal. There were still people to thank: Nory and Rette, her sister and mother, and the brave creatures in the FOM. Most of the members of the Council of the Nest had declined the invitation to the festival, eager to resume their quiet existence as wild and independent animals. But, there was one Hinge Forester that Tess was most anxious to see.

Careful to avoid Linden's eye, Tess slipped away from the bustle of the market square and passed through the lighted walkways under the colonnades. She alighted a narrow staircase that led to a small guest room above the southern walkway. To Tess's surprise, Judge Cedar had invited her to stay in one of these prestigious rooms. After speaking with Headmaster Holly, she no longer wondered why. Tess tugged at an old, solid door and sighed with relief when she could finally rest her back against its interior side.

"I warned it would be most unpleasant, my lady," said Wyndeling, who yawned on the windowsill. Tess pulled her *shenil* from her waist, pressed it against her stomach, and threw herself on the bed. She buried her face in a dense pillow.

"I don't mean to complain," Wyndeling said, "but I had not thought of acclimating to a human schedule when I made the oath. It seems I sleep much more often than I used to, and yet I feel twice as sleep deprived."

Tess rolled over on her back and smirked. "If you like, I'll take more naps during the day, and we can stay up together at night, talking about our feelings and our friendships, our hopes and our dreams. . . ."

"Oh, for pity's sake. I'll take sleep deprivation, thank you very much." Wyndeling fluffed up her feathers in protest.

Tess chuckled weakly, placing her hands over her eyes.

"My lady, when do we leave for the cliffs? This hubbub is affecting my health. And the close air of this city is stunting my feather growth."

"You may have to get used to those bald patches," Tess said, her hands still clasped over her eyes.

"What on the continent do you mean by that?"

"I've been offered a position here in Redfoot. I know I said the dione would be safer if we were somewhere remote, but . . ."

"This *but* had better be very convincing." Wyndeling hooted unsympathetically.

"But, if I am isolated, I won't know when something is going amiss, will I? I'd be the last to know if there was a threat to Glademont. Plus, Tynaiv is being held here, and there's no telling what mischief he'll be up to, even in a cell."

"I believe you know my opinion of *that* one," Wyndeling said. "The farther you are from him, the better."

Tess uncovered her eyes and went to the window. Looking at the bright winter stars, shining on the joyous feast, she felt a pang of loneliness.

"We can winter on the cliffs, Wyndeling. But I'm afraid I wouldn't be carrying out my duty as the thane if I stayed there forever."

The red owl sighed and blinked up at the stars with her large mesmerizing eyes. "I admit, it's comforting to know that great oaf is watching us," she said wistfully.

"Who? Osiris?"

"Didn't you notice?" Wyndeling said. "There's a new constellation. See it there? A bear by a tree."

Wyndeling extended a wing upward, and Tess squinted at the sparkling navy blanket. "I don't see it," she said.

"He's there," said Tess's bondfellow. "He's watching."

ACKNOWLEDGMENTS

Some who graduate from a modern American college fall into what can only be described as a depressed stupor of the least sympathetic kind. This describes yours truly in the summer of 2009, and by October of that year it was clear I would have to find an occupation, or my parents might get ideas about kicking me off their deck chair. So, wanting to enjoy the best of the north Georgia autumn breezes, I took up a pencil and some loose-leaf paper and endeavored to write a fantasy novel . . . from the deck chair.

This fantasy novel contained sweet sentiments and did wonders for my emotional heart, but it was never worth reading until the following people got their nimble fingers on it.

First, my dear friend Adair and I met weekly over tea and snacks to discuss in great detail each character and scene. I believe a developmental editor would charge a house on Valley Road for the amount of time and energy Adair put into that evolving draft. The most valuable gift she gave me was that she loved the story it could be and strove to bring out the best in my writing.

When my own dashing prince, Hill, and I were married, I got up the courage to share my work in progress with him. Endless bolstering and rousing speeches followed and continue to this day. It was Hill who convinced me to leave behind my job as a full-time theology teacher to write books. It was Hill who helped me make the leap into indie publishing. And other than my Lord, it is Hill whom I wish to please most, and have always wished so, since I was seventeen.

Once I made public my desire to become an author, many, many loving souls graced these pages with their attention. My most committed beta readers, Caki and Aunt Marta, have never hesitated to read and acclaim my words. Paul made the manuscript's first professional developmental edit. Rayna celebrated my small successes. Sweet Morgan read a huge stack of loose printer paper out of a box. Sarah and I discussed our fledgling books over coffee. Molly made me feel like a real-life writer. Jill and I became instant bosom friends at a writers' conference. And so many cherished friends, old and new, have reached out to offer their support, even without yet knowing Tess and her story.

Next came the dream come true, which was to sign with a literary agent. Julie Gwinn of the Seymour Literary Agency championed this story and eventually encouraged me to publish it on my own. I am honored to be among the authors she represents. A special debt of gratitude I owe to Leah and Meg, who so kindly brought this novel to Julie's attention.

I wish to recall the aforementioned parents, who claim to have loved the time I spent moping in their house from 2009 to 2010, who then gladly agreed to send me back to school for another degree, and who have shamelessly advertised me as a graceful saint, though we all know the reality to be otherwise. They, along with my siblings and their spouses, are perhaps the best members of the domestic church Atlanta has ever seen. Mom, Dad, Sylvia, Scott, Rachel (see exquisite illustrations throughout), Thomas, John, Caitlin—I love you.

Since becoming a bride, I have experienced the joy of a family doubled. And it seems Hill's family has decided to catch up with my own by squeezing decades of support and encouragement into the last seven. Ginger, Big Hill, Hartley, and Chris—I love you, too.

Lastly, Girl Friday Productions must be zealously congratulated on the editing, designing, styling, and general execution of this book. I am particularly grateful to Devon, Tegan, and Georgie, all of whom have given me reason to hope that this book will bring joy to more than my family and friends. If you are a writer with a book worth reading, break that piggy bank and hand the coins to GFP. You will not be sorry.

All these souls are part of this book, and I hope it is a little part of them. If you are wondering whether any characters are based on individuals from my life, the answer is "yes."

Wally, you may have only been a miniature schnauzer to the groomer who banned you for biting him, but you will always be the Colonel in our hearts. RIP.

ABOUT THE AUTHOR

Photo © 2018 James Ting

E mily H. Jeffries is a theology teacher and speaker with bachelor's degrees in drama and religious studies from the University of Virginia and a master's in sacred theology from the Dominican House of Studies in Washington, DC, where most of her classmates were wizards—that is, friars. She loves wandering through forests and cathedrals, and her hidden magical abilities include performing improv comedy, evading cardiovascular activity, and singing all of *Les Misérables* from memory. She currently lives in Atlanta, Georgia, with her husband, baby daughter, Aussie-doodle, and herbs.

THANK YOU so much for reading my debut novel, *Fyrian's Fire*. I hope Tess's journey has inspired you to be faithful and courageous, even if no one sees your goodness but those who know you best. My own journey as a writer has just begun. I hope you'll follow me on social media @emilyhjeffries. You can also go to my website at emilyhjeffries.com to sign up for writerly updates, and be the first to learn the scoop about the next book in The Fate of Glademont series, *The Last Thane*, coming in 2021. Much love and tah tah for now!

—Emily

CPSIA information can be obtained
at www.ICGtesting.com
Printed in the USA
LVHW110825090919
630389LV00001B/29/P